WHEN HER POWER AWAKENS

Brenna Bustamante

Saving Taiamen series

DEDICATION

Some people think that low self-esteem is just something that goes away. It's like anxiety, biting at you every chance it gets. It never goes away. At least, that's how it was for me. To every woman who feels like they are never enough. It will take time, but soon, you'll realize your worth.

To my husband, who every day helps me realize my worth.

CONTENT TRIGGERS

Your mental health matters.

Content triggers include: poverty, abandonment, adoption abuse, anxiety, self-harm, sex work and sex slavery, child abuse, violence, trauma, death and dying, sexism and misogyny, classism, torture, gambling addiction, starvation and dehydration, disappearance of a loved one, kidnapping, massacres and mass murders, earthquakes, bushfire, tornadoes.

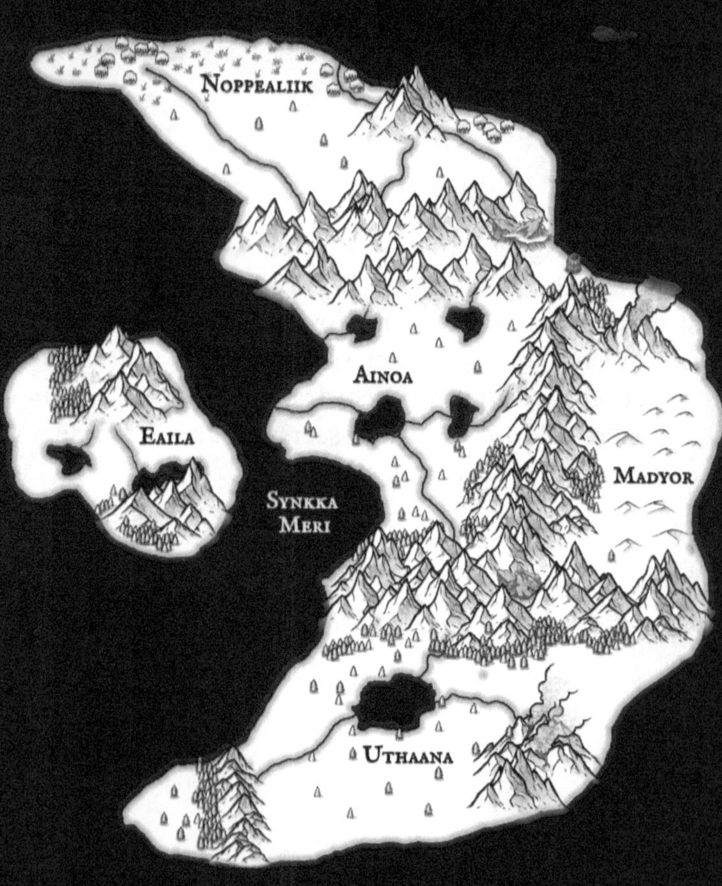

Noppealiik
Ainoa
Eaila
Synkka
Meri
Madyor
Uthaana

KENNA, 8 YEARS AGO

"You useless, worthless nobody!"

I look up from the desk, my eyes widening at the accusation. The mayor stands at the entrance of the inn, his eyes narrowed, bulging with anger, his face red, his fists closed.

"Uh… Mayor Winston?" I respond immediately, bowing to him as always, just as everyone in Madyor is expected to. "Can I help you find someone?" I tilt my head.

He approaches the desk, his fist landing on the top with a thud. "Who do you think you are to do this to my daughter?"

My eyes widen again. "Uh––I'm not sure what you're talking about, Mayor. I-I just got here. I've been asleep all day. I've been working sixteen-hour shifts all week at night," I explain.

The mayor's jaw tenses, lines on his forehead creasing as he closes the distance between us, stomping across the hardwood floors to grab my arm.

"Ow!" I protest as he drags me out of the inn with a tight grip on my arm. "I don't know what I did, I promise, I've been asleep all day!"

But the mayor didn't hear me. Or didn't want to hear me. After all, I'm a useless, worthless nobody. He stomps across Madyor, his face red, his grip tightening by the moment. People stare at us, whispering quietly to themselves. Heat rises to my cheeks as I look down. I can't even imagine what Peter will do when he hears about this.

The mayor continues to drag me across the entire district until we make it to the front of his house, where his daughter, Amara, sits at the edge of the stairs to their house's entrance. Her long, blonde hair is clumped and matted, pulled to one side in unnatural sections like someone had glued them together. My heart sinks. I saw Zander with glue yesterday.

"You stupid, dumb girl. You think you can just do this without consequences?" the mayor yells, pulling my arm and shoving me at his daughter. His daughter recoils instantly, like I'm some kind of disease she can contract with a touch. The way she looks at me very much felt like it. Her nose scrunches, her upper lip curls, and her head pulls back with her narrowed eyes.

"I didn't do this," I maintain.

"Sure, sure. You're only really jealous of me," Amara accuses, her lips pursed.

The mayor grabs the hair at the back of my head.

"Ow!" I yell.

"I'll be docking five pera off your pay for the entire month," he spat out.

My mouth drops. "No! Please! We need that money, please. Please, Mayor," I beg, dropping to my knees, scraping them against the ground. Not only will Peter beat me up for this, but we won't be able to eat anything for days!

"Please, Mayor," I plead, touching his hand to my forehead.

He pulls his hand back, his face twisting. "You disgusting, worthless human being. Nobody wants you. Not even Madyor," he snaps, his eyes glaring at me for a moment before he shoves me away, then pulls his daughter back into the house.

When I'm back at the inn and Zander drops by, the first thing he says is, "I'm sorry!"

I round on him quickly, my eyes blazing with anger. "Do you know what you've cost us? Do you know how I'm being punished for this? For something you did?" I spat.

"I'm sorry! I didn't think--"

"I know you didn't think, you ass! That's the problem with you; you don't think about anything else but yourself!" I exclaim, cutting him off.

"I'm sorry! I didn't mean for this to happen, Kenna!" Zander protests.

"You never mean for anything to happen until something actually does happen. And you know what the problem is? I seem to be the one constantly taking the consequences. Not you, Zander. Me!"

"Oh no, Miss Perfect, I'm sure you're the only one taking consequences, huh?" He steps back, his contrition turning into anger. "How about the many times I took on the tasks you couldn't do at school?"

My face changes. "I didn't mean I don't appreciate those things. You just don't think about how your actions impact me. You're too impulsive; you don't think before you act!"

"Oh, I'm sorry, I'm sorry for actually having a life outside of just work," he snaps. "Other people actually like to have fun. Like to stand up. No, wait, I forgot; that side of you is gone."

My eyes narrow. "I have to take care of my siblings. You know that."

"And yet you can spend an entire day with Kane, but never me," he spat out.

My face falls.

"You know why you're so mad, though? You're so mad because you can't do these things anymore. You've become so pathetic that you can't even defend yourself anymore," he continues.

"That's––that's…"

"Nothing to say?" he spat.

"I––"

Zander turns on his heels, leaving the inn and me.

But when he returns that evening, his shoulders are slumped, his eyes are wide and red, his jaws are tight, and his lips are pressed into a thin line.

"Zander?" I ask the moment he enters the inn. I tilt my head, frowning. I've never seen him like this before. He walks slowly, his eyes never leaving mine. I realize instantly he's shaking. I shoot up from the chair I'm sitting on, approaching him slowly. "What is it?" I ask cautiously.

He buckles, his whole body seeming to lose all strength, gravity pulling him down as he slumps to the ground. I rush to his side, checking his neck and forehead.

"Zander? Zander, what is it?" I ask, forgetting everything we talked about earlier, forgetting the anger, the horrible words he and I said to each other.

"Kenna," he says, his voice shaking. "Kenna, he's gone."

I frown. "Who's gone?"

"Kane. They took him. They took him, Kenna. He's gone!" Zander's tears come, and so do mine. He pulls me to him, and I slump against his chest, my body realizing this faster than my brain was. I burst into tears, crying, my body shaking uncontrollably as I grieve the loss of our other best friend. Someone we grew up with. Someone we played with constantly. Someone who endured the bullying, the stares, the gossip with us. The family we grew up with. Our only family.

"They took him," Zander cries into my hair.

"It's just you and me now. We can't let him take you, okay?" I say, momentarily looking up at him. "We can't let them take you too. Please, Zander, I can't lose anyone else."

"The moment they realize, we run, remember?" He cups my cheeks and looks into my eyes.

"We run. No one takes either of us. Never the government," I agree firmly, nodding. A promise we made as a group when we were younger. A promise renewed.

"It's just you and me now." His arms tighten around me. "I promise I'll be better. I promise."

Kenna

The day I burn down the inn would have to be the day I die.

I suck in a deep breath, and it almost feels like a chore to force the fresh air through my lungs.

I scoop my shoulder-length auburn hair carelessly into a bun, blowing stray strands away from my face. A single feeble source of light emits from a small candle on my desk as I work. Out of boredom, I wave a finger through its flame. It casts ghostly shadows onto the uneven stone walls, making the lobby of the inn that I work at feel even eerier.

This is my seventh night shift in a row. We hadn't had visitors in a week, and the gnawing emptiness in my stomach mirrors the three days I've gone without food. I only took the night shifts because no one else wanted them, and I can always use the extra pera. Even when no one's staying at the inn, the mayor requires someone to be here for at least twelve hours throughout the night, just in case important visitors drop by the district.

I pull out the coins I've earned over the last few days and count them. When I accidentally drop one, the sound of it hitting the floor echoes throughout the room. I bend down and pat the floor, feeling for the coin.

After I've retrieved it, I spread the coins on my palm to count. I've earned twenty pera in the last two days and saved two pera from my previous trip to the store. What do we have left to eat in the house? Maybe three or four eggs and a couple of potatoes? My belly rumbles. I crave bread. In Madyor, bread costs twenty-five pera. My family and I haven't had any fish or meat in the last few months, either, maybe more, but I also didn't have enough coins to buy any of those things.

Again.

Tagapamigay. The thought of fish makes me salivate. Like the god who gives will actually give anything. Not to me anyway. I wipe my mouth with my sleeve.

Maybe I could use some of my savings. The pera is supposed to be used for emergencies only, but over the last few years, I've dipped into it multiple times. Luckily, I've had this job since I was eleven years old, right after Lena died.

A low rumble rises from my stomach, and I wince. I've only had water from the inn. Existing mostly on water and the odd morsel of food used to make me feel dizzy and sick, but after years of practice, my body has adjusted a little. Good, I guess, although I've probably lost a good amount of weight.

I wonder what Zander's doing tonight? Zander's my best friend. He's my only friend, really. He and I have the same background. We could even be mistaken for siblings, with our olive skins, a stark contrast to the paleness of everyone in Madyor.

I have green eyes. Zander's are blue, while everyone else in Madyor has brown eyes. We're the outsiders, the unknowns, left in front of our adoptive parents' houses when we were babies with five hundred pera. Our parents had no choice but to take us in. There was a third baby, too: Kane.

We were all friends until we were sixteen years old, and then Kane disappeared. Zander and I still live in Madyor, a district of the country of Taiamen, probably the poorest district of all.

We are the no-ones, the leftovers, the hardest to reach in all of Taiamen, and the farthest from Eaila, which is the most beautiful district, with wonderful weather, bountiful land, producing all the resources our people will ever need.

But it's cursed.

Every time I crave the sunshine there, I remind myself of all the reasons not to go.

1. Only six hundred people live there.
2. People can only get pregnant if someone dies.
3. No one can leave Eaila, and if they try, they die immediately.
4. The Synkka Meri, an enchanted sea where monsters and creatures of all kinds live, surrounds Eaila, preventing people from escaping unless Conjurers and Soturis are there to fight them off.

If I long to live anywhere around here, it would be Ainoa. Ainoa is our capital, and because it's where the king, queen, Leaders, and all Soturis and Conjurers live, and because it's the closest to Eaila, they get to have all the resources first.

We get the longest winters and the harshest summers, so our land can't grow anything. Our oceans are freezing, so we can't produce seafood either. Instead, we have to rely on Ainoa's deliveries. If Ainoa can't spare a Conjurer to use their powers to keep food and resources fresh by the time it gets to Madyor, then we get nothing. Old food, rotten vegetables or fruits. Hard meat.

We get scraps.

So everyone in this district has to get the food we need when we have it, and if we don't, we have to figure out a way to save or get food so we survive. The other problem is we don't always have the money. That's why I do this. That's why I kill myself to get as many hours of work as I can get.

I sigh again, staring into the candle--my only source of entertainment. I fight the urge to run my finger through it again. Instead, I settle my chin and arms on the desk and watch the flame flicker once… twice… swaying with the soft breeze that blew from the slightly opened window behind me.

The silence is deafening.

I think about Peter and how he hasn't given us any pera for food for many months now, even though he's had a steady job in the mines for years. How, despite the fact that I just turned twenty-one years old, I've had to take care of my sisters ever since Lena died, almost ten years ago. My sweet, younger sister Katleya is getting bullied for not having the pera to buy new clothes or good meals during school.

He asks me every now and again, but he knows the entire family needs the pera more than anything else. Instead, he's signed up to work but hasn't been drafted yet. Open jobs in Madyor are extremely rare and work on a drafting system. People who need jobs put their names up for work. If they get drafted, they get the job. If they lose the job, they go back to the draft board.

My younger sister, Inez, who's only fifteen, had put herself up for work when she was just eight, but because of how few job opportunities there were here in Madyor, she still didn't have one. My other sister, Soleil, was drafted to work in the mines when she was ten, but without proper food, she didn't have the strength to keep the job.

Katleya, at twelve, is my youngest sister, and she's too sick to work. Heaven forbid she gets even sicker, as we don't have the pera to get her any medical care. Aelin Praer, Zander's adoptive mom, has suggested we take her to a Conjurer to get healed, but Peter conveniently disappears every time the Conjurers come to visit.

Conjurers are her only hope of healing. They're people born with the power to manipulate elements, though I can only imagine what they'd require from us in order to heal her.

And guess where I usually am when Conjurers visit? Yes. At work. Krag Vinde is the only week when Conjurers come to visit, and I typically get sixteen hours of work a day during that week. That means an extra five pera for each day.

An angry hiss jolts me back to attention. I stand up quickly, pushing the chair back so violently that it topples over.

Niada.

I gawk at the flame that swells almost three times its original size, growing by the minute, casting eerie shadows that dance ominously across the room. Within seconds the flame grows quickly and intensely, forming a fiery vortex that devours both the candle and the table. I blink, then hesitate. I really must be going crazy.

The table or candle wasn't actually burning. I lean forward; the heat blasting unforgivingly on my face, and squint, struggling to focus on the details, especially with the flames flying around me. I smell a slight singe of fire on my auburn hair, so I pull it back from my face, holding the short length of it hostage and away from the flames. The raging inferno consumes the table in the center, and yet, the table just stands there, unscathed. It seems like someone intentionally placed the fire around the table for decoration.

What?

My heart races as I cautiously step toward the flame, a hand raised to touch it. I gasp as the intense heat of the flames burns into my palms.

I shake myself. I'm seeing things. I really should eat something.

I spin, grabbing the wool jacket that hangs behind the chair, getting ready to throw it over the fire to snuff it out. When I turn back to the flames, my jaw drops.

It isn't raging anymore. Instead, it's doing something I've never seen before. I take cautious steps toward the desk and examine the flames.

Am I going crazy?

The fire draws itself back into the candle slowly, flame by flame, crackling and flickering back into the original small flame floating above the candle. In its wake is a cloud of black smoke, slowly disappearing into thin air. Hesitantly, I wave a hand over and around the candle.

Nothing but cold air. I take a step back, narrowing my eyes at the candle and table, which look exactly as they had minutes ago.

Niada.

I hit my forehead with my palm and exhale, suddenly realizing the gravity of what might've happened. I definitely don't need to get fired from this job. This is our only source of pera. Without this, my entire family will die.

"*Niada,*" I curse at myself. "What an idiot."

I shut my eyes, grimacing, images of what could've happened playing in my mind. There isn't anyone here, but I'm ashamed that I let something like this happen. This could've easily been a disaster. I can envision it in my head. The worst possible scenario.

Me burning down the inn would be the worst thing that could ever happen. It is the only inn in the entire district. I'd lose my job. I'd get branded as the girl who burned down the inn. I'd never get a job again. No income. No food.

I can't even imagine the look on my siblings' faces if that were to happen. I don't even want to picture how Peter would look at me, or how many times he'd hit me for not bringing back food for the family.

I blink wildly, eager to get the images out of my head.

I reach over the desk and frantically pat around the candle and the walls, checking to see if the flames have left any debris behind. My eyes close and I sigh, relieved at the same cold, hard cement. I make a mental note to check again in a few hours when daylight comes to see if it's left any soot or color on the walls or desk.

I turn back to the candle. The flame floats and flickers as if nothing's happened.

I shiver, but I'm not sure if it's from the soft breeze. I turn to the window anyway, and push it closed, feeling stupid for thinking there was anything else that could cause the fire.

Obviously, it was the wind.

I pick up the chair, sink into it, and bury my face in my hands. *Tagapamigay.* I'm so tired. And hungry.

I guess I don't die today.

2

Zander

After a long day at work, I cross the street, glancing around for incoming carriages. I nod at a man I recognize from work, instantly slowing my pace to make sure he doesn't follow me. It's unlikely. No one really notices me or cares about what I'm up to. I've never been anyone.

I'm a pariah. Mostly. If it weren't for my best friend Kenna, and maybe even my sisters, no one would even know who I was. I could disappear, and no one would even look for me. In some ways, that's empowering. But most of the time, it doesn't feel like enough.

There's only one place I feel good enough here in Madyor.

As soon as my coworker disappears into a building, I walk again, speeding up to gain traction. I pull my hood over my head. I don't want anyone else to see where I'm going. I turn a corner into a back alley, scanning behind me quickly to check if anyone is around. I dip back into the alley, stopping at a trash box with old and decayed half-eaten food, broken glass bottles, ratty clothes, broken furniture, and used items.

A pungent smell assaults my nose, but I don't wince. I'm used to it, having come here looking for food so many times. I run my eyes around the trash, spotting an old piece of meat that looks like it might still be edible. I think about taking it, but it wouldn't be a good idea to take it where I'm headed. I make a mental note to check back later.

Instead, I push the trash box away from the wall, revealing a door almost hidden by dead, overhanging vegetation. The wooden door is old and weathered, with a faint eye marked in white chalk drawn in the middle. I turn, scanning the alley again, before turning back to knock three times.

A hole in the middle of the eye pops open.

"Password?" a voice croaks.

I step toward the door and whisper, "Redeem the sin."

Silence.

Then, a loud click, and the door swings open slightly. I slip through the doorway, shutting the door quickly behind me.

The atmosphere is different inside. The room is dimly lit, with only tiny lights lining the aisle. Cement walls divide the room into separate sections, but instead of doors, long, sheer curtains create not-so-effective barriers between the halls and the rooms. A soft, soothing sound echoes across the cement walls, there to camouflage the sounds of pleasure that come from each section, but clearly failing.

I walk through the halls, ignoring the shadows of bodies bonded together through the translucent curtains. Even the ambient noises don't bother me anymore. I can still remember how I'd felt coming in the first time, about three years ago, and how embarrassing it was to listen to people making that sound.

I follow the man through a few more halls, down a flight of stairs, and across another area of sections separated by the same sheer curtains. Finally, the man stops in front of a door. I nod at him before entering.

Once again, my surroundings change. Unlike the area before this, this room is bright, open, and well-ventilated. I blink a few times, trying to get my eyes used to the brightness. Inside the room are three big, round tables, each manned by a local worker holding playing cards. People crowd around the tables in groups of at least three, watching each other's moves closely as they gambled.

This is the only place I like in Madyor. The only place I feel like I actually have any power, or something to offer. I come here every now and again. There isn't really anywhere else to go. I don't like being at home because my adoptive mother, Aelin, hates me. I don't have any friends outside of Kenna. I don't drink, so I don't like bars.

And this is the only place where the Winston kids might find me, and I'd end up getting my ass beat if I were to run into them.

A worker at a table motions for me to join just as another person walks away. I glance around, casually scanning the table for anyone I know. Luckily, most people who come here are visitors or people I don't have to deal with daily. At least here no one sees me as that kid who was dropped off at a random person's front door. I'm a foreigner in the land I grew up in and a foreigner in the only family I knew. Within minutes of being here, I always show them that I'm someone people would want to know and respect.

The worker shuffles the cards and distributes them to each of the players. There are three of them on the table: a strange, dark-haired woman, wearing a black cloak; and a burly, light-skinned man with blond hair and incredible blue eyes, wearing a thin, rundown shirt, which is a bit odd for the time of the year. The dark-haired woman barely speaks. I can't see her face, but from a few glances at her in the right light, I glimpse a tattoo on her neck. That makes me slightly nervous. Most people who have tattoos are Soturi, Ainoa's soldiers. It's a rite of passage, according to elders within the community. It isn't Krag Vinde yet, so if she is, her being here is curious.

The man has a gnarly scar on his left cheek. He must've been in some kind of battle to incur such an injury. He also looks very confident, which isn't common, especially in a place like this. People hide themselves and wear cloaks or hoods to make sure they don't get recognized. The man isn't wearing a cloak or hood. He looks at me, his eyes searching, so I look away. I always assess my opponents just to make sure I can do what I need to do to win. But I don't want them assessing me back.

I scan my cards, making sure I keep a blank face. That is important. In the game of Yusod, it's all about hiding your emotions so your opponents can never guess what your hand is. I visualize my goal, then breathe, blinking evenly, keeping my heart rate steady to avoid anyone noticing. It takes a few seconds. Then, the letters on my cards shift. It happens quickly and seamlessly, the change barely noticeable.

I hide a smile, feeling triumphant. Instead, I take a deep breath, forcing myself to celebrate the fact that I'm getting better at this later.

I may have no idea who my parents are, but at least I can manipulate certain things. The Conjurers haven't caught me yet, but I hide it--mostly to spite those same Conjurers, who I don't believe do a good job of actually protecting us. I don't want to be one of them. I don't want to be part of an organization that bows down to a corrupt government.

When it's my turn, I lay my hand, my triumph erupting from my body in a slow, sly smile.

"Congratulations!" the worker proclaims blandly, a forced smile breaking into his bored expression. Workers at the brothel earn ten pera a night. They never notice anything. If they did, they'd chalk it up to alcohol they no doubt take on their breaks to relieve themselves of the constant tedium.

The worker starts counting pera. I beam, slowly scanning the table for reactions. I always love the look on their faces when I win. It's exhilarating.

The woman next to me hangs her head, a reaction I relish. Oddly enough, the burly man, a faint smile playing on his lips, is peering at me with a curious expression. I frown.

"Five, six, seven," the worker mutters, counting the coins as he passes them into my outstretched palm.

I place the coins in my pockets, preparing to leave.

"Again?" a deep and commanding voice says.

I laugh, turning to him. His intensely sapphire eyes flash with an air of intimidation. "You want to lose again?"

This isn't normal, not here at the brothel. People hate losing. If you win, they encourage you to play again so they can have another go at making you lose your pera. It's visible in their eyes: the desperation, the hunger to win back the pera they lost, the desire to win, maybe not just pera but also dignity. But this guy… there's nothing. He's just lost seven pera, and he doesn't seem fazed at all.

I scan his expression, curious if I'd see some kind of emotion or thought that might give me an idea of who he is. I get ready to respond, but a slow knot builds in my stomach. Instead, I turn, pushing myself out of the room. I can almost feel his eyes burning into my back. As soon as I make it out of the door, I sprint out of the brothel as quickly as my legs will take me. Outside, I keep my fast pace before disappearing into an alley, then jumping over a fence, pulling myself onto the roof, trying to be quiet to avoid making any noises for the people inside to hear. I walk across the rooftop, peering over the edge to the street.

No one's there.

I jump, then continue walking briskly, determined to distance myself from the brothel without drawing attention. I walk into another alley and immediately duck under some trash boxes. I wait, then peek behind it, looking specifically for the burly, blue-eyed man.

He's nowhere to be seen.

I jump up and started sprinting again, making my way across the street and into another alley. I know I'm being paranoid. But there's something about that man that made me uncomfortable. I haven't felt like that before, either. It almost felt like he… knew? I sigh. That can't be possible.

No one knows.

We don't have Conjurers who live in Madyor. Conjurers barely even visit outside of Krag Vinde. We're too far, too out of the way, too poor for the powerful to visit or even care about.

I circle the streets a few more times before finally making it back to my house.

I'm not even inside yet, but I smile when I hear the shrill, loud voices coming from inside the house. I feel better almost instantly, and I tuck the memory of the burly man into the back of my mind. I can deal with him later. My sisters are home.

"Hi!" an airy, but soft voice quips as soon as I enter.

"Ugh," I groan, as a tiny figure forces herself into my arms. I kiss her forehead, wrapping my arms tight around her.

"Eww!" Jana Praer giggles. I settle across from her, next to my other sister, Maris.

"Whatchu doing?" I ask playfully, leaning against her. Her short black hair frames her delicate features, untouched by the hardships of this place, at least for now.

"I'm eating," she says, smiling widely, her toothy grin bordered by bits and pieces of food.

"Ew." Jana wrinkles her nose from across the table. She stabs a fork into her potatoes and meat. "Mom made us dinner. Do you want some?" Jana motions to her plate.

Of course, on the table, there are only two plates of food.

Classic Aelin. She has three kids, but you'd never know. My adoptive mother has never been very warm toward me. Yes, she took me in and put a roof over me. She put me through school and fed me.

But the difference between how she treated the girls compared to how she'd treated me was like night and day. It didn't hit me until Jana came into the world. In my eyes, she was just the type of mother who was frequently mentally and emotionally absent. I had to learn how to feed myself, clothe myself, and find love and care from anywhere else outside of this house

And then, Jana was born. Suddenly, she was extremely caring and sweet. Aelin took care of Jana's food, clothes, and made sure she was comfy. There's always food and drinks ready for them in the morning and at night, always something to snack on. For many years, I thought it was me. I started spending most of my time out of the house so that the pain wouldn't be so obvious. I spent more time with Kenna and Kane, and I started gambling. Anything to keep me out of the house so I wouldn't feel that neglect.

Then Maris was born. The shift in Aelin continued, but never changed toward me. She was always cold, calculating, and indifferent toward me. Eventually, I accepted the truth and attributed my feelings of detachment to the fact that I was adopted and not her biological child. So while I live here, my family remain the girls and Kenna, but that's it.

But every now and again I'd wonder. Will Aelin ever see my worth? Will anyone?

3

Alistair

Light shines through my window, warm on my face, and a gentle breeze escapes into the room. My face feels cold, but I like that. I'd left my window open again overnight. It isn't a problem, but it can be dangerous, depending on the weather, season, and politics within the Highline in Ainoa. The last time I opened my window, it got smashed with a brick by a protesting Soturi who'd just got laid off from their position.

I bury myself under my blanket, enjoying the cool air and the glow of the sun as well as the warmth of the heavy, thick wool blanket.

Gone are the days when I couldn't afford a blanket. Gone are the days when I couldn't just lay here and enjoy the beauty of the sun because I had to head out into the mines at the break of dawn just to make sure I had something to eat. Gone are the days when I had to worry about someone yelling at me or waking me with a fist on my face.

I reach over to my nightstand and peek at the clock. It's almost time to get up. I enjoy a few more moments under my blanket before finally forcing myself to get up.

After closing my window, I walk to my washroom, grabbing my toothbrush. There was a time when I had to create a toothbrush from cloth and sticks when I was young. I couldn't afford to buy one, so I'd made one myself. Now, I have a toothbrush made of bamboo and soft bristles, costing at least fifteen pera.

I'm much better off now. I have a beautiful apartment, my own bedroom. Despite the walls still being cold, hard cement, my living situation has been much improved since moving to Ainoa. Ainoa has better buildings, insulated and brightly decorated. I love the modern, expensive-looking space in my apartment. It's a huge contrast with the place I grew up in.

I live in Ainoa, the wealthiest district in Taiamen and the closest to Eaila. Because we have many Conjurers and Soturis in Ainoa, we're the only district that can send a ship across the Synkka Meri, a sea of monsters that borders Eaila, to get resources and still make the trip back. Ainoa is also where Soturis and Conjurers live and train. Soturis are Taiamen's protectors against creatures, invading countries, and rebel groups. They go to school to learn about dangerous creatures, notable plants and trees, and learning skills like knowing when to visit certain areas in Taiamen. Then, they train extensively to fight and protect the country against all potential enemies–including Conjurers.

Ainoa also takes people from each district to train as Soturis. Most of the time, they are prisoners, people who don't have families or friends, or people who are deemed useless within their district. This was me once upon a time. I was deemed useless, so they took me.

But now I'm a Soturi, and my life is entirely different. I'm much better off. I'm richer; I actually have things now. I can afford to eat.

After brushing my teeth, I slide open the glass door to my marble-tiled shower. Again, something I never had growing up.

After showering, I change into my Soturi uniform, grey pants lined on the side with a triple sun (Ainoa's logos), matched with a grey, plain, *Protego* shirt over a thick, white, sleeveless, cotton undershirt with a round neckline. The grey shirt is made of thick, quality fabric, with a pointed collar, and a front opening that fastens with a series of gold buttons. We call it *"Protego"* because Conjurers enhanced it to protect us from powerful Conjurer attacks and keep them warm on cold, miserable nights traveling across Taiamen.

Luckily, I haven't had to travel much. I can't even imagine leaving Ainoa. The idea of the unknown is uncomfortable, and the thought of going back to where I grew up is unbearable. I like my comforts in Ainoa. I like my new apartment, the abundance of food, and the beautiful weather. I enjoy being able to have friends, have influence, and drink alcohol. I even like the Soturi. And some Conjurers. Most of all, I enjoy not having to wake up to my adoptive father telling me I'm useless. If only he could see me now.

Suddenly, her face appears in my head. Short, wavy, auburn hair cradling her face, green eyes. She was one of my best friends when I was growing up, but after I was taken, it didn't make sense to think about them anymore. I'll probably never see them again. How would I? I'm here in Ainoa, and they're a few months of travel through unpredictable and dangerous mountainous regions, far, far away. Why would I? Who would give up the comforts of Ainoa just to be with someone somewhere else, let alone in a district of nobodies? That was why I never wrote to either of them, even though I knew where they were and even though I could actually afford to do it now.

Sometimes, it's best to leave the past in the past.

I button my *Protego,* pat down my uniform, scanning myself in the mirror to make sure nothing is out of place. My uniform always makes me feel smart and timeless. But what I'm actually proudest of is the yellow badge on my left chest.

A yellow badge means I have access to more than most Soturi. That means I have power, control, and the ability to train other Soturis. I'm only two levels away from making it to the top leaders, in just four years. After yellow, was gold, then black. Most people don't even make it out of Soturi training after four years. It usually takes six to eight years to get through it, and two to make it to a purple badge, another two to make it to white, then two to yellow, two to gold, then to black. But I made it to yellow within four years.

I follow instructions to the tee, make sure I talk to the right people, and I've learned how to speak and influence people by always saying the right words. Only two weeks after earning my yellow badge and I'm already making all the moves to get into gold, which means I could become a Leader one day. I have a plan, and regardless of how I got here, I am dedicated to seeing it through.

I finish getting dressed and head into my kitchen, which is almost as big as my entire house was back where I came from. I grab a slice of bread to toast and pick up some fruit to snack on.

Gone are the days when I had to count my bread and fruit. A servant of the Soturi regularly fills my kitchen with plenty of food, including lots of meat I never used to have, and alcohol I could never afford. I used to save my bread up to the last crumb, just so I could survive. I used to pick up food from trash boxes.

If my father could see how every punch made me more obedient, how every slap strengthened me, how every belt I felt on my back made me the perfect Soturi, strong and resilient, he'd regret every single word he'd said. He'd regret telling me I was useless and would die unknown. He'd regret all the pain he ever caused me.

If I ever had to come back to where I came from, that would be one of the first things I'd do--show him how much better I am without him.

I grab a pan and place it on the stove above the fire. I close my eyes, letting a warmth build in my chest, filling my thoughts with the goal of the pan sizzling. My arms stretch toward the fire, releasing carefully. When I open my eyes, I beam instantly, proud to see that the fire is hotter, and the pan is sizzling, a sliver of smoke rising in the air.

That's exactly what I want to happen. I'm not great at Conjuring yet, but I'm getting better by the day. I don't practice often, but when I do, I can feel myself getting stronger.

I crack an egg, then a second, and a third into the pan. Luckily, I can afford eggs now. Eggs are so expensive these days. I mix the eggs carefully. It would be easier to have a cook, but I don't enjoy having people intrude on my home. It's the only place I can practice Conjuring safely, without anyone noticing. I could be one of the very few Leaders who's a Conjurer and a Soturi at the same time, which would give me a huge edge over others.

I spoon my eggs onto a plate before eating, glancing quickly at the time.

This has been my routine every day for the last few years now. It's day and night difference from where I grew up. While I spent months hating training and missing home when I first got taken, I don't regret it anymore. So much has changed for me, and I only hope my friends are doing just as well as I am. But truthfully, I try not to think about them anymore. Not if I want to keep moving forward. Not if I want to achieve my goals and become a Leader.

I finish eating, grab my bag, and take one last look in the mirror. I'll clean up later. But before I leave, I look directly at the fire, stretch my arms out toward it, and a burst of energy releases from my hands. A smile of self-satisfaction spreads across my face as the flames retreat into the coals.

As I walk out of my building, I exchange nods with the caretakers before making my way to the Soturi training center. I wave to a variety of people along the way. I've deliberately worked toward becoming popular, and I'm pleased my efforts have paid off. To become Leader, I have to have support.

I turn to a group of women huddling together in a corner, whispering to each other. I smile and wave at them. Even from across the street, I can tell two of them are Conjurers just from the *abayas* and jewels that they're wearing. Making good impressions is important. Most Conjurers dress in *abayas*, but the really rich and important ones always have badges and jewels to indicate status. These women dress beautifully, wearing crisp, gently pressed green *abayas*, not a strand of their hair out of place. But they also adorn themselves with glistening gold or emerald jewels hanging just above their breasts, and they have a yellow badge pinned over their left chests, which indicates their status. I don't know what the levels are for Conjurers, but I know to smile and make sure they notice me.

I spot the building I'm heading toward and instantly swell with pride. A huge gold castle towers above everything else, easily noticeable, outlined by majestic and colorful jewels, glowing in the sun. The castle is called the Iklead, and it's where the king and queen live. The Soturi training center, known as the Koltuskus, is only a few blocks away. The Koltuskus is a dome-shaped building, not as tall as the Iklead, but wider. Inside, each floor has a different atmosphere or ecosystem, so Soturis get to experience and train in unfamiliar terrain, environments, weather, and even cultures. One floor accurately replicates the harsh climate in the ergs, deserts, and mountains of Madyor, while another floor is designed to resemble the mountains, lakes and seascapes of Uthaana. On the third floor, Soturis can explore and train in Noppealiik's mountains, swamps, and coastal areas.

There are also floors dedicated specifically to mountainous regions, volcanic surroundings (where sometimes there's a volcano erupting), and dark seas, mimicking what they might experience going through the Synkka Meri. Behind both buildings, practically as tall as the Iklead, is the impressive outline of a building called the Voi Makkas. In the right light and angle, it's visible as a white tower twinkling in the sun. Otherwise, it's only reflected in the mountains behind, making it easily concealed. The Conjurers use their powers to change how the building looks on purpose so they can hide the knowledge of where it's located.

The Voi Makkas is where Conjurers train. Most powerful Leaders, who are also Conjurers, spend a lot of time there, too. I've never actually been inside.

I walk toward the dome, my mood instantly lighting up as soon as I see their faces. Two people I consider my friends, even though they knew nothing about the real me. Two people I've been most honest and upfront with--except for the fact that I'm also a Conjurer.

"Jack! Oliver!" I greet.

They turn, smiling back.

"Hey, Alistair!"

4

Kenna

I scrub the walls of the inn that I'd almost set on fire just a few hours ago. I want to make sure there's no proof that I've done stupid things. Stupid things like setting the table on fire. Surprisingly, the wall looks fine. There are no signs of soot on it at all. But I really need to do something to keep me awake, or distract me from wanting to eat my own hand.

I look out the window, sighing, the fresh breeze a welcome feeling in my lungs.

The sun slowly emerges from the horizon, painting the clouds a beautiful orange-pink. I hope it will be a good day today. It rained for the last few days, and it's starting to feel like I will never see the sun again. I sit back down on the floor, the length of my skirt scraping the wet floor. I ignore it. I don't really care right now. I need sleep, I realize. Like a long, dead-ass sleep where I can forget about this life and all of my problems.

I get up to finish scrubbing the walls, and drop the sponge into the bucket, patting my wet hands on my skirt.

I get up, my knees buckling from kneeling on the concrete ground. I grab the broom and bucket and haul them into the storage room behind the desk. The room is filled with metal shelves holding cleaning supplies, buckets, and firewood for our guests. After grabbing a bottle of water, I use the rest of my energy to haul it down the stairs into the alley.

I'm not really allowed to do this. The canals lead to the one tiny reservoir we had here in Madyor, so any wastewater should go in the bathrooms. But it always clogs the toilets, so every now and again, especially on nights like this, I take a chance on the back canals instead. I know. Disgusting. But let's be honest, many things in Madyor are more deadly than the contaminated water. It's the least of anyone's concerns here.

No one can see me, and no one would care anyway, except the mayor and their kids, who seem to have a penchant for pointing out the things I've done wrong.

I carry the bucket over and tilt it into the canal. It's been a tiring day. I can feel the little muscles I have complaining from lack of sustenance. I heave a sigh as the murky water spills slowly, combining seamlessly with the continuous flow of water. The sound is almost calming.

Suddenly, a force knocks me from behind. I drop the bucket, and my body skips across the path.

I groan, the sting of a rapidly growing bruise echoing throughout my body. I push myself up from the ground, brush my elbows, and turn, ready to meet that force with an ugly face and some choice words.

Instead, my eyes land on a figure masked in straw bending to collect something off the ground. I'm slow and weak, but this is Madyor, and so is everyone else.

"What are you doing?" I yell at the figure, even though I know exactly what he's doing. I hear my voice echo throughout the alley, and I wish to *Tagapamigay* that someone would hear it. Hot tears burn my eyes, and I do the only thing I can think of doing.

I crawl over to the figure, hanging onto their coat as tightly as my muscles can afford.

"Please don't," I beg. My voice cracks, but that doesn't compare to the fear I'll have when Peter finds out that I've lost all the pera I've earned in the last few days.

"Please don't. My family and I need that pera." I will myself to look into the eyes of the masked figure. "I haven't eaten in days," I add. I'm not just crying now. I'm sobbing pathetically.

I force myself to look at him again, hoping my desperation and hunger will actually show through my eyes.

"I really need this pera. Please don't take it."

The figure starts to walk, and I continue hanging onto his coat so tightly that I feel myself being pulled. The sting of the concrete scraping my legs is nothing compared to what this will do to me and my family.

The masked figure stops, and I can tell they're conflicted by the way they hesitate--at least for a moment. But then, they wriggle their coat out of my hands, drop a coin into my palm and vanish into the main street.

I don't have the strength to get up and run after him.

My body is numb. Tears stream down my face, and I can't see anything. All I can do is sit there, shaking violently with nothing but a single coin after working three fourteen-hour nights.

I don't hear the rumble that resonates through the heavens, like a snarl of a celestial creature seeking vengeance.

I don't see the sky open up with huge raindrops, covering my surroundings in a blur of motion.

I don't feel the freezing rain drenching my shirt, sticking to my skin and hair, seamlessly mixing with the tears that drip down my cheeks.

I scream.

I am pathetic.

I am weak.

I am tired.

5

Zander

I'm not a good friend.

I know this because I don't have any. I spent many years trying to find friends, trying to make friends, and it's damn difficult. The truth is it's hard to care for people who don't care about you. It's hard to care for people who look at you and immediately see an outsider, someone who doesn't belong, no matter how hard you try.

I *do* have Kenna, though, and the position of the sun in the sky tells me it's the time she would be finishing her shift at the inn, so I pull on some shoes and start making my way over there.

The only person who's really ever stuck by me is Kenna. I may have gone through some shitty times, and we may have lost our other friend, Kane, but ever since we realized we had similar backgrounds, we've stuck together. She's always been good to me. When we were young at school, she defended me from the mayor's family, the Winstons, and we've stuck together since.

I typically walk her home from work, mostly because knowing her, she probably hasn't eaten in days. She has a whole family to take care of, so she saves most of her money for them. That's Kenna. Martyr to a fault.

I turn a corner and immediately spot her small frame on the ground in front of the inn. Her hair, tangled and matted, glistens with water droplets, while her stained, muddy shirt clings to her body. She looks like she's been rolling around in the canals. I catch her puffy eyes and tear-stained cheeks. My walk turns into a trot, my heart softening at the sight of her.

"Hey, hey," I say, kneeling to see her face. She's definitely been crying.

"What's wrong?"

She looks at her feet, and her eyes look like they're about to tear up again.

"What's wrong?" I ask again, pulling her into my arms, momentarily wincing at her ice-cold skin.

Tagapamigay, she's dripping wet. She must've been out during that random rainstorm.

She collapses into my arms, sobbing, her tiny body trembling.

"It's okay." I gently pat her damp back and tighten my hold around her, a slurry of feelings creeping as I watch her break down. I want to hurt the people who did this to her. But this isn't the first time I've found her like this. Kenna cries pretty often. She's not the type to fight back. The girl who used to speak up when we were younger? She disappeared long ago, probably after Lena, her adoptive mother, died. Or perhaps after Kane was kidnapped. It's my job to take care of her.

"Let's go get you something to eat, huh?" I wrap my gloved hands around hers, blowing some heat into her hands. I rub her hands a few more times, eventually slipping her hand into one of my pockets, where it's warm.

I put my arms around her, hoping to share some of my warmth, lead her up on her feet, and start moving her toward the store. She doesn't say anything. But I've known her long enough to know that there's only one thing that could upset her this much.

"I-dov-hab-pera," she stutters in between sobs.

"I know." I pause outside the store. "Wait here." I wipe her cheeks with the palms of my hands. Then I turn to enter the store, patting the coins in my pockets. I won today. Within Madyor, there's only one small store that sells food and other necessities. It's early, so there isn't anyone in the store outside of Roger, the security guard, a big muscular man with light skin, a glorious mustache, and a beard. Supplies are delivered from Ainoa to Uthaana, to Madyor, and it's Roger's job to make sure the deliveries are stored to sell to locals.

It's bright inside the store, courtesy of a long, large bulb on the ceiling in the middle of the store. There are three aisles, divided by a row of shelves. One row of shelves stores fruits and vegetables, the second shelf stocks bread and eggs, and the third is for meat and fish. At the front of the store, right at the entrance, is a desk where Roger usually sits to watch anyone trying to steal. Stealing isn't uncommon in Madyor. People starve to death if they don't know how to scavenge for food or if they haven't tried stealing. I've stolen from the store a few times. Roger knows that, too, so the moment he sees me, he frowns, his eyes following even as I pass the desk. Luckily, today is a good day for pera. I won twenty-one pera from gambling, and I had an extra thirty from work in the last few days. My eyes scan the options available, then I walk over to pick up a loaf of bread and a bag of meat. I'm pretty sure she hasn't eaten meat in a long time. Meat's expensive. Even Aelin only brings meat home every once in a while. I count the total in my head before walking towards Roger.

He nods at me, then gestures at Kenna, who's standing outside the door, looking like a drenched bird, trembling in the chilly morning wind.

"Is she okay?" he asks, his voice low, rough, and raspy, and his eyebrows furrow. Unlike me, Kenna's liked by people around here.

"Yeah." I drop coins into Roger's open hands before making my way out the door.

"Hey," Roger grunts, and I pause, mentally recounting to make sure I dropped enough coins. Instead, Roger approaches me with an arm stretched out.

My head tilts, but I curiously accept his offering. I open my hand to find five coins. I look back up, about to say something. Instead, his eyes meet mine, and I understand. I nod, then turn, pushing the door open.

My arm wraps around Kenna, leading her towards her house, cradling the bags with my other arm. She sniffles, but she sinks beneath my arm.

Suddenly, she hesitates right outside her house and turns towards me. In the soft morning glow, I can see her disheveled hair, swollen eyes, and flushed cheeks.

"I can't go home, Zander; I lost all my pera. I don't have food to give them," she says, her head hung. She sounds so ashamed, even though I know that she's just spent most of her nights working this week. My heart clenches.

I pull her to me, softly touching her forehead with my lips, a familiar warmth sweeping over me. I push the bag of meat and bread into her arms and slip the pera Roger had given back.

She blushes, her eyes avoiding mine. "I can't take this."

I can see her fighting back tears, and for a second, I think she might start crying again.

"Yes, you can," I respond firmly. I grab her hand and forcibly wrap it around the bags of food. Then I push her gently towards her door.

She looks at me, somber and weary, but her eyes glow.

I nod. She doesn't have to say anything. I know and understand.

Kenna

"Did you have enough?" I ask my younger sister, Katleya.

She nods, licking happily at the meat juices on her fingers. I pick up her plate and wipe her messy end of the table.

"Thank you, Kenna, that was delicious!" Katleya chirps, looking happier than she's looked in the last couple of months.

My sisters giggle. "You're disgusting, Kat."

Inez rolls her eyes, but chuckles anyway.

I feel a soft tug at my heart as I watch my youngest sister acting like an actual child. It rarely happens, but when it does, I'm reminded that he's only eleven years old.

A low grunt emanates from the far end of the table, and the girls fall silent. We enjoy our dinner so much that even Peter, seated at the end, remains expressionless, likely oblivious to the ongoing conversation, like he usually is. That's a good thing. I prefer he remains quiet. It's better than shouting at one or all of us. I count any dinners where violent threats don't come until after actual food a roaring success.

Peter slams his empty bottle on the table. That's his third bottle. I've counted. He's always more violent by the third bottle.

Time to go to bed, I guess.

"Another!" he roars, his voice reverberating through our tiny home, drowning out any other sound, like the fire crackling next to us.

"I-I don't think we have anymore," Katleya says, her voice meek against the overpowering volume of our father's voice.

Peter grunts, then clumsily gets up from his chair. He clings to the back of it to maintain his balance.

Peter, our dear father and head of this household, every day at dinner: drunk before we even get to say grace.

"Papa," a voice pipes up, and he turns, a tad gentler.

"What is it?" he responds, looking directly at where the voice had come from.

Katleya rarely speaks up, but when she does, Peter always looks at her. Out of all of us, Katleya is the only one he responds to this way.

Katleya's face flushes. She looks like she's regretting his decision to call out to Peter over the dinner table.

"Can I get some pera to replace my shoes?"

Silence. No one moves. I don't dare breathe.

"My shoes have been broken for months," Katleya adds, looking embarrassed.

Peter glowers, but he controls his voice.

"Why don't you ask Kenna?" He bores his amber eyes straight into me, and for a moment I forget that I have no spare pera to give.

"Papa, I worked every day last week, and we still don't have enough money for food. Why don't you give her pera?" I flush instantly. I didn't want to anger him, not right now.

The room is silent. Is it just me, or is that clock ticking louder? I scan the room. The girls avoid my eyes.

Peter whirls, his eyes blazing, mirroring the fiery dance of the crackling flames in the fireplace. "What did you say?" his voice thunders across the room.

I cringe. I don't want this. I don't need this.

Katleya darts across the room, her tiny fingers gripping Peter, while he stomps over to me, dragging the little girl with him.

"I don't need it after all, Papa." Her voice quivers.

Peter dismisses her with a sharp shrug. Katleya loses her balance, tumbling onto the ground, her body hitting the hard concrete, creating an echo through the room. Soleil and Inez jump from the table to help her.

I glare at Peter, a warmth rising in my belly. "Did you have to do that? You could've hurt her!" I accuse, glancing between Peter and Katleya.

Peter's jaw tightens, and his brow furrows. He's too drunk. His eyes glaze with today's alcohol, his face scrunching as he slowly turns to me. Uh-oh.

"Don't. Tell. Me. What. To. Do," he stutters, emphasizing each word.

He steps, grunting and stumbling. His hand shoots out with lightning speed, striking at my face with a force that echoes through my ears.

My body freezes. From the corner of my eye, I see orange spires spinning within the furnace.

Probably a result of the hit.

"Don't you talk back to me. I fed you, I housed you, you ungrateful little bitch. You don't get to talk to me like that." He seethes, his voice dripping with venom.

I close my eyes, mentally preparing myself for another blow from his palm or fist, whichever one he decides he'd like to bless me with this time. But nothing comes. I open an eye.

Peter spins around instead and stomps out of the house, his muddy boots leaving a trail of dirt on the cement floor.

I breathe a sigh of relief.

Soleil and Inez run to me, looking over my cheeks.

"Are you okay?" Katleya asks, patting my cheeks gently. "I'll go get some ice," she offers and disappears behind the ice box.

"Is Katleya okay?" I motion to the little girl across the room.

She looks ashamed, staring at her feet.

"Yeah, she tore some skin on her elbow, but I think she's a bit more embarrassed at what she caused than anything," Soleil says, exhaling.

I push myself up, Inez giving my arm a helpful lift.

"You have a bit of a death wish," Inez mutters to me.

I chuckle and pat the top of Inez's back. I hobble across the dimly lit room straight for my younger sister and pull her into my arms. Katleya sobs.

"I think you put something weird in here, Soleil," Inez cut in. She's inspecting the fireplace, where the flames have noticeably stopped their little dance and are back to the normal-sized blaze.

"I thought it was going to jump out of the furnace, actually. That was so strange!" Soleil agrees, joining Inez by the fire. "It looked like it was dancing!"

"Probably the wind outside," Inez counters, looking up into the chimney, "what a coincidence, though. It made everything look even more intense!"

Soleil chuckles.

They turn back to Katleya and me. She continues to cry, her little body shaking, her nose dripping.

Soleil grabs an old rag and hands it to Katleya to blow her nose.

I pat her back gently. "It's going to be okay," I whisper into her ear. I kiss her cheek and look at her solemn face.

"Are you hurt?" I ask.

She shakes her head and sniffles. The child, who was happy just moments ago, now has red and swollen eyes. How quickly things can change.

"Tell you what," I say. I reach into my pocket and pull out the pera Zander gave me. I slip it into her tiny hands. Sometimes, it's easy to forget that she's only twelve years old.

"But Kenna," she protests, her cheeks turning redder.

"It's not much. But I'll earn more. We'll figure out food. I know it's hard right now, but we will get through it," I tell her.

Soleil and Inez join us on the floor.

"Yes, it will be okay, Kat," Inez says encouragingly, as she shoots me an approving look.

"We will find jobs and we'll get our family out of this mess," Soleil adds.

I pull Katleya into another hug, sorry that I can't protect my siblings from this. Guilty, because this is the best I can do.

Alistair

I left for work early the next day. Yesterday, I received an invitation to attend a Leaders' meeting, and I can't wait to socialize with as many people as possible. Instead of turning left to the dome where the Soturi typically train, I make a right turn. I don't get to do it often, but when I do, I can't help the excitement in my stomach. I feel like I'm getting there. I feel like I'm actually getting to my goal.

I present myself to the guard in front of the gates of the majestic castle, showing my badge for the guard to check, and wait. The Soturi disappears into the sentry to check before stepping out again, motioning for me to enter. I nod, giving a distracted smile before walking through the gates, marveling at the incredible architecture and expansive gardens that spread in front of the castle. A few other Conjurers and Soturis hung around the entryway, casually chatting with each other. I smile again, just in case an important person sees me.

"Hello," a voice greets me, and I turn to see her pace matching mine.

I grin back instantly, making sure my expression looks genuine. The woman's short, but has a commanding voice and aura. She has short, curly black hair, dark skin, and piercing black eyes. Her white *abaya* had a hood that hung loosely over her hair.

"Hello," I greet her. I've seen her before, and based on the many jewels on her, I know she's important and high-ranking.

"I'm Avery Bilson," she introduces herself.

"Right! My name is Alistair Strong." I reach my hand out to shake hers.

Her gaze is a critical one, and she frowns, looking down at my hand like it was something to be wary of. Finally, she nods at me, then speeds up, passing me quickly.

I try not to take it personally. Many Conjurers are wary of people. Wary of anyone they haven't known since birth.

Guards in their polished armor guide incoming people to the meeting room. A mix of Soturis and Conjurers head the same way.

"Welcome to Krag Vinde celebration planning!" a man calls. He's at the center of the room, wearing his blue *abaya*, adorned with sapphire jewels over his neck and hands, similar to Alanna's. That's Leader Chen Savier. He has the power to nominate a Leader.

That's who I want to get close to.

"To all of you who aren't aware, Krag Vinde is the annual week of celebration at each district to identify and collect any person who might be holding Conjurer powers. To protect our people, we need to make sure they get to the Voii Makkas so that we can train them and make sure they don't pose as a problem to our society," Leader Savier adds.

I remember Krag Vinde differently. I remember everyone being extremely careful during that time. I remember fancy parties and people buying nice clothing that they couldn't afford just to impress Conjurers. I remember people disappearing, and families not knowing where they were. Of course, now I understand that people were being brought to a better place, to Voii Makkas, where they undoubtedly have better lives, like I do.

"By the next moon, each group will head out to each district to spend a week to observe and identify any potential Conjurers. You will be discreet. You will be silent. You will act as if you're invisible when observing and taking the person from their place. This allows us to make sure this process continues on and we equip Ainoa with only the most powerful Conjurers we can have," Leader Chen says.

"Once you've picked up these people, they need to understand that they are not to contact their families or friends by any means, unless they actually make it through their studies. No letters, no visitations, nothing. This allows us to make sure we do not get blamed for their family members dying," Leader Chen continues.

Finally, he pauses dramatically, scanning his audience.

"Remember, to the public, Krag Vinde is still a celebration of love, community, and friendship. There cannot be any talk or disclosure of finding and picking up people with power. Is that understood?"

"Yes, Leader," everyone responds, me included.

"Now, everyone can go, unless you have been tapped to travel to each district. Please stay behind so we can discuss your travel plans," he finishes.

I get up to leave.

"Oh, Alistair Strong," the same voice starts, and I nearly trip over. I look back at the man in the middle of the room. I didn't even know he knew my name. For a moment, I freeze.

Then I stand straight, bow formally, and then respond, "Yes, sir?"

"You will be in charge of Soturi training while everyone is gone," Leader Savier declares.

My mind whirls, and a surge of joy pulses through me. I can barely contain my grin.

"Yes, sir!" I say immediately.

I bow again in respect, then head out with the rest of the Conjurers and Soturis.

It's a little later in the day before I get some time with my friends.

"It's odd, don't you think?" I say as I tell them about the meeting, and the two nod. I pick up a piece of steak, munching on it thoughtfully.

I've arranged for a cook to make a meal for the entire group. It saved me time and allowed me to spend time without having to worry about food. Our spread includes soft, delicious bread, a variety of juicy and fresh fruit, corn and potatoes, steaks, and pig meat cooked to perfection. A meal like this could've easily fed a family of six where I come from.

"You know, I've never actually understood how Conjurers make it to Ainoa. No one actually comes to be a Soturi on their own. Usually, it's prisoners, good fighters, people who get caught doing something. Are there even Conjurers who come here of their own volition?" Oliver wonders aloud.

"Why would anyone not want to come to Ainoa?" I furrow my brow. I owe everything to the Soturis for giving me a much better life.

"Family. Home. You don't get to see your own people anymore, and anything can happen to you. It's a long journey, and unless you don't have a home, you won't want to come here just to train for another district that will only exploit your strengths." Oliver shrugs.

I can resonate with that. If I'd stayed where I grew up, I probably would've died. But if I had a family, maybe that would feel different.

"Plus, most people die on the way. These mountains are treacherous. Weather is incredibly unpredictable, and there are creatures in those mountains that I've never seen before in my life." Oliver chews his lip.

That was true. The journey to Ainoa took a couple of months, and it was harsh. We went through multiple storms, our carriage got run over once, and the rest of the children died during the journey. I was the only one who survived.

"I was sent here by my father. It wasn't my choice, I didn't want it to happen, but my father said it was the best way to make sure I'm trained for any kind of danger," Jack remembers, chuckling. "It feels like a lifetime ago."

"My father sent me here too," Oliver adds, looking angrier. "He put me on the next horse coming here without even getting a chance to say goodbye to my sisters and mother. That was right after I found my mother. I don't even know where my siblings are today."

"And to think Ainoa just picks up people from the street that they think have powers. They don't get to say goodbye, and they don't get to tell anyone." Jack scoffs.

"Like they're not human beings that deserve to know the truth," Oliver agrees.

They both look at me. "How did you get here?"

I hesitate. I knew they'd ask this question one day. I stare them in the eyes, making sure they can't see anything different in me.

"I don't actually remember," I respond.

"I wonder if Conjurers take your memories away?" Jack suggests suddenly.

"I bet they do. That's not good," Oliver agrees, shaking his head.

I don't say anything. I have an almost uncontrollable need to defend the Conjurers, but my friends wouldn't respond well to it.

I don't think it's that bad. After all, I made it here.

8

Kenna

It's finally the first day of the celebration week for Krag Vinde. Madyor is bustling with action. Anticipation fills the air, and my anxiety is through the roof. This is every Madyoran woman's or man's opportunity to find someone of higher ranking to buy them out of this district. I know. It's disgusting. But that's the only way to get out of the poorest district in all of Taiamen—to get bought by a richer family. I've never wanted to be bought, nor do I plan on it. No one would buy me anyway.

I'm nobody. I'm just me.

Colorful banners and bunting line our streets, creating a vibrant and festive atmosphere in comparison to the usually dark and gloomy surroundings. Local artists display their handmade crafts on tables outside their shops and along the windows. The inviting aroma of freshly baked bread and pastries permeates the air, tempting everyone—especially those who can't afford it.

A crowd gathers on the streets, some by the walkways awaiting the grand parade, others circling a makeshift stage where musicians and performers will entertain with lively melodies and captivating acts a little later in the day. High-pitched laughter fills our tiny district as children enthusiastically engage in traditional games, like sack races and tug-of-war.

Later, Madyor will be filled with cheers and applause as soon as the parade of Conjurers and Soturis passes. Everyone's excited about it.

Everyone except me.

It was only as I got older that I—and many other folks in the district—realized the yearly event happened to coincide with many incidents of people suddenly disappearing. Many theorized that the Soturi and Conjurers were kidnapping people from Madyor.

For what?

The theory is that Conjurers look for people with power. The power to Conjure is genetic, but people have been known to breed purposefully with Conjurers so they can pass down power, so it's not uncommon to find powerful people in other districts.

Then they bring anyone they think has power to Ainoa so they can hone it and use it to the government's benefit.

I look around at the crowds, wondering how many people are hiding a quiet dread beneath their cheer.

Because some cover their powers for that reason. Or some may not even be aware they have them. Some powers become evident later in life, or are only released when a Conjurer finds themself in danger.

So, no one is completely safe from the threat of abduction. Soturis look for people who are alone and have no family, so they can train more soldiers.

While most people enjoy the free food, celebrations, parties, and opportunity to climb the ranks, there are families that walk on eggshells, say goodbye to their kids every day with the expectation that one or all of them might suddenly disappear.

After all, there's nothing that Madyor can do if Ainoa chooses to take people. We don't have the resources or the people to fight. We don't have Conjurers or Soturis. We don't have pera.

We have nothing. Peter, Inez, Soleil, Katleya, and I stand by the store, along the sidewalk, waiting for the parade. Inez and Katleya whisper excitedly to each other, while Soleil just looks bored. Soleil is like me, never one to be impressed by these once-a-year celebrations that the government imposed on us, just to make us look and feel even more inferior than we already do.

"This is our year. I promise you," Peter says. Even he looks excited. He turns to the girls, mostly Inez and Katleya.

"You need to find husbands. It'll get you out of Madyor, and you'll be able to have a much better life somewhere else. Maybe even Ainoa," he encourages.

I look away, then roll my eyes, afraid he'd catch my reaction. He paints such a beautiful picture of Ainoa to us, but the truth is, he came from Ainoa and left it once upon a time for Lena.

He bends to push a strand of hair away from Katleya's face.

I catch her tense, unable to resist scowling this time.

"My beautiful girl. You're going to find someone this year. I know it," he says. "All you have to do is be on your best behavior."

I have to get out of here. This once-a-year bullshit from Peter will kill me.

I scan the area, looking for Zander's familiar figure. He typically doesn't like being around Soturis or Conjurers, so he likes to hide himself in places where people won't see him. I climb up a block, scanning the rooftops, my scowl softening into a smile as I spot Zander's familiar face on top of another rooftop. Even with his head beneath a hood, I know it's him. He's the only one who likes to climb roofs and prefers to spend his time hidden, looking over others, instead of joining in on the activities.

I jump down, then study Peter intently, waiting for the perfect moment to escape. When he gets distracted by one of our neighbors, I slip behind another person to make a quick escape.

I head toward the store and turn into the alley where I know there'd be gutter posts and trash boxes I can climb to get onto the roof.

"Hey," I greet him as soon as he's within hearing distance.

He turns. He has a dark look on his face, his brows furrowed, lips pursed, and the creases on his forehead have deepened. A face that isn't as excited as every other Madyoran for this holiday is a welcome sight to me.

I'm the only other person who knows about Zander's Conjuring powers. He released his power about seven years ago, saving us from a landslide in the mines. Like me, he doesn't trust the government, so he avoids using his powers.

He avoids being around Conjurers so he doesn't get kidnapped, which I'm relieved about, as I don't know what I'd do if I lost Zander, too.

As soon as he sees me, Zander's face softens, and he nods. He had his back to the roof, his long legs folded, hanging over the side of the roof.

"Peter finally out with the girls, huh?" he says.

I sit beside him, leaning an elbow on his arm to stabilize myself.

"Yeah." I sigh. "He gave the speech again about finding husbands and getting out of here."

He shoots me a look, and I shrug.

"Same old shit. You'd think Kat wasn't twelve years old."

Lively, upbeat music pierces the atmosphere, greeting the excited cheers of the crowd. Zander and I look up, and I squint to see where the music's coming from. Every spectator gathers along the walkway, awaiting the participants of the parade. Children stand on tiptoe, craning their necks for a glimpse.

In the distance, the rumble of a bass drum resonates through the air. People cheer. The sound draws closer, and the melody becomes more distinct, keeping everyone's attention on the approaching musicians. The rhythm is infectious, so people tap their feet, moving their hands, and dancing to the beat. I've never actually danced before, nor have I ever gotten into music the way most people did.

With colorful uniforms and gleaming instruments, an attractive and impressive marching band comes into view, illuminated by the sunlight. The drummers establish the tempo with powerful and rhythmic beats, while the brass and woodwind players add a triumphant and celebratory feel to the melody. The music swells and envelopes our surroundings, filling every corner of the street with its infectious energy. I might start clapping, too, but I despise Conjurers and Soturis just as much as Zander.

They'd rather drown in their own shit and piss before actually doing anything for us poor people of Madyor.

The crowd claps and cheers. Young and old folks match their steps to the cadence of the music. I catch sight of my sisters in the crowd, laughing, enjoying the moment. It's hard not to smile. I may not agree with the festival, but I don't see my siblings having fun as often as I'd like. Everywhere, balloons, flags, and streamers bob in time with the melody, adding to the visual and joyous spectacle. It looks fun, especially from where I am sitting.

The first float comes into view. A beautiful woman with enigmatic cerulean eyes and long, flowing jet-black hair, wearing a striking blue *abaya* had her arms out, making various shapes in the air with liquid. Next to her is a man with mesmerizing azure eyes, his muscular frame barely fitting into his blue *abaya* as he skillfully created shapes from the water in the bucket.

In the second float is another woman with fiery auburn hair, wearing a red *abaya,* juggling flames in an impressive incandescent display. She's accompanied by another man with spiky red hair, dark features, and amber eyes. He's big and heavy, his muscles defined especially in his red *abaya.*

I squint to get a better look, and notice a scar on his left cheek and a vertical line that runs down the middle of his left eyebrow. He has a dark expression, his eyes shifting through the crowd like a snake trying to find its target. I shudder. He looks like one of the men that haunts my dreams sometimes. Like someone who could really do some evil.

On the third float, a dashing, dark-skinned man, wearing a yellow *abaya*, stands tall, his hands outstretched over a tornado of leaves. Oddly enough, he looks like he's having the time of his life. A big smile spreads across his face as he engages his audience diligently. I didn't even realize Conjurers could smile. He's joined by a woman on the float, also wearing a yellow *abaya*, creating shapes with the light that surrounds them.

Next is a young man wearing a green *abaya* that swallows him whole. Vines crawl all over his body, as if they've grown from inside of him. The plants act as an extension of his arms as he freely touches and plays with the spectators' hair or heads. His display clearly tickles people the most.

"Look at them," Zander pipes up, his unimpressed voice cutting through the music, "looking down at us, like we're nothing." He scoffs, his blue eyes looking darker than ever.

I barely hear him. I'm preoccupied, catching sight of the group of Soturis and Conjurers on another float, who are looking at my sisters and any other young women they pass. Each woman looks pleased to attract their attention.

I roll my eyes. No matter the age or look of the Soturi or Conjurer, young women from Madyor continue to fawn over them. These people come to Madyor only once a year to show that they have power and that they can control anyone who rises against them. To take people from their families giving nothing back.

"It's disgusting," I agree, scowling.

I turn and quickly catch sight of my sisters talking to a Soturi. I tense immediately, my upper lip twitching and tightening as I watch the scene unfold. The warm smile on Soleil's face, the flirtatious grins from Inez. Even my twelve-year-old sister enjoys the attention.

"Are your sisters here?" I ask Zander.

He shakes his head, and my shoulders sag with relief.

"My sisters have to go to a dance class at the meadow today," I mention, just remembering the tradition of learning how to dance to prepare for Nights of Aava.

The Nights of Aava is a huge ball that takes place over three nights during Krag Vinde, where every eligible man and woman is invited and encouraged to go. For those eager to leave Madyor, it's a great time to get a Conjurer or Soturi to notice you. For those eager to avoid worrying about sustenance for the next few weeks, it's a great way to get free food.

"Are you going?" He turns to me. I can feel his eyes burning a hole.

"To the ball or the dance class?" I scoff, avoiding his eyes.

"Both."

"What's the point? I'm working. I also don't have anything to wear. It's not like they'll let me just barge in wearing work clothes," I snap, then immediately blush. Why do I always have to be so crass?

He chuckles, looking away.

"You don't want to go, anyway. It's just a bunch of Soturis and Conjurers preying on people."

The parade and festivities end at dusk. Zander and I wait on the rooftop for some time before heading down. I feel him reach behind me to raise my hood before taking my hand as he leads me through the streets to our homes. We stop when a haunting, mournful cry emanates from somewhere. My skin crawls, the hair on my arms prickling at the sound. It's so intense, so eerie, and Zander and I follow the sound to a window of a house.

After peeping through the glass, I see a woman lying on the floor, her shoulders shaking, her face a mask of tears and pain. Three other people surround her, their eyes also moist, faces crumpled. One of them kneels on the floor next to the woman, pulling them into their arms as the woman continues to cry. I shudder as the woman lets out another ear-piercing wail, her wordless, guttural sound conveying her anguish and despair, saying the words every other person who's lost someone would want to say but never could in times like this.

Tears burn my eyes. I remember the day Kane was taken, like it was yesterday. If I'd had the capacity to break down like this, I would've. But I had my siblings. I had my family to think about. I muffle my sobs. This isn't the first time I've seen something like this, but it's always heartbreaking. I look at Zander. He glances back at me sadly, conveying words he and I always share but never talk about. He extends his arm, wrapping it around my shoulders as he slowly pulls me away.

It is Krag Vinde, after all.

9

Kenna

My sisters and I enter the dress shop; excited chatter, curious demands, happy squeals, and disappointed groans fill our eyes and ears. I've always found it overwhelming to be here at the dress shop. I wish we'd had the idea to come here earlier so they could've skipped all this excitement--and pricing. Today, the dress shop is bustling with mothers and kids, trying on different styles, looking for dresses they like, getting fitted, everyone getting ready for the upcoming Nights of Aava. Since this is the only dress shop in Madyor, it's absolutely packed to the brim.

I follow my sisters around the store as they look at different dresses. I've never been interested in dresses. I've never had the time. When I was young, Lena used to take me to places like this, and it always cost her so much that it made me feel bad. Our entire family couldn't have meat for a few months just to make up for a single dress that I got.

So I never asked to go to a dress shop. When Lina took me, I tried not to want things that would be costly, tried not to want things I couldn't have, so I didn't have to be disappointed. I'm not pretty, so it isn't worth putting a nice dress on me, or filling my face with colors, just to prance around for boys to look at. There's no point trying to look attractive when there's nothing under it. Lipstick on a pig, my father would say. It is irrelevant whether I wear a nice dress or not; I will always be seen as no one, an outsider.

"How about this?" Inez excitedly pulls a dress from a rack.

Soleil rolls her eyes. "Do you mean for you?" she says sarcastically, pointing at the low neckline.

Inez giggles.

"Maybe one day." She smiles slyly.

Soleil and I look at each other and laugh.

Soleil runs her hand down a dress from a different aisle. "How about this, Kat?" she offers.

But Katleya is already on another aisle, deep in thought in front of a light-green dress, her hands slowly trailing down the neckline, admiring the blue ruffles and lace that run along the shoulders and arms.

Soleil, Inez, and I walk to her. My heart pounds, worried she's looking at an outrageously priced dress.

Katleya looks at us, her eyes filling with hope and excitement.

I peer at the price tag over her head, and immediately my heart sinks. Just from the look of this dress, the intricate designs of the lace, and the delicate jewels along the waist, I already know it will cost too much. There's a short, awkward silence between us sisters, amidst the wild chaos behind us.

"Actually, I think you'd look amazing in this dress, Kat," Soleil cuts in, holding up a different dress and breaking the sad silence that spread across Katleya's delicate features.

"Oh… yeah!" Katleya offers, her voice breaking.

I can tell she's trying to keep her voice steady. Katleya grabs the dress from Soleil and dashes into a dressing room. I can hear her stifled sniffles.

Soleil, Inez, and I look at each other sadly. None of us says anything. There's nothing I can say or do to make anything better.

Finally, I turn, disappearing behind an aisle of dresses, before I approach the dressmaker as quietly as I can.

"How much is the dress with the nice lace and jewels?" I ask the dressmaker, already dreading the response.

I've known the dressmaker for years. She'd even worked here when Lena used to take me. The dressmaker hesitates, and for a while, I thought she wouldn't say anything.

"Please," I beg desperately, "I'll do anything."

"I'll give it to you in exchange for six full months of cleaning at night. Can you do that?"

I quickly calculate my next six months in my head. It's not like I have anywhere else to go or anything else to do. I might as well. For my sister.

"I'll take it. I'll be here," I promise, already thinking about how I'd make it here in time after my shifts at my current job. It makes me tired just thinking about all the extra work, but at least I'll be somewhere other than the inn, right?

The dressmaker nods.

I grin, grabbing her hands to thank her. I head straight for the dress, plucking it out of the racks, before handing it to Soleil and Inez.

"I made a deal with the dressmaker. Do you want to go help her get into this?" I say excitedly.

The girls throw an arm over me, then excitedly run into the dressing room where I can hear my sisters shrieking with excitement.

I look over at the dressmaker, shooting her a smile. I'll be forever grateful for this. I can think about how to work an extra couple of hours in addition to my already scheduled fifteen hours a day at the inn later.

I join my sisters in the dressing room to help Katleya. My heart softens at the smile on Katleya's face. I think it's been a while since I've seen her smile like that. I take the dress from Soleil and Inez and kneel, holding the blue puffy dress in my hands, steering the opening of it towards my youngest sister. Katleya puts her hands on my shoulders, aiming to balance herself before stepping into the dress.

I spread the dress out further, pulling on its ends to showcase the fullness of the skirt. I'm careful not to pull too hard.

"Lift your feet," I tell her, as Katleya slowly eases into the dress, finding her footing under the mounds of fabric and dress beneath her. I shake the dress to make it easier for her, then lift it over her bodice. I grab the shoulders and pull it over Katleyas head, so she can push her arms through it. As soon as I get both shoulders on

Katleya's arms, I pull the back in place, making sure the fit's right before I pull the lace to create a snug, but comfortable fit for my sister. I tie the corset back, then step away to look at my work. I adjust the layers of fabric to make sure they fall gracefully and maintain their shape.

"Beautiful," I breathe.

Katleya beams. She walks to face the mirror, her hands grabbing the sides of her dress. She slowly turns, carrying the dress with her as she watches her reflection in the mirror.

I study her face, my heart softening at her expression. It's very rare that my sisters feel beautiful, and I'm here for every moment of it.

"You look great, Kat!" Soleil adds.

"If only we had some kind of jewelry," Inez cuts in, throwing me a look. She knows very well that I don't have any jewelry or pera to buy that kind of luxury.

Inez rolls her eyes. "I was just saying," she adds, her voice trailing.

"Okay, we got one down. Who's next?" I say brightly, puffing Katleya's dress one last time before looking at my other sisters.

"Me!" both Soleil and Inez offer at the same time, giggling.

My sisters enjoy these nights. I've never been to one, but I've always gotten the chance to enjoy all the leftovers brought home by my sisters. They always bring home quite a bit of food, usually feeding our entire family for at least a week.

"Are you sure you can't come, Kenna?" Soleil asks, sounding disappointed. She asks every year, and every year, I've always had to turn her down.

I shake my head.

"I'm sorry, girls. I can't get out of work tonight." I shrug. They know how I really feel about it.

"You don't have a dress, either," Inez adds as she works herself into her own dress with Katleya's help. Soleil glares at Inez.

"It's okay," I appease her, tapping her gently on the arm. "It's true; I don't have a dress."

I press my lips together. There's no point in dwelling. This is my life; this is my future. This is what I'll be doing for the rest of my life before I die. I put all my energy into helping Inez into her dress.

I force a smile as my sister twirls in her dress. "You look beautiful, Inez."

Hours later, we head home, my sisters drunk on the happiness of getting a new dress. On the other hand, I'm counting how much pera I have left for tonight's dinner, and realizing how much work I have coming up in the next week. Katleya stops suddenly, Soleil instantly bumping into her back.

"Hey!" Soleil says, glaring.

But Katleya just points to a home on her left. She walks toward a similar haunting sound to the one I heard the other day.

"Oh, it's the Crenzies' son," Inez whispers.

We watch a family cry through their window. The mother's bent over, her face wrenched as tears run down her cheeks. The father's eyes are also red, but he stands there quietly, watching the mother as she falls apart. Two other young girls sit beside the mother, studying her as they hug each other. A different family from the one Zander and I saw the other day. Another day in Krag Vinde, another family affected.

"What about him?" I ask.

"You haven't heard? He was moving things around last week in class!" Inez whispers back.

I swallow. "He's a Conjurer?"

I watch the mother wail in agony. She's clutching onto the father, her cries getting louder and louder by the minute.

"He definitely has powers of some sort. Apparently, there's talk the mother cheated on the father, and that's why he has powers. It was bound to happen, especially when you show off powers like that." Inez shrugs.

"If I were him, I would have hidden it. Why would anyone show their powers, knowing Conjurers would want to take you? You never get to see your family again, so what's the point?" Soleil's mouth ticks up and shrugs.

"I would have run away," Inez adds.

We all turn to look at her.

"You'd leave us behind?" Katleya says, her chin starting to shake.

"Only for you and your safety, dummy. What do you think would happen if Conjurers found out that you guys were hiding me? They'd hurt you—kill you, even. I'd run so they never find me, and you won't have to worry about protecting me." Inez rolls her eyes, shrugging like she actually knows what's outside of Madyor.

"Why wouldn't you take us with you?" Katleya says after a moment of thought.

She manages a weak chuckle. "You'd be too much trouble. If it were just me, I know what I can do. But if I have all of you, it would be much harder."

Her eyes widen. "Wouldn't you be lonely?"

"I'd rather be lonely than be taken. Who wants to be the government's puppet? Nobody. I sure as hell don't. Poor Conjurers think they're doing good, when in fact they're all just fucking puppets." Inez lets out a hollow laugh, but Katleya doesn't share the same sentiment.

She frowns.

"Don't worry, Kat." Inez pats her shoulders. "I highly doubt any one of us has powers."

Kenna

The sounds of music echo playfully throughout Madyor. I can hear it from where I'm sitting. Lights from the ball flicker throughout the walls of the inn, bringing some entertainment to what otherwise would be another boring night at the inn for me.

Tonight is the Nights of Aava, a celebration at the Takkia Rakken, a symbol of the Ainoan government right here in Madyor. On most days, the Takkia Rakken is closed, standing tall and still with vines growing on its gates and all over the walls of the building.

Some Madyorons would parade themselves willingly in front of the Conjurers and the Soturis, hoping for a proposal before the end of the night. A promise of an escape from Madyor, a promise of a better life somewhere else, where they won't have to worry about food anymore.

The proposal can be given to anyone who attends the Nights of Aava, no matter how old they are. Most commonly, they are marriage proposals, especially to anyone over the age of eighteen years old, but sometimes—and this turns my stomach to even think about—if a Soturi or Conjurer feels like a child has potential, then they'll propose to give the child a future, with the caveat that the proposed person would be marrying into that family in the future, chosen by someone of the family, or becoming their slave. The family of the proposed person gets a good amount of pera, most likely enough to feed them for a few years. The proposed person leaves at the end of Krag Vinde with their new family to a new life and district.

Just the sight of the Soturis and the Conjurers is enough to make me tremble with fury. They have the power to make a difference, and none of them do, all because they're under the orders of the King in Ainoa, a king who has never visited Madyor, not in the last three hundred years. A Leader who can't even be bothered to visit a district they govern.

Even the mayor's sons and daughters attend every year, hoping to be sold to someone. Lena never allowed me to attend when she was alive. My sisters go because it's fun, but the more they do, the more it feels like they've accepted that part of life, that they won't amount to anything unless they get sold.

I jump, falling off my chair at the sound of a knock on our door. It opens, and a head pops in, a goofy expression on his face.

I look at him, confused. Zander's usually out and about and away from the Takkia Rakken during days like this.

He chuckles at the look I give him, a slow smile spreading from one side of his face to the other. In the moonlight, his blue eyes looked purple, and I just catch sight of the flash of dimple on his right cheek.

Honestly, Zander and I have been friends for so long that I've never seen him in a romantic light or thought about how attractive he is. But these days, especially after all the ways Zander has protected and provided for me, I've been squashing some thoughts I never thought I'd have. Thoughts I don't think I should have.

Especially if I didn't want to be disappointed.

"Hi," I say, tilting my head toward him.

Zander steps forward, pulling a long package behind him. He looked particularly proud of himself tonight. I turn to the package in his hand. It looks a lot like a dress.

He takes a few steps towards me, and the package glimmers in the light.

My jaw drops.

He lays the package down on the table, and I trace my hand along the fabric of it.

Beautiful. I breathe deeply, my eyes furrowing at the exquisite dress.

The lace is intricate and soft beneath my rough fingers. I've never felt anything like it.

I look up at Zander.

"What's this for?" I ask, pulling up the bottom of the dress to get a better look at the silhouette.

I run my fingers slowly, feeling the satin fabric and lace details. The dress is a beautiful emerald green, with a V-neckline and low back. It has delicate yellow flowers made out of lace that run across the chest and around the abdomen.

He sits on the desk, and I feel his palm press down on my hand. I look at him again. My cheeks burn at his touch.

"I know how much you could use a night off." He squeezes my hand. "I know you want to go."

I do. I really do. I've never been to a Night of Aava, but I've always been curious. Even though the idea of it is disgusting, I've always heard how much fun it was, how there's so much food and drinks, how there's dancing. It's just one night. Maybe I can forget my morals just for a little while, so I can dance and forget my problems, right?

Right?

After all, I work so much. I deserve some time off, and I can keep an eye on my sisters and make sure they're not getting proposed to by random men.

He squeezes my hand again, and I look at him, willing down the bug-like flutters in my stomach. He smiles at me, his eyes twinkling in the darkness, his dimple deepening, and the fluttering instantly returns.

"Even though I think it's a bad idea," he adds slowly, giving me a look, "I think you deserve to forget about life for a moment. Even if it's just one night."

I don't really know what to say. I've never had a dress this nice, nor had the chance to attend the Nights of Aava.

"Zander..." I begin, my mouth still wide open at the shock.

I look at him for a second, then throw my arms around him. He smells like fresh earth, like it's just rained, but with a hit of iron tang, probably from working in the mines all day.

My heart skips, and for a moment I'm vaguely aware of his body so close to mine. How close I am to his chest. The sound his beating heart makes.

"Go ahead. Put it on," he encourages, picking up the dress, gently pushing it towards me.

I hesitate, and he pushes it again, the lace tickling the sides of my arms.

I take the dress and shoot him a smile before turning and disappearing into the closet behind me. As soon as I shut the door behind me, I squeal, biting my bottom lip. I feel silly, but I don't care. I've never had a dress this nice. I'm actually going to the Nights of Aava tonight!

I pull the dress over my legs, wishing I'd actually bathed and done something nice to my hair today. Oh well. At least I'll somewhat look the part. I didn't really want to get sold, anyway. Who am I kidding, though? Who'd want to buy someone like me? Gingerly, I bring it up over my shoulders, feeling the lace all over my body. It's soft and comfortable. I can't reach the back, so I shuffle myself toward the door, reaching a hand out to Zander.

"Can you?" I point to the zipper I can't quite reach.

My back is turned, but my body tenses as I realize I'm half naked in front of Zander. He steps closer, and I feel the heat from his hand down my back. My cheeks flush immediately, even as the dress tightens around my chest and closes on my back. I can't see myself right now, but the way the dress hugs my body makes me suddenly aware of my full breasts and the curves I didn't know I had.

For the first time in the twenty-one years I've been alive, I actually feel beautiful.

I turn around to face Zander, immediately blushing, remembering I was just half naked in front of him. We've been friends for so long, but we've never actually thought about each other like that. At least, I don't think he has.

I walk out of the closet, smoothing down the dress over my hips, looking straight so I avoid his eyes. I'm afraid I'll just be regular Kenna to him, and for just a few more seconds, I'd like to feel beautiful.

"You look stunning, Kenna," he murmurs.

I look up, surprised, and he's blinking like he's never seen me before. I blush under the weight of his gaze. He's never looked at me like this.

"I wish you could come with me," I tell him shyly.

He chuckles. "I know I talk a lot of shit about the people who will be there tonight." He swallows. "If it's your dream to have better things, you deserve to have them. You have to have the courage and bravery to do what it takes to survive—even if it means things I don't like." He caresses the side of my cheek, leaning closer ever so slowly. Time stops for a moment.

My entire body heats up, and my heart pounds in my ears. I close my eyes, feeling the warmth of his breath on my face.

This is it.

I wait.

Instead, I feel a soft touch on my forehead.

I swallow, fighting back disappointment. After all, I can't blame him for not wanting to kiss me. There's nothing about me that anyone would want to kiss.

I open my eyes, but I don't look at him.

"You should go," he says, stepping back and motioning to the door.

"What about you?" I ask, finally getting the courage to look at him.

He runs a hand through his tousled hair, his cheeks slightly red. It might just be the moonlight.

Zander chuckles, settling himself in the chair. "I mean, someone has to keep an eye on the inn, right?" He shrugs, winking at me.

I smile. "Thank you," I mouth to him and turn to the door.

"Be careful. Don't accept any proposals." I hear him say as I close the door behind me.

The Takkia Rakken is lively tonight, the atmosphere filled with dancing lights and echoes of rousing music carrying through the air. The pathway to the main door is lined with a luxurious plush red carpet that shimmers with an assortment of dazzling gems. Soturis stand along the gate, dressed in matching grey buttoned shirts and pants, adorned with intricate designs on the sides. They look so serious, looking out into the distance, pretending that Conjurers haven't already conjured the entryway to only accept people who meet certain criteria.

I cautiously enter the vicinity, my heart thudding in my ears. Despite the fact that I have a beautiful dress on, I still feel out of place. I gaze at the Soturis at the entrance, waiting for instructions, but they don't even glance my way. I keep going and make for the main doors. A few people loiter around the entrance and look at me like they've never seen me before. I can't blame them. I bet I wouldn't recognize myself either.

The massive double doors gleam with gold, crowned by a magnificent arch carved in the same intricate patterns as the building's sides.

Someday, I'll know what that means.

I take a deep breath, then push open the double doors and reluctantly step inside. No going back now.

I'm immediately blinded by captivating lights that run across the ceiling, shooting colorful lights onto the floors. The ceiling is so high it seems to touch the sky. I scan my surroundings, immediately catching sight of the dance floor in the middle of the room. It has open spaces, though it feels like everyone from Madyor is here.

Conjurers look absolutely stunning, with their expensively designed *abayas* gleaming in the lights. Madyorans look radiant and beautiful, everyone wearing their best dresses and outfits. Some also wear jewelry to accentuate their dresses and show their status, setting apart the few families who can afford such extravagance.

I scan the room again, this time, for my sisters.

Amara Winston leads a group of women with dazzling jewelry on one side. She's older than I am and hardly speaks to me unless it's throwing around some snarky comments about what I'm wearing. Miles Winston, who's the same age as Zander and I, leads the men in another area. He roars with laughter over something someone has said. They haven't noticed me come in, which I'm glad about—I don't want their attention. I shift from looking for my sisters and decide to find food instead. I'm starving. I walk along the aisle, ogling and running my fingers gingerly over the writings on the wall. Even the inside walls are decorated with aesthetic carvings. What could they mean?

Suddenly, I see a bright light over some tables. Bingo. Food time.

I hope there's fish. It's been a while. I start for the table immediately, passing other Madyorans who are definitely already sauced on the dance floor.

I reach the food, and I can't help but smile. I've never seen this much food in my life: rows and rows of different types of meat, lots of fish, soups, stews, and finger foods. A variety of pastries and bread. Cakes and desserts. Vegetables and fruits that look so fresh they might've just been plucked out of a farm. We don't have farms in Madyor because of the weather. All vegetables and fruits have to travel all the way from Ainoa or other districts. I've never seen anything this fresh.

I start with the drinks. There are many beverages: orange juice, grape juice, alcohol, apple cider, and more I didn't recognize, like wine, punch, and energy drinks. In Madyor, people are lucky to have apple cider and alcohol. Juice requires a lot of fruit, so it can get expensive, too.

I grab a cup and settle on hot apple cider before heading back to the food again. I stop for some crispy rolls. Yes, please. The description in front of it says "beef rolls." I pick a few and add them to my plate. Then, I pick up a few fish cakes. I grab a few of each type of food

I recognize. By the time I make it to cakes and desserts, I've already eaten the fish cakes, the beef rolls, and some delicious pastries.

Suddenly, the smell of the food makes my stomach churn. I haven't had this much food in a while. Stuffing my face probably isn't the best idea.

I place my plate and cup on an empty table and head out of the area, eager to get away from the smells. I'll come back for some leftovers later.

I walk around the Takkia Rakken, admiring the beautiful architecture and the conjured surroundings. A lot of those on the dance floor are people I grew up with. They wear beautiful gowns and jewels, their bosoms exposed just enough to catch attention, parading themselves around the Soturis and Conjurers, who looked radiant and dominant in their *abayas* and uniforms. Some appeared to be under the influence, stumbling and slurring their words. Others had a more visible agenda.

I find an empty couch and sit down, nursing my stomach. A sudden commotion draws everyone's attention to the middle of the dance floor. Other women crane their necks to watch a woman who's dancing with a man already, yet other men of all ages keep reaching out towards her, clearly hoping to get some time with her. She barely gets the chance to dance long with one man before another cuts in. I can't see her face from here, but she looks like she's having the time of her life. The shadows on the dance floor make it difficult to see exactly who she is, but from afar, the woman looks pretty young.

She must be very beautiful. A tinge of jealousy sparks, but I sigh it away. I can't change the way I look. I have to accept, even though I'm wearing a beautiful dress, that this is all I am, and all I can be.

I bet she'll get a proposal tonight.

A man twirls the young woman, and she laughs aloud, her laughter echoing throughout the halls of this beautiful building. I freeze.

I stand up so sharply that the people next to me glance up. I don't care. The crowd of dancers around the young woman is still too thick for me to see her. I walk around, my heart palpitating faster and faster as I tiptoe around the crowd, eager to see her.

And then there she is.

In the middle of the crowd. Her long brown hair flows in the soft breeze, swaying with her every move as the man, who's far too old for her, spins her around. Her lips are wide with joy and delight as onlookers watch with adoration. Her familiar brown eyes glow with laughter under the dazzling lights of the room. The dress accentuates the girl's moves, highlighting curves she doesn't even have yet. But in the dancing lights within the Takkia Rakken, the weight and volume of the dress I'd bartered sleepless nights to work double shifts for gave her such a regal presence, a presence everyone clearly admires. Then, in the vibrant lights of the dance floor, the sparkling jewels and gems above illuminate her face. My heart sinks.

It's my twelve-year-old sister.

Kenna

I wake up slowly, the nightmare from last night still lingering in the dark shadows of my eyes. I brush the corner of my lips with my wrist and groan. My stomach complains, and I feel nauseous.

A hasty bang sounds at the door, waking me up to the consequences of my actions last night. I turn over just as a dress disappears behind the door. It slams shut, the sharp sound echoing through the walls of our tiny room.

I grimace.

Last night did not end well. The moment I saw Katleya in the middle of the dance floor being ogled and surrounded by powerful, but older, random men, I lost it. Like, *lost it*, lost it. I grabbed Katleya mid-dance and dragged her out of the Takkia Rakken, kicking and screaming. By the time we made it to our house, Katleya had shouted every single curse at me, slapped, kneed, elbowed, and hit me in the face countlessly. The pain in my eye isn't as painful as the words that had fallen from Katleya's mouth. I don't think she's ever talked to me this way before.

It's too painful to remember exactly, but something about ruining her chances, wanting to control her every move, not liking it when someone else gets the attention, and how I'd wasted her opportunity to leave this shithole.

I bury my face back under my blanket.

When did the idea of being sold to a richer family become so important to her? I can't remember. I wish Lena were here. Lena would know what to do. If Lena had been here, this would've never happened.

I lightly pat my bruised eye. I hadn't seen myself in the mirror just yet, but I bet my eye had turned purple.

I will myself out of bed and immediately want to crawl back in. Facing the reality of last night is emotionally draining.

I sigh, my lungs grateful for that extra oxygen to help push me out of bed. I listen to see if there is anyone outside the room. My sisters are in the kitchen. I know I'm going to have to face this sooner rather than later.

I pull on some clothes, rehearsing an apology in my head. I shouldn't have to apologize. But my sisters have grown up thinking they have to impress these people. They never had the protection that Lena provided. By the time Lena passed away, Inez was only four years old, not nearly ready to be out and about. When Inez turned six, Peter put her in a nice dress and paraded her out and about during Krag Vinde. The only reason he never pushed me is that I was already working at that age.

As I head out of our bedroom door, I pause, catching my reflection in the mirror, and grimace at the purple reflection that was once my eye. I sigh again, and then brace myself to open the door.

I head directly for the ice box to grab a pack of ice for my eye. Only Soleil and Inez are in the kitchen.

"Hi," I say, struggling to look them in the face.

"Hey," Soleil greets me, with a half-smile crossing her face. The house seemed painfully quiet today.

"Where is she?" I ask, cringing at the ice on my eye.

Inez points toward the back door. "She's outside."

I sit next to her and sigh.

"You know she's just doing what she's been taught to do all these years, right?" Soleil offers. "This is the situation we're in at the moment. We're being trained to impress these people so we can go somewhere—anywhere."

"That's what I find so upsetting, truly," I respond. My eyes well again, painfully.

"I think you are all worth more than just that, Soleil. I hate that we have to get married and be sold off just to find something better," I protest.

She smiles warmly.

"I know. But at the end of the day, we can't do anything about it. That's just how we are; that's how we get anywhere. I love you, and I appreciate everything you're doing for us. We don't intend to be here forever, though. If that means we have to get sold to someone, then that's what we'll do." Soleil shrugs, eyeing Inez.

When your thirteen-year-old sister is willing to give herself up just because that's what society has told her to do, it breaks your heart over and over again. The even sadder part is I can't do anything to save her. I can't do anything to make her life better.

"We aren't blessed like Maris and Jana, Kenna. Aelin protects them from all of this. We don't have anyone shielding us from that," Inez looks me in the eye, "and you can't protect us from that either. You can barely feed yourself." She shakes her head.

I feel like I just got slapped. My eyes grow hotter, and tears start running down my cheeks. I heave a sigh, resisting the heat rising in my belly. Soleil and Inez just look at me.

"We don't mean for that to hurt, Kenna." Soleil eyes me carefully.

I work so hard to give them as much as I can, and it's not enough. It will never be enough. How does anyone do it? How does Aelin do it? I look away, casually wiping the tears from my cheeks.

Soleil gets up from her chair and moves closer, taking my hands in hers. "Truly, Kenna. You cannot play mother to all of us. You need to live a life, too. Have you even thought about what you want to do in the future? Like, get married? Have kids? Do something else outside of working your life away?"

I haven't. I live on a day-to-day basis. I never think about my future. Truthfully, I've never thought I'd have one. I've honestly always thought I was going to die in Madyor, probably in the next few years. I mean, seriously, with the hours I work and the climate here.

"I mean, you and that tall guy always seem to hang out. What about him?" Inez pipes in suddenly, sounding excited.

"Ooh, right! He's super cute!" Soleil adds.

I blush instantly, remembering our moment from last night. Zander and I have been friends for so long that it barely occurs to me that we can be more than that. Okay, that's not true. Sometimes I hope, every now and again, just like I did last night. But Zander's never made a move; he's never done anything to show he might be interested. I mean, again, why would he? I'm just… me.

"You like him," Inez teases. They look at me, and I falter before responding.

"I've always had to take care of you. I've… I've never thought about it," I lie, shrugging.

"But that's why we need to do this, Kenna. So you don't have to. And you really don't. This is our choice. Our life. We want to do this. I hate that you put so much pressure on yourself just for us," Soleil explains. "We need to do this so you can have the courage and time to go be yourself, be who you are meant to be."

I wrap an arm around my little sister, wincing at the muscle pain on my shoulders. Sometimes, it is difficult to remember who she is when she says such insightful things.

"You think I can go talk to her?" I ask.

Soleil shrugs.

"You can try. Truthfully, I think she is just embarrassed. I would be too if my overprotective sister dragged me out to a ball that every single Madyoran attended." She chuckles.

I turn red and looked at her sheepishly. I kiss Soleil on the forehead and nod at Inez.

Then, I breathe deeply before heading outside.

"Hey," I say as I come out the back door.

Katleya is sitting on a chair, her head buried under a hat. For a second, I worry that she won't respond. Instead, she sits up at the sound of my voice.

She looks so tiny in her chair, so young with her soft features, dark round eyes, skinny legs. I want to protect her, want to keep her safe. Want to prevent things from happening to her. And yet, I'm powerless.

I sit next to her.

"You know I love you, right?" I begin, any rehearsed words immediately disappearing from me.

She smiles. "I know," she answers. "I'm sorry about your eye."

I shrug. "I talked to your sisters," I say. "I'm really sorry."

Katleya grins, her front tooth peeking out of her lips. She looks so much like Lena.

"It's okay. I understand. I know you're only looking out for me." Katleya reaches out and pats my knee.

"I never meant to embarrass you, you know. I just didn't like how every older guy there was ogling you," I admit, fighting back tears painfully.

Katleya laughs. "Don't worry. I really only liked dancing. I don't think I'm ready to leave yet, either."

"Really?" I smile, hope rising back up.

Katleya giggles. "I'm only twelve, Kenna. I think you'll have to put up with me for a little longer. I was just embarrassed. Everyone's going to talk about it at school. I'll always be the girl whose sister pulled her off the dance floor at Nights of Aava. Isn't that embarrassing?"

"I'm sorry," I apologize, nodding sheepishly. I can only imagine. I must be the laughingstock of the entire school at the moment. I can't even imagine what kind of insults the Winstons will hurl at Inez or Soleil.

Katleya grins.

"It's okay. I'll get bullied either way, so it doesn't matter. At least I know you're here for me," she assures me.

I reach for her hand. "I'll always be here for you," I promise, squeezing Katleya's hand.

A sudden commotion erupts from the house. Katleya and I look at each other.

"Uh-oh. What now?" Katleya says. She jumps and starts for the house. I follow.

Inside the house, Peter is waving his hands, looking pleased with himself. His alcohol-infused eyes glisten with a glossy sheen. He reeks of alcohol.

"What happened?" I demand, instinctively planting myself between Peter and the girls. Whenever he gets drunk, he has a tendency to start throwing punches at anything and anyone in his path. Especially when he's 'happy' drunk.

"You did it! My beautiful girl. You'll be the one to get me out of this place!" he drawls, his thick accent making it difficult to understand.

I look at the girls. They look as confused as I feel.

"We're going to be rich!" he continues to rejoice, moving back and forth, looking like he's about to fall over.

Dread spreads over me. "What do you mean?" I insist, taking another step toward Peter.

Peter barely looks at me. Instead, he looks past me and onto the girls, like he's looking at a prize. I stare at him. Then at the girls. Then back at him.

"What do you mean?" I repeat, a sinking feeling creeping up to me. Warmth rises in my belly.

"You will get us out of this place," he says again, his eyes pinned on the girls.

"Who? Who, Peter?" I urge, planting myself firmly between Peter and the girls, mostly to get his attention and actually get an answer.

Peter moves closer to the girls, shoving me out of the way. I stumble and hit the floor, my lips busting on the concrete. I taste blood, but I ignore it. Peter is unsteady and irregular. He sways with every step as he tries to balance. His pace is inconsistent, sometimes aggressively accelerating, then slowing down suddenly. The girls try to shrink as small as they can, but they're already backed up to the stove behind them.

"Kenna," Katleya pleads, and I catch her eye.

I know I need to help her.

I get up immediately, ignoring the pain on my side, taking the now-tiny space between Peter and the girls.

"What are you talking about, Peter?" I demand. I motion for the girls to leave while I distract him.

He beams. "I sold your sister to a rich Conjurer who needs a wife. He's going to pay ten thousand pera for her now and another ten thousand when the wedding happens," he slurs.

My stomach knots, and bile rises in my throat. That's enough to feed us for many years, but I can't let this happen.

"What?" My voice thunders across the room so loudly that even my sisters look surprised.

Peter's eyes narrow, and his lips purse. I can see his muscles tightening as his fists start to clench.

A piercing scream escapes one of the girls, shattering the tense air. The girls scramble in different directions, desperate to flee the palpable sense of danger emanating from the escalating confrontation between me and Peter. But Peter reaches out and grabs Katleya's arm, his fingers tight around her skinny little arms.

"This little bitch is going to save us," he slurs, dragging Katleya behind him.

"Let me go, Papa," Katleya whimpers, tears rolling down her cheeks, fear brimming in her eyes.

I lunge between them, wrangling Peter off of Katleya. He's heavy, but mostly drunk. His fingers clench so tightly around her arm that his knuckles are turning white. Katleya's arm is red from Peter's grip. I pry his fingers off of Katleya and jump on him to prevent him from coming after her again. "Go!" I hiss at her.

Katleya scampers off to Inez and Soleil, who stand at the corner, trembling as they watch me and Peter.

"What did you do, Peter?" I demand, pushing him onto the ground as I stand up.

Peter waves me off, stumbling as he tries to stand and steady himself with the nearby chair. He looks at me, then at the girls. His eyes glaze over, but his expression is triumphant.

"I sold your sister, Kenna. And you can't do anything about it." He looks at me.

I look at him.

Silence.

Then, I lunge at Peter, growling.

"Kenna!" the girls scream.

I aim for his face, but Peter's too strong, and too quick, even in his intoxicated state. He meets my face with his palm and pushes against me. His fist lands on my cheek, and I stumble across the room, finally hitting the floor, hard.

"Kenna!" the girls scream again.

But Peter isn't done.

He staggers across the room, his eyes laser-focused on me. He charges, his hand finding the neckline of my shirt. I can see the veins in his wrist throbbing with rage. His hand trembles, and I brace for impact. As his hand lands on my face, the sound echoes in my ears.

Alistair

As I watch the group train, I keep a closer eye on the Soturis that have the least experience. The Soturis have a specific set of moves they have to repeat consecutively. A mistake means the entire group has to repeat the entire set again. This helps the team master the moves and gives them the chance to work together more harmoniously.

Today's a big day. A majority of the Leaders have left to travel for Krag Vinde. They won't be back for many months, especially since there are many, many treacherous paths to cross just to get to one district. I've been tasked with my first real leadership role, a role that could essentially put me up to be a Leader in the future.

I'm excited because I'm getting closer and closer to what I've always wanted. One day, I'll be a Leader. I'll be someone my adoptive father would never even fathom.

I'm enjoying leading the training of a group of Conjurers and Soturis. Typically, Conjurers and Soturis train separately, but every Krag Vinde, when there are significantly fewer Conjurers and Soturis in Ainoa, we combine training, allowing Conjurers and Soturis to actually get to know each other and work together. Conjurers train Soturis to ward off their attacks; Soturis train Conjurers to strategize and fight physically, if they need.

Last year, someone else led the group. That person eventually moved on to a job within the Iklead. This time, Leader Chen actually reached out to me directly to give me the task. ME!

I've never been tasked with something this important before, but I'm excited to have the job.

I feel like I'm doing something important, something real, something that allows me to give back to the people that gave me everything I have today. Besides, I really like having people look at me the way they do now—with respect and admiration. Everything I say matters here. I bet I'm the only one from where I came from that's made it this far. It will only be a matter of time before I become one of the most important people in this country.

When I first joined, this was the way I was trained. The repetition, the sacrifices, the consistent orders. The better you follow, the better you become. After all, we train good Soturis, not rebels.

I was skinny and thin when I arrived. The journey was harsh and long, and by the end of the journey, we barely had anything to eat. I struggled so hard to keep up with the training. My arms were weak. I couldn't even hold a sword, let alone carry the heavy buckets of water or bricks that every Soturi had to train with in the early stages of their training. Because I was so small, I got beat up a lot for not being able to follow training sets and making everyone else have to repeat the set again. It took time for me to build muscle, so I actually spent the first few months doing overtime. I woke up every morning a few hours earlier than everyone else, and got a head start on training. I did it to be stronger, better, faster than everyone else. I carried bricks and buckets of water, and did laps around the lake until I was ready to pass out. That was how I met Jack and Oliver. Jack was getting beat up by another Soturi, and even though I was nowhere near the size of the guy who was making fun of Jack, I ran over to help.

Of course, my hero complex got me nowhere. I broke my jaw, busted an eye, and a couple of ribs. While I was transported to the infirmary, Jack called me Alistair, a known name for a defender of people in Noppealiik. I never corrected him. From then on, I was Alistair, and I honestly liked it. Being the defender felt really good, like I was someone. Someone who could make it somewhere. Someone worthy to be looked at. Suddenly, with that new name, I was a different person, a different human being, not the one plagued with thoughts of the past, and horrors of my upbringing.

After all, here in Ainoa, I didn't have a safety net. I didn't want to fail at becoming a Soturi—that would prove everything my adoptive father used to say. Everyone who fails Soturi training ends up becoming a servant for the Conjurers, and I don't want to become someone that another powerful person just orders around. Besides, as a Soturi, I'm trained to find and aim for a goal. Becoming a Soturi has trained me to aim higher, speak up for myself, know, and understand my purpose in life.

The group repeats the set a few more times before I dismiss them for a break and head into my tent. I have to fill out some forms to complete my application for my next badge. Yes, I'm already applying for the next level of Leadership, not even a full month after getting promoted.

"Hey," a soft but pleasant voice interrupts.

I jump from my seat, turning, and laughter erupts from me when I see who's at the entrance.

A woman with beautiful blonde hair walks in. Her tall figure and captivating features make her impossible to miss. Her eyes, deep as the ocean, are accentuated by the contrast of her elegant royal blue *abaya*. Nestled within a delicate silver setting, a row of exquisite sapphires adorns the center of her breasts, making it very hard for me to avoid looking at her cleavage. She has a similar bracelet, each gem catching the light as she turns, reflecting it with a dazzling display of brilliance. The colors dance and shift with the change of light at every movement—from rich navy to the clearest cerulean. The sapphire gems are a sign of stature: appropriate, because Alanna is the daughter of Leader Chen Savier, who's the current *Ranyatira*, or Leader of all Conjurers.

I smile. I like having her around. It feels important to be around someone of such standing. I stand up to face her, pausing for a second to take in my surroundings before inching closer, my body leaning towards her. I pull her towards me, immediately smelling the delicate and floral aroma of her skin. Her fragrance is subtle, but leaves a lingering impression.

She chuckles slightly, holding her breath as I draw closer, my lips just inches away from hers. I brush her long, blonde, silky hair away before cupping her face and leaning in. Her lips part ever so slightly, her sapphire eyes watching my every move, and I tilt my head, aligning my head with hers. I can feel the warmth of her breath against my skin, instantly triggering impulses throughout my body. Our lips connect, and for a second, everything else disappears.

I shut my eyes, but then flinch involuntarily. I never meant for it to happen, but suddenly, another female face appears in my head. I swallow back the memory.

I've never even thought of her in that way. We were just kids. She was my best friend, and she's probably dead now. People where I come from don't survive.

"You okay?" Alanna asks, her eyebrows furrowing.

I shrug off the thoughts of her. I smile again, willing my face to act as my head demands. I'd never hurt the daughter of a Leader. Never.

"Yeah, yes! Sorry, it's just been a long day," I say, looking away, as if that would brush away the sudden intrusion.

We are casual, but we've been seeing each other more often lately. I don't socialize with many Conjurers, but it's easy to spend time with Alanna. Besides the fact that she's incredibly beautiful, irresistible, in fact, I'd be stupid not to try to take things further with her, especially if I want to become a Leader one day. Alanna is my way into the inner circle. She'd also make the ideal wife of a Leader: powerful, rich, beautiful. Everything a Leader would want.

"Ready to go to dinner?" she asks, peering over my desk.

Her eyes narrow, squinting as she trails her fingers along the piece of paper.

"Application for the gold badge." She nods approvingly, but I can see the hesitation on her face.

"Impressed?" I chuckle.

She laughs.

"Wow, you've only been a yellow badge for what? A month?"

"No better time than now," I respond confidently.

Alanna was raised in Ainoa, right at the heart of politics. She didn't have to make it anywhere. She was born already *there*. On the other hand, I have to fight for everything I have, everything I might want. I come from the poorest, lowest background any Leader could ever have, and I constantly need to prove myself.

"Dinner, then?" I interrupt, purposely avoiding a longer conversation about this. She doesn't understand what it's like to constantly be fighting for space, for privilege, for everything that's better.

Alanna nods.

"Ready," she confirms and leads the way out of the tent, her royal blue *abaya* flowing in the wind, trailing behind her long, blonde hair.

I follow, hoping someone of a higher stature sees us. No better way to make it up the ladder than being around the people already standing at the top.

Kenna

I didn't think I was going to die today. I mean, it's not like I woke up wanting to die or even planning to. Yes, I might have woken up feeling like I got punched in the face, which I actually did last night after pulling my screaming and kicking little sister Katleya out of the Nights of Aava.

But here I am, lying on the ground, with Peter's large body hunched over mine, his fists making contact with my cheeks in an erratic pattern dictated by his inebriated mind.

I grunt, feeling a throbbing sensation radiating from my cheeks. I can't breathe. I gasp for air. I'm disoriented and confused, but just as I'm about to get up, Peter slams me back down. His latest punch lands on my nose, and I hear a crack. I thrash to get out of his grip, but I'm too weak. Peter's eyes are glassy and translucent, and he seems to be in some kind of trance. His intoxicated rage consumes him. His punches are wild and uncontrolled. His form and stature are menacing.

I open my eyes, the rhythmic pulsating of my head echoing the beating of my heart. It feels like something is pressing on my head. The pain radiates from one side of my face to the other. I see blinking lights in my eyes, and I'm nauseous and dizzy. Fear and anger are the only things I can focus on aside from Peter's fists.

And then... I feel it before I even realize it's happening.

Something pulsates from me, erupting like an explosion of energy and will. Peter is lifted off the ground, an overwhelming force propelling him across the room, his eyes wide as he desperately tries to regain control. His body slams into the wall, and a distinct crashing sound reverberates throughout the room. He hacks and groans, and then ultimately falls quiet.

But that warm feeling in my stomach feels wonderful.

I sink into it. I'm so tired, and the feeling is so pleasant, like a hug. I'm comfortable here. So I let it take me.

Kenna

"Kenna, Kenna, you have to wake up. Kenna, we have to go," a desperate voice says.

I blink. I'm so tired and dazed.

"Kenna, we have to go. Come on, they're going to take you. We need to leave now," the voice says again, and I feel a gentle pat on my cheeks.

I grimace. That stings.

"Kenna, Kenna," he repeats.

I cough, blinking rapidly. My eyes hurt as they open to the blinding light. I fixate on the brilliant and dazzling glow. And... it is radiating from...

From me.

Me.

I scream. The light continues to glow, and I wave my arms at it, trying to get rid of the light bursting out of my stomach.

I continue to thrash, eager to get the light away from me. What the *Faahi* is that?

"Kenna!" a voice yells, and I look up.

A pair of hands grabs my shoulders, shaking me.

His face comes into focus. I know him. His face brings a cool breeze breaking into the steady warmth of the light. I float toward the breeze.

Toward him.

Finally, I recognize him, and my eyes fill with tears.

Zander is here. I grip his arms tightly, my entire body instantly grateful for his presence. My cheeks are wet, but I hold tight, forcing myself to focus on his face.

The light vanishes back into my body.

Kenna

After the light leaves me, I can feel myself sinking back into unconsciousness, and my mind keeps taking me back to the past, as if to remind me of my place. That no matter what's just happened, I'm never going to amount to anything. Not only have I grown up thinking I'm ugly, socially inept, and generally inferior to the other women around me; I've also spent a lot of my life believing I'm stupid. My school days hadn't helped that, of course. The only people who talked to me were Kane and Zander. Whenever my teacher would ask a question, I never had the right answer. My entire class always laughed. I could never even remember what the question was; all I could think about were the pairs of eyes boring through me from every corner of the classroom. I just looked down at my feet every time, my ears turning red.

I'm stupid, I kept thinking. I wish I was smarter. I wish I could retain information better. That when I'd look at my books I'd see the words right. I wish I knew the answers. I wish I knew what to say and had the courage to say it.

It wasn't even that I didn't try, it was more that I just had a hard time with books and reading. My brain didn't function as well as others' did. I didn't learn quickly enough.

One afternoon, I'd run into a group of kids who always liked to gossip about me. I was on my way back to the house when Amara Winston and her group approached me. They were always together, she and four other girls with two guys. I'd always see them laughing together, hanging out. Amara invited them to her parties. She and her family had enough food to share, unlike most Madyorans. Our entire class wanted to be her friend. I wanted to be her friend, too, but I was never good enough. I mean, who wouldn't want free food?

"Are you stupid?" Amara asked in that high-pitched voice of hers.

I didn't respond, but I couldn't pull my eyes away from her. I tried so hard not to cry, but I couldn't help it. My eyes immediately started brimming with tears.

She smirked. "We haven't even said anything yet," she said, rolling her eyes. She shrugged her beautiful, long hair off her shoulders. The other kids giggled.

"Why are you stupid? Maybe because you're the daughter of some random creature? Are your parents stupid, too, do you think?" she said.

They all laughed. On my bad days, I still remember this laugh. It echoes in my mind like a constant reminder of who I am. Of how much I don't know who I am.

"You're so ugly, too. Where did you come from? A hydra?" another quipped.

They laughed again.

My lips quivered. I opened my mouth to say something.

"What? Maybe you're from a bakawa," Amara sneered.

I didn't look up. I didn't dare respond.

"Kenna, you know you'll never amount to anything, right?" she continued, jeering.

Her group of bandits continued to laugh.

"You're going to die here. You're going to be nothing. No one will look at you because you're nothing. You're not pretty. You're nothing," she repeats.

"You're nothing," the rest of them agreed.

And that's what I'd continued thinking about as I ran back home.

Honestly? I still think they're right.

16

Kenna

"Kenna, we have to go, we have to go," the voice repeats.

I cough, straining to get up, but my body resists. I'm in so much pain I can't even feel parts of my body anymore. "What?" I ask, peering at him through the one eye I can open. He looks back at me, his eyebrows knitted, eyes wavering, shifting restlessly with nervousness.

"You just showed incredible power, Kenna. The Conjurers are going to come for you. We have to *go*," he repeats, emphasizing the last part of his sentence.

I scan my surroundings, immediately spotting Peter across the room, unconscious, his head slumped against a wall. The girls huddle on the other side of the room, their eyes also closed, their chests heaving up and down from labored breathing.

What the *Faahi* did I do?

"They're alive, but we need to go. We can't let them take us. They'll kill us and our families," he snaps impatiently. "You and me, Kenna. Remember?"

I look at Zander again, my brain recognizing his face. It takes another second to realize that he's scared and panicked. I can't wrap my head around what is happening.

So, instead, I follow directions. Zander pulls me up. Rather than head toward my sisters, I run into the bedroom and grab a rucksack, stashing some clothes and my thickest coat.

I'm overwhelmed. I can't think straight. My head aches.

I pat under my clothes until I feel coins. I snatch a handful and drop them into my pockets. Then, I pick a piece of paper and a pencil, quickly scribble on it, and place it on top of Soleil's pillow. Outside, I can hear Zander's footsteps echoing as he paces back and forth.

I leave the room with my rucksack on my back, slamming the door behind me.

In the kitchen, my sisters and Peter start to wake. I head for my sisters, kiss their cheeks, ignoring the burn that comes along with my tears. I never thought I'd be the first to leave.

"I love you," I say, my voice cracking.

They look confused and dazed. I open my mouth to say more, but Zander grabs my arm.

"I'm sorry," I tell them, taking one last look, before turning and running out the door.

I don't bother saying goodbye to Peter.

I follow Zander out of our house, past a few streets and across the main street when suddenly, he stops.

"We have to make a stop," he says.

He pulls me into a dark alley and behind a huge refuse skip.

Zander pulls off his coat and wraps it around me, pulling the hood over my face. I let him. I'm still processing. My mind's still where I left my siblings.

"Stay here," he says, pushing me behind the trash. I don't resist, letting myself fall into the small space behind it.

"I have to go pick up some stuff. I'll be right back. Do not move," he hisses at me. He grabs another board and places it in front of me.

In the silence of the trash bags, I'm left alone to catch up to what's happening.

I look down, patting my stomach gingerly, right where that light had come from only moments ago. I look at it, feel it, question it. What's inside me?

I'm leaving my sisters. I'm leaving Madyor. Where am I going? What am I? What did I do?

My head is spinning, the pain of Peter's punches reverberating behind all the thoughts threatening to take over.

What the *Faahi* have I done?

I jolt at the sound of a board being pushed from the trash box. I brace for danger, but sigh in relief when I see Zander behind the board. He reaches over and pulls at my arm.

"Let's go," he says. "Keep your hood up. I saw a few Conjurers out."

He pauses and looks left and right before turning into the alley. Lucky for me, Zander knows these alleys like the back of his hand.

"Where'd you go?" I ask, trying to steady the fear in my voice.

He hesitates before opening his rucksack. I look inside.

His rucksack is filled with food—fruits, meat, pig meat, fish, even eggs.

"Zander! Where did you get that?" I hiss, even though I know exactly where he'd be able to get that food.

Zander rolls his eyes.

"Never mind where I got it," he snaps, rolling up his rucksack, and he throws it over his back before he starts to walk.

"Zander!" I scold, trying to catch up to him. I ignore the pain shooting up my legs.

Zander whips around. "We're on the run now, Kenna. How do you think we're supposed to eat?"

I stare back, stunned. That thought hadn't even occurred to me.

He's right. We're running now.

Without Zander, the Conjurers and Soturis would've found me by now. I'd be on my way to wherever they take people. And if I resist, they'll probably kill me.

So despite the fact that I feel bad for Roger and the store, I reach out, grab his hand and continue to follow Zander as we pass through Madyor.

Most people haven't made it out of bed yet because of Nights of Aava. We see a few Conjurers staggering around, looking pale and weak, but Zander pulls me into an alley before they notice. We make it all the way to the meadow across the rooftops from Takkia Rakken under the hot morning sun. When we make it to the last house, Zander climbs down as quietly as he can. He scans for people and for any other signs of life before he signals for me to toss my rucksack. The rucksack lands in his arms.

Then, he looks up, motioning for me to come down. I get down on my knees and look down, my arms shaking. I can't tell if it's from the running or if I'm finally succumbing to the blows Peter had subjected my head to.

"Whoa," I say as my world suddenly spins.

"I'm coming," I tell him, blinking quickly so I can grab hold of reality as well as the drainpipe running down the side of the house. With my better arm, I hold tight and jump, hauling myself down. My heart races, but I keep holding, my body sliding down as carefully as I can.

It feels like forever. Pain sears through my body, throbbing angrily as I make my way down.

I can't take the pain anymore. My arm slips, and I lose my balance and flail, losing my grip on the post altogether.

I'm free falling, looking up at the soft sky with sore eyes. I brace for impact, expecting to hit the ground hard. What's a little more pain, right?

Instead, I land on soft arms.

My eyes heat, and another streak of pain sears through my body from my eyes.

"Hey," he whispers.

I need to close my eyes. Just a second. Just for a moment. I don't know if I have any more fight to keep it open.

"I'm awake," I respond. "I'm just having a really hard time opening my eyes."

Zander nods as he puts me down. I feel the ground beneath my feet, but my legs buckle and I fall, crumpling onto the ground.

"You okay?" he asks.

I nod. I'm so tired.

He opens his rucksack and pulls out a piece of meat.

"Here," he says, handing the meat to me.

I stare at it. It's uncooked red meat.

"I'm not hungry," I tell him, struggling to keep eye contact.

He chuckles. "It's for your eyes. Put it over them. Carry your rucksack on your back," he instructs.

I grimace as I turn my head to put on the rucksack. Even my neck is not having it. Peter has done this so many times to me. If it isn't my eyes, it's something else: an arm, a bruised rib, a sprained ankle. I used to always just sleep it off. This time, I can't.

I shift my shoulders to hold my rucksack evenly.

"Ready?" he asks.

I nod.

He turns, gets down on his knees, and motions for me to get on his back.

I stare at him blankly.

"Kenna, we have to get far, far away from Madyor now. While everyone is still asleep. The sooner, the better. I'll carry you; you get some rest," Zander tells me.

That makes sense. Besides, I'm too tired to argue.

I climb onto his back and rest my head on Zander's shoulder.

Zander struggles to stand up, and for a moment, I'm worried he can't. But he endures, and as soon as he stands, he adjusts me on his back.

"Thank you," I whisper with as much strength as I can.

I hold on to him as tightly as the pain will allow.

Finally, everything is dark, and I let myself drift.

Kenna

The heat of the sun is harsh on my face. My cheeks burn, and my forehead is dry and raw. The sun is scorching, and the rucksack chafing across my sunburned back isn't helping. My back trickles with sweat. I pray we get a breeze or wind. I imagine water. Even a cold shower would be welcome right now.

I blink slowly, my injured eye still shut tight. I don't dare try to open it so I can avoid feeling pain. As soon as my one eye stabilizes, I realize we're out of Madyor.

The erg is an endless stretch of sand dunes, sculpted beautifully by the wind into curves and peaks that seem to last forever. In the morning light, everything looks orange and brown, except for areas where the sun's rays cast a magnificent golden glow on the sand. It's quiet and still, so peaceful, not even a whisper of the wind. Under the harsher sunlight, the erg's curves and peaks create light and shadow, emphasizing the seamless contours.

"Hey," I start, but my voice croaks, as a dull, burning ache itches deep in my throat.

Zander doesn't look up, but he pats my hand. I don't bother holding on or responding. The skin to skin contact is almost unbearable, and talking aloud just takes away the energy I don't have.

"You need to drink some water," he says, his voice also cracking.

My throat is dry and sore. "We need to keep going," I respond stubbornly.

"Well, can you get me some?" he asks.

I immediately wake. He hasn't had water since we left? I open the rucksack in front of me, pull out a bottle and hand it to him. He pauses to drink before passing the bottle back to me.

"Drink," he croaks.

I grab the bottle and do what he says. Cool water washes down my throat, instantly giving me a slight reprieve from the heat. I sigh. I needed that.

"Thank you," he says.

"How are you feeling?"

"I'm okay. A little sunburned, I think." He chuckles. "How about you?"

"Better. I slept a bit," I respond.

"You did. I was worried for some time," he admits.

"How long was I out?"

He pauses. "It's been about three nights since we left Madyor, I believe."

My stomach drops, and my eyes bulge. He's been walking for three full days? Guilt gnaws at me. Not only am I a burden on his life now, but I'm literally burdening him by being on his back.

"I can walk for a bit. Can you let me down?" I tell him.

He hesitates, but then nods.

Zander bends down slowly and grunts as his knees touch the sand. I get off as quickly as I can manage, suddenly feeling the weight of my rucksack and my body again. My knees threaten to buckle, and I hold as strong as I can, forcing myself to remember how to stand. I watch Zander stretch, then I take a deep breath, hands on my knees as I mentally and physically prepare myself to walk. My knees tremble as I force pressure onto them.

I take another deep breath and pull myself up, groaning, as pain sears through me again. I ignore it. Instead, I reach over and pull on Zander's arm to help him up. "You okay?"

He nods, patting the front of his pants to shake off the dust.

I shrug my rucksack around, feeling my muscles awaken. They're not happy about it.

"Do you want me to take anything from your rucksack?" he asks, motioning to my back.

I shake my head.

He scans my face, and I immediately look away. There's nothing worse than being uglier than you already were, and I'm sure the last few days have done my features no favors.

"I'm okay," I tell him, balking at his gaze.

He looked like he was going to say something, but he resigns. "You ready?" he asks instead.

"Yeah, let's go." I nod and turn.

We start walking under the sweltering heat of the sun.

It's nightfall by the time we consider stopping. Zander's too scared and too worried to stop, so we eat and drink while walking and barely even stop to take bathroom breaks.

After walking all day, we find a cave, buried under the curves of the erg. There are no trees or any plants, but it's hidden enough to give Zander some peace of mind.

Zander leads the way into the dark cave, his hand enclosed around mine, patting his way around with a foot as he continues deeper into the cave. He finds a sturdy patch of ground and drops his rucksack. I do the same, the pressure of the rucksack lifting, my body rejoicing in the lightness. I settle myself on the ground, next to my rucksack.

My eyes blink repeatedly, straining to adjust to the darkness. I can still only see with one eye, but I catch Zander walking around the cave, probably looking for signs of danger in the area. Finally, he seems satisfied and takes a seat next to me.

Zander pulls his own rucksack open and fumbles inside it.

Moments later, he pulls out a long stick and a matchbox. He sighs, and I echo it.

What the *Faahi* would I do without him? How did he even know to bring matches? I'm impressed. I probably would've died by now if I were doing this alone.

He gets up on his knees and moves, turning away from me. I hear him strike the matchbox, but instead of a flame on the matchstick, the flame rolls into a ball and floats onto the ground.

I gasp.

The flame grows, shining a soft light around the cave.

I curl back up, staring at the fire.

Then I look at Zander. Then back at the flames that are now twice the size of the original one.

My jaw drops, but I don't say anything. I saw him Conjure once many years ago when he saved us from a mining incident, but I didn't realize he'd been practicing. Holy shit.

Like *holy shit.*

I recoil sharply when Zander gets up, his rucksack and items falling around him. I look up quickly at him, suddenly embarrassed by my reaction. I hope he didn't see. If he did, he doesn't show it. Instead, Zander circles the flame, scanning our surroundings one more time. I watch him with my one working eye. The cave isn't deep. It's shaped like a crescent and has no nooks or crannies for creatures to hide in. His face is blank, so I can't read it to know what he's thinking. He continues to pace around the cave, his eyes searching.

I can only imagine the pressure he must be under having to take care of someone like me, having to leave his home just to make sure someone like me lives. I don't even know if I deserve to live.

Finally, he looks at me, and my face heats up.

He drops next to me, but he doesn't say anything for a while.

"Don't worry, I've been practicing. We need it tonight," he says without looking at me.

I know we need light to see if the place is safe. We need something to make food and keep us warm for the night. He is here after all, spending his nights carrying me, taking care of me, thinking about things I never thought about when we left Madyor.

Who am I to complain? I can barely walk at the moment.

So I don't say anything. Instead, I fix my eyes on the flames and rest my chin on my folded knees. Beside me, Zander starts preparing the meat.

He turns back to me and grabs my coat, patting the ground to indicate a place for me to lie down. He sets my rucksack at the top, moving things around in the bag so it'd be comfortable enough to lie down.

Then, he gets up and extends a hand. "You need to rest. I'll let you know when the meat is cooked."

I accept his hand and settle it on my coat. He kneels in front of me and hands me another piece of meat. "Put that on your eye again," he orders.

I do what he says, lying on my coat and setting my head on the rucksack. I accept the meat and place it over my closed eye. Its coolness is refreshing to the stinging skin.

I close my other eye, but not before I catch a glimpse of distress in Zander's eyes. I feel guilty. He's so against

Conjurers that the idea of even practicing it isn't like him at all, so that can't have been easy for him.

My eyes burn, and I flip to my other side to hide my face from Zander. I flinch as an agonizing sting surges from my eyes, and I slowly place my cheek on the rucksack. I'm exhausted. We are so far from home, and I miss my siblings. I grimace, the stinging sensation vibrating as hot tears stream down my cheeks.

I feel a hand pat my back, and I force myself to avoid recoiling.

I know he's trying to comfort me, but for some reason, knowing he's just Conjured makes me feel even lonelier, and… maybe even… scared?

Is he still the Zander I know?

How powerful is he, exactly?

What else can he do?

What else isn't he telling me?

I sob for the life I left. I sob for the family I abandoned.

At this moment, the realization of what's happened over the last few days finally comes crashing down on me. I slump over my rucksack, my entire body trembling as my tears fall uncontrollably.

I've never been away from home. I've never had to figure out where to go, where to sleep, what I'm supposed to do next. I'm scared. I don't know where we are or where we're going. I don't know what I'm supposed to be doing.

Up until now, my nights were always filled with working.

But tonight? Who knows what it will bring.

18

Alistair

My heart sings as I make my way through the streets to meet my friends. I haven't seen them in days. I've been so busy with work that I've missed our regular dinners and drinks. It's been odd not seeing them so frequently.

I nod at a few people I pass, and a surge of triumph hits me when they all nod back. A Soturi even bows to me. That excites me. Before this, I could walk around Ainoa and be completely invisible. I'd wave to people I knew, but most wouldn't even remember me.

Today, I can feel them staring as I pass them. It'll only be a matter of time before everyone knows my name, and I'll command everyone's respect.

I look up, catching the name of the restaurant we'd agreed to meet at, and I immediately cross the road. Before I enter the building, I wave at a few more people. They wave back. My mouth hurts from smiling. I enter the restaurant, and my eyes adjust quickly to the darker atmosphere. It's different inside. Multiple tables with people and their friends, a bar on the corner, music playing loudly over their conversations.

I scan the area for familiar faces. I'm excited to see my friends. It's been a while. I'm nervous about seeing them, though. I hope they're as excited about my successes as I am.

I scan the restaurant a second time, finally getting a glimpse of Oliver's blond hair and outrageous laugh and focus on that. I spot their table and start walking over.

"Hey!" Jack and Oliver say in unison, standing up to greet me and pat me on my back.

"How are you guys doing?" I greet them, motioning a bar girl for a round of alcohol.

"Us? It's you that's been missing the last few weeks!" Jack claims, chuckling. "What have you been up to, Alistair?"

He raises a bottle, and we all respond by lifting ours into the air.

"We hear you've been slumming it with the Conjurers all week. What, you too good for us now?" Oliver sneers before chugging his alcohol. He slams his jug on the table and settles back in his chair, running a hand through his hair. He catches the eye of a woman across the room and winks.

Jack and I laugh.

Oliver's a ladies' man. He brings home different women from pretty much everywhere he goes. From bars and restaurants, to training, to random walks along the lake, he meets people quickly and easily and has a long line of women yearning for his company.

"Yeah, I've been training them. It's been a bit chaotic. I'm not just managing one or two classes, there are fifteen groups that I've been training simultaneously." I beam proudly.

"Oh yeah? How did you get that gig?" Oliver asks, watching me closely.

I pause, but I can hardly keep my excitement in control. I lower my voice.

"Leader Chen asked me personally before Krag Vinde," I whisper.

They pause, their gazes sharpening, and their eyebrows raised.

"I don't know why they chose me, or what I did to catch their attention, but they approached me after the last meeting with the Soturis and Conjurers," I continue.

Jack and Oliver look at each other.

I try not to feel disappointed about their reaction. Jack and Oliver have always had the same view of the government. To them, they're not doing enough, and are taking advantage of people, neglecting to use their powers for good.

I've always been on the fence about it, especially because I owe a lot to Ainoa and the government. Without them, I wouldn't be where I am today.

They don't understand.

"Look, they're training me to take on more responsibilities. I want to be put up for Leadership. I think I can be a great Leader. And everything you say about the government I can help with as long as I get up there, you know?" I watch their reactions carefully. I can't help but feel a little anxious about their responses. I need friends to make it to the top; otherwise, it will be a lonely ride up.

"I can help the government be better, I can help to prevent all these kidnappings, and I can make better processes for all of us, can you imagine?" I protest.

They exchange glances again. They said nothing, but their silence is enough; after all, this is something we've talked about for many, many months.

"The government gave me everything I need. I have to give back. They gave me a home, a goal, a place where I can prove myself, and soon, I'll lead the entire government so that I can give more people like me a chance to make it in life," I tell them.

I feel like I'm alone and that I'm the only one who wants to change this government from the inside.

I hate when my friends look at each other like that. It reminds me of the kids who used to beat me up and make fun of me. They always had a silent communication.

"I can do this. I can be better than our current Leaders," I say.

There's another long pause, and both of them just stare at me. Jack swallows awkwardly.

I sit back down, a warmth rising in my belly, making itself at home. I fight hard not to show the disappointment on my face, but I can't help it. After many years of going through the same thing with my adoptive father, four years of trying to prove myself, and my closest friends can't see what I see?

"Why don't you believe me? Why can't you trust that I can do this?"

Jack and Oliver roll their eyes.

"Alistair, it's not that we don't trust you; it's just that many others have tried, and there's just no way to make that kind of change overnight. You can't do this alone. Have you even tried asking other people within the resistance to see if they'd support you? I didn't even know that's what you were trying to do," Oliver says, scratching his head.

I didn't even know there was a resistance.

"I don't need them. I can do this on my own. We just need someone like me in the government," I counter. I can already see the king and all the Leaders bowing to me in my mind's eye. I have enough power to do that.

"Alistair, you've never really been against the government, though. You've always supported them," Jack adds.

I suppress a pout. "Just because I do, doesn't mean I can't make an impact, you know that, right? I can be influential. I can be the difference."

"Did you hear about Nesta Carrinos?" Oliver asks.

I flex my hands irritably, feeling the warmth crawling through my veins. "Who's that?"

"She's a low-level Conjurer who was taken from Madyor a few years ago," Oliver responds, his eyes switching between me and Jack. "According to some Conjurers, she disappeared."

"Maybe she went back to Madyor?" I offer.

"No can do. The girl was so excited to be a Conjurer. She was the first in her family to make it anywhere. She was actually excited to be taken."

The heat in my palms dissipates. That felt familiar. I'm the first and only one in our family to make it here, too.

"She arrived here and made so many friends. The problem was, she was just not that powerful. One of the women I was with the other night said she was so excited because she was picked for a special project. Then suddenly, the next day, her entire apartment was cleaned out. No trace of her at all, anywhere."

A beat of silence stretches between us. "Maybe she ran away," I supply.

Oliver laughs thinly, clearly stalling.

I study them carefully, frustration rising in my belly. I force it back down, but it's difficult, with all the negative emotions and insinuations that I'm getting from my two closest friends.

"Alistair, you have to admit, something's not right. The government is not right at all," Jack says, shrugging. His eyebrows scrunch, like he feels sorry for me.

Sorry I believe in a government they think is so fucked up. Sorry I can't see things their way. Sorry I'm not powerful enough to be the Leader that I can be.

But that's just it. They have no idea. I'm powerful. Not only am I a strong Soturi, but I'm also a powerful Conjurer. I can be a Leader. I *will* be king.

The fire in the middle of the restaurant makes a loud, crackling pop, and people nearby shriek.

I look down at my hands. They are warm and pink. I shut my eyes for a moment, taking a deep breath to calm myself.

Then, I look at them.

Oliver pops a nut into his mouth and winks at a woman behind me. "She's not the only one, Alistair. There are hundreds of Conjurers and Soturis that just disappear. Do you remember Frank from Uthaana, second year? He was also excited to be here. Then, he just disappeared. The government is definitely doing something to them. What? I have no idea."

Kenna

"Kenna!" Kane calls. He waves his arm frantically, his eyes glistening in the low sun.

I blink wildly, confused. I'd almost forgotten how handsome he was, how different he was from every other kid in Madyor.

My back is slick with sweat, and my hair sticks to the back of my neck. We're back in the mines, the smell of iron pungent in my nostrils.

"Come find me!" Kane's laughter echoes in the mines. I'd almost forgotten how his laugh used to sound.

"Come on!" another voice yells, and I feel a slap on my back.

But Zander appears behind me, giggling. I watch him laugh at me, then he disappears into the mines, chasing after Kane. I step forward, unsure of what to do.

"Kenna, come find us!" I hear another call.

Where am I? Why am I here?

"Kenna!" a singsong voice taunts.

I start down the steps, following their voice.

The entrance to the mines is merely a hole in the ground, propped up by wooden beams.

I drop to my knees, noticing I'm wearing blue pants. Pants Lena made for me when I was eleven, before she passed away.

I crawl into the entrance.

The entrance is tight, but short. Once I make it through, I slowly drop myself onto the ground. Inside is much bigger, but the air is scarce. I can barely breathe in here.

The mines have three different pathways. One has rail racks that lead somewhere within the mines. A lamp lights the entrance to that side, but it darkens further in. The second pathway is fully lit with many lamps. The third is smaller and has no light at all.

"Kenna!" the voice calls again.

I can tell this time that they're definitely in the third path.

I laugh.

"I'm coming!" I yell back to them.

I enter the mine, letting my eyes adjust to the darkness. I don't feel fear. I don't feel worried. So, I keep going.

"Kenna!" the singsong voice says again.

My eyes adjust, giving me the ability to see the outlines of this path. It gets smaller and smaller, but I guess I'm small again too, now, so I just keep walking.

It's pitch-black by the time I see a slight outline in the dark.

"Boo!" I yell.

CHAPTER 19

They both jump, laughing. I laugh too. The earth heaves beneath my feet, a deep guttural sound preceding the tremors. We look at each other. The ground quakes and shudders, emitting eerie groans and creaks that send a chill down my spine.

I scream.

The world lurches, a sickening crackle of stone echoing the frantic thumping in my chest as the earth rips open; brief, blinding shafts of sunlight slicing through the chaos.

I scream again, tucking myself into the ground, cowering as if my hands could do something. I brace to die.

But instead of impact, the world is quiet. I peek open an eye. It's bright.

I look up.

Rocks hover above me, just floating in the air.

My mouth drops. I turn. Kane is on my left, still cowering. I spin to the other side.

Zander is on my right, but he's standing, his hands outstretched, palms upward like he's carrying the rocks.

"Whoa," Kane says behind me.

Zander pushes his arms, and the rocks start creaking.

I scream again, cowering.

The rocks rearrange themselves, carving a path away from us, before tumbling down the hill, a loud boom echoing around us as each rock hits the ground.

I turn to Zander, my mouth still open. His blue eyes were shining in the sunlight. With the last rock echoing away, Zander's eyes, wide and frantic, mirror the terror still clinging to the air.

"What do I do now?" he asks.

"We can't tell anyone," Kane says immediately.

"Kane's right, Zander. They'll take you away from us," I hear myself say.

"I don't want to be taken," Zander says, his eyes blurring.

"We won't tell anyone," Kane promises, patting Zander's back.

"We won't tell anyone," I repeat.

"I don't want to be taken. You're my only family," Zander says again, tears streaming down his cheeks.

"We won't let them. I promise. We'll be together forever. If they find out, we run, okay?" Kane suggests.

Zander and I nod. I can't even imagine leaving my sisters, but I'd do it. I'd do it to keep Zander away from those Conjurers. To keep him with me.

"If they find out, we run," I repeat.

Kane throws an arm around each of us, and we huddle like we used to when we were much younger.

Then, Zander's entire body shakes. When he falls to the ground, I scream again, and my eyes flutter open.

Kenna

I can smell eggs as I wake up. Images from my dream flutter behind my eyes, so I blink furiously, eager to get rid of the image of the mines. I grunt as the pain in my neck starts seeping back to me. It looks dark outside, but I can hear movement.

I look over my shoulder, grimacing, pain shooting up the sides of my neck and head. My eyes feel like lead weights after crying all night.

When my eyes adjust to reality, I see Zander by the fire. I watch as he cooks the eggs using some sticks.

It's been a few days since we left Madyor. Dark bags line Zander's eyes. It doesn't look like he's slept at all. His forehead is scarred and scaly from being sunburned, and his neck is peeling. He's deep in thought, staring at the egg in front of him.

I grew up with this man, and I thought I knew everything about him. But looking at him right now, I don't absolutely know if that's true.

When Kane, Zander, and I promised we'd look out for each other when we were young, I never imagined it would be like this. Yes, I thought we'd fight the Watsons every now and again. We'd get in trouble with the Mayor, maybe even Peter or Aelin. I never imagined it would be us against the country. I never imagined Zander would have to choose between me and his family. Me and Madyor. And here he is—choosing me. Choosing to be here, despite the unknown, despite the fact that he'll probably die when the Conjurers and Soturis find us.

In the warm glow of the firelight, I can see the young boy I grew up with. The boy I promised to protect. The boy who promised to protect me. It feels like we're the only two people left in the country. It's us against the world.

Zander continues to stare at the fire and the egg. His dark hair is lightly tousled and greasy, the harsh sun on our walks contributing to the dirt and dust on his head. He had creases on his forehead, like he's many feet deep in thought. His arms are bruised and red, and I can see the lines of his toned muscles. I don't even remember when he started getting them. His blue eyes are purple in the dark light and glimmer in the firelight, shadows of his worries crossing his pupils every so often. He is beautiful.

My heart does that fluttering thing it does where I'm rendered motionless and I can't figure out what I'm supposed to do next.

"You're staring," he says, and I practically jump.

I didn't even realize he'd noticed I'm awake.

CHAPTER 20

He turns to me, and I hope the darkness has shadowed the redness creeping up my cheeks. I don't want him to think I expect anything from him. After all, I'm just me.

He moves closer and lies down in front of me, with an arm under him to support his weight. He raises his other hand, tracing his fingers gently across my cheek.

My skin tingles. My mouth feels dry.

His fingers move gently, caressing the outlines of my wounded eye and the bruises around my cheeks. I flinch.

"Sorry," he whispers. I'm tongue-tied. Mostly because my heart is beating too fast for me to think.

"This is what? The fifth time this year?" he says softly.

I blink. I know he's referring to the black eye. "I don't think it's going to happen again." Even I'm surprised by the sadness in my tone.

Zander looks at me, his eyes also sad. His fingers push my hair behind my ear. He's so close, I can feel his breath on my face. He looks into my eyes, and I feel like he's trying to tell me something, but I don't understand what it is. We look at each other for a long moment, and I pretend time is standing still. Pretend nothing is happening. Pretend we won't be dead in the next few weeks. Like I didn't just put his life in danger.

Then, just like that, he gets up and turns back to the fire.

My heart sinks.

I stare at the back of his head, a realization washing over me, weighing on my heart. Reality sets back in.

What happens if Zander gets killed? What if Zander dies because of me?

The most powerful people are coming after us. I get up slowly and move myself closer to him by the fire. I reach for his hand and hold it tightly.

"Thank you," I tell him.

I stare at him, hoping to send everything I feel about him through my eyes.

"For everything," I continue, squeezing his hand. "You ran away from everything, including your sisters. You walked for days and carried me on your back. Now you're here, running from them, when you didn't have to be."

He pulls his hand away, but only to pick up the egg that had just cooked. He peels the egg then hands it to me.

"I'd do anything for you," he responds.

I smile, and yet, a sinking feeling continues to root itself in every part of me. I don't think that's a good thing.

Kenna

We've been walking for hours. I'm tired. I can barely feel my face, what with the harsh winds whipping across the desert landscape. The wind howls loudly, and fine particles dance and swirl in the air. A dull sepia fog envelopes our surroundings as curtains of sand and dust spread throughout the horizon. Struggling to see through the haze, I wince as tiny particles assault my skin and eyes. Our eyes and bodies are defenseless against the swirling dust and debris, even with the protection from our clothes. As we continue to walk, the soft sand seems to swallow our feet with every step, making it harder and harder to move forward.

I hung onto Zander as we both trudge along the soft sands, each step becoming more and more of a chore. I can feel the wind pushing at me. I'm afraid that the moment I let go of Zander, it will take me. I don't look up because every time I do, sand assaults my eyes. It's been hours since we stopped, but we can't now.

Then, Zander ducks, pulling me to the ground. He tugs at my arms, and we crowd together, creating as little space between us as we can under our coats. The desert comes alive as tornado-like columns of dust whirl around us, whipping sand particles across our uncovered faces, slapping our skin aggressively. Zander plants his palms over my shoulders, trying to put as much pressure on my body as he can.

I'm scared. I'm useless.

But it isn't enough. The winds are fierce, roaring through the landscape, as the dust particles dance in the air, creating a hazy, otherworldly light that barely illuminates the surroundings.

I can't see anything.

Suddenly, the wrathful wind rips me away from Zander's arms.

I scream.

I lunge for Zander, but his hands slip away.

I'm midair, my heart pounds in my chest, my body is frozen with terror as gravity momentarily abandons me. The chilling wind stings my cheeks and hair. I can't see anything but the back of my lids, occasionally being forced open by white pressure from outside. I hold on tight to nothing but my hope that I'll actually survive this.

I don't know how long I'm in the air for, but at some point I crash onto the ground, my tailbone smashing into the soft sand.

"Ugh," I grunt, coughing. I can taste the salt and feel the hardness of the particles in my mouth. I'm too afraid to move in case I get taken by the wind again, so I curl up into a ball as small as I can, praying to *Tagapamigay* that the winds stop.

I wait a while; I don't know how long.

Gradually, the hissing subsides, and the powerful gusts slowly fade away. I stay still.

I wait until I can't feel anything else but the searing intensity of the sun on my neck.

Finally, when everything feels calm, I look up slowly, half expecting sand to sting my face once more. I look around me, searching the wide expanse of golden brown for any trace of another being, desperately hoping to find signs of Zander.

I pull myself up, brushing down my clothes to remove the sand and dust. I take another sweep across the horizon, hoping to see where Zander might have made it.

"Zander!" I yell.

The desert landscape responds with an echo. But that's it.

No. My brain responds immediately, even before my fear washes through my body.

No, no.

"Zander!" I try again, wandering aimlessly, my footsteps digging into the sand.

No. No, this can't be happening.

"Zander!" I bellow, then succumb to uncontrollable coughs. My throat is sore. I refuse to think about what I'd do without him. What I can't do without him. I look around again.

"Zander!" I call again.

Again, it's just the desert landscape that responds to me. My eyes sting, hot and heavy with unshed tears. I furiously blink them away.

"Zander!"

No, no, no. This can't be happening.

"Zander!"

I call a few more times, continuing to pace somewhere, nowhere, anywhere. I don't even know where I am! How am I supposed to know where I should be going?

My entire body freezes. My heart's pounding in my ears, and I can feel it in my legs. I fall to my knees, and my body lets out a wail from the depths of my soul I didn't even know existed.

I bury my face in my hands.

What have I done?

I continue walking through the erg; the heat blasts my face, but I don't care. I'm busy having an internal battle with myself. I want to find Zander, but my brain is foggy, and I can't think straight. My back and butt hurt, and a throbbing pain keeps shooting up my leg. A grain of sand is stuck in my eye. I don't even know how to start with finding Zander or getting myself to safety.

Tagapamigay, I hate being so stupid. *Idiot, idiot.*

I slap my forehead.

I have to focus. I have to find Zander, I tell myself.

How? You know nothing. A cold dread washes over me as a cold reply from somewhere inside of me echoes in my head—a viper striking before my rational self could react.

Okay, Kenna. You can do this. I blink, eager to ignore the other voice in my head.

Do what, exactly?

You got this. You can problem solve. You've done this before.

Yeah, no problem, my sarcastic internal nemesis responds, breaking into the little confidence I've been trying to build in myself.

For Zander. Kenna, you can do this, I tell myself, repeating it over and over until a sliver of hope reveals itself to me.

When I was young, Zander, Kane, and I used to play in the mines all the time. We'd play hide and seek. I used to panic if it took me too long to find them. But then eventually I'd talk myself into calming down. I started thinking about who Zander and Kane were, where they usually hid, where their favorite spots were, and started from there.

I take a deep breath; the heat of the erg is unwelcome in my lungs. I need to calm down.

My heart slows, and I can feel myself returning to my body.

Which way is the wind blowing?

My body starts walking in the direction of the wind. I don't know if this is correct, but I tell myself it's okay. I remind myself that it's just the first step. If this doesn't work, I'll figure something else out. I keep walking.

And walking.

And more walking.

"Kenna!"

My head jerks up, my heart skipping a beat. I've been walking for what feels like hours, and the silence is deafening, but I swear I hear something in the distance.

"Kenna!"

I hear it again. I spin, turning towards the source of the sound. The pounding in my chest is a wild rhythm that shakes my whole body. I strain my ears and look around frantically, trying to locate the source of the sound.

"Kenna!"

My vision blurs from the burning pain and tears. *Where is he?* I spin around more slowly this time, my eyes darting back and forth, searching for any sign of movement.

"Zander!" I call.

"Kenna!"

I stumble across the hot sand; the grains burn my feet as I follow the sound of his voice.

"Zander!"

And then, as the curve of the erg settles, I see him. A coated figure appears out of the golden-brown curves of the sand.

A sigh of relief and then a sob escape my lips like a whispered prayer. I run toward him, the burning in my legs a distant second to the relief and joyous pounding of my heart.

I throw my entire body over him, and he topples backwards onto the sand.

"Ouch," Zander grumbles, but his arms close around my body, and I've never been more grateful to feel his presence.

Zander releases me, but I hold on longer. Words often fail me, and I never seem to talk about the right things. So instead I hold on, hoping to *Tagapamigay* that Zander can feel how much I care about him with this hug.

I give him another squeeze before I hesitantly let go. I study him carefully as he struggles to get back up on his feet. His face is red and raw from the harsh sun, and a deep gash mars his forehead. His cheek has a ragged, angry gash, and his lips are a startling blue, dry and cracked, with flecks of dried blood.

I don't give myself time to question. Or to hesitate.

I reach for him and plant my lips on his.

The moment our lips touch, a fiery blush creeps up my neck as a jolt of electricity courses through me. My eyes widen as the nemesis inside me reminds me of who I am and what I just did, and I brace myself for rejection.

But then, an arm snakes around my back, and he holds my neck with the palm of his hand. His lips are back on mine, and suddenly it's not pain that I feel.

He's warm. He smells of crisp air and sand. The hair on the back of my neck rises, and I sink into this feeling. Into him. His hand caresses my neck, slowly coming down my back, and as his touch moves onto my legs and thighs, I feel heat warm my core. His lips devour mine, exploring, caressing, his tongue playing with mine. I'm alive and awake, my tongue doing things I've never done before.

Right here, right now, I feel home. I feel whole.

"Ugh," he groans, pulling away. My heart sinks, but it's quickly replaced by concern when I hear the strain in his voice.

He clutches his side, wobbles, and stumbles onto the ground. I reach for him, but his weight is too much, and he falls. His eyes close, and I crouch down next to him, looking for any visible wounds.

"What's wrong?" I croak.

His face contorts, and he grunts in response. I pat gently around his side until his grunts turn into whimpers. I pull open his coat and raise his shirt. He grumbles, but he raises his arms, anyway.

I fight a horrified gasp. Zander's torso is dark purple. His skin is intact, but it might as well have broken with how gruesome his abdomen looks. I glance back up at him.

His eyes are closed, and he breathes slowly.

Niada. What do I do?

"I think you broke a rib," I tell him, forcing my voice to stay as calm as possible and moving closer so I can help him sit up.

He nods, his eyes still closed, but he accepts my help and sits up, grimacing the entire time.

"Just give me a moment," he wheezes, each breath hitching in his chest, his body trembling.

I reach for my rucksack and pull out the bottle of water for him.

I feel useless, and I'm embarrassed at how little I know about life. He takes the bottle and sips in between carefully drawn breaths. I sit down next to him, watching him take slow breaths.

This is all my fault. I need to get us somewhere safe.

"Can you walk?" I ask after a moment.

Zander nods. I help him up, putting one arm around my neck.

Kenna

Finally, we make it to a forest. I've only seen woodlands like these in picture books and paintings at the inn. The towering trees create dense, cool shade, a completely different world for Zander and me, one filled with the scent of damp earth. Madyor only has four trees, and they're all artificial, Conjured to look that way so that Conjurers and Soturis have a nice place to look at when they're visiting Madyor every year. Something to match the beauty of all other districts. Something to make us worth a visit.

Zander and I find another cave at the foot of the mountains, just on the outskirts of the erg. From there, I can see the peaks of the sand dunes, and even the tiny tornadoes created by the harsh winds and sand particles. We don't have a lot of food or water left, but we had a piece of meat, some eggs, and fruit left. We'll have to look for food, and the sooner we can find water, the better. We set our rucksacks down, and Zander does his usual checks to make sure we don't have any companions in the cave. I help him set up a place to lie between our coats. He tries to fight back after I tell him I'll sort the food, but he doesn't have the strength to argue much longer. I pick up some kindling from right outside the cave, and carry it inside, creating a pile near Zander. Then, I wander, eyeing the trees and plants around us. I hesitate to pick anything at first—after all, I've never tried to find food out in the wild. Hopefully, they aren't poisonous. I really wish I had gone out more with Lena when I was younger to study plants. It would've been such a useful skill to have today.

The forest is a cathedral of towering trees, their limbs a dense latticework against the sky. Smaller shrubs, thick with tiny, dark berries, fill the spaces between the trees, and I collect them in the pockets of my shirt. I light up, catching sight of the mid-size trees bearing heart-shaped pears. They look like pears I've seen at Roger's store.

I grab the fruit firmly, pulling it from the branch, before tossing it into my backpack. I guess if I don't pick up this fruit, we'll die anyway.

My rucksack feels heavier when I make it back to the cave. I look for a match in Zander's rucksack, praying to *Tagapamigay* that he has more. Unlike Zander, I don't have the power to do what he did. Or maybe I do; I don't know. I barely remember or understand what I did before we left Madyor, so how the *Faahi* am I supposed to know what to do with actual flames?

Stupid. Dumb. Weak. *Worthless.*

I sigh when I find a match in Zander's rucksack. Thank *Tagapamigay.* I light the match, immediately placing it near the kindling, sending another silent prayer to *Tagapamigay* that it works. I don't know how many more matches Zander has.

The flame slowly catches onto the kindling, and the wood, and I almost cry with relief.

I reach into the rucksack again, patting around for another matchstick. If this is the last, I'll have to make some tomorrow. I count a few more. Thank *Tagapamigay*.

The wind whistles outside, and I look back at the erg. I didn't even realize it, but the wind has picked up again. I'm grateful for the walls the cave provided for the night.

I grab the remaining piece of meat and use a stick to pierce it in the middle before placing it near the fire to cook.

The figure next to me moves, and I glance at him. His hair is disheveled, his face red from sleep, and dark lines border the crooks of his eyes. He grunts but heaves himself up to sit next to me.

"How are you feeling?" I study his face. He didn't look so good earlier when we found the cave, but the nap he took seems to have given him back a bit of color.

He breathes deeply, grimacing as he stretches out his arms.

"My chest hurts. But I think I'm okay." He chuckles as he clutches his ribs.

I nod slowly. "I picked up some fruit outside. I don't see any rivers or lakes nearby, so we have to conserve water until we find our next water source." I hand him the water bottle to drink. There isn't much left. He takes the bottle and sips before handing the bottle back to me.

Zander pulls himself closer to the fire, folding his long legs in front of him.

"Do you want to talk about it?" he asks.

"About what?" I tilt my head toward him. I can tell just from the look in his eyes that he's talking about Conjuring. "How long?" I breathe in, the smoky air engulfing my nostrils.

"Since I found out," he responds almost instantly.

I stiffen. Since he found out? That was years ago! He's been practicing all this time? I can feel the weight of his gaze, heavy and intense, but I'm afraid to meet his eyes, fearing my judgment will show.

He holds up a hand to the fire, the flames dancing and flickering in response to his every gesture, growing and shrinking with his slightest movement.

I jump back, the roar of the fire deafening as the flames leap higher, and a stark realization hit me—I knew far less about Zander than I'd believed.

"Stop it," I hiss.

Zander pulls his hand back.

"I know how you feel about it, Kenna, but really, where would we be if I didn't use it at all?" he says. "You can't be scared of this. You have it too."

"I didn't even realize you were trying," I mutter, my gaze on my feet, anything other than him.

I'm grateful; I really am. But I also feel betrayed. Who is he? Who am I? Who were we, and why do we have these powers?

My head aches.

"I know we said we wouldn't. But I can't help it. It just started coming out every time I was angry or upset, and it was easier to control it than try to hide it. Have you never had a time when you were so angry you made something happen that you didn't want to happen?" Zander explains. "It's easier to control it than to let it happen all the time."

I stay quiet. I don't know what to say.

"What do you mean?" I ask.

"I don't know much about Conjuring outside of what I can do. But I control my Conjuring using my emotions. I'm more powerful when I'm angry or sad," he adds thoughtfully. "If I don't know how to control it, then every time I'm angry or sad, I do things I don't intentionally want to do."

He looks at the fire, a memory clearly circling in his mind.

"I accidentally broke a branch right after the Winston kids tried to beat me up at the park. The more I know how to control it, the less I do random stuff like that."

I stare at the fire too, letting myself remember the day it happened.

"Do you think all that light came out of me because of Peter? Because I was angry at Peter?" I say finally.

He nods, chewing his lip. "Maybe. But it's not just that. I bet you were hungry. Sad. Desperate? All those feelings can be overwhelming. The more you try to hold those emotions in, the more it grows, and the more you can't control it."

"Do you--" I pause. I don't even know if I want to know the answer. "Do you think I'll be able to control it?"

I'm afraid of the answer.

"You'll have to learn," he says after a while, his tone kind.

I look back at the fire. What if I can't control it? What if it comes out again? What if I kill somebody? What do I do now?

Maybe it's good that I ran away. At least my siblings won't be in danger from me.

Kenna

Our surroundings have changed from the golden-brown peaks and curves of the desert to the tall trees with vibrant green leaves that create a verdant canopy overhead. The forest floor has come alive with splashes of color from the blossoms of the wildflowers. Without the sun bearing on us constantly, the temperature drops, the air is cooler, and we enjoy the melodic chirps of songbirds. Every now and again, the sunlight breaks through the canopy, casting intricate patterns on the forest floor and filling the woodland with a warm and enchanting ambiance. Unlike the erg, it is much easier to hide from the intense heat of the sun, and luckily easier to find drinkable water.

We walk for a few days, taking refuge in caves or under dense trees. Zander's torso has turned from a gruesome purple to black. He struggles to sleep and sometimes still takes forced, shallow breaths, but he's staying strong.

It's late in the afternoon on another hot day when Zander finally admits defeat for the day. We find a secluded spot nestled amongst the trees and bushes. We set our stuff down, creating our usual setup to lie with our coats and rucksacks. I find wood and create a space to build a small fire. Zander sits down, stretches his legs, and watches me light a fire with a matchstick. The starter flame catches on slowly, so Zander raises his hands quickly, Conjuring the tiny flame to grow. I've seen him do it a few times now, but I don't know if I'll ever get used to it.

"How does it feel?" I ask as I hand him a piece of fruit to eat. We ate meat the day before, so today's dinner is fruits, berries, and whatever other food I can find within the area.

"How does what feel?" he responds, sinking into his pear. The laceration on his forehead is beginning to scar. I'd stuck a leaf on his cheek yesterday to help the gash close.

"Conjuring. What does it feel like?"

Zander looks up and eyes me carefully. I blush.

"I need to learn, don't I?" I say softly. I look down so he doesn't see the fear in my eyes. My chin quivers. He scuffles, and I feel him settle next to me. I hold back tears, but this is Zander. I don't have to hide anything from him. He cradles me and pulls me close. I push through a sob and casually wipe a stray tear. He pats my back gently.

"Well, it feels like your stomach is hot. It starts slow, so it's warm, and then as you Conjure, it gets hotter and hotter," Zander starts.

My breath hitches. "Do you get scared?"

CHAPTER 23

"In the beginning, yes." He shrugs. Then his eyebrows narrow thoughtfully. "I didn't know what I could do, so it used to scare me. But now that I've practiced a bit more and I've done a couple of things, I don't feel so scared. In fact, the more I do it, the more comfortable I am with it."

Maybe that's what I need to do. Maybe all I need to do is do it more. Easy for me to say. Hard to actually do. I don't even know how to start.

"Do you want to try?" he asks, looking at me carefully.

I swallow. "I should, right?"

Zander chuckles. He reaches for my hands and aims my fingers towards the fire in front of us.

"Okay, are you ready?" he asks.

I nod, unsure.

"Think about the fire," he instructs.

Okay. I think about fire.

He looks at me warily. "Close your eyes, Kenna," he says.

I shut my eyes.

"Don't just think about fire in general, think about this specific fire. How it's small, keeping us warm. It's sitting on some wood and kindling; it's soft and low and it's keeping us warm, right?"

Okay. Weird, but okay.

I think about the fire in front of me. Its flames are small, whipping softly in the faint breeze. It gives off a soft warmth, mostly on my hands since they're closer to the flames. I think about the flames, their bright orange color in the shape of tongues. How each flame sways with the breeze.

"Focus on how it makes you feel. How it's warm against your skin, how it makes you feel safe."

This fire is keeping us alive. It's a bit scary to have because it can draw light and possibly attention, but we've cooked with it; it's kept us warm, especially when we were at the ergs during those windy nights. It's cooler in the forest, so even during the day, sometimes we'd light a fire just to stay warm.

"Okay, Kenna, back it up," Zander says suddenly, his voice breaking into the monologue I'd started in my head. I feel his arms pull me back, and I fall backwards.

My eyes snap open.

The trees, leaves, branches, bushes—everything in front of me is on fire.

Kenna

"Move!" Zander yells, pushing me away from the fire. I fall backwards, crawling on my feet and butt, eager to get away from the roaring fire I'd started. The heat is intense, scorching the tips of my hair.

Zander plants himself in front of me, his eyes closed, his hands waving at the fire.

I blink furiously, my eyes overwhelmed by the flaming orange. What's he doing? He's so close to the fire, it'll burn him.

"Zander," I start, grabbing onto his pants to get his attention. His fingers are already within the flames, and he's going to get hurt. Yet, Zander doesn't budge. He continues to make movements with his hands, his eyes closed.

"Zander…" I say again, warningly, pulling on his pant legs more ferociously.

He doesn't acknowledge me and kicks me away.

I pull myself up, preparing to throw myself on him to get him away from the flames.

"Zander!" I scream at him. He's unmoved, standing as still as ever, and continues to wave.

How the *Faahi* does he not *see* the flames in front of him? *Okay, that's it. I have to save him.*

"Zander!" I yell. I give myself a running start, then hurl my entire body over him.

Zander loses his balance, and we fall, crashing straight into the tree behind us. A tree that's fully intact. A tree that isn't on fire.

"Ouch," Zander grumbles beneath me.

"What the *Faahi*!" I smack him. Zander cowers behind an arm and scowls at me.

"Ow!" he says again, grimacing.

I roll over him and bring myself to my knees, wiping the dust off my pants. I glance around us.

The forest looked like it had before I had set the fire. The tree trunks are brown, towering with beautiful, verdant green leaves, looking just as vibrant as ever. Near us is the small fire he'd kindled earlier, still the same size as it was.

"What the…?" I swear. I look back at Zander.

He's crumpled on the ground, by the tree, clutching at his ribs. I immediately feel guilty, so I move to him, holding out a hand. He grunts, but takes it, and I use what energy I had to pull him up.

"What the *Faahi*, Kenna." He glares at me.

"I thought you were in danger!" I protest.

"I was working on not being in danger!"

"I…"

Zander looks back at the forest, reaching out to a bark to scan his work. His face lights up, and he turns to me, a wide smile breaking out across his face.

"I did good," he says, chuckling. "I've never done that before."

He looks proud. I try to smile at him. I want to celebrate with him, but I can't stop thinking about the fact that I just set a forest on fire. Like lots of fire. Fire that could've easily killed us. I plop down on our coats, burying my head between my knees.

"What's wrong?" Zander asks, taking a seat beside me.

"I nearly killed us," I speak slowly with a sigh.

"This is your first try, Kenna. You're not going to get it right immediately. I had to practice a *lot*. Like I lot," he tells me, playfully pushing me.

"I just…" I look at him, heaving a sigh. I manage a small smile. "I don't know if I can do this."

Zander

It's almost sunset when we decide to make the next stop, just a few hours after I almost burned down the entire forest. We stumble onto a massive maple tree, its long and winding branches reaching out into the ground, curving around some shrubs and bushes, enough to create full cover on one side.

I drop my rucksack beside Kenna. She picks out leaves and stashes them by the rucksack, molding it into some kind of bed for later. It's my turn to find food, so I walk around, looking for fruits and leaves that we can eat. Despite my lack of experience, I've learned how to hunt in the last few days. I killed a squirrel yesterday and a rabbit the day before that. I've also had to learn how to clean it and prepare it for cooking, which was disgusting. The longer we're out on the road, the more we have to rely on each other for food and survival. I've never eaten squirrel or rabbit before either, but here we are, trying different meats to survive. Kenna, who's done nothing remotely adventurous before, has also had to try different things. The other day, she'd cleaned the squirrel. Her stomach wouldn't accept it in the beginning, but by trying little by little, she got some protein that kept her for a few hours before needing more food.

I walk further, looking at different trees and fruits to pick. It's nice to be in a place where we actually have options for food. Not the food we're used to, but food we can eat and survive on. I don't know when we'll see districts again, or if we're anywhere near civilization.

I examine a fruit on a tree. I don't recognize it, but I tighten my hold on it, ready to pull, before I hear a loud hiss. I spin around, scanning my surroundings quickly.

By this time, the sun is beyond the horizon, casting a dim and hazy light. Darkness is about to loom.

"Hello there," a shy, small, ethereal voice says.

I whirl around, desperately trying to look for the source of the voice. "Hello? Where are you?" I call out. I turn, squinting my eyes to get a better view of my surroundings.

"Hello, handsome," the voice says again. The voice echoes throughout my surroundings like an angel.

"Who are you? What do you want?" I demand.

"Don't worry, I'm not going to hurt you. I'm a friend," the voice responds, so angelic, so nice.

I smile. I feel relaxed. "Show yourself!"

A beautiful figure appears, floating out of the mossy and lush greenery. I step back, stunned, some of it from surprise, the rest from her beauty.

The beautiful woman had long, wavy and blonde hair, wearing a green dress that almost melds into the greenery she came from. She has striking jade-colored eyes that blend so beautifully with her surroundings; a slender nose, high cheekbones, and luscious lips. Her entire being glitters in the sunset.

"Who are you?"

"My name is Elisa." She positions herself directly across from me.

Her eyes are so gentle, so kind. She's having a strange effect on me, I realize, and I suddenly feel like everything's going to be alright. Even my tense muscles feel better.

"You must be exhausted." Her melodic voice echoes so beautifully across the forest.

"I am," I agree.

Her smile is enchanting. "I am here to help you."

I can barely form words. "Help me with what?"

"Anything you need," Elisa responds, smiling, and I feel my worries melt away. "But most of all, I'm here to make sure you get what you deserve."

That feels nice. I've always wondered what it's like to get what I deserve. I got Aelin for a mom. Was that all the love I deserved as a child?

"You're so beautiful," I blurt out, so imbibed in her and the atmosphere she creates.

"Thank you." She laughs. Her laughter writes beautiful music in the air. "Don't worry. I'm here now." Her voice almost glistens.

I feel a tug at my heart, like a voice at the back of my head telling me there's something I'm supposed to be doing—some kind of responsibility.

"What are you?" I ask, ignoring any feeling of alarm or warning. I feel lightheaded, a bit foggy, even, but I don't know why. I'm not even sure I care why.

CHAPTER 25

"I'm an angel. I come here every now and again to watch over people," her ethereal voice says. "I just want to make sure you're taken care of. You're such a good, powerful person. You deserve the best."

I nod. She is right. I *do* deserve better. "I deserve the best," I repeat slowly.

"You are more powerful than anyone."

Oh, how I enjoy that. The idea that I'm more powerful than anyone. That not even Kenna, who showed immense power only a few days ago, wouldn't have the same power as I do. That I don't need her to be powerful and great. That I don't need anyone to be powerful and great.

"I'm more powerful than anyone," I repeat slowly. Oh, my brain feels even foggier and weirder now, but it just feels so good, I can't resist.

"You deserve all the power in the world, Zander. You're very good at what you do," she says.

"I do?" I ask. "I'm powerful. I'm not as powerful as Kenna, though."

"No?" she responds, her voice floating in the air like a wonderful drug. "You're more powerful than she is. You know that. You have all the power, the control, the desire to be the most powerful person in this country." Elisa plants a soft palm on my hand.

She is electrifying. I fall to the ground, my back landing on some soft leaves. I don't feel anything. I don't notice anything else.

"You don't need her," she says.

"But she's my friend," I respond instinctively.

"Is she? She always slows you down. She's preventing you from starting the things you should be doing."

"She is?" I ask.

"You could be the most powerful man right now, but you've had to protect her."

I think about all the times I've had to save her. The moments when I've had to stop doing what I was doing just to make sure she was safe. Moments when I've had to sacrifice what I had to do just for her. Times when I've had to steal or do something unlawful just for her.

"I've had to protect her," I repeat.

She smiles and nods. "You need someone who will lift you up."

I think about the times when Kenna made me feel bad about my choices. My gambling. My use of Conjuring. How I treat our bullies. How she looked at me when she found out that I had stolen from Roger. I look back at the beautiful woman.

"I need someone who will lift me up," I repeat.

My head is so foggy now that I can barely form thoughts. My muscles are so soft and relaxed, and I can't remember the last time I felt like this. I feel so comfortable and pleasant. The beautiful figure floats. I can feel her now, her warm breath, her grassy clothing.

"You don't need her," Elisa repeats.

I look at her, enchanted by her alluring face. "I don't need her," I confirm.

"You are better without her."

"I am better without her," I repeat.

"You are stronger without her."

"I am strong," I agree.

"You are more powerful than her."

"I am powerful," I repeat. I stand up slowly. I grab my spear and start walking back to Kenna. "I am powerful," I murmur.

"You are powerful," Elisa says.

I nod, her voice ringing repeatedly in my head. "I am powerful and I don't need anyone," I agree. My feet start walking.

# Kenna

I'm so tired. I lean on the shrubs, finding a fairly comfortable spot for my head. Zander has been walking around for food for a while now, and I know I should start setting up the fire, but it feels so nice and cool in the leaves.

"Hello," a shy, angelic voice says.

I look around, alarmed. I don't see anyone.

"Who are you?" I demand, raising my spear.

The sunlight has dimmed, fading through the crevices of the thick foliage, but I blink furiously, trying to help my eyes adjust to the shift in light.

A woman with long, wavy brown hair appears, emanating so seamlessly from the vegetation. She is magnificent, her features so striking and ravishing, it's hard to look away. Her eyes are doe-shaped and enigmatic, so blue they look like the skies on a good day.

"Hello, Kenna," the woman says, settling herself in front of me. She floats in the air, casually stepping over random brush and roots.

My entire body relaxes, and I feel all the pain washing away. "What's your name?" I ask.

"My name is Daphne," the angelic figure says.

"What are you?" I ask.

"I'm your friend," she says in a singsong voice that radiates through my body.

Friend. Such a nice word. I've never had enough of those. I feel wonderful and comfortable. My mind is air, floating away from all my worries.

"I'm here to make sure you get everything you deserve," she says.

Aww, that's sweet. Sure, I'd love to get everything I deserve.

"You deserve everything, Kenna. You deserve the best of the best," she says, reaching over to smoothly pat my hand. Her touch is electrifying. Even my tired muscles ease.

"Why? I haven't done anything that great to deserve everything. If anything, my sisters deserve it. And I never got to give them any more than I had," I ask.

She tilts her head, sympathy dripping from her features. It makes me feel so… seen. "You deserve everything because you've been a wonderful daughter, sister, and friend," the woman says.

My back pain is gone. I feel… happier. More relaxed, less worried.

I worked seven days a week in Madyor to make sure my siblings always had something to eat. I put in extra hours so my sister could have a beautiful new dress for Krag Vinde. I constantly had to catch up on sleep. I'd never been to Nights of Aava because I was always working. I made sure Katleya had the last piece of meat, even though I was starving and could really use the extra meat. There were many days when I didn't eat so my siblings could. Why shouldn't I deserve more? Don't I deserve more for all the sacrifices I've had to make over the many years?

Oh shit. She's right. I nod. "You're right. I do deserve more," I confirm, and there's a sudden rise in my self-confidence.

"Yes, you do, Kenna. You deserve everything," Daphne says.

I like that. I smile, thinking about the many things I can't wait to have. I'm committed to this now, excited for what I might be able to have.

"Yes, Kenna. Think about it. You should get everything you deserve," Daphne continues.

Oh, what a beautiful thought. I feel shivers down my spine, a surge of energy coursing through my entire being.

The idea of getting more, having more, as a reward for everything I've done and sacrificed in the last few years. It's exhilarating. I stand tall, squaring my shoulders.

"I should get everything I deserve," I repeat. It feels slightly awkward, but the thought goes away. Excitement takes its place, and it's almost intoxicating. "What do I do, then?"

Daphne beams. Oh, she's so beautiful. Every time she smiles, I feel even more relaxed, like I'm floating on a bed of clouds. I think of all the things I want in life. How good it must feel to get all of that. To be able to achieve it. My sisters are successful, doing everything they want to do. We don't have to worry about food and eating all the time. No worrying about money anymore. I'd be strong and useful. I'd be worthy of something—worthy of love, of life, of happiness. I'd be beautiful. Someone people can look at and actually admire. Someone a person like Zander deserves.

"I think you know what you have to do," Daphne says softly, her voice ringing softly in my ear.

I smile, still reeling from my imaginary world where my troubles didn't exist, my insecurities were at bay, and I had all the money in the world to forget the fact that I am ugly and unwanted.

And then, Daphne's words settle and I see a break in the clouds. "Wait—what?" I pause, heading for that break.

Daphne approaches, her green, leafy dress hovering above the leaves. She kneels in front of me and places a palm on my hand. I don't back away. Instead, I feel calmer. It's instant. Everything just feels all right now.

My brain feels mushy, heading straight back into that beautiful dreamland. A life where I have enough pera, where I can easily support my siblings and they don't have to marry and get sold into rich families. A life where I haven't put Zander in danger. Where Conjurers or Soturis could never separate us. Where I don't have powers or anything that makes me different. A life where Lena is alive and Peter isn't the Peter we know now. Where Peter doesn't beat me up, or see me as a constant disappointment. How wonderful would that life be? But how do I get from here to there?

I look at Daphne.

"What do I do?"

Tagapamigay, I want that. I want that life so badly. I can feel it within my reach. In my hands. So close.

Daphne smiles sweetly. The ravishing being holds out her hand. In the palm of her hand lay a sharp knife.

I look at it for a long moment, then I grab the knife and stand up. The clouds are pretty, and all I want to do is be here. Be like this, be wonderful, even though it feels unnatural. I feel like each movement is so seamless, and everything I do is right. Like this is what I'm supposed to be doing. I start walking.

In the clearing, I see Zander come out of the bushes. His eyes are glazed but they lock with mine as he approaches. He raises a knife.

Instantly, I see an image of Zander waking me up after that power escaped me in Madyor. The look on his face, his gentle touch. I see the Zander who gave me a dress to wear for my first and only Nights of Aava. I see the Zander I grew up with, the one who gave me his food, the one who took me home at night, bringing leftover food, just because he knew I hadn't eaten yet. Zander, who'd been my friend, my only friend, for many years.

I remember our first kiss. It was sweaty and dusty, but he made my stomach feel funny, like something keeps jumping around. But it also made me feel warm. No one's ever looked at me the way Zander looked at me when we kissed. He's the only person I've ever confided in. The only person who knew my deepest, darkest fears. He's the only one who shares a similar background, the only person who knows what it's like to feel like an outsider in the only place they've ever called home.

The cloud gets a break again, and I feel a tear run down my cheek. I head toward that break, shaking away the fog. My mind clears, and I swallow and glance around. We're still in the forest, but I'm not exactly sure how I got here.

I glance down at my hand. My knuckles grip a knife. I jerkily drop it, and it slams onto the ground with a soft thud.

Why do I have a knife? I turn. But Daphne grabs my hand. The picture of Zander fades.

There I am again, in that beautiful dream. Confident, strong. Rich. Loved.

"You're holding me back," Zander spits out at me. His eyes blaze, his purple eyes dark and angry.

A wave of rage crashes over me. "I never asked you to, Zander," I snap.

I steel myself, ready to protect this image in my head.

"Without you, I can be more powerful," he threatens.

Why aren't his cruel words making me crumble? I feel nothing other than anger and pride. "Without you, I won't have to do illegal things," I fire back. There's a break. Why? Why did I say that?

"Without you, *I* wouldn't have to do illegal things," he counters.

I clench my fists. "Without you, I could do so much more."

The light shines through again. What am I saying? *Why would I say that?*

"I could be so much more," Zander retorts.

I hear myself hiss. I'm not sure where that even came from. "I'm more powerful than you." My voice doesn't even sound like me. The clouds open even more. That takes me by surprise. What?

"Are you sure about that?" Zander sneers. "You can barely do anything. You can't even control yourself. You couldn't do what I did today."

My face contorts into a snarl before I can stop it. "You are nothing. You are nothing to Aelin. You were nothing compared to Kane. I don't have to prove myself to you. You saw my power the other day," I retort angrily. Oh, I'm so mad. I want to say so many things.

But suddenly, Zander's eyes widen and a glimpse of pain crosses his glazed eyes. A knot unravels in my belly as the vivid image of Zander's pained expression plays on a loop in my mind. The cloud dissipates completely. Whatever it was, it's gone.

My mind is mine again. I look down at the knife in my hands, feeling the anger that isn't mine leaving my body slowly. The grip of the enchantment loosens.

I glance up at Zander. He still holds the knife in his hands, and his eyes are still glazed.

"Zander? Zander, it's me," I call to him, raising a palm to stop him from approaching. He continues to walk.

I step back. "Hey, Zander, remember when we were young? You broke your arm at the mine, and Kane and I brought you some food at the park. Do you remember?" I start, my mind looking for memories I know only Zander would remember. "How about when you gave me a dress for Nights of Aava? Do you remember how I was so surprised and impressed because I never told anyone how much I wanted to go, and yet you knew. You knew," I continue.

He steps forward.

I stumble, landing on my butt, and I start crawling back. "In the desert. I kissed you, Zander. I… I love you," I say, my voice trailing, desperate for him to hear.

To hear me.

The words hang in the air like a heavy promise. Seconds feel like forever. "I love you," I repeat, my voice soft, but clear.

And then… the glaze in his eyes washes away.

He wakes perplexed. He looks down at the knife in his hand, puzzled, and drops it immediately. He looks at me.

"What happened?" His voice shakes.

A low growl fills the atmosphere, and the earth shakes. I grab the closest tree and hold tight. The forest comes alive as the trees around us start to shift and sway, as if waking up from a peaceful sleep. The huge branches move, shaking loose from the ground. Like the fingers of a hand, the tree's limbs extend, stretching and curling, until it finally wraps itself around Zander, embracing him tightly.

The echoes of our screams ring around the dense forest.

The trees ominously shift and reach towards Zander, wrapping around him like serpents, lifting him into the air, his terrified howling reverberating through the canopy. The gnarled tree roots wrap tightly around Zander's body, constricting his breath.

I spin around to face the woman, my mind clear as day, nourishing a warmth in my belly. "Leave him alone!" I yell at her.

The woman who'd once exuded tranquility now stands tall and rigid, her fiery expression betraying a deep sorrow. The darkness in her eyes mirrors the weight of her heart. The tree roots connected to the limbs that hold Zander in the air, replacing her soft hands.

"No," the woman lashes out, spitting the word out with disgust. She glares, her eyes thirsty.

"Leave him alone," I explode, the warmth heating up.

The woman laughs shrilly.

"You say you love him, and yet you're ready to kill him. He doesn't deserve you," she sneers, her eyes blazing in her violent anger.

She cackles out loud, her voice ringing throughout the forest.

"Say goodbye to your friend," she mocks. Then, she prepares to snap his limbs.

My heart races. Suddenly, the warmth in my belly is hot, spreading like a virus through every vein until it seeps into every bit of my body. I scream again, but this time, I let my body feed that warmth.

My body emits a golden light, flowing outwards as if it has always been a part of me. It leaves my body, shooting directly towards the danger I face, before it balloons to cover the surrounding trees.

The light beams at the branches holding him, burning straight through them until they flicker and break, releasing Zander's body to the ground.

Zander hits the ground with a thud, the impact jarring his bones despite landing on the soft, green grass. The tree limbs convulse and tremble, then squirm into place before finally nestling back into the ground.

I burst into tears, feeling weak, as I fight to control the energy that I've released. It's so strong, so powerful. But how do I control it?

I continue to let the light in, feeling the radiance in my arms, my fingers, my legs, my toes. It swallows me. My muscles start to cramp, and I'm tired. I close my eyes and think of Zander. Maybe this will save him.

It feels so warm, so nice, almost like home. As long as I'm in this light, I'm safe. I'm comfortable. So, I let myself sink into that feeling.

I don't even feel it when I collapse onto the ground. But before my eyes shut, I watch the faint rays of sunlight filter through the dense foliage. Then, it is dark.

27

Kenna

I'm a horrible person. Add that to the many things I already know about myself.

Weak. Stupid. Dumb. Horrible.

How did I say those horrible things to my friend? To the one person who's always there for me? It plays again and again, over and over in my head.

Even though I'm weary and tired, my head continues to play it, concocting alternate scenarios where I could be worse.

Zander refuses to talk to me. Understandably. We slip into a wordless routine just to keep each other alive. Every other day, Zander will look for food, and I get us set up for the night. Then the next day, we'd switch.

In the meantime, every time I'm alone, I practice a speech, but I fail to speak up whenever I see Zander. I'm crippled by guilt when I look at his face and see the sadness and anger in his eyes.

I play out the scenario every single time. There are so many reasons for me to apologize, so many things I said, and yet, I can't find the words to say. I can't find *any* words at all.

Many years ago, when we were children, Zander was constantly compared to Kane, constantly told to be like him, by Aelin, all our neighbors, our elders. I'd said the same once to piss him off, and it ended up turning into one of our biggest fights. It hurt him, and I knew that. Even the woman who'd possessed me knew that.

It also doesn't help that every time I look at Zander, it looks like he is two seconds from exploding. His face is worn and fatigued, his lips perpetually pursed and his cheeks slightly swollen. His shoulders are so tense he could cut our meat with them. He sleeps away from me and won't turn when I try to make conversation.

Suddenly, I pause when I notice smoke rising among the trees. We haven't seen anyone in days. It's too far away to have been the fire I'd lit.

I glance up at Zander. His eyes are wide. He stops walking too.

"What do you think it is?" I ask, my voice shaking. I'm afraid he won't respond.

Finally, I hear: "I don't know."

I nearly jump when he takes my hand. We haven't touched each other in days. He leads me, and we keep walking, but we maintain a slower pace. While it's nice to see signs of life, it's a reminder that I'm being hunted. Hunted for something I don't even truly understand.

I eye him carefully. He's walking slowly, but his eyes move from one area to another. I can almost see the wires moving in his brain as he strategizes his next move.

Zander stops. He grabs my hand and starts pulling me in a different direction, parting the undergrowth and brushing away branches to make way for us. My heart clenches when he squeezes my hand. It feels like forever since we kissed. I'm afraid I've lost him. And yet, he's here, holding me like he still wants to protect me.

Zander starts to walk faster, deeper into the heart of the woods, where the trees are getting thicker, and the shrubs and bushes are getting denser, filling the environment with lush undergrowth.

"Let's find a place to rest for now. We can pass whatever that is tonight instead," he decides.

I stare at him.

He can still barely look at me. A part of me wants to yell at him, to make him look at me. But that part isn't very loud.

His eyes roam the area, scanning for caves, or anything that could keep us hidden for the next few hours before sundown.

"Let's keep walking," he says suddenly, his hands tightening around mine. He starts speed walking, and I can barely keep up, tripping over the many bushes and shrubs that we pass.

It's unnerving to see him so nervous. His eyes keep moving around, and he constantly looks over his shoulder and around us.

Maybe he'll get past everything I said. Eventually.

I want to say something nice, something sweet. Something to help him calm down.

And yet, nothing comes.

I remain quiet and let him lead us deeper into the lush, green forest, going around whatever produced that smoke. By the time Zander stops, it's already dark. We find a little area covered by shrubs and big willows, their drooping branches creating natural cascading curtains as a cover. I let Zander nap for a bit and then took over for a short while. We don't make a fire to avoid attracting attention, so we snack on fruits and berries instead.

The smoke is coming from a tiny village nearby. It's small, with only a couple of houses, bunched close to each other, creating a break in the denseness of the forest. One house has an attached barn and land big enough to grow vegetables and other types of food. The houses are small, made of stone with flat, wooden pieces covering the roofs. The wooden pieces are old and moldy, with verdant moss weaving through their seams. They're different from the houses in Madyor, not as boxy, or concrete, built to withstand Madyor's harsher elements. We're definitely in a place with a different climate.

Once we finish eating, Zander and I walk through the tiny village. We pause at the back of one of the houses, keeping ourselves in the shadows of the building, away from the moonlight. I watch Zander peer through the windows, dropping to his knees as he scours the inside of the house. It's late and way past bedtime, so the main areas are dark and empty. Zander hadn't talked to me in days, but I still know what he's doing. I don't like it, but I understand it.

I take in our surroundings, training my eyes to catch silhouettes of people or even any other sign of movement. But it's quiet, just the soft breeze blowing through the big trees and the rustling of leaves. I glance back at Zander. He's focused on his view, his brows knitted, his eyes still searching. His muscles are tense, and it looks like he's about to sprint into a run. Suddenly, he turns and reaches out a hand to my shoulder. I jump, half expecting him to pull me into a run. Instead, he looks at me, his eyes softer than they've been over the last few days. I nod, taking a slow, deep breath. His face tightens again, and he ducks under the light, slowly pulling the door open. The wooden door creaks, and he pauses. He waits until it seems safe, then continues, shooting me a quick look right before he disappears behind the door.

I exhale, the pounding of my heart right at my ear. My feet tap softly, eager to silence the worries I can't afford to indulge. Just when I'm about to burst into the house myself, Zander comes out, his rucksack over his back. He grabs my hand, and we move onto our next house. We do this with a few more houses until the rucksack that had finally become manageable to carry is filled with food and water again. Once we've split the weight, we make our way onward through the forest, with only the moon to light the way.

Kenna

It's been a few weeks since Zander and I left Madyor. At least, I think. Our nights had merged into days, and after we got more comfortable walking at night, we only actually stopped when my knees finally gave out. After a few days of walking from our last village, we make it to our second; more proof there are other people in this world.

Zander grabs my hand as we walk through the village. It's bigger, with more houses, more farms. It isn't as busy as Madyor is at night, but it has more people than the last village we passed through. Zander's pace switches, and he pivots. I follow.

"What is it?" I ask.

"I know it's been a hard couple of days. How about a nice bed and hot shower?" he suggests.

"Can we afford it?" I ask immediately, looking down at my pockets where I'd collected some pera for our journey. I don't even remember how much I took, but I can't imagine being able to pay for a room at the inn.

Zander grins.

For a moment, I recognize the boy I grew up with, and my heart flutters. Sly, funny, not a care in the world, but just me and him.

"I have some pera. And surprisingly, the cost of a room didn't look too bad," he responds, pointing to a sign behind me. I spin, almost giving myself a headache. The sign is big, bearing the large letters: INN, next to *twenty pera a night.*

Whoa. That's so much more affordable than Madyor. That's less than what bread costs! Our rooms cost fifty pera a night in the off-season, and up to a hundred pera a night during Krag Vinde.

"I don't know if I have twenty pera." I pull out the coins I have, but Zander's already pulling me towards the sign and into the inn.

As soon as we enter, the smell of freshly baked pastries wafts toward us, and I can't tell if I want to eat them and then be sick, or be sick first, then eat them.

Their inn is much nicer and bigger than Madyor's. Madyor's inn's foyer would be dwarfed by this one; it's at least twice as large, with soaring ceilings and ample space. A bright color is spread over the walls and doors. Dark, heavy wood beams crisscross the ceiling, drawing the eye to the center of the room, while a crackling fireplace to the right casts a warm, inviting glow and gives off a pleasant scent of wood smoke. A single bright beam of light from the ceiling illuminates the room, dust motes dancing in its path. Even the desk has two lamps, casting a warm, inviting light on the room. I have a candle, and that's it.

A short girl, who appears to be around our age, wears an apron and sits behind the desk; her youthful face framed by long, yellow hair pulled back into a bun. She smiles, her gentle, friendly eyes lighting up in a welcome. For a moment, I forget she knows nothing about me. I'm not the foreigner who grew up in the area. I'm no one to her.

"Hi, Mamser," she says, her voice echoing across the room.

"Is it one room or two?" she asks, a bored sigh escaping her lips.

Zander glances at me, but doesn't give me a chance to answer. "We're married, so we just need one room," he responds.

My face flushes, and I avoid eye contact.

The girl nods.

As she rummages around the back, he leans close. "It'll be safer this way," he whispers, his breath catching on the sensitive skin behind my ears, and I shiver, goosebumps rising down my spine. I don't argue.

The girl hands us a key.

"Here you go. You're in room five, across the hall, up the stairs to the left. Have a great stay!" she says in a fake, cheerful tone.

Zander accepts the key and heads toward the hall. I follow, my knees protesting when we climb up the stairs. We find the door with a number 5 on it, and Zander uses the key to enter.

Our room is small, but adequate. It's about the same size as the rooms the inn in Madyor offers. There's only one bed, bigger than my old bed, and a small couch under a window that overlooks the street. We have a desk and chair by the door to the bathroom.

I remove my rucksack and settle on the couch, pleasantly surprised at the softness of the cushions. Our cushions at the inn were old and weren't this soft at all.

Zander puts his rucksack down on the chair and then starts taking his boots off. I do the same, pitying myself for the scars and scratches I've developed all over my thighs and calves.

"Do you mind if I take a bath first?" I ask, glancing at him across the room.

He's already plopped onto the bed, his eyelids looking heavy. He shakes his head, grunting what I think is a "no."

I nod, then grab the only clothes from my rucksack before disappearing into the bathroom. I turn on the water, cupping my hands and dipping my face in the cool water. It even smells clean. I remove my clothes, my entire body screaming in pain. I sit on the toilet's closed lid, catching my reflection in the mirror. *Tagapamigay*, I am thin. I must've lost weight over the month, too. My face is darker, and I have a cut on the far left of my chin. My auburn hair is matted with sweat. I sigh.

I pull the hair tie off my hair and turn on the faucet. I bury my face in my hands as I wait for the tub to fill. I haven't had a bath in weeks.

Once the tub is full, I get in, the warm water like heaven to all the pains and aches my muscles have.

I wash the rest of my body, then get out of the tub, once again glimpsing my body in the mirror.

I'm so short. I barely make it to Zander's shoulders. I'm stick-thin, and I can see my bones poking out of my neck and stomach. My breasts are small, my nipples taut from the cold. I can't even imagine anyone being impressed by my breasts; they're certainly nowhere near Amara Winston's size. Everyone I know from Madyor who has gotten proposals always had breasts that spilled out of their dresses. My hair is limp and wet, clinging to the back of my neck. It's cleaner, but I've never known what to do with it besides keep it in a rolled bun, away from my face. Amara Winston always had beautiful braids in her soft, shiny hair. When mine's dry, it's wavy and frizzy, falling just past my shoulders. As I glare at my body in the mirror, warmth builds in my stomach, and for a moment, I think I see gold around my pupils. I blink and shake it off, and it disappears. Of course. There's nothing about me that's pretty. Nothing about me that's powerful. Nothing about me that's worth all this.

A sinking feeling washes over me, and I turn, wrapping a towel over my body, feeling silly I even spent that time thinking about myself.

I have nothing to offer. Nothing to show. Nothing. I don't look in the mirror again after that.

I dress in the only clean clothes I have and get out of the bathroom as quickly as I can. Zander is already in bed, buried under the sheets. I tiptoe around the bed, pulling the curtains closed before climbing in on the other side of him. My heart pounds as I sink into the mattress, his warmth radiating through the crisp cotton sheets. He and I have slept next to each other every day since we left, but this is the first time we'd actually been in a real bed together.

"Is this okay?" I hear across the bed.

I turn to face him, flipping the blanket carefully to cover my back. I'm inches away from his face, and I can feel his breath against my face. "I'm sorry," I say softly.

I study his face. His eyes are closed, but I can see the dark lines underneath. His forehead is still healing, and the cut on his cheek is now a scraggly line. Zander forces an eye open as I run a soft trail across his jaw.

"I know you're sleepy. But I just wanted to say it. I'm sorry, Zander. I didn't mean any of the things I said. I didn't, I swear."

He doesn't say anything, but his second eye flutters open.

"You know I love you. I'm grateful to you and I would never have survived this without you. There's no one I'd rather be with right now than you."

That's true. No one I know who'd do what he'd done for me in the last few days. No one would take care of me the same way he has.

He studies me, the same way I study him.

I lean over, crossing the tiny space between us, and I press my lips against his, a rush of surprise coursing through my body. For a moment, I'm terrified I'm afraid to lose him, and afraid to be rejected. But then, his mouth opens, and I feel his tongue on mine, and I'm on fire.

He brings his hands behind my neck, pulling me closer. A shock of energy pulses through every part of my body. I'm hungry, hungry for him, his lips, everything about him. Everything we've been through melts away, the tiredness, the anger. I don't even remember what I just said.

His hands find my back, pulling me into the hard, warm press of his body. The feel of his skin, rough yet comforting, sends shivers down my spine. Oh *Tagapamigay*. I want him.

His hands venture along my neck, my back. I wrap a leg around his, and I'm encouraged by the heat protruding from his center. I can't get enough. I need him closer.

I dig my fingers into his back, and he jerks suddenly, waking me from his expedition through my body. I look up.

"Are you okay?" I ask, my eyebrows narrowing.

Zander sits up, grimacing as he pulls up his shirt. I hold back a gasp and look at him before going back to examine his wounded skin. He winces the moment I run a soft finger over his torn skin.

"Sorry," I whisper.

Zander's back is a horrifying tapestry of purple and black bruises, crisscrossed by multiple deep scratches, and a long, gaping laceration across his spine, revealing the underlying muscle that glistens with oozing liquid each time he moves. His skin is swollen and red; the inflammation is uneven, some areas a deeper crimson than others.

"Why didn't you say anything?" I demand, my face red, but not from irritation.

"I didn't realize it was that bad." He shrugs. He pulls me playfully, capturing my mouth in his.

"Stop," I say, giggling. *Tagapamigay*, I can't think. Not with me on him like this.

"Didn't you grab something from the last village for sores?" I ask, ignoring the protruding outline from his pants and the wild idea to jump on him and go back to what we were doing.

I pull away. I need to think.

Zander sighs and points to his rucksack.

"Yeah, I took a bottle of the green stuff that Aelin used to put on wounds," he says.

I get out of the bed, suddenly feeling cold, and start going through his rucksack. I find it; it's a small green jar that I'd seen at Zander's house multiple times. I squeeze the jar open, the odd and unpleasant smell catching my nose. I wince.

"Sorry, it's smelly. But it's effective. Aelin used to make it," he explains, turning his back on me as I approach the bed.

I reach for some with a finger and lightly pat it over his back. He groans.

"I didn't feel it until you touched it, honestly. Or maybe I'd just chosen not to feel it."

I spread it across his back gently and close the jar before placing it next to the bed. Then, I pull down his shirt and help him get back on the bed before tucking the blanket tight around him. I kiss him one more time before settling beside him.

"I'm so sorry," I whisper again. *I'm sorry for ruining your life. For taking you away from your family. For putting you in danger. Because you'll likely die with me. I'm sorry.*

He traces the outline of my jaw with a finger, his blue eyes studying me. "It's okay, Kenna. Get some sleep," he says, caressing my cheeks. I snuggle up next to him, bathing in his warmth.

It's really not, though.

Kenna

Zander and I walk through the village the next day. It's nice to be in an area where no one knows who we are. Back in Madyor, people often stared at us. We were the kids dropped off in Madyor once upon a time. The kids with no parents. The kids who didn't come from Madyor.

This village has its own seamstress, little grocery store, pub, and a small mine at the end. It also has a few farms with cows, pigs, and chickens.

After making it around the village, we head to the pub. No better place to find people ready to talk than the ones already talking.

I glance at Zander. He looks confident. I scan the pub quickly. A group of women sit by the bar, their laughter and animated conversation filling the air. Zander spots them first, leading me to the table next to theirs.

"Hey!" Zander greets them.

It's weird seeing Zander in this environment. A wide smile spread across his face, the slight dimple on his left cheek peeking out. I look at the ladies. They looked enthralled with him. My muscles tighten.

"Oh, hello! Are you from out of town?" one of the women responds, turning to our table. She leans over just enough to give a casual glimpse of her cleavage.

I fight the urge to look at the non-existent one beneath me. They don't even see me. I mean, this isn't the first time I've seen Zander flirt. He's flirted with a few women in Madyor. This time, it feels different. Heat rises in my belly, and suddenly, I don't feel so chipper anymore. I fidget with a fingernail behind my back, hoping the pain will distract me.

"We are! This is my sister, Kenna," Zander says, gesturing to me.

I can't help the smile that fades from my face.

The woman's eyes brighten. She leans towards Zander, the curves of her breasts showing. She flashes him a wide smile.

My jaw tightens. I know he's only saying that because the more interested this girl is, the more she'll likely talk to us about this place, but I can't help the pang of jealousy.

Her reaction when she realizes I'm not competition. The way she looks at Zander like he's something to eat. The way they possess everything any man would want. The way that I'm none of those things.

I wish I was her. Pretty, with actual bosoms, and the confidence to respond to a stranger.

"Oh wow! That's cool. Where are you both headed off to?" one of the other ladies asks, eyeing Zander like she's about to strip him of his clothes.

"We're not sure. What's this place?" He smiles at the girl.

Oh, *Tagapamigay*. I press a fingernail onto the skin of my index finger, forcing myself to keep smiling. How do I snap myself out of an emotion I don't even understand?

"Oh! Oh my goodness. Ya'll never have been here, have you?" one lady says, her voice so high-pitched, it contributes to the irritation I feel. She touches his arm, ever-so-slightly, her chest heaving heavily as she leans closer. She might as well be on top of him at this point.

"No, this is our first time traveling," Zander says.

"This place is called Malina. We're in the mountains between Uthaana and Madyor," the lady explains.

Zander shoots me a look. I didn't realize we'd gone that far at all.

The girl by the bar comes over, a notepad and pen in her hands.

"Can I get a glass of alcohol, please?" Zander says politely, then turns to me. "Maybe water for my sister here?" I nod stiffly.

The girl nods, then turns to the group of ladies. "Anything else?" she asks.

The lady by Zander shakes her head, waving her away rudely before turning to Zander instead.

"Where did you guys come from? Did you meet any dryads on your way here? They're all over the place! They're everywhere, so travelers in town often have insane stories about them. We've never seen them, of course. I've never left Malina," the lady says.

"Callie has! She came from Ainoa," another girl pipes up.

"Shh!" another girl cuts in.

Everyone at the table gazes at the striking woman; her dark skin glows, her almond-shaped eyes sparkle, and her bouncy curls frame her high cheekbones.

Even in the darkness of the pub, I notice the muscles outlining her shoulders and arms. Damn, I've never seen anyone with muscles like that. Clearly, this girl had a job that put her body to the test.

"Make it more awkward, would you?" The dark-haired woman shoots an annoyed look at the other ladies. From the looks on the women's faces, this girl definitely has some kind of influence over them.

"I worked for the government back in Ainoa. When I got away, I found this little village and thought it was a great place to stay," she continues, studying Zander and me.

Zander shoots me another look. His brows furrow, and his muscles tense up. I feel his grip on my hands tighten.

"I'm Callie," the girl introduces herself. She stands up, her limbs rising out from under the table, and reaches out her hand to me.

I shook it hesitantly at first. She has a very strong grip.

"Minnie," another girl offers.

"Tanya."

"Melissa."

"Petra," the girl with the high-pitched voice quips.

"You worked for the government?" Zander repeats.

The girl must've sensed the fear in his voice because her aura shifts, and she gives an encouraging smile, walking past her friends, and then she sits down on the chair next to me. She motions for me to sit. I do, hesitantly.

"I used to be a Soturi," she explains, looking up at Zander, who stiffens. "Don't worry, I don't participate in any of their functions anymore," she adds quickly. She glances back at me, her eyes boring holes through me, like she's trying to read me.

I adjust uncomfortably, avoiding her eyes.

It's surprising to see that Callie doesn't appear to share the same fascination with Zander that the other women do.

"Many people are angry at the government here," Minnie explains, shrugging.

"That's why people move here. To get away from the districts. The government doesn't always find these places easily. The desert and forests are so vast it's hard to get here unless you've been here before. Most people die on the way here, too, because of the dryads," Callie adds.

I force my shoulders to relax. "Why are they angry?" I ask. I release the fingernail that pokes my index finger.

"Well, my family is from Uthaana. Before we came here, one of my aunts ended up getting taken by the Soturis. They denied it, of course, and my entire family looked for her. But no one would admit that it was the Soturis that took her. After we had a few more family friends get taken, my parents decided to run for it. I was born here," Tanya says.

"Same, really. Except my family had a Conjurer. It skipped me, of course, but they took my grandmother. My family took me and my brother here," Minnie agrees.

"I found this place after running away from Uthaana, too. I'd seen enough families get ripped apart by the government." Melissa shrugs, tutting irritably.

I empathize. It's only been a few years ago that Kane disappeared.

"Do you know what the forest going to Uthaana is like?" I ask.

"Oh! Are you headed there?" Tanya responds, her eyes taking on an excited sheen.

"We're not yet sure. It depends on how rough the travel is, I think," Zander cuts in, shooting me a look. I don't think he wants people to know where we're going.

"Well, none of your options are great, really," Melissa says. "The forests are treacherous. You have the volcanoes, the glacier, the weather."

"There are so many creatures that roam these forests, too," another girl adds.

"You have to be prepared for everything that you're going to go through," Callie says.

She looks at me. "Are you prepared?"

I don't say anything. I just look at her, stunned.

Zander laughs.

"We'll make do," he responds. At least he's confident.

"No, really," Callie forces, her voice firm this time, "you have to make sure you're prepared. The elements out there are harsh and unforgiving. You need to be able to fight, to help yourself. Help each other," Callie responds to Zander, but her eyes remain on me.

I frown. Should I be worried? I shoot Zander a look.

"Ooh, Callie can teach you!" Petra pipes up, and I glance at her, grateful for the distraction.

"Callie taught us a few ways to protect ourselves," Tanya adds proudly. "I've never had to use it, but it feels good to know a few things."

"I'm not as scared to venture out anymore, either," Melissa agrees.

The ladies are right. I need to be prepared. I need to learn how to fight back, to protect Zander. Fight *with* Zander.

"What did you teach them?" I ask Callie.

"I used to train Soturis. I can teach you to fight." Her eyes fixate on me.

I share a look with Zander. Zander frowns.

I glance at the spot where his wound is. Callie is right. I need to step up. I need to be able to fight.

I look back at Callie and nod.

Kenna

Callie kicks at my shins.

I yelp, jumping to separate my legs. My arms stretch out with my hands balled into fists. I feel silly. I catch my wrists and think about how thin I am. I scoff. How much damage can I actually cause being this skinny?

It's been two hours since Callie took me out to the middle of their property. I'm glad Callie offered to teach me, but after only a few hours, I'm already getting irritated, the realization that I'm nowhere near built to be a fighter dawning on me like a slap on the face. As a trainer, Callie is vicious and straightforward. Gone is the girl with the gentle eyes and encouraging smile that Zander and I met at the bar. Instead, this woman is strong, bossy, and unforgiving. She notices every single thing, from the slightly incorrect movement of my hips to an angled ankle that apparently would never give me the right strength to move.

Callie owns a wide, expansive property with a huge barn, plenty of land, and chickens, cows, and pigs. She barely lets us meet her kids and her husband, but she makes an exaggerated motion to them to let them know she isn't to be disturbed. We have the entire barn to ourselves, surrounded by clucking chickens, neighing horses, and the occasional mooing of the cows.

Zander sits on a tree branch right outside the barn, his sapphire eyes piercing through me every now and again. He refuses to come in. He's worried that Callie will eventually produce a Soturi and prevent us from escaping. This way, he can keep his eyes on me, our surroundings, and Callie.

"You have a very protective friend," Callie says, her gaze shifting momentarily from me to Zander on the tree.

I immediately notice Callie didn't say "brother." I eye her suspiciously.

Callie chuckles, breaking the tension I feel toward her from the last hour. "I can tell," Callie answers gently, even though I didn't ask.

She touches my hand softly and guides my fist and wrist to a position parallel to my chest. "Do you feel that?" she says, wrapping her hands around mine. "You can have more power just by having the right stance. Even though you're practically skin and bones," she adds.

I scowl, crimson creeping up my neck.

She holds onto my arms and guides the motion to stretch my arms out with a force. "Remember that," she instructs, doing the motion again a couple more times, "keep doing it."

I continue to make punches in the air. "What can you tell?" I urge after a while.

From all the scary stories I've heard, I can't imagine Callie being a Soturi. Outside of being a trainer, Callie seems so kind, so gentle, and genuine. But to be fair, I've never truly met a Soturi. They stay at the inn, but the mayor always made sure to check them in himself, so I never got to talk to them. All Soturis do is stroll through town, looking (and probably thinking) they're superior to everyone else. Soturis have a reputation for punishing people for minor offenses, like getting in their way or accidentally bumping into them, or even for stealing small items. They're infamous for being the culprits behind the abduction of children, and well-known for their wide range of methods for inflicting pain. I hear whispers and agonizing cries throughout Madyor, but really, I've never seen anything actually happening. Soturis are too smart and skilled. Anything they do, they hide.

"The way he looks at you isn't the way that anyone would look at their sister," Callie answers as I continue punching at invisible things.

I feel my cheeks hot, an image of us in bed last night appearing in my mind.

Callie laughs. I ignore her and continue to punch the air, trying to focus on memorizing the stance instead of the growing heat in my belly and center. "I don't just mean that, though," she adds quietly, her voice dropping to a whisper.

My eyebrows furrow. I avoid her gaze, terrified of what I might see on her face and what she might say next.

"I *know*," Callie repeats.

I freeze.

"I won't tell anyone, I promise. We've been waiting for you," Callie whispers.

I mentally prepare to yell at Zander to run. "What does that mean?" I demand. My voice shakes, betraying me.

Callie holds up a hand in defense and motions for me to calm down. She catches the change in my position and points at my hips before placing her hands to reformat them properly. "When I was at Ainoa, I trained and worked daily with Conjurers. We're trained to notice them, trained to feel their power, trained to *know*," she continues, emphasizing her last words again, before piercing her dark eyes through mine.

I cave first, blinking before looking away. She plants herself in front of me, her eyebrows knotting together.

"We can feel the energy you give out—especially if you don't know how to control it," she says.

My jaw drops, and I blush again, a sense of uneasiness increasing in my belly. "You can feel it?" I repeat.

"The more powerful you are, the more you give off an energy, a pulsating emotion that I can tell isn't mine," Callie explains, motioning for me to continue my invisible punches. "With training, you can start telling what's yours and what isn't. The moment that you can feel something that isn't yours, you know there's someone who's unintentionally giving it."

I don't respond. I knew the Soturis have some way of tracking people with power down. That's how they end up kidnapping kids from Madyor. But I didn't know it was something I was doing.

"We might be days away from Madyor. But we all saw it, Kenna," she adds.

I pause again, my arms dropping to my sides. "S-s-saw what?" I ask, my knees trembling violently, mirroring the frantic beat of my heart.

Callie puts a hand on mine. "We all saw the light, Kenna. The light you produced. I don't know why or what happened, but we all saw it. I know why you're here," Callie says.

My jaw drops again, and a part of me debates running to Zander right now.

"Why do you think I wanted to teach you? I know you're running. It's good that you are. I don't think the government would be too happy to know you exist," Callie says.

That I exist? What does that mean? All I know is that I'm running because I don't want to be a puppet for the government. I don't want to be a Conjurer. I don't want to be away from Zander.

"I can also feel your friend," Callie adds, her nod motioning towards Zander.

I don't think Callie is any kind of threat, but this just means Zander and I are in a lot more danger than I think. It doesn't matter that I'm running away from the government. I'm leading them right to me—and Zander.

"I-I-I don't know what to say," I say.

"You don't have to say anything. Just keep practicing. I'm just telling you I know. Anyone who has experience with Ainoa or being a Soturi or Conjurer will also know," she says.

"How do I prevent you—or anyone else—from feeling us?" I ask.

"I don't know. You'll need a Conjurer to teach you," she answers.

"I-I don't know any Conjurer who isn't going to turn me into the government," I say, the realization coming to me slowly. I will die. I'll definitely die. I'll be the reason Zander dies.

My body shakes. The heat in my belly bubbles.

Callie holds up a hand, her eyes locking with mine, a silent reprimand in her gaze. "Hey! Just breathe," she says firmly, but my eyes widen when she takes a step backwards. "Let's get you ready to fight first," Callie encourages firmly.

I note a hint of fear in her almond eyes. What would she be scared of? Me? I can't even do her exercises!

Callie turns and walks back towards the horses. She grabs a long, rounded stick leaning over the fences separating the horses from the rest of the barn. She throws the stick toward me. I catch one end of it, but the other end smacks the side of my face. I stumble forward, catching myself before I hit the ground. I wince, rubbing the side of my face that the stick hits. Yep. That is going to bruise.

Callie chuckles.

I scowl again, my face red.

"You okay?" Zander yells from outside.

I hear him chuckle, so I shoot him a glare.

"Get up," Callie orders.

I brush the straw from my pants and pull myself up, picking up the stick on the way up.

"You okay?" Callie asks as soon as I am back on my feet.

I nod. I balance the stick in my hands. "How do you even hold this? It's so heavy. How am I supposed to wield something twice my size?" I can feel the strain the weight of the stick is putting on my arms.

Callie smiles. "Remember, I trained for many years. It didn't take more than a few hours," she says.

I sigh. I'll probably be in training for my entire life. I hold the stick parallel to the ground and walk with it, letting it weigh heavy on my nonexistent arm muscles. I'm only a few steps away when I catch sight of something odd. Something I've never seen before.

"Oh," Callie says as she watches me drop the stick.

Inside the barn we've been practicing in is another room with plants, fruits, and vegetables growing. It looks like an entirely different world in there.

"It's a greenhouse," Callie tells me.

My eyes widen. "What is it?"

"It protects plants and vegetables from outside elements so they can grow, despite the harsh elements. It's how we haven't had to rely on districts for food, unless it was for meat. Every family here has one, so we haven't had to bother with the districts at all. This is how we've been able to keep living costs down."

I pat the window to the greenhouse, catching sight of pears, apples, lettuce, and more growing inside. This is amazing. If we could do something like this, Madyor would never need to wait for food from Uthaana. My sisters would never need to be sold. They can live a life without it being an exchange for money. One day, when I'm not dragging danger with me, I'll come back to tell them all about this. I'll make sure Madyor can rise, just like Malina did.

"I don't understand. Why don't districts do this more often so we don't have to rely on Eaila or other districts?"

Callie sighs deeply. "I was a Soturi when I realized this was possible. The inventor and everyone else who knew about this was killed before anyone else could find out. The only reason I know is that I was part of the crew that cleaned up the mess. She had notes about it. What it's made of, what it needs. What our ground needs. So when I ran away and found this place, I realized it was a great way to be self-sufficient. It took years, of course. Probably about five years to get all the supplies we needed, especially since we had to keep it secret. But each family has one, and we all make sure we have our plants growing and healthy."

"I wish Madyor had those," I say thoughtfully.

"It would probably lower the cost of living, and you won't have to get supplies from Ainoa all the time. Especially since people really don't like going to Madyor." Callie nods.

"We always ran out of food. I used to work constantly just to make sure we had pera for when the deliveries came in. Sometimes, we'd get nothing."

"Yeah, I remember there would be calls for people to go to Madyor and help make deliveries. Getting them to Uthaana was hard enough, and getting someone from Uthaana to deliver to Madyor was harder. By then, the Conjurer would have already gone through so much with the travel from Ainoa to Uthaana. It's a rough road."

For a moment, I think of my siblings. I bet Soleil took over my job at the inn. The job was always too dirty for Inez. I wonder if Katleya did ever get sold. I wonder if Peter ended up giving her some pera for new shoes or if he just kept it for his alcohol. My heart grips at the thought of Soleil shouldering all the burden now. I wonder if Inez finally found a job. Maybe she'll take over the bargain I had for Katleya. I think she'd like it; she's always had an affinity for clothes. My biggest hope is that no one has hurt them. If I ever get the chance to come back, I'll make sure to bring this knowledge back.

I let myself feel it for a moment.

And then I move on. Let's be honest. I'll probably never make it back.

31

Kenna

I wake up to loud banging on our door at the inn. My eyes blink, slowly getting used to the soft, but dim light pouring in from the half-opened curtains. Hm. It's not even sunrise yet. It can only be one person. She's been doing this to us for the past few days since she started training me.

"The sun isn't even up yet, Callie," I complain. I pull open the door.

Callie barges in, her normally friendly eyes lit up like fire, panic spreading across her face. My chest tightens. This doesn't look good.

"We have to go," she says, already cramming food and clothes back into our rucksacks. It doesn't take long before I realize we're finally living my worst nightmare.

"What's going on?" a sleepy voice calls out from the depths of the sheets.

"Zander, we have to go," I croak.

He immediately rouses, getting up to get dressed and help Callie with the rucksacks. My sleepiness vanishes, replaced by a cold wave of panic and fear that constricts my breath and quickens my pulse. I immediately dress, putting on my coat, and grabbing the makeshift spear I had created with Callie's help. We leave the room, closing and locking the door behind us, and then follow Callie down the stairs.

She pauses halfway down before turning back to us. Callie holds a finger to her lips, her steps becoming lighter and lighter as she takes each step.

"What is it?" I whisper, adrenaline rushing through my veins.

Callie responds with a hand, shushing me. "Follow me," she whispers back.

We turned the corner into the main lobby and down a hallway where we watch her count the rooms before stopping at a locked door. We wait as she plays with the lock until she pushes it open. She motions for us to enter the room.

The room is empty and clean. Unlike our room, this room looks out over a roof instead.

Callie locks the door. She walks over to a dresser and easily lifts it to plant the dresser in front of the door. Then, she walks over to the bed. She motions for Zander to take the other end and does the same thing, planting the bed right in front of the dresser.

"What's going on?" I hiss.

"I feel them," Callie says, eyeing me. She crosses the room and opens the window, looking out to scan the area. Callie lifts herself easily, squeezing her legs into the window.

She disappears onto the roof for a moment, and Zander and I look at each other for the first time since she woke us. I see the stark terror in his eyes, a chilling sight that does nothing to calm my racing heart. After a few moments, she reappears, motioning to us.

"Give me your bags," she orders.

Zander pulls off my rucksack and pushes it through the window, followed by his own.

She pulls the rucksacks and tosses them to one side before reaching out to Zander. "Come on. Then you can help Kenna up. I'll scan the roof for a path down," she instructs.

Zander holds out his hand and lets her pull him up. He makes it up onto the roof with ease, and I'm impressed by the strength this woman has. She just pulled him up onto the roof like he weighed nothing.

I've been cautious with her the last few days, but with that show of strength, I'm glad she is on our side—at least for now.

Callie doesn't wait. She disappears behind Zander. Zander turns and holds out an arm to me through the window. I grab it, grunting, as I kick off the wall to get onto the roof. I use the roof to lift myself up with Zander's help, ducking instinctively to avoid hitting the top of the window, even though I'm too short for it. My knees hit the concrete, and I grimace before pulling myself up, just in time for Callie to make it back.

She puts a finger on her lips again and points to our feet. We nod, sharing a look. This isn't our first time running on a roof.

She kneels back down and reaches over to close and lock the window.

"Follow me," she whispers as soon as she gets back up on her feet.

She walks, her head hunched down, her face a picture of concentration and focus, like there are other things she's considering concerning our escape. We cross the roof as quietly as we can, then move to the next roof, with Zander helping me to make the transfer.

"Keep your heads down," Callie hisses, waving a hand at us.

We cross a few more roofs until we reach one with a greenhouse at the top. Callie crouches beside the garden, her eyes continuing to scan the area. She motions for us to stay low, and we follow, kneeling beside her. I didn't notice it before because it's dark, but with the soft light of the dawn, Callie's wearing her Soturi uniform. She looks so beautiful, so strong, so ready for battle, and incredibly intimidating, that for a moment, I forget she's with us.

"I felt them this morning," she starts, her eyes moving from me to Zander. Her brows are knitted, the muscles in her cheeks and jaw tight.

"You what?" Zander asks, frowning, running his hand through his hair.

"I can feel your power," Callie adds, looking at Zander.

Zander's jaw drops and turns to me, raising an eyebrow. Ah. I didn't tell him because he'd worry and make us leave. I wanted to train and be ready to fight with him, instead of him having to carry all the burden.

"I didn't know you could," Zander responds, his gaze back on Callie. But I can tell he's pissed.

"It doesn't matter right now," Callie snaps.

She's right. I shoot an apologetic glance at Zander again before looking at her again.

"This morning, I felt power outside of yours and Kenna's. I can tell they're coming. They're still a bit far out, but there's more than just a couple. I've never felt this much power before. Our community—this village—has never been found by Soturis or Conjurers before," she explains.

"I created a couple of false scents for us, but we need to keep going. The problem is…" She pauses and looks at me. "You're giving out a really strong pulse. We need to get you to someone who can teach you to control that. Without that, you're always going to be in danger. Without that, they can find you anywhere," she says.

My face flushes under Zander's glare.

"I don't know how to stop it," I tell her, my chin quivering as I fight the urge to cry.

Callie turns to Zander, whose face is still scrunched in confusion.

"As a Conjurer, you give out a pulse, most likely every time you use your powers. Yours isn't as strong. But Kenna isn't even using her powers, and she's still giving out twice as strong of a pulse as someone using full powers," Callie explains quickly.

I focus on Zander's face, wincing as I see the panic cross his eyes.

"It's okay. We'll get you to someone who can help you," Callie says reassuringly. "It's going to be a bit of travel, and we'll have to keep going with no stops for a few days. But I heard of a Conjurer in another village who might be able to."

Zander's face turns to stone as he nods.

"We?" I repeat.

"Yes, I'm coming with you," Callie says.

"But what about your kids?"

"My kids can protect themselves. I've been training them since they came out of my womb. You," she says, planting her hands on my shoulders, "you're important to the future of this country. You need protection, and I'm going to help you get as far away as possible."

Wait. What? I'm so confused right now. Who's the future of this country?

Kenna

After escaping the village, we walk for days through the forests, making as few stops as we can manage. Zander wanted to rest and hide at night, but Callie knows these forests so well that she's convinced him she'll protect us from the dryads that roam the forest. I can't even remember the last time I sat down. My heels hurt so much I can barely walk.

"We're going to need a horse, maybe two, I think," Callie says, interrupting the self-pity I'm about to dive into.

I look over at Zander. He hasn't spoken to me since we left the village. Outside of occasional answers and some questions, he's been quiet. I know he's pissed at me for not telling him. I can't blame him.

I should've known better.

We reach a pass in the mountains, glimpsing another village just below. Lucky for us, Callie knows these mountains like the back of her hand. She knows when to turn, where the monsters are, which villages to avoid. It's impressive, and curious, especially considering her background. We stand on the pass, taking deep breaths of the cool mountain air.

I've never seen anything quite so breathtaking before. The mountains are a picturesque sight, with different shades of green intermingling to create a captivating panorama. If I look really carefully, I can even spot hints of blue that might be a lake or a source of water. The clouds hang low, creating a mysterious shadow surrounding the mountainous range.

"Welcome to Uthaana," Callie says.

I can't help how excited I am to be in a different district. I actually made it. I'm actually out of Madyor.

"It's beautiful. So different from Madyor. There's so many trees here," I respond, marveling at the sight around me.

"Yes, it is," Callie agrees. I hear a hint of regret in her response.

"Do you miss it?" I ask.

"My entire family was killed by Soturis when I escaped," Callie murmurs, keeping her eyes down.

My jaw drops.

"There's nothing there anymore for me. Except for a lot of heartache and regret," she continues, sighing.

"Did you ever come back?" Zander asks.

I glance at him, hoping to catch his eye. Instead, he avoids my glance, and my heart sinks. He must miss home. He must miss his sisters.

"No. I knew they'd get to them as soon as I left. No one escapes the Soturi without consequences. My mother wrote to me and encouraged me to leave. She kept writing for a while until I found the village.

Eventually, she stopped. I got word that my entire family was dead soon after," Callie croaks.

"I'm sorry," I tell her. *I'm sorry this government failed you. I'm sorry your family had to die.*

But Callie looks at me, a smile spreading across her face. "That's why we need you."

Wait, what? Why me? What does she need with me? "I don't understand, Callie. I don't understand what you mean when you say that."

Callie chuckles, quiet for a minute, though her eyes still glisten with tears from the bombshell she just dropped on us. "It's fascinating to me that you don't know that. When I was younger, this was all they talked about," she says.

"We grew up orphaned, Zander and I. We were dropped at our adoptive parents' front door in Madyor when we were babies," I explain.

Her eyes widen. "So, you grew up in Madyor?"

"Yes. Lena was great, but she passed away many years ago, and Peter wasn't exactly the fatherly type." I turn to Zander. "He's my only friend." I catch Zander's eye, but he looks away.

"Is it Peter who gave you that?" She gestures at my eye.

I'd almost forgotten how sore my eye still was. I nod. "I have no idea who my parents are or where I actually came from," I tell her.

Callie kicks a rock to get it out of the path. I follow closely behind, Zander at my heels. "My mother used to tell me this story. But I've heard it told many different ways, especially as I got through becoming a Soturi and met different people," she starts. "There's a story about someone who will break the curse on Eaila and the government. Someone with incredible power." Callie pauses, looking at me. "The savior of this country. Of this life." She continues walking, brushing away large roots and shrubs.

"Me?" I laugh.

Callie and Zander stop to look at me. My stomach hurts. I don't think I've laughed this hard in a while.

"I'm sorry. You think it's me?" I ask in between laughter. I'm coughing now.

Callie smiles.

"Callie, the Nagiisa is supposed to be powerful and able to help everyone. At least, that's what we know of her. I only heard about her once in my entire life. No one likes to talk about things that are unlikely to happen."

Callie keeps walking, that same sure smile spread across her face.

"No," I say definitively, as I follow her, watching, waiting for her reaction.

She doesn't respond.

"No," I repeat, glancing at Zander, who shrugs at me. "No, you can't think it's me."

She looks back at me, a weird smile still on her face. I'm so confused. "I know it's you," Callie responds finally. There is a definitive tone in her voice, and I can't tell if I should be afraid.

I laugh again, but not as wholeheartedly. "You think I'm going to save this country? Eaila? From the government?" My voice is getting shriller by the second.

Boy, what have they been feeding people from other districts?

Callie doesn't look fazed by my laughing at all. If anything, she just looks more… certain.

"Are you serious?" I ask finally, my laughter dissipating until it's completely replaced by something else.

"As a heart attack," she responds. This time, it's her turn to laugh.

Me? Save the country? Me? I mean… maybe the country *should* be scared. If I'm who they think will save them, they should *definitely* be scared. I can barely save myself. I couldn't save my sisters. I can't even save Zander.

I reach out and grab her arm, and she stops, looking at me with gentle eyes.

"Why do you think it's me?" I demand.

She puts a hand over mine, looking directly into my face. "I wish I could show you. I wish you could feel how much power you're giving off at the moment." Callie's brows furrow.

My mind whirls. She can't be right. This can't be true. I can't be whoever she thinks I am. I mean, if I am, Taiamen is definitely doomed. I mean, look at me. I'm nobody. I'm… I'm me. Nobody.

"Are you sure it's not Zander you're feeling? Or both of us combined?" I ask.

I'm almost positive she is going to say it is. She has to. She needs to. Anything. Anything to get me out of this… this responsibility, this weight.

"Yes. When we get to the Conjurer, I'll have her show you," Callie promises.

My heart sinks. I take a deep breath and look up. We've reached the village.

Callie pointed to the stables at the end of the street before heading toward them.

"Should we wait until tonight to grab and go?" Zander suggests, hesitating.

"What for?" Callie's eyebrows raise, but she doesn't stop.

"So we can grab the horses?"

Callie laughs. "That won't be necessary. Follow me."

We follow her to the stables, where Callie calls out, "Greer."

A young woman comes out of the stables, her long, blonde hair in a braid behind her back. She lights up seeing Callie, her face breaking out into a smile, and she heads over to wrap her arms around her. They talk, their voices so low, neither Zander nor I can hear what they're saying. After a few minutes, Greer disappears into the stables.

Callie approaches Zander and me.

"Greer is an old friend. I've had my share of my travels here, and I've needed help multiple times. Greer has helped me out of several hairy issues," Callie explains, gesturing at the woman walking out of the stables, pulling two beautiful, majestic horses.

"They're beautiful," I breathe, as Greer hands one to me and another to Callie.

"Can you ride?" Callie asks.

Zander nods. I shrug. No, I've never ridden a horse. Add that to the many things their supposed savior *can't* do.

"It's going to be a painful couple of days." Callie chuckles.

"We've been waiting for you." Greer turns to me, a huge smile on her face.

I freeze. What the *Faahi* do you say to someone who tells you that? That they've waited for absolutely nothing? That they should probably keep waiting?

"Thank you, Greer," Callie says, nodding.

Greer nods at her before turning and disappearing into the stables.

"What did you tell her?" I hiss at Callie, the warmth in my belly rising.

"I didn't," Callie responds quickly, turning to me. She reached up and fixed the saddle on top of the horse.

"Here." She motions for Zander.

Zander takes the reigns and gets up on the horse easily. He reaches out to me. Callie waves for me to grab his hand. She points to her knees, and bends halfway. I hesitate. Then I stand on her knee and launch myself up.

I hit the horse square on my chest, falling backwards and stumbling on the ground. *Great.*

Zander and Callie fight a laugh, but they don't do a great job at it. I scowl at them.

Yeah. I'm the savior, alright.

"I'll find us a place to rest after this, I promise," Callie offers as she helps me up again. She gets up on her own horse and leads us out of the village and back into the wilderness.

We ride for a few hours before Callie finds a place to rest. By then, my inner thighs are burning and cramping, and I struggle to dismount, my muscles screaming in protest. So much for being their savior, huh? I don't even have the muscles to ride.

Callie makes me stay put with the rucksacks while she goes to find water and food for the horses. Zander wanders off to find some fruit and hunt. He's been in a very pensive mood, and it's hard to read.

The rustling of leaves startles me, and I spin immediately, looking for a dryad in the trees.

"Hello," a deep, but kind voice reverberates around me.

I get up, scanning the area.

"Don't worry. I'm not a dryad," the voice responds.

I wheel around to the voice. My mouth drops, and I back up slowly, eventually stumbling onto a tree.

"You don't need to be scared. I'm not going to hurt you," the creature says.

I open my mouth again to speak, but nothing comes out.

"It's okay. You don't have to talk. I can read your mind. You're not going crazy," the thing responds, even though I don't say anything. My heart pounds painfully.

"Wha-wha-what are you?" I stutter. I grab my makeshift spear and pose to defend myself.

And then my view completely changes. From the trees and bushes that I'm looking at comes a slow outline, then a figure. First it's orange, and then green, getting bigger as it eventually draws closer, encompassing my entire surroundings. Its head towers above even the highest tree, and its tail curls around the trees to my left.

I don't know whether to be scared or enchanted. I've never seen anything like it.

The creature before me is massive. It has the body of a serpent, but with giant wings, flapping softly in the breeze. The creature's skin is emerald green and orange, perfectly mimicking the colors of the surrounding foliage and sunlight. Under the sun's rays, its form is embellished with magnificent feathers that shimmer brilliantly with each movement of the light. The creature moves elegantly, gliding along the ground with a slender, sleek, and sinuous form. Its magnificent feathers form a crown on top of its head, accentuating its piercing green eyes and regal appearance. The creature's eyes are humongous, yet hold a gentle, soothing gaze.

I swear it's looking right at me.

It proudly extends its grand, expansive wings, basking in the warm sunlight. Despite its size and intimidating presence, I feel calm, like I know what it is, and that I'm safe with it.

"I'm not a monster. I'm a creature. I'm a couatl. And no, I'm not making you feel that way," the being says, answering the question I have in my mind.

"You can really read my mind?" I repeat.

"*Yes,*" it responds, fitting itself on a rock.

"My name is Cersei."

"I don't understand. What are you?" I ask.

"An ancient being, created from the dawn of time, to look over and help powerful beings. Like yourself," Cersei explains.

There it is again. Who the *Faahi* is powerful? Me? I can't be powerful. I'm not powerful. I can't even ride a horse! What kind of powerful person can't ride a horse? I sigh.

"*It's okay. You're just starting your journey. You might not feel it yet, but you are,*" Cersei says.

"I'm not powerful. I-I-I don't know what I am. I don't know why you're here," I stutter, trying to convince Cersei.

"*I'm here because of you,*" the couatl repeats.

"But why? It was only a few weeks ago that I released whatever that was. I don't even know how I did it. I don't know what happened. I don't know where it came from. You have the wrong person!" I tell Cersei.

I jump as Cersei waves her massive tail. She's so elegant, it's mesmerizing, and the sunlight reflecting off of her scales creates shapes across the verdant heights of the trees.

"*I know you're scared, Kenna. It'll be okay. You are who you are. You've already shown such immense power that nobody's seen in many years.*"

"It's a one-time thing. I swear to you, I'm not capable of doing anything like it again. I think you have the wrong person. I'm not who you're looking for."

Cersei just huffs.

"Right, now you're quiet," I snap, exasperated.

"*Why are you scared of who you are?*" she asks.

I pause momentarily, feeling like someone just slammed their palm against my cheeks. "I'm not!" I start unconvincingly. "I'm just... I'm just not who you think I am."

"*Why do you think that?*" she asks.

I don't know what to say. "Well, Cersei, don't you think if I were powerful I'd have known sooner? Right? Like maybe I wouldn't have been made fun of so much. Or maybe, maybe, just maybe, Peter wouldn't have beaten me up half to death as often. Just maybe, I don't know," I say sarcastically.

"Or maybe, those experiences have made you even more powerful," Cersei responds.

I blow out a long, shaky breath. "I don't feel powerful, Cersei. I think if I were powerful, I'd feel it, wouldn't I?" I scowl.

Cersei laughs, and it sounds like music echoing through the forest.

I roll my eyes.

"You have incredible power. You just haven't discovered it," Cersei says.

"But why do I have it? Why me? I don't want it!" I plead. The heat in my belly rises, and suddenly, the earth starts to shake aggressively, moving every tree like a flag in the air.

"Breathe, Kenna. Breathe," Cersei says.

It might be my imagination, but I think I just watched a serpent teach me how to breathe. I gaze at the giant creature.

"Breathe," the creature says again, boring her beautiful and enchanting, lush green eyes into mine. I stare at her.

The ground shakes violently, causing the earth to shift and a crack to form between Cersei and me. But Cersei keeps her eyes on me, and I follow her lead. The horses spook, neighing loudly, climbing on their hind legs. Both of them break out of their tethers and sprint off.

"Just keep breathing," she tells me. *"Close your eyes."*
I do.

"Think of something that calms you," she instructs.

I breathe in, force myself to keep the air inside my lungs, and think of the only thing I can: Zander. Then I breathe out. I open my eyes slowly. The earth is still.

"Kenna!" I hear a voice and spin around.

My eyes well up. Screw him being mad at me. I do the only thing that could ever make me feel better. I run into his arms. It seems to surprise him for a moment as his body tenses. But eventually, he wraps his arms around my body, and I feel warmth and calmness wash over me.

"Are you okay?" Zander asks, his brows furrowed.

Callie is right behind him.

"We have to go," she says. She looks at me suspiciously, eyeing where the horses were just moments ago. Her forehead scrunches, but she doesn't ask. She whistles. A neighing sound surrounds us, and we turn to our right as the horses sprint back, stopping near where Callie stands.

"You're lucky I planned for this," she hisses, rolling her eyes. She grabs the horses' reins and motions for me to get on one of them.

I turn, expecting to see the serpent-bird I was just talking to be there. Instead, in its place, is a huge crack in the ground, revealing a deep crevice where some trees had cracked and settled. Am I going crazy? A serpent-bird? I scoff.

Taiamen's rumored savior is going crazy.

Kenna

When I wake up, Zander's snoring beside me. I'm on a bed, in a dark room, somewhere in the middle of who knows where. I must have fallen asleep hours ago; the last thing I remember is seeing trees as I drifted off on Zander's chest.

A sudden hiss makes me jump. I look up and see the serpent-bird again by the door.

Tagapamigay. I am crazy. How did she even fit in here?

I get up from the bed and follow the green-eyed being. It leads me toward stairs and out a steel door. The door leads to a rooftop overlooking the little village we're staying in. It's twilight. I must've slept all day.

"How are you feeling?" the serpent-bird asks.

I'm definitely dreaming.

I sit down on the ground, facing the village. We're deep in the mountains now. This village is in a valley surrounded by mountains on all sides. The mountains are blocking any early signs of the dawn sunlight. I see silhouettes of trees swaying softly in the breeze. Smoke is rising from a few chimneys, and a light is on in a room in a house at the far end. I look up at the sky, onyx black, lit up by small dots of stars. I don't think I've ever actually been out looking at the stars like this. I look back at her, her feathers glistening in the darkness.

"Are you real?" I ask.

The couatl nods. *"I am. They just can't see me,"* she responds, floating elegantly towards the edges of the building.

I bite my lip. "Why not?"

"Only you can see me, Kenna. I'm attached to you because you're the person I'm following. I have to choose to appear to other people. At the moment, I have no reason to."

She looks so majestic in the dawn light; it's a pity no one else can see her.

"How do I know you're real, then?" I demand.

Cersei chuckles. She floats towards me. *"You can touch me,"* she suggests.

I gape at her at first.

"It's okay," Cersei urges.

I reach out, partially unsure of what I'm doing. I expect to touch air, but instead, my hands connect with something. She's smooth and supple to the touch, dense, even. It feels like human skin, except much thicker. Cool and smooth beneath my fingertips, and as soon as I touch her, Cersei's evergreen-colored skin transforms, radiating a captivating glow that illuminates the waking sky.

"What's that?" I ask, marveling at the light show.

"It's you," Cersei says gently. *"It's your power, Kenna. Your power connecting with mine."*

I jump back immediately, and the coloring on Cersei returns to normal. "I don't want this power," I mumble, avoiding her eyes. I feel so much lighter just from saying that. Yet, saying it aloud also makes me feel like I've just disappointed every single person in this country.

I bury my face in my palms. "I just want to be normal. I just want to get my siblings out of Madyor. I just want them to have a good life. I just-I just want to be able to eat," I tell her. "That's all I want."

It seems so long ago since that was my daily goal. Since the days when I'd wake up, hoping something good would happen, so I didn't have to be hungry by the end of the day.

"Can I tell you a story?" Cersei asks. The serpent-bird sits beside me, its majestic wing fluttering once, sending a soft breeze across my skin as its feathers brush the ground.

I look up at her and nod.

"Once upon a time, there was a great Conjurer named Emer. He had all the powers of a Conjurer easily. Emer could wield water, earth, fire, air. The prophecy spoke of him, the one who'd lift the curse from Eaila. That one day, Eaila could be a normal district, where people from Eaila could be anyone they wanted, go wherever they wanted. That they won't die if they try to escape Eaila. Emer was such a kind Conjurer that all he ever asked for was to help release Eaila from their fate. So he gathered the rest of the Dominums, the other Conjurers who also had the powers to wield all elements. They agreed and planned to do that."

I roll my eyes. "I know this story, Cersei. Yada-yada, he accidentally broke the Conjuring powers, and that's what created the Synkka Meri. We learned this in school," I interrupt.

Cersei's face remains impassive, as if she hasn't even heard me. "*The day of the event, Emer had a dream about his mother. You see, something had happened to his mother many years before this day. She went from being the most loving person to suddenly not being reactive. She stopped talking, stopped moving. On the day of the event, Emer realized who the real culprits were. The real villains that destroyed his mom.*"

I nod slowly.

"*So instead of using his powers to release Eaila, Emer redirected the entire event towards something else—the destruction of Ainoa. Because his intentions changed while he and the rest of the Dominums were Conjuring, the power meant to release Eaila backfired. It strengthened the curse over Eaila and created the Synkka Meri, along with every single monster that guards it.*"

"Is that what actually happened?" I ask, skeptical. I've heard multiple versions of it already.

Cersei nods. "*I was there. I remember it happening.*"

My eyes widen. "Did Emer ever avenge his mother?" I ask.

"*He never did. He died that day, same as every other Dominum in the country,*" Cersei finishes.

I fall silent for a bit, staring at the dawn. "I don't know what this has to do with me, though."

"*You, Kenna. You're the only descendant of a full-powered Dominum. You are the one and only descendant to bring about the full power of all the elements. There are no other Dominums left. The others who died that day weren't married and didn't have any kids."*

I'm a *what?*

"I'm a descendant of *who?* Cersei, I'm no one. Somebody dropped me off in the poorest district in Taiamen, like they didn't care about me. If I'm a descendant of a Dominum, don't you think I would've been part of a famous or rich family?" I argue.

"No one knew Emer had a daughter. Emer had a secret partner. She was pregnant when he died. She gave birth to a daughter after Emer died. You are a direct descendant of Emer," Cersei reveals in a serious tone.

I think I'm going to vomit. "Me?" I scoff. Laughable! All these years of having no idea who I am. Now, here's this serpent-bird telling me my great-grandfather is Emer. What a joke. I'm a joke.

"I'm not a Dominum, Cersei," I tell her.

She ignores me. *"So far, you've wielded all four elements. You aren't even trying. You just happened to have an emotion so strong it wielded the strongest element in the area. You aren't even trying, Kenna. And you've already done it—just by force of your feelings,"* Cersei reminds me.

My stomach rolls, and I resist the urge to gag in front of her. "Four?" I repeat, forcing a laugh. This is ridiculous.

"The earth was the earthquake and the ground. Air was the light. Can you guess what the third one was?" Cersei asks.

My brain scours the past few weeks. It feels like a blur at this point. Everything happened so quickly; my mind picks up only the significant parts.

"It was fire," I whisper.

Oh *Tagapamigay*. My head aches. The image of it comes back to me slowly, but it seems so clear now. The fire had turned itself into a tornado from a small flame of a candle. I was thinking about Peter at that time and almost burned down the inn. I'd forgotten about it, and honestly chalked it up to hunger.

Cersei's big head nods, and I swear she smiles at me. *"Do you even know what the fourth one was?"*

I wrack my brain. "I… I don't remember," I tell her.

"That's because I don't even think you realize you did it. You were in Madyor, this was the same day that you Conjured fire. You were in the alley behind the inn when someone stole from you," Cersei starts.

No. No. I give an awkward chuckle. No.

"Yes," she responds.

My brain hurts so bad right now I feel like it might explode.

"No, Cersei. That was weather. That was rain; that was not me. I can't… I…" I stutter, failing to give a reason.

"Yes." Her voice reverberates around and through me.

Can it be true? Am I actually a Dominum? Am I really powerful? But why don't I feel that way?

"But, Cersei, you weren't there yet. How do you know about that?" I ask.

Cersei chuckles. *"I've been following you since you were a child, Kenna. We couatls are always drawn to power. I've been with you since you were a baby."*

My mind whirls, and my mouth goes dry. This is all too much. "But you never showed to me until now," I argue.

"*You never needed me until now,*" the giant serpent-bird responds.

I fall quiet. "How do you know it's me? Why not Zander?" I ask.

She doesn't miss a beat. "*I'm drawn to you. We're drawn to the strongest powers,*" Cersei answers nonchalantly.

I look at my feet. I'm exhausted. "I don't know if I'll ever meet your expectations, Cersei. I really don't think I'm the person you're looking for," I say finally.

But the giant serpent-bird isn't there.

"Hey," a voice says, and I turn to see Zander. "Are you okay?" he asks, eyeing me suspiciously.

I scan around him for Cersei. The celestial being is gone.

"Who are you talking to?" Zander asks.

I stammer, hesitating to tell him about my surely imaginary friend. "No one," I finally answer before getting up.

"It's time," Zander tells me.

Kenna

Zander and I wake to a loud bang coming from outside our room. I jolt awake, instantly catching each other's eyes under the sheets.

My heart pounds as we spring out of bed and pull on our clothes as quickly as we can.

I stop for a moment, and as the remaining sleep weans off my senses, I recognize the desperate sounds of screaming and crying. I glance at Zander quickly. He's busy with our rucksacks.

A heavy, resonant knock shakes our door. Zander walks to it slowly, trying to listen for any indication of who might be on the other side.

"Let me in," a steady but familiar voice responds.

Zander opens the door, and Callie slips in before quietly shutting the door behind her. She crosses the room to the solid-looking dresser, bends down to grasp it in her arms and drags it over to the door before pushing it up against it. She quickly motions for Zander and me to do the same thing to the bed.

"They're here," she says, scanning our faces.

"What? How?" Zander hisses, his jaw dropping.

My stomach lurches.

"They masked themselves. I didn't feel them at all. There are two Soturis and two Conjurers roaming the streets. There's another two of each on their way here. I got a couple of rooms to block the doors like this, so it might take some time to find their way here. They can feel you, though, so they know you're here." Callie springs open the window and gestures for Zander to get up onto the roof outside.

Zander pulls himself up easily. He reaches out a hand to me.

"Callie, what do we do?" I ask as soon as I join Zander on the roof.

"Zander, take her across the roof, toward the sunrise. Once you get closer to the forests, go left. The horses are there. Take them both and keep riding toward the sunrise," she orders, looking at Zander.

Zander nods grimly.

"Do *not* stop. Do not grab food. Do not grab supplies. Do not deviate from that path. I've masked it from the Soturis and Conjurers so they won't feel that area for a bit. There will be a village about a few days from here. The Conjurer isn't here, but she might be there. I will catch up with you—if I can." She pauses.

Her odd expression makes me even more nervous.

"If you need food or supplies, approach anyone along the way and tell them Callie Shane sent you. They will protect you as much as they can, but you have to keep going. Getting to the Conjurer is important so they can help mask you," Callie continues.

"How do I know if they'll help me?" I ask. I fight hard not to let tears come, but they do.

"They will. Trust me, they've been waiting for you," Callie assures me. She gives Zander a look, and he nods.

"But, Callie, what about you?"

I'm afraid I know her answer. There's a reason she came with us. And I'm afraid this is it.

"I have to fight and delay them. There's no other way. I need to buy you as much time as I can, and I'll do everything in my power to keep them at this village for as long as I can," she says.

My heart clenches. "Can we come back to find and help you?" I suggest.

Callie smiles, hope flickering in her dark eyes. "You say you aren't worth it. You say you aren't who we're waiting for. But I say we've got more than we asked for. It's been a pleasure, *Nagiisa*. I can't believe I was there to see you grow." She looks at me, her eyes dark but confident. She raises her palm to me, and she bows. I jump back immediately, my mind flaring in protest. I don't know how to react to that.

Callie turns away from me, her eyes piercing through Zander. "Zander."

Callie reaches out her hand, and he accepts it. "Spray this every few steps as you get into the forest with the horses. It will strengthen the smell of the horses, masking you and Kenna's pulses. There's two bottles, and they should last at least until nightfall. It's all I have left, but it should get you far enough to get away from here. I'll create a separate trail leading somewhere to distract them here, too," she instructs.

Zander nods, slipping the tiny bottles into his coat.

"And Kenna?" Callie burrows her big brown eyes into mine. "Do not try to help anyone. Not even children. You can't help them. Not right now. Not yet."

I don't understand. What am I about to see? My cheeks are wet, but I can't feel anything outside of the pain on my chest. I nod quickly, and she gives me one last look. Callie gestures for us to go. Zander pulls my arm and starts walking. I follow blindly, refusing to look back, afraid I'd see something I shouldn't.

As we walk through the roofs, the pain in my chest grows as the harrowing noises make their way to my ears. In the midst of chaos and the loud beating of my heart, the air resonates with cries of women and children, their prayers to *Tagapamigay* mingling with the sounds of fear and desperation. I can hear clinging of swords clashing and strained grunts of effort. The unmistakable sound of bodies being flung onto walls filled the air, then silence, reminding me of what I had done to Peter.

I grimace.

What have I done? Why is everyone willing to die for me? Why is Callie willing to sacrifice herself? What did Callie mean when she said "Nagiisa?" Who the *Faahi* am I?

I follow Zander across the roofs until we reach an area where the tree line starts. Zander walks around, looking for a way to get down from the roof. Just like the roofs in Malina, the roofs here are sloped. On one side, they angle closer to the ground. Zander jumps down first, then motions for me to follow. He catches me as I slip down the roof.

He takes my hand, leads me a few blocks, and then turns left, just as Callie instructed us.

Zander pauses and ducks. I do the same, hiding behind his frame. A man and a woman scream, running past us. The man is clutching his arm, blood dripping on the ground as he and the woman make their escape. The woman looks pale and terrified, looking back every few steps, eager to make sure whatever she was running from wasn't right behind her.

My mouth drops, my eyes grow wide, and my brows furrow. I stifle a gasp.

What the *Faahi* is happening? I squint, eager to see what they're running from.

It's dawn, but the light isn't bright yet. From where I'm crouching, I see it.

Large, orange flames that lick at the sky have swallowed the buildings, including the one we just spent the night in.

In the middle of the chaos, a Conjurer controls a blazing orange inferno. The flames dance in the Conjurer's grasp, as if taming a wild creature. His arms move as he selects a target for each flame. The flame soars through the air, latching onto its target, devouring it, and reducing the pieces of wood or concrete to ashes. The Conjurer has a scar on his left cheek and a vertical line that runs down the middle of his left eyebrow. The same Conjurer who'd performed at Krag Vinde. I remember his dark expression, just like I'll remember the look on his face right now—like he is enjoying this, like he doesn't see people screaming around him. Like everyone in this village deserved to die.

I scan the area, horrified at everything else I see—a man lying on the street, his skin black and smoldering. A few people run across the street, one holding a child, another carrying a chicken. Just across from the man on fire, a young child stands in the middle of the road, desperately crying for their family.

No. My heart clenches. That's a child. I have to help her. I start for her.

"Don't," I hear a whisper that makes me stop. I turn to see Cersei behind me.

"*You can't help them. Not yet. If you reveal yourself right now, they'll take you. Do you see that Conjurer? He has more control over his powers than you do right now,*" Cersei warns.

I turn back to the child, my heart breaking at his cries. "But Cersei," I protest.

"*Do not help. You do not have the control you need to help. If they find you, they will lock you up or kill you. Then you really can't help anyone.*"

"But you can help them!" I hiss at her angrily.

Cersei only looks at me sadly. "*I can't because my power is tied to yours. Right now, you can't help them.*" There is deep regret in her eyes.

I glare at her. She's certainly big enough. Why can't she go and help them? I turn back toward the town, and my feet step forward. But Zander's hand slips over my wrist, holding me firm. His eyes lock on mine, unwavering. I don't even try. At this moment, his eyes scare me. I take a deep breath, back down, and fight the urge to look back at the child.

Zander pulls me across the street into the forest. We spot the horses immediately. "You okay to ride?" he says, but he doesn't give me a chance to answer. He picks me up by the waist and helps me up onto the horse.

I climb onto the horse and settle on it, but I can't seem to take my eyes off the horror behind us. Zander climbs onto his horse. He reaches out for my horse's reins and starts to trot.

"Hey, hey," he says.

I pull my gaze away from the village, toward him. I feel tears streaming down my cheeks. Is this because of me? Are they dying because of me?

"Stay with me," he says. "I'm going to keep you safe."

I nod, biting a lip. I clench my fists and look forward, determined not to give in to the overwhelming desire to turn around and see what's behind us. Instead, I take the reins from Zander, and concentrate.

"Get ready to run," Zander says.

He gives a soft kick, and his horse speeds up. My horse follows, and we both ride off towards the sunrise.

"Do you think we'll see Callie again?" I ask Zander some time later.

Zander turns.

I swivel around to look as well. We haven't been riding that long, yet there are no traces of smoke or sight of any village.

Or any life.

"I don't think we'll see anyone from that village ever again," Zander responds without looking at me.

Zander

The moment Kenna let out that light after Peter beat her, I knew we were going to run. I knew we could die. I knew it was going to be difficult. I was scared, yes, but there was no time to actually process or even think about my fear. All I could think about was what would happen if the Conjurers took Kenna? I was sure they'd kill her. I'm still sure they will the moment they find her. No one could be that powerful and still be able to survive without being some kind of puppet to the king. I would do anything to make sure we'd never be apart, just like we promised each other when we were younger. To make sure she lives. To make sure she has a future.

Callie called Kenna the "Nagiisa." I've only heard that story maybe once when I was younger, while I was at school. Kenna, Kane, and I had just laughed it off and forgotten about it. People in Madyor don't like to talk about things they don't believe will actually happen. There's no point. We're too busy trying to survive.

If Kenna is the "Nagiisa," who am I? And am I worth being by her side? Am I worth anything?

I look over at her. She's looking straight ahead, her eyes fixed to the front. I can tell she's thinking about Callie .If Kenna was dropped off at Lena and Peter's house and she's special, could I also be special? Who am I? Is Kenna asking the same thing about herself? Who are we? Why does she have so much power? Why were we dropped off in Madyor, like we were nothing?

I look down at my hands. My adoptive father always made me feel like I was never enough. Like I wasn't worth anything. If my best friend is the Nagiisa, I have to be someone, too. Otherwise, how do I protect her? How do I make sure she lives?

I look at her again. She's lost so much weight since we left Madyor. To make sure Kenna is protected, I need to hone my powers. I need to practice. I need to be better. I have to be powerful. So I can be worthy of her.

36

Kenna

Zander and I ride for a few days without stopping, except to pick up food we see along the way or refill our water from the streams we pass. My legs are in so much pain, I don't think I can feel them anymore. I'm terrified of getting off the horse, because I don't know if I can get back up. *Faahi,* I don't even think I can get down without falling.

"I think we can stop here for a bit. Let the horses get some rest," Zander says as we approach a stream, three days into our ride.

He stops, slipping off his horse. He ties the reins to the tree by the stream with enough leeway for the horse to drink.

Then, Zander turns and reaches up to help me down. I hesitate, my face scrunching in fear.

"I got you," he says, giving me a weak smile.

I take a deep breath. Then, I hold out my hands and let Zander reach for me, but my knees and thighs buckle. I crumple to the ground as soon as Zander lets go. My entire body shakes as I crawl my way up onto a rock.

Zander looks through our rucksacks for food and water.

"*You need food and water,*" Cersei says.

I know it's her because she's been talking to me more and more. Zander can't see her, so I try to hide my replies to her as much as I can. "I know that," I snap at her. I can't see her at the moment, so I glare into the air.

I grab a rock and pull myself onto it, feeling the struggle of my muscles. Everything hurts. I pat myself down before looking back up at Zander. He's looking at me weirdly. I look away.

"You should eat," Zander suggests, walking over to hand me a fruit.

I accept, coughing before I take a bite. "Thanks," I manage a little after.

I watch the water flow in the stream, letting the peace and sound take over my mind. I refuse to think about the village. I refuse to acknowledge that Callie is dead. I refuse to believe that all those people, those kids…

"*I'm sorry,*" Cersei says. I can see the glimmer of her feathers in the verdant forest background. I blink, and her outline seamlessly disappears into the colors behind her.

I glance back at Zander, who's busy rummaging through his rucksack again. "For what?"

"*I'm sorry about Callie.*"

A lump builds in my throat, and I blink away the pain. But I can't do anything about this tightness in my chest. I look at the stream again, allowing the sounds to fill my mind.

I sigh and move to make room for Zander as he sits next to me. "I put you in so much danger. I didn't know this would happen. I didn't know they'd be this determined just to capture me," I tell him, and a sob escapes.

Zander touches the soft skin on the back of my ear, pushing back the hair from my face.

"You are in danger because of me, Zander. They can kill you. That Conjurer—he… he killed those people, like it is nothing. Like they were nothing. That could be you," I say.

He wipes away the tears from my cheeks. His hand cups the back of my neck, slowly massaging the muscles at the base of my head.

"I think they'd kill me regardless," he responds. "I'm not going to be their puppet. I'm likely going to be first on their kill list. After all, the government doesn't like rebels."

That's true. Zander has never been one for the government. "Maybe I should just surrender?" I wonder aloud.

He spins on me, his eyes darkening. Okay, I guess not. I don't know what to do. How do I save everyone? How do I save Zander? How am I supposed to be the person this country needs me to be if I can't?

I close my eyes. I'm trying to feel for that warmth, that thing that I usually feel in my abdomen right before something happens.

The problem is I don't know how to make it happen. In the times I've accidentally done something, I was either upset, overwhelmed, or hurt.

I try making movements with my hands, just like that Conjurer was doing, hoping it might spark something.

Nothing.

"*Try again.*"

I jolt, my eyes popping wide as I turn to see Cersei behind me. I scowl at her. "Geez, Cersei. Try to scare me less, will you?" I snap.

The beautiful creature glows in response. "*Try again*," Cersei repeats.

I nod. I close my eyes and try to mimic what the Conjurer was doing again.

"Trying to practice?" someone else says.

My eyes open, and I turn. Zander's back from looking for more food. I quickly scan the area for Cersei, but she's gone. I turn back to Zander, who wears a skeptical look on his face.

"I'm trying. But I don't really know how."

Zander sits down next to me, placing the fruits he'd picked next to us. "Well… I'm not an expert either, by any means. I have no idea how to mask us or how to do bigger things. But what I *do* know is that it starts with a bit of imagination," he explains.

He bends quickly to pick up a rock. "Hold out your hand," he instructs, and I do it.

He places the rock in my hand. "Now, close your eyes. Think about this rock in your hand. You can feel it. You know it's small, and you know it's a hard rock." He pauses.

I nod, feeling a bit self-conscious. I can feel his eyes on me.

"Okay, now, imagine the rock lifting. It's moving up; it's just a bit above your finger, so it's not too far away. You can still feel its energy and shape; it's just not connected with your hand anymore."

I follow Zander's voice, imagining the rock lifting from my hand. I can feel a slight burn in my stomach. I open an eye. The rock is still in my hand. *Yes, I'm so powerful.* I sigh, my heart sinking.

"It's not working," I say, disappointed, holding back the urge to throw the rock. Seriously. I can't even do this one little thing?

Zander gives me an encouraging smile. He lifts my hand, the rock still sitting on my palm. "Try again," he tells me.

I frown. I steady my hand with the rock, lifting it to level my neck, and close my eyes again. I focus on the rock. I feel it in my hand; it's slightly heavy, and it's cool to the touch. I close my fingers around it, feeling its odd shape, feeling the smoothness of the surface. The skin on my palm sweats, and my wrist shakes with the weight. I feel it. Warmth starts in my belly, and I relish it. I see the rock in my head so clearly. Then, I try it. I imagine the rock slowly lifting, giving my sweaty palms relief from the weight and pressure. I feel air on my palm as the rock lifts further and further.

I crack an eye open. My spirit plummets, and I heave a sigh, looking at the rock with dismay.

Zander pats my arm. "Kenna, look," he says.

"It didn't work, Zander," I grumble, about to go back to closing my eyes to try again.

"*Look*," he repeats, a hint of amusement in his voice.

I open both eyes and follow Zander's gaze. My mouth drops, my eyes widening at what I see. I wheel around slowly, cupping my other hand over my mouth as I clasp the rock that hadn't moved in my hand.

It's so beautiful. I'm here surrounded by some of the most beautiful trees and flora that I've ever seen in my entire life. But it isn't just that. Decorating the verdant colors of the trees are rocks that defy gravity, hovering and dancing in the air. It's hypnotic.

I've never been able to make anything like this happen. Never. I did this. I. *Me*. Like, *me*, Kenna from Madyor, a girl who's never been able to do anything remotely close to this. Maybe I'm not just an ordinary girl from the desert, after all.

A tear rolls down my cheek. I turn to Zander, and I can't contain the pride and happiness. I beam at him. Everything I felt over the last couple of days washes away. The tiredness, the exhaustion, the fear, the sadness. It vanishes into thin air, and all I can see is beauty—and it's all because of him. With this man, I feel like I can do anything.

I fling my arms around him, wrapping my legs around his waist, pressing my lips on his.

He steps back, catching me in his arms, his eyes opening wide before I sink into him. His hands move to my waist, climbing up to my cheeks, cupping my face in his hands. I feel hunger, like I can't get enough of him.

Behind my closed eyes, I see a streak of light. I open my eyes and momentarily pull away, my eyes turning to where the light is coming from. My jaw drops again, and my eyes widen, marveling again at the beauty around me.

The rocks aren't just floating now. A myriad of lights dance around the rocks, bouncing off of the bobbing rocks and trees around them. It's magnificent.

I start laughing.

"I think..." I marvel at our surroundings, the light continuing to dance around us, in beautiful shapes and shadows triggered by the rocks and trees. "I think this is us."

37

Kenna

Zander and I continue our journey through the forest. It feels like ages since we left the small village and district of Madyor, and the echoing silence of the forests now contrasts sharply with the lively chatter that I remember. After my first success at Conjuring, I feel more confident, so I put more effort into practicing. I'm still not great at it, but I continue training, switching from carrying and moving the stick Callie had given me to trying Conjuring again.

Training my body had been easier than practicing Conjuring. I still follow the technique Callie showed me, trying my best to replicate the proper foot positioning and feeling the strength in my stance as I wield the stick. Even though my entire upper body strains and complains about the weight of the stick, I do it. Even though I feel a throbbing pain spreading from my wrists and elbow. I do it because Callie thinks I'm worth it.

Someone thinks I'm worth something.

Zander sometimes practices with me, and we "fight" with the sticks. He's gentler and slower than he usually is, but it helps me move and feel the difference. I watch him train on his own sometimes, and he's just so much quicker and faster, even though he's injured. He moves the stick with ease and strikes faster. He's even pierced through trees he practices on, showing just how strong he is.

I can barely make a dent in the trees here.

I think I'm getting slightly faster, though. Eventually, I get accustomed to the pain in my wrists and elbows, and by nightfall, I'm scratching my wrist on a trunk to give it some much-needed friction to help alleviate the pain. I don't even think Zander's doing anything for his. His body just seems to welcome and adjust to it as he sees fit.

I wish my body was more able to adjust, build muscle, and recover like a normal person. Instead, I have to work twice as hard, practice twice as much and still not get the same results.

For someone who's supposed to be the Nagiisa, you'd think I'd find these things easy. But they're not. So... am I really who they say I am?

I sigh, looking at the bush I'm trying to grow. I see it in my head: the slight bulk of its leaves; the branches lengthening. For a second, nothing happens. Suddenly, the ground reverberates, the sound low and hollow. The stems branch, growing longer and longer.

"Zander," I say excitedly

He looks up and chuckles. The sound of the splitting earth gets louder and louder. As soon as the bush grows to twice its size, I panic.

"I don't know how to stop it." I shoot Zander a pained look.

Zander approaches me, his hand wrapping around me. I don't pull away, but my body reacts the moment he touches his hand to my stomach. My body shivers, the hair on my back rising from the contact. I'm giddy, and I beam at him. Ever since we kissed and made the rocks dance, every touch, every look makes me feel like this. Like I can do anything.

He motions toward the overgrown bush, but all I can feel is the phantom pressure of his lips against mine, igniting a pleasant chaos in my belly.

I finally look back at the bush. It's stopped growing.

Zander chuckles. "I didn't mean to distract you," he teases, bending down to kiss my forehead quickly.

My cheeks burn.

"When I Conjure, I feel a warmth in my stomach," Zander continues, gesturing to my abdomen, increasing the flutters beneath it. "When I need to stop, I typically have to pull back or change the way I feel about it. So, the goal is to change that warmth in your belly. The more you focus on it, the more it grows and empowers it. By distracting yourself, you change your focus to something else."

"So, to make something happen, I have to focus on it, and to stop whatever I was doing, I have to focus on something else," I repeat.

"Correct. Something powerful enough to distract you, change that focus, pull you out of whatever you're trying to do, or doing."

I think about the last few times I've done something big. Like when I first released that light. It was difficult to get out of that focus. It was so beautiful, so warm and nice that I found myself sinking into it more and more. How did I get out of it? How did I stop?

I look up at him suddenly. "I think of you," I say, taking in his beautiful features, despite the dirt and injuries his face has suffered over our adventures. His blue eyes glimmer in the sunlight. The sharp curve of his jaw. His dark eyebrows and thick eyelashes. His now much longer, wild, dark hair.

"What do you mean?" He pushes a strand of hair from my face.

"When I first had my outburst in Madyor, or the time when I caused that crack in the ground," I remember. "It was you. It was you who brought me back." I meet his eyes. I don't know if he feels the way I feel. But I do it anyway.

I tiptoe, pulling his face towards mine, and kiss him.

Kenna

The light radiates from above the verdant leaves of the tall trees that surround us. I rub my eyes as I rustle from where Zander and I slept overnight.

Tsk. Tsk. Tsk. I hear a sound rustling through the leaves.

I rub my eyes again, groaning, as I pull myself up.

Tsk. Tsk. Tsk. There it is again. I sit up, my eyes getting accustomed to the light around us.

And I see it.

I scream.

Zander jolts next to me, quickly rising and grabbing our makeshift spear. He places himself between me and the creature.

"It's okay. It's not going to hurt you," Cersei says.

I don't see her, and I want to believe her, but I've never seen anything like it before.

A tiny creature hovers in front of us, floating gracefully in the air like a gentle breeze. The creature is round, with long, jelly-like tentacles, and big, kind eyes at the end of stalks that protrude at the top of its head. It has vibrant green patterns that shimmer and shift as it moves, creating a mesmerizing display of color. Its tendrils sway and ripple as it moves, and with the soft breeze, they almost look like ribbons.

It drifts slowly towards Zander and me until Zander points the spear toward it.

"Don't come any closer!" I warn.

"What are you?" Zander asks.

"Hello! I will not hurt you," the creature tells me, but it doesn't have a mouth.

"How are you doing that?" I demand, looking around to see where the voice came from.

"I'm not talking. I am in your head," the creature responds. Its voice is chipper and loud.

I stare back at it for a moment. "How are you in my head?" I press.

The creature's eyes are so gentle and empathetic that it's hard to see it as a danger. "I am a flumph! I am a creature of the forest. Hello!" It bounces.

Zander scoffs.

"Most creatures will hurt us. How do we know you won't?" I ask.

"*It won't*," Cersei says, and I glare at her invisible outline.

"Do you think I will?" the creature asks. Its eyes grow wide, and it blinks so slowly.

Suddenly, the green patterns on its body softly move and change into a soft pink.

"What are you?" I ask again, my brows furrowing.

"I am a flumph. I am sorry to wake you. I just had to feed a little," it says.

"Wait. You fed on *me*?" I demand.

"You fed on her?" Zander repeats, raising the spear again.

"Just a little. Do not worry, I just need some strength. I didn't hurt you, I promise," the creature defends itself. "I promise." It plants its big, gentle eyes on me.

Zander drops the spear, but he holds it in his hand, ready to strike, if needed.

"We feed on other creatures' mental energies. We don't take too much, and we never hurt anyone we feed from," it explains.

I approach it slowly.

"Are you… are you real?" I ask.

"You can touch me," the flumph offers, bobbing a little closer.

I reach out, my fingers gently touching the creature. Zander kneels down next to me and does the same. The creature had soft, gelatinous skin. When I was at the Takkia Rakken, I'd tasted a dessert that had a similar texture.

"What do you need from us?" I ask.

"I am here to help," the flumph says. "I'm here to tell you about the things I have heard in the past."

"Help?" I repeat. "Help with what?"

"My name is Tika. I have been looking for you," the flumph tells us.

Zander and I share a look, then glance back at the flumph.

"Why me?" she presses.

"Because you're *Nagiisa*," the flumph declares.

That word again.

"I do not know what that means," I protest, getting up on my feet with frustration.

"It means 'the one,'" Zander interrupts, turning to me as he sits down next to the flumph, crossing his long legs.

I heave a sigh, turning from them so they don't see the tears welling in my eyes—the only way I know how to expel my fear and frustration.

"Everyone keeps telling me what I am. I don't even know what I am. I don't know where I came from, who my parents are, or where I came from. How am I supposed to know who I am?" I start, immediately jumping, hiding behind a tree, as leaves rise from the ground, spinning with nonexistent wind.

"Kenna," Zander says, jumping to his feet to avoid my tornado, laying a hand on my shoulder.

I startle, looking up at him, blinking as I work to calm my racing heart. I breathe deeply, continuing to hold his gaze, as I keep my focus on my breaths. The leaves twirling in circles settle themselves on the ground softly.

The flumph bobs back to us, his big eyes gentle. "I need to tell you something."

Zander and I look back at the tiny creature in front of us. Its body's shade goes from soft pink to blue, and then to red.

Its big eyes look like they're about to bob out of his eye sockets as it switches looking from Zander to me, then back again. "Someone is planning to kill you."

Zander and I stare at each other.

"What?" we exclaim at the same time, then look back at the tiny creature in front of us.

"Do you mean the government? Yeah, we've been trying to outrun them," Zander says.

Tika's tendrils shake. I frown. "I think this may be above that, my good sir," it says.

I approach the creature and sit down in front of it. The deep line in Zander's brow furrows, but he follows, settling himself next to me. He pats my knee in encouragement. I look at him and smile wanly.

There are moments when I'm truly grateful. Who else would do this for me? Who else would risk their own life just to protect me?

"You see, I hail from all over the country. Flumphs like me generally travel, roaming the country, looking for creatures to feed on and dark secrets to find. Then, we look for good people to share these secrets with so we can expend that negative energy. I come from a cloister that is focused on doing good for the *Nagiisa*. For you," the flumph says.

I hate that word. The responsibility of it.

"We have been roaming the country, feeding on dark creatures to get an idea of any plans for you," the flumph continues.

For me?

"We have flumphs who are tasked with covering the north, the south, the east, and the west. I was tasked all over. But now, I'm tasked to find you and show you what I have seen," it says.

"Show?" I repeat, my eyes widening.

"Do not be scared, okay?" the flumph warns. "Close your eyes. I will show you what I have seen in the last few years," the flumph says.

I look at Zander in a panic. He shrugs. Then he takes my hand and squeezes before his eyes close. I look around us before I do the same, disappearing into the darkness behind my eyelids. But instead of darkness, I'm in a different scenery.

My muscles tense, and I fight the urge to open my eyes. I feel a squeeze in my hand, and I convince myself I'm okay.

We are on what looks like a field of poppies, along a mountainous range, overlooking raging seas. Water turbulently hurls itself against the rugged rocks, and I shift through the drops of water spray. Waves create thunderous crashes, the sound echoing across our surroundings. The rocks are weathered and worn, filled with moss, bearing scars of countless battles with the tempestuous waters. Everything is gray—even the skies.

My heart pounds. I don't understand how I'm seeing this.

"Do not open your eyes. It is okay. You are safe. You are in my memory," the creature says.

I shift, trying to relax, and squeeze Zander's hand back. I can't see him in this memory, but I can feel his presence next to me.

"I was deep in the mountains of Ainoa, close to the coast. I can sometimes see Eaila from here, but it is a bad day today, so all I can see is this. It is not abnormal, really. Most days are bad days, especially when there are boats coming from Eaila or going to Eaila."

The roar of the waves cracks in the air, reverberating through me. The sound echoes in my ears. My grip tightens.

"This is kind of scary, Tika. How do you stay in places like this?" I ask.

"I have been in scarier places," the creature responds nonchalantly.

The view of the coast moves, and I float across. I gaze at the wild tango of the sea crashing against the rugged rocks, its resilient beauty leaving me speechless. I'd seen many things in the last few weeks, but nothing like this. I've never been to the coast.

"Please do not be scared," the flumph warns again as we slowly move. "You are about to see some creatures I feed off, and most of them can be frightening."

My grip tightens, my heart races, and we turn. I gasp, clamping my other hand over my mouth as I grip tighter on the other.

The enormous serpent's tail rises in and out of the tumultuous waters, its body stretching all the way across the mountainous coastline. Its head juts over the rocks, resting over the grassy expanse. It groans, and the ground beneath my feet shifts and trembles, filling the air with a deafening sound. Its breath creates a wind so strong, I might just get blown away.

I gasp and shudder, my body freezing in terror, as the foul stench of the monster's breath invades my nostrils. I cough, feeling the smells suffocate my chest.

The monster's head is unlike a serpent's. Its monstrous scales slither down the top of its head, and its wings stretch out like jagged shadows behind. Its head towers above me, a bridge to the sky, taller than any other tree I'd seen.

If this creature moves, I'll likely die.

Its monstrous teeth, sharp and menacing, jut from its gaping mouth; its breath fills the air with a putrid stench as it unleashes a horrifying roar.

My muscles tense, and I shift uncomfortably. I feel another squeeze.

"Tika, does it not see you?" I ask.

"I'm small, you see, I do not register as something that will hurt it," Tika responds.

We move closer to the creature.

"I fed from it, so you might feel the taste of terrible emotions right about now," Tika warns, but a little too late.

I grimace, suddenly feeling heavy and nauseous.

"What is it?" I ask Tika.

"This creature is called a bakawa. It is an ancient creature that I have not seen for many, many years," Tika responds.

I looked up at the creature in front of me.

Oh, that hurts. I clutch my stomach and gag.

"Why do we have to experience this, too?" Zander asks, his voice so far back in my head I almost question if he's real.

"The worse you feel, the more evil I'm consuming. I don't become evil, but I feed off of that energy," Tika says. "It's important that you know just how evil this creature is. That's the only way I can make sure you're ready and you can prepare."

I groan; the pain in my stomach is so bad I can barely keep straight. Oh. There it is. I retch and vomit to my left, away from Zander. I fight to keep my eyes closed as I wipe my mouth with the side of my arm.

"I think I got it," I say, disgusted.

"I do not know if you know this, *Nagiisa*. Bakawas aren't common in this country. We have not seen any in five hundred years," Tika says.

I think I hear Zander gag too.

"Why?" Zander asks.

I pat my forehead as heat rises from my stomach to my head.

"Bakawas are not your normal dangerous creatures. They only have a single purpose in life," Tika explains, over Zander's gagging and retching. Finally, Tika stops feeding and bobs away from the monster. "Their primary purpose in life is to kill you."

My heart sinks, racing at the same time.

I feel another squeeze, and I squeeze back, in between sharp breaths.

"I don't understand. I don't understand what everyone wants from me," I say quietly.

"Right now, you are the most powerful person in this country. The bakawa has no choice but to come for you. And it will," Tika says.

I exhale, staring at the huge monster. This thing *will* kill me. How do I survive this? Can I even? Why don't I just die now? Then maybe I won't even have to worry about being killed brutally.

"You have exceptional power. Because of that, nature thinks it is only right that there'd be something to correct that. Your biggest and most dangerous enemy is the bakawa. They will try to make sure you cannot travel across the Synkka Meri. They will make sure you cannot make it to Eaila so that your powers cannot release the island," Tika continues.

Oh great. It's not like my next destination was going to be Eaila. "I haven't even been outside of Madyor until now." I scoff. It feels like everything I do is a mistake. My very existence is a mistake.

"But please keep watching. Do not be scared. You are in my memory. There is nothing they can do to you in my memory," Tika encourages.

I watch the coast, sighing.

Suddenly, my surroundings change.

"Tika?" I say, unsure.

"Do not worry. This is still my memory," the creature responds.

The raging seas and mountainous coastline are replaced by a dark area, surrounded by rich, wide, reddish-brown stalactites all over the ceiling.

The walls tell a story of many years, with deep scars on their rugged surface. I walk deeper into the cave, where the rocks are smooth and slick, while in most parts they are rough and jagged, each telling a unique story of the past through intricate patterns and formations. Layers of sedimentary rock form a variety of colors that weave through the rock like threads in a tapestry. In some places, the rock shimmers from the very little light that escapes from the small holes above. A sudden sloshing of water over the rocks catches my attention.

I squint, looking hard ahead, trying to make out a figure.

There's someone here. They're tall, wearing a long, thick, dark cloak over their head. It drags behind them, floating over the water carelessly.

"It is time, my dear friend," a voice erupts from the figure, echoing thunderously throughout the shallow walls.

I walk closer, trying to get a glimpse of its face—if it even has one.

"Do you feel it?" It cackles. The voice is hoarse, deep, and thick. "I've been waiting for this for so long. I can't believe it's finally here. You, my friend, have been asleep a little too long." The voice booms across the cave.

"But don't worry. It's almost time. You can feel it, can't you? You can feel that power, that strength. I can feel it too. It's coming. Soon, we'll be able to take back what's ours. Soon, we'll be able to take back the power they've stolen!"

The figure moves, its arms stretching in a wave of victory.

Finally, it turns.

I gasp, and my hands grip so tightly onto Zander's hand, I practically cut through his skin. The figure isn't human. Or is it?

In the dim light of the cave, the face of the figure looks like that of a human skeleton. Most of it is just bone, with remnants of skin clinging to his cheeks and above its eye sockets. Its cheekbones sink so deeply, I can see the emptiness inside—even from a distance.

But then… then… I feel different.

I'm not sure what it is, but I know something has changed. I wiggle my fingers, hoping to feel the warmth and familiarity of Zander's hand. But I don't. Instead, I feel the cool air pass through my fingertips as a small wave of water brushes against my legs, sending a shiver down my spine. My heart races and I fling my eyes open.

I'm in an identical setting to the one I've just left. The air is filled with a distinct, earthy scent. It is musty and cold, tinged with the unmistakable smell of decaying matter. I know this because it's the same as the smell in Madyor.

I wheel around, my gaze turning everywhere. Stalactites loom above me, their sharp edges casting eerie shadows in the cave's curves and contours. I look around, my eyes locking onto the longest stalactite in the cave, where a cluster of black roses, resembling a majestic crown, adorns the tips. I catch the small holes in the ceiling, where beams of light escape. The opening is concealed by flourishing green vines that move gracefully, as if dancing. Limestone walls enclose the area, full of character, with undulating contours and rough, bumpy surfaces.

I feel cold water pass through my feet and legs. Harsh humidity hits my face like a slap. I feel cool droplets of water trickling down from the ceiling. I lift a trembling hand to pat my cheek, feeling the heavy humidity clinging to my skin.

"Who's there?" the figure calls.

I jump, and my eyes widen. This can't be happening. What is happening? Where in the Faahi am I?

"Who's there?" An angry voice echoes again through the cave, causing the walls to tremble and awaken with a booming sound.

I close my eyes and bury my face in my arms. I beg *Tagapamigay* to let me feel Zander's hands again. I beg *Tagapamigay* that I'm sitting on the grass again, just like I was before this.

Please, *Tagapamigay*, please let me back anywhere but here.

And then, suddenly, amidst the sound of the crashing seas, I hear Zander's voice. I eagerly attach to that sound, his voice, and continue to think about it, pleading with *Tagapamigay* to send me back where I was.

I feel a hand on my face. I open one eye first. I see Zander's outline, and it's all I need. I burst into tears and throw my arms around him. I don't even realize I'm dripping wet.

"Hey," Zander whispers into my hair, pulling me close and tight.

I have never felt more at home than right here with Zander.

"I'm sorry, I'm sorry, I'm sorry, I don't know what happened!" another voice begs. It is gentle, but shrill, and I almost forget where I am.

My eyes clear, but as soon as I see the tiny, bobbing creature, I roll as far away from it, my body shaking with the memory of the humid cave and the foreign body cackling in my veins.

"Stay away from me!" I yell, getting up, but only to crawl behind a tree. I don't want anything to do with this creature. Not anymore.

"Get away from me!" I scream again. My eyes are hot with tears, my brows furrow, and my cheeks flush. I'm sweating. I hold up a hand to the creature to put space between us.

Zander walks to me slowly, his hand also raised towards me. "Kenna, it's me," he says before taking slow and careful steps toward me. "It's me," he repeats, inching closer.

I'm shaking. I don't see anything else but that creature. That creature is evil; I'm sure of it.

I train my eyes on the tiny bob, its big, gentle eyes also filled with tears. I look at Zander. "It took me somewhere. It took me there!" I exclaim, pointing at the jelly creature.

39

Kenna

Zander approaches me slowly at first, then takes me in his arms, sitting with me, while he clutches me tight. I sob as he caresses my back and hair, rocking me slowly.

"It's okay. I'm here. It's okay," he repeats into my ear.

"I'm sorry, I don't understand. That's not how my memories work," the creature begs, its eyes still holding giant tears.

"What happened?" I hear Zander ask the creature. He holds me in his arms, and I grip his chest tight.

"That's not how my memories work," the creature repeats, sounding confused. "I show you my memories, and that's all," it says.

"Alright, alright," Zander says, patting my back softly as I continue to crumble. "Do you know what happened to her?" I hear him ask the creature.

"I was showing her my memory, then suddenly, she transported herself there," Tika explains.

I lift my head, my eyes still red and swollen, my nostrils spilling snot on his shirt. "What does that mean?" I ask.

"I… I don't know. I've never had anyone do that. I've never known anyone who could do that!" Tika admits.

"You're safe in my memory, you're safe, I promise! I don't know what happened!" the flumph's body shakes. "I only know this because I saw it happen in her mind. She saw everything. She felt everything. She was in the cave with that creature. That water is from the cave," Tika explains, pointing its several tendrils to my legs.

Zander takes a piece of my hair and smells it. I shift, doing the same thing. The creature is right. My hair smells salty and musty.

Zander trails slow kisses on my forehead, continuing to rock me back and forth. I'm still shaking. "I'm here," he repeats, and I wrap my arms around him, tightening as I crumble again, the memory still clutching to the depths of my dark shadows behind my eyes. Finally, I think I've cried it all out. I sit up between his legs, tugging his arms around my body.

"Are you okay?" he whispers.

I nod. "It wasn't you?" I ask Tika.

"No, I promise," the bobbing creature responds solemnly.

I exhale, but I watch the creature suspiciously. "What was that?" I croak. My eyes are so swollen I can only peek out of them.

"We don't talk of it. Those beings are of extreme evil," Tika explains. "Do you understand what happened in the memories?"

I shake my head.

"The first memory is mine. That was of me feeding on the creature. The second memory is the memory of the actual creature," Tika explains. "That is the creature's secret. It met this other being some time ago."

"I still don't understand. What does that mean?" I ask.

"It means something is controlling this bakawa. And whoever it is wants to take your power."

I take a sharp breath, and I bury myself against Zander's chest.

"We'll have to head out soon. Are you going to be okay?" he asks.

"Can I ride with you? I don't want to be away from you right now," I ask him, sniffling loudly.

He nods.

Zander helps me up and onto his horse. He grabs our items, sets them on our horses' sides, then hands me the other horse's reins before he climbs up behind me. We trot, with the bobbing creature trailing behind us.

We ride for a few more days, avoiding any rest as much as we could. We ate while we rode and rested only when the other person was riding or leading.

"Hello!" a voice greets us, and Zander and I snap into attention. I didn't even notice the encampment as we came atop the mountain. We've been so tired, we've neglected looking out.

Zander's hand moves to his hip where the spear is tied.

"Hey-o!" The man stops, throwing his hands up in retreat.

"Don't mind him," another voice pipes back. This time, the voice is female, and much kinder.

Zander and I turn to where the voice had come from. A woman appears behind the man, looking sheepish.

"Hello!" she greets.

The woman is beautiful, with olive skin, long, brown, wavy hair tied back with a clothed band over her forehead, and slanted eyes. In one arm, she carries a basket, and she cradles a baby in the other.

"Forgive my husband. He didn't mean to scare you. We're a friendly lot, and you look like you could use a hot meal," she says in a heavy accent I don't quite recognize. "Come on." She motions for us to follow her.

Maybe it's the fact that we are tired. Or how kind her voice is. Or the idea of hot food. But we follow her anyway.

"Oh! You have a flumph! How adorable!" the woman says, noticing the tiny creature behind us. "How did you get one?"

"I…" I start.

"You don't have to tell me now. Let's get you some food," the woman says, chuckling. Another woman approaches us. "This is my sister, Aaliyah," she introduces the girl as she hands the baby to her.

The woman nods at us before she headed into a tent.

There are about fifteen to twenty tents, all big enough to house multiple people, set up around the mountaintop. In the middle of the tents, a wood-burning fire burns, alongside a tall pile of logs. A few people sit around the fire, chatting. Some of them glance over at us, curious.

"We don't want to impose," I say.

"I think you need to." The woman chuckles again, her smile empathetic. "I don't want to be mean, but you both look like you haven't eaten or rested in a long while."

"Thank you," Zander says.

He dismounts and then reaches up to help me. I haven't said anything to Zander, but I seriously need some rest.

"I could just use some sleep," I say. "Would you have a place for us? If not, we can just lay our bags down."

The woman touches my arm, smiling. I feel a slight jolt of energy, but I can't shrug it off. I'm too tired. "Don't worry. We have a tent for guests. You can get some rest after we get you some food," she assures us.

Zander follows her. I don't think I've ever seen him so willing either. He must be tired too. Near the fire stand a few tables with a variety of food and drinks. It reminds me of the Nights of Aava feast. The spread isn't as luxurious, but to Zander and I, who haven't had a real meal in days, it feels like heaven.

The woman grabs plates and hands them to us. "Here. Take what you need," she says, gesturing for them to round the tables.

We share a hesitant look.

"It's okay. It's not poison, I promise," the woman teases.

A few people near the fire start chortling too.

Zander and I eye each other again before we start to take some food. "We're grateful, really," Zander says, taking a huge helping onto his plate.

The woman nods. "Join us over there when you've gotten your food," she invites, pointing at a table by the fire with her husband and another man.

Zander and I nod. We pick up some biscuits, some meat, beans, and fruit before settling beside the woman at the table.

"My name is Aminah," the woman introduces herself. She points to the people in front of them. "This is Gregor and Andrew."

The two men nod at us. They watch us curiously, so I make sure to eye them as well.

Zander starts to eat. I do the same. *Tagapamigay.* I didn't even realize how hungry I was.

It feels like it's been a while since I've eaten hot food. I'm not even sure if this is a dream.

"Are you always here?" I ask as soon as I come up for air. The food is delicious.

"Do you mean this area?" Gregor asks.

"Yes. Is this an established village, then?" Zander repeats.

"No, we're what you might call travelers. We constantly move, mostly so we can avoid Soturis and Conjurers from finding us. We travel all over the mountains and coast within the country," Andrew explains, his brows furrowing.

I'm not sure if he is suspicious of us, or the nut he's eating.

Zander and I share a look.

"Are you… running away from them?" I ask.

"I think the question is who isn't?" Gregor responds as he glances at Andrew.

I might be really tired, but I think I spot a scowl. Is he angry with the government, too? I look back at my food and continue to eat.

"We're from a variety of backgrounds. Most of us are running from them because we did something. Some of us are running because they've taken our family members," Andrew offers. "We change locations every few days, so they don't catch us."

I nod slowly, my tired brain fighting to take it all in.

"You don't have to tell us your story right now. I know you're tired. But we'd love to talk once you're ready," Aminah says graciously.

Zander nods before he takes a huge gulp of water.

I do the same, the feel of cool delicious liquid filling my throat. Oh, water. What a luxury.

"I'll show you to your tent," Aminah offers.

Zander and I take one more drink before we stand up to follow Aminah. We pass a few different tents, then stop. She points at a small, grey tent.

"We usually offer these to our guests. It'll be nice and warm inside. There's a bed, too, so you can get as much rest as you need."

I nod and push open the door of the tent.

"I should tell you I'm a former Conjurer," she says suddenly, her voice dropping low.

I stop. We turn back to Aminah. She stares at us with kind eyes.

"I didn't realize you could escape being a Conjurer," Zander responds, frowning.

"You can't," Aminah confirms, chuckling. She puts a hand on my arm, but Zander pulls me away.

She nods at him, also placing her hand on his elbow. "We can talk tomorrow. But for tonight, I will protect you. I will mask you. Get some rest, and we can talk tomorrow."

Alistair

I open the door, breaking into a wide smile.

"Hey boys! I haven't seen you in a while!" I greet them, taking turns with a pat on the back. I step back, motioning for Jack and Oliver to come in.

Luckily, my apartment is in great shape for company. I hadn't been home enough to mess it up, and Leader Chen has been sending over gifts.

I watch Jack and Oliver walk into my living room and sit on my brand-new grey feather couch, a gift from the king himself. Jack holds a pack of beer in his hand and places it on the table in front of us. A gentle blaze dances in the firepit, providing a pleasant heat. Oliver edges close to it, rubbing his hands by the fire.

"What a nice surprise! What are you guys doing here?" I ask, grabbing one of the bottles. I chug it and burst into a fit of coughs. "You cheapskate." I scowl at Jack.

"We still can't afford the good stuff, you know. We don't work as hard as you do," Oliver teases, and we all break out in laughter. He grabs a bottle for Jack and another for himself. "What have you been up to?"

I wonder if they've noticed my new couch. "Oh, you know. Lots of work," I say. I can't really tell them, unfortunately.

"Redecorating?" Jack comments, pointing at my new furniture.

"Personal gift, actually. From the king." I beam, looking at my living area proudly.

Jack and Oliver exchange a look.

"Ah. That's still going on, hey? No wonder you don't have time for your friends anymore," Jack responds.

I notice the light shake in his words.

I smile.

"You don't pay me very well," I tease, triggering another laugh.

"Sadly, I don't get paid very well, either," Jack adds, grinning, before he chugs his alcohol. He shoots Oliver a look, and I feel like I might be missing something.

"So, Jack and I met some new Soturis a few days ago," Oliver starts.

"Oh yeah? Do they remind you of the brats we were when we were younger?" I muse. Those were the days. I didn't have plans back then. But I do now.

"It actually reminded us a little of the past, I guess. Oliver comes from Uthaana, I was sent here from Noppealiik. Surprisingly, most of the new Soturis were from Madyor. Where are you from again?"

"That's not that surprising, though, right? I don't remember many of us surviving in my journey. Those roads were treacherous," I start, memories of my past coming to haunt my present.

For a second, my old, dear friend's face flashes through my mind. Her green, soulful eyes. Auburn hair falling over her eyes. She was never really the bright-eyed beauty everyone would've considered drop-dead gorgeous in Ainoa, but I always appreciated her for who she was. We got really close, especially before I got taken. But I don't even know if she's alive. Her father used to beat her up, and she worked so much; there's a high chance she's already dead.

"Oh! Who was that?" Oliver catches me in my thoughts.

"Who was what?" I say, willing myself to come back to the present.

"You were thinking about somebody! I can see it in your eyes!" Oliver claims. Jack's jaw drops, and I roll my eyes.

"I don't remember much," I begin.

"Come on, you never tell us about your past!" Jack urges teasingly.

"There was a girl," I continue, hanging onto her memory for a bit longer.

"We used to hang out a lot. We grew up together. I get glimpses of her face every now and again. Just now, I got a glimpse of her. I'd forgotten how pretty she was. When we started talking about the past, it was the first thing I remembered."

"Was?" Oliver repeats.

"I don't know, honestly. She's probably dead by now. We didn't have a lot of money. Neither did she. Her mother passed away a few years before I left. I remember she used to work days and nights, even with school. She barely slept. She was working for her entire family, and she used to get beaten by her father. I can't imagine having survived this long with him around."

"What did she look like?" Jack pushes.

"She had beautiful olive skin. She was very small, tiny, really. Short, wavy, auburn hair. Really, it's her piercing green eyes I remember the most." I don't realize I'm blushing until I look at them and see their reaction.

I don't like thinking about the past.

"Did you love her?" Oliver asks, edging closer to me. "Was she your first love?"

"I-I don't know."

Suddenly, I feel a sharp pain in my chest. I don't recognize that pain. It's unsettling.

I look back up at them. "Let's talk about something else," I say brightly. As the memory lingers in the recesses of my mind, I struggle to get out of it.

Jack grabs another bottle and hands one to each of us. I accept immediately, opening it to take another chug. Nothing that alcohol can't fix, right?

"I'm curious, Alistair. Especially with the work you do for the king now. What do you believe in?" Jack says, leaning forward.

"What do you mean?" I narrow my eyes at him.

"You know, we've always had that conversation of how we wanted to grow older and how we believed that the government was doing some shady things," Oliver jumps in.

Hm. Odd change of subject.

"I still believe they are. But I also think they do some good. For example, my life wouldn't be like this if they hadn't done what they did. I wouldn't have met you, for a start." I shrug. "Look, I know it doesn't feel like it right now. But I'm still your friend. Nothing's changed for me. I want to make it up there so I can make some changes to the government from the inside. I can do it."

Hm. Again, they look at each other. I frown. They're asking me about my past. They're asking me about what I believe in. This is Conjuring lessons, third year. Do they think I'm being Conjured?

"Wait a second."

Jack and Oliver stiffen in their seats. I glare at them. Warmth rises in my belly. Tension builds on my forehead as I tilt my head to face them, trying to find some kind of response in their eyes.

"Alistair—" Oliver starts.

I finally start making my way up the ladder, and they think I'm being Conjured? What, I'm not good enough otherwise?

Jack and Oliver exchange a look again.

How dare they think I can't make it up on my own? This must be Alanna. After our date went awry the other day, after I spoke of my support to Leader Chen. What a waste. We could've been great together had she not been so adamant about hating her father.

"We—" Oliver tries again.

"You couldn't even take the chance and just ask me. You've known me for many years. We've gone through so much together, and you believed the words of a scorned woman?" I accuse, my jaw tightening.

"You know," Jack says. It wasn't a question. It was a statement.

I did know. I knew someone was following me. I'm a skilled Soturi with Conjuring powers. Of course I know.

I narrow my eyes, feeling heat course through my veins.

"Of course I know. You've been following me for days. Alanna hasn't wanted to see me since that night. She hasn't spoken to me since I told her I was working with Chen," I spat. "Why don't you understand it? Why can't you understand that I'm doing this for you? Why can't you understand that this is a good thing? Once I make it up there, I'll get to change things. I'll be able to make things better; I'll be able to control things more." My nostrils flare.

Jack and Oliver just look at me, their eyes wide.

But it isn't me they're looking at. The blaze behind me grows steadily, captivating their attention. What had started as a tiny fire had transformed into a massive inferno, consuming half of the living area. I can't seem to focus on it, though. It just feels like background noise to me.

"Alistair—" Jack starts again, this time pointing behind me.

"You don't understand what it took to get from where I came from to this. You don't get to judge me for wanting more. You don't get to judge me for wanting to change it from up there. I will be a Leader. I will make it so the king looks up to me and only me," I say darkly.

Jack and Oliver's faces twist in horror, their focus shifting from me to the fiery tongues behind my back.

I don't care. I'm going to get what I want. I will become a Leader. I will become someone everyone looks up to—even if it means I have to be their villain for a minute. I stand defiantly, unaffected by the chaos.

The fire continues to crackle in the background, barely registering in my mind.

"Alistair!" Oliver yells, his voice tiny among the crackling of the flames.

They exchange another look and nod. "Alistair!" they yell in unison.

Finally, I look at them. I feel the fire in every part of me. I feel the heat around me. I'm drinking it, living it. I am a powerful goddamn Conjurer, and no one can stop me.

I hold up a hand and motion to the flames. They gradually calm down, diminishing until they eventually return to normal.

Jack's jaw drops. Oliver's eyes dart anxiously from the fire to me and back again. Neither of them knew I could Conjure.

"Get. Out," I spit.

Oliver and Jack don't try to argue with me. They're gone within seconds.

Kenna

I wake up a few days later, but not by choice. Aminah knocked on our tent a few times just to make sure we were still alive. I've slept for almost three days straight before I'm hungry enough to get out of bed and go get food.

"Thank you," I say to Aminah as she sits down at the table. It's midday. Most of their encampment is out hunting. Aminah smiles.

"I hope you got some rest. I cloaked the tent from any sounds to make sure you didn't get woken up too often," she adds.

"I was wondering why I didn't hear anything." Zander chuckles.

His hair is disheveled, his cheeks lined with sleep, but he looks much more rested, even with the bags under his eyes. He definitely sounds a lot more energetic than he was when we first arrived at the encampment.

I bite into my bread. My stomach lurches in appreciation. *Tagapamigay*, I needed this. Food and rest.

Zander has already finished his first plate, so he heads back to the tables to grab more.

"Are we keeping you here? We're sorry," I say after some time, finally looking up.

Aminah smiles. "It's okay. We understand. We want you to get some rest before we move again. You both definitely needed it," she responds, nodding empathetically towards Zander.

"How long has it been?" Zander asks Aminah, sitting himself back down next to me with his second plate full of food.

"Since?"

"You left Ainoa?"

Aminah pauses to think. "A while. I broke out after about fifteen years as a Conjurer. I'd had enough at that point." Her eyes glaze, her memory zeroing in on what seems like a painful situation.

"I was born in Ainoa. My parents were Conjurers. They worked in government, too. They already had reservations about being a Conjurer, even as they were growing up, but they were too scared to speak up when they were at their peak. When they had me, they made me go through training. They knew I'll need it, regardless. If you find the right mentor at Ainoa, you get to learn quite a bit," she continues.

"I learned as much as I could as fast as I could. I learned it all on the sly, too. I made alliances secretly, and didn't tell anyone about why or what my plans were. I learned from some of the most powerful Conjurers. If I'd had the ambition, I would've made it up the ladder in as quickly as two years. But I didn't want anyone to notice me. The more you get noticed, the harder it would be to escape, and the quicker I'd die. I wanted to live a life, if I could." Her face falls, filling with pain and sadness.

"I got to leave first. I was sent to travel to Noppealiik for Nights of Aava. I caused an accident on the way back and faked my death." She looks directly at us, and I see pain rising into her eyes. She doesn't tear up, though. She stays focused and looks at us as if this is crucial to know.

I lean forward, showing her I'm paying attention.

"I killed twenty-four other people. I tried to escape from them, but I couldn't. I needed to make sure no one knew I was alive." Her dark eyes focus on me, and mine well with sudden tears. "After some time, my parents killed themselves. Conjurers were getting a little too close, and they didn't want to be tortured for information. One day, they made a pact, and just took their own lives. They sent me a letter before that. It was by chance I got it, too, and it wasn't until a few years later."

Her face is hard to read, outside of the occasional lines of pain that show up every now and again. Is it being a Conjurer? Is it growing up in Ainoa?

I cry at everything. I'm helpless and useless most of the time. This girl spent years plotting her escape and can somehow still look at me like it's some distant history that she was never a part of. How am I supposed to be their rumored savior if I can't even control my emotions?

"What made you and your family want to escape? What was so bad?" Zander's empathetic, but he's never been a fan of Ainoa, anyway.

"What do you know about Conjurers?" Aminah asks.

Zander and I share a look. "I don't really know very much," I admit. That's the truth.

"We're both from Madyor," Zander adds.

"Ah yes, they tend to keep things from Madyor. That's just another of their goals. Another one of their plots." She scoffs.

My head shoots up. "What do you mean?"

"Conjurers visit each district every year, right?" she starts.

"Yeah, it's a huge party in Madyor. It's the only week when we can get free food. My sisters would attend all three nights of it just so we can eat comfortably for a month after that without me having to work myself to death," I remember, feeling a tightness in my chest the moment I mention my sisters. How are they managing for pera and food without me? Is Soleil doing okay with all the responsibilities? What a stupid thought. Of course she isn't. I wasn't.

"Have you ever noticed any families in anguish after the celebrations?" she asks.

"Yes, it's usually because they have a family member disappear. Rumor is they take them." I shrug. Aminah looks at me, her eyes grave and serious.

"They do," she confirms.

It isn't necessarily a shock. But it is also the first time anyone has ever confirmed it.

"But that's not the problem." Aminah sighs. "They take them on with the pretense that we will give them a good life. We'll teach them how to Conjure or how to protect and become a Soturi. We'll give them good food, drinks, medicine, everything they need. It's a worthy cause, and some might even have that wonderful life after they get taught and go up the ranks.

"Some of them, the lucky ones, become Conjurers or Soturis. They become an army for Ainoa and the king. Once they are, they're given nice houses, all the food and drinks they need, a nice warm bed. They follow the king and are blinded by the beauty of their lives."

Aminah takes a sip of her drink. "But there's more of them that are looped into the worst parts of it. There's a reason the king keeps getting strong. A reason he's still alive. There's a reason the stronger Conjurers get stronger. And there's a reason you never see them take on dangerous missions like this.

"They don't just build an army, Kenna. They take," she says. Her entire body tenses up across the table, her hands closing into fists.

My brow furrows. Zander looks confused. "What do they take?"

"They take. They take *everything.*"

Suddenly, a carousel of Kane's images spins across my mind, leaving me breathless. I wince, squeezing my eyes shut in an attempt to block out the sudden painful memories. My mind is a blur, and my temples are throbbing.

What the *Faahi*…

Aminah is talking about what the government is doing when the memories appear, one by one, so visible, it almost feels like I'm there again. It started slowly at first. From the first time we met, to when we played together, to when we became friends. Our many days of hiking the mountains of Madyor. Then, it's the memory of the last time we were together, when we hiked up the mountain in Madyor. I didn't feel too good, but he carried me all the way down the mountain. That's the first time I'd ever felt anything for a boy. The memory is so intense that it completely overwhelms my senses. It feels as though the emotions I experienced that day have resurfaced, transporting me back to that very moment.

I close my eyes, massaging my temples slowly.

"Hey, are you okay?" Zander asks, placing a hand on my back.

I squirm, my body tensing up involuntarily. A shiver runs down my spine as a wave of anxiety washes over me. I can't help but feel guilt, knowing Zander is right beside me.

"Yeah, I'm okay," I lie, my voice choking with tears, and I blink rapidly in a desperate attempt to erase the haunting images of Kane from my mind. I rub my eyes.

Aminah frowns, then pushes a glass of water towards me.

I ignore it, but continue to massage my temples. I close my eyes again, engaging in a mental battle, desperately trying to keep the memories at bay and stay focused on the present moment.

Strange. This has never happened before. I think about him every now and again, but nothing as strong as this. Nothing as forceful as this. I didn't even start it. It just happened.

"Ugh. Random headache, sorry," I respond, peeking an eye out at Aminah.

Zander cups a hand on my neck, massaging the tense muscles on my neck.

"Can you—can you keep talking? It's probably just because I'm tired," I tell Aminah, with one eye open.

Aminah nods. "Are you sure? Do you need to go lie down again for now?"

"No, no, I'm fine. Please continue. What do they take?" I ask.

The memories gradually fade, and I reach for Zander's hand, giving it a gentle squeeze to express gratitude. It's confusing to have memories of Kane swirling in my mind. I reach for the glass to drink, reluctantly, but also to prove I'm fine.

Aminah looks hesitant, but she continues. "At first, we just thought they were taking people's lives. Did you know they take twice the average number of people in Madyor than they do elsewhere? It's because they're training people, but they're also taking people that don't have family, don't have a lot of potential, so they can send them through the Synkka Meri as food for the monsters that lurk there."

Bile rises inside me.

"The more bodies that are there, the less likely the strong ones will also die. They spend money to train the people that have potential, but those that don't, they give a good moon's training and decent food before they send them out to die. Half the people they take from all other districts have a good chance of being dead by the time they reach Ainoa. They feed the other half to the monsters so they can get their resources. Why do you think they can afford to do the Nights of Aava every year?"

My jaw drops. Is that what happened to Kane? I feel sick.

"That's not the worst part. Within the Conjurers, there's a type of power we call siphoners. These are Conjurers who can take one Conjurer's power for themselves or for other people. If they give them to other Conjurers, the Conjurer who receives it becomes more powerful. If they give it to a human—the king, for example, they become younger, stronger. Have you never wondered why our king looks exactly the same at his age today? Even though he doesn't actually have powers?"

I don't know how much more my jaw can drop at this point. I've never seen the king, honestly. But she's right. The king has been king all of my life and much of Lena's because she talked about him.

"How old is he?" Zander interrupts, his brows furrowing in thought.

"Three hundred and twenty-two years old," Aminah responds quickly, without so much as a blink.

"People who don't have powers don't live that long. The last king only lived until he was a hundred and fifty-six years old, and I bet he did something similar, too," she continues.

"That's horrible." I gape. My eyes narrow.

"You haven't seen what happens to those people that lose their powers, Kenna." Aminah's eyes blaze with a sudden intensity as she declares, "You haven't seen horrible yet."

"Do they die?" I guess.

"It would be better if they did. Once a Conjurer loses their power to a siphoner, they're stilled. In their current state, they become completely helpless, so they can't talk or move. They can still think. They can still feel you, hear you, and understand what you're saying. But they can't do anything. They live a life of a vegetable—no movement, no interaction, nothing," Aminah explains.

"No Conjurer can help?" Zander asks.

"Not that we know of," Aminah replies. "My family was in charge of all those who would get siphoned. They were usually the weaker ones, or the ones who liked to break laws or rules, or people the government didn't like. My family saw them get put in dungeons under the Iklead." Aminah pauses.

I'm not sure how much more of this I can handle. I take a long, slow breath and force myself to keep listening.

"For someone who has never seen the Iklead before, you'd think it is beautiful. You'd admire it and love how beautiful it is on the outside. But that's all it is. Beautiful and magnificent on the outside. The horrors that happen on the inside are on an entirely different level. The men, women, and children that have died inside that castle have been numerous," Aminah says.

She glances up at me, and her lip trembles as she continues. "I grew up killing people. I can never take that back. I can never fix that horror in my head," she finishes, looking remorseful at both Zander and me.

My chest tightens, and I feel desperation for Aminah. Like there should be something I can do, but I don't really know what. So much for a rumored savior, huh? Can't even help others. I can't even help myself.

"But you have a family here now," I offer after some thought.

A slow smile spreads across Aminah's face as she looks towards her encampment and the few people that have just come back from hunting.

"I do. But those days will haunt me for the rest of my life," Aminah admits.

Then, she looks back at me, her eyes grave. She takes my hands and squeezes tightly. Her eyes are heavy with meaning.

"That's why we need you," she declares.

I pull my hands back quickly, my lips pursing, my spine straightening. Callie mentioned that Soturis can sense powers. I shouldn't be surprised that Conjurers have their own method of detection.

"You know?" I ask. But I already know the answer.

"I've been feeling you for a couple of days now. There's a reason why we're here. I knew you'd make your way out. I'm here to help you," she tells me.

I don't say anything. But there it is again. The weight of responsibility. The weight of the future. I can feel my stomach lurching. The bleakness of my future. The unknowns.

I stare at Aminah. "You'll teach me?" I ask.

"It would be my pleasure, *Nagiisa*." Aminah drops the plate she is holding. "Be prepared!" she yells to the encampment.

She pulls us towards the rest of the encampment, scanning us with her dark eyes. She grabs a shawl from one of the women nearby and wraps it around my head, pushing my hair back.

"Soturis are coming," she whispers quickly, keeping her voice low. "Our group is prepared for them, and I'll be hiding you both with air, but you need to keep still.

No movements, no sound, no reactions," she instructs, her eyes heavy on me.

"Family! You know what to do. They will come here to intimidate us, to scare us. They will look for our friends here. We must protect them. Be ready," she announces.

To my surprise, everyone nods. Some even give us reassuring pats on our backs.

The entire crew comes from the south, the same path that we had come from. There are twelve of them, all in their uniforms, with the same expression on their faces— grave and unimpressed. The Leaders approach Aminah, Gregor, and Andrew first, while the rest of their crew scan the encampment carefully. Everyone stands in formation, almost as if they've done this before.

"Hello," the captain greets. He walks ahead of his group by a few feet and starts pacing in front of us, like a teacher patrolling the class. He keeps a stern expression, his eyes aloof and disdainful.

"Hello, Captain," Aminah says pleasantly, smiling at him.

"What is this?" he demands haughtily, looking at their setup.

"We're traveling to Madyor from Uthaana. We've found ourselves having a bit of a hard time with costs in Uthaana, so we're moving our entire family there," Gregor responds immediately. He doesn't look bothered at all.

The captain's gaze pierces through the group. Everyone is frozen in place, their backs straight, watching the Soturis like a hawk. The captain patrols, staring each person down carefully.

"We're looking for two people," the captain says, looking back at Gregor, Andrew, and Aminah.

"What do they look like?" Andrew asks without missing a beat.

"One of them is a girl; the other is a boy. Both young and from Madyor," the captain begins, his eyes assaulting the rest of the group.

"The girl's hair is reddish brown, and she has green eyes. She's short and skinny." The captain slows down to assess the smaller girls in the group. "The boy is much taller, with blue eyes," he says, eyeing the men now.

"What do you need them for?" Gregor asks.

A look of pure disdain, sharp as a knife, crosses the captain's face as he glances at him. "Now that's not any of your business, is it?" he says in a condescending tone.

The rest of the Soturis laugh, sounding phony and hollow.

The captain walks towards our table of food. "You even have food," he observes. The captain picks a chicken leg and takes a bite.

Aminah coughs. "With all due respect, Captain, our group hunted and made that for our family," she interrupts.

The captain lets out another fake chuckle before taking another bite. His group echoes him, diving into the rest of the food on the table. He glances back at Aminah, his eyebrows narrowed, his lips curling into a contemptuous smirk.

He makes his way toward her, staring her up and down.

I see Gregor stiffen.

The captain switches his gaze to Gregor, his expression full of condemnation. He raises his hand and motions to his group of Soturis.

The Soturis march toward the tents. They enter each tent, tossing and turning the tent inside out. The camp members look at them with wide, horrified eyes.

The captain saunters toward the food table again. "I think I'll eat for a while," he says, eyeing the group, goading them for some kind of response.

The captain takes a bite of his food, keeping his gaze on Gregor, who in turn, also has his gaze fixed on him.

We watch in fear as the rest of the Soturis turn up at the encampment, ripping tents, tossing clothes, lighting things on fire. None of us moves, just as Aminah had instructed. But it's a struggle as each tent comes crumbling down, some completely torn down the middle.

The captain watches his soldiers do the work. "Do you see what we can do?" he taunts, turning back to us. "We can do more to all of you, especially if you don't tell us where those two people are. We know they came this way. If you're harboring them in any way, we will know," he threatens, his voice calm and steady.

He grabs a bottle of alcohol and takes a chug. "If you must know, these two committed some terrible crimes in Madyor. They killed some of our Conjurers and Soturis and..." he pauses, suddenly approaching one of the kids in the group, "cut up some little kids," he finishes, mockingly threatening the child.

The child burst into tears.

The captain jeers again, his laughter shrill and empty.

I shut my eyes, terrified of losing control. I hate seeing this. I hate that these Soturis take advantage of these wonderful people.

The captain keeps going, sauntering back to Aminah.

"If I find that you're harboring these criminals, We. Will. Kill. You. And. Everyone. Here," he says, emphasizing every word, pushing his face mere distance away from hers.

Aminah doesn't retreat, her face blank.

"We haven't seen anyone like that, Captain. If we did, we'd tell you," she says, planting her dark eyes on him.

"Would you?" He scoffs, mockingly in her voice.

It happens in an instant.

The captain raises his hand and strikes Aminah's cheek with a forceful backhand. Gregor and the encampment step forward, but Aminah raises her hand, a clear sign to refrain from doing anything.

The captain laughs. "What?" he eggs them on, eyeing Gregor specifically.

No one responds or moves. Not even Gregor.

He looks back at his soldiers, who are still ransacking the tents, a satisfied smile spreading across his face.

I feel sick. I sneak a peek at Zander, who's clearly struggling to stay put.

The captain turns. But as his face turns, it meets Gregor's balled-up fist. The captain wipes the blood with the back of his hand, grinning wickedly. This is clearly what he wants.

"I was waiting for that." He spits blood back at Gregor triumphantly.

He motions for his soldiers to approach. Five of them surround Gregor.

The captain surveys the group, his face twisting in a mask of hatred. "See, this is what I like. I want to show you that there's nothing you can do," he says, his voice calm and steady, like he is telling a story to a child.

He kneels down next to the child he scared earlier and looks her in the eye. The child recoils and wraps her arms around her mother. The trembling mother pats her, but doesn't move.

"There's nothing you can do to fight us. We rule the country. You have to do as we say," the captain says, his eyes grazing from the child, to the parent, then the rest of the encampment. He motions to his soldiers.

We watch as the five Soturis who surround Gregor start to beat him. Andrew, who's standing right next to Gregor, tries to push them all back, only for the other Soturis to beat him up, too.

Aminah looks pained, but she holds a hand up to the encampment, keeping everyone at bay. After what feels like forever, the captain holds up his hand, too. He glances back at Aminah.

"You and your group better not be hiding those two fugitives. If we find out you are, we will skin your daughter alive," he snarls. He spits in her face.

Aminah barely flinches.

Then, he cackles again. He grabs another bottle and motions for his Soturis to have their way with the food. He keeps one eye on us as the Soturis savaged the food the encampment had cooked.

My fists clench tightly, and my face flushes as I struggle to contain my rage. These people, who selflessly disregarded their own safety, took us in without questioning or hesitation. And yet, here they are, protecting us like we're one of them.

Once the Soturis have had their fill, the captain takes one last look at us before marching away, his band of trouble following close behind.

42

Kenna

Aminah keeps her hand raised, even after the Soturi are out of sight. No one moves. Even Gregor and Andrew lie still on the ground, their eyes bruised, skin cut, and bleeding.

After what feels like forever, Aminah finally drops her hand. She rushes to Gregor and Andrew's side. Everyone else starts moving, too, like they already have a set of things they have to do, even after what happened.

Zander and I rush to Gregor and Andrew.

"What was that about?" I ask.

"I was following their heartbeats to see if they're actually moving on or coming back," Aminah explains quickly. She strips cloth from her jacket and presses it onto Gregor's stomach to stop the bleeding. She tosses another strip of cloth to me, and I wrap Andrew's leg.

"Thank you," I say to Andrew and Gregor. I keep my head hung, avoiding the annoying voice in my head that keeps telling me this is my fault. Gregor grunts as he sits up, and Andrew accepts my help to get back up.

"What can I do?" Zander asks.

"I guess we're just going to have to start your training now," she replies, glancing at Zander.

"You know I can conjure, too?" he asks, surprised.

"Of course," Aminah says. "Do you know what elements you can conjure yet?"

"Fire and air," Zander responds.

I shoot him an odd look, but he doesn't see.

"How much can you control?"

"I can do the little things, I…" Zander pauses.

"Do you know the concept, though?" Aminah asks.

"I think so. I practiced on my own. I never got any sort of training." Zander shrugs.

"That's impressive. I wouldn't have known what to do with mine had I been left alone with it," she says, nodding approvingly. Aminah motions for me to wait with Andrew and Gregor, and stands up, making her way to the tents. Zander follows her. I watch them as Aminah teaches him.

"You'll learn, too." I hear Gregor say, and I turn, blushing. "I hear you're having trouble with it."

I turn beet red again, feeling the heat in my ears.

"It's okay," Gregor offers, chuckling. "Every powerful Conjurer struggles in the beginning."

"It's just that…" I begin, looking back at Zander's attempts at fixing the tent. "I've never been good at anything, Gregor. Never. Now people are calling me Nagiisa and the One, and I don't know what to do about it. Zander does this so easily, and I can barely Conjure it. How am I supposed to be this person?"

I don't even think I've told anyone about that. I turn to Gregor, who's looking at me with an odd expression on his face. "What?" I ask, blushing.

"Everyone has to start somewhere. You can't expect to be that person if you don't work at it. Yes, it'll be long and hard, but you just have to choose to be," Gregor says.

He's right, of course. But what if I don't want to be that person? I don't even know who I am today.

"You just found out about your powers not so long ago. You just have to keep trying," he says.

We watch Zander fail a few times until he finally makes a really impressive attempt on one of the tents. I clap, and he shoots me a look of pride. It must be nice to be so good at something that you only need to try a few times. It just comes so naturally to him. He didn't even have a teacher.

"Hey," Gregor says.

I turn back to him and Andrew, who are still watching me with great intensity.

"Aminah can teach you," Andrew says kindly.

"I don't think she'll like it," I mumble under my breath.

"Your friend's doing really well," Aminah reports, pleased, as she heads back to us.

"I know." I glance back at him, grinning widely.

I'm proud of him. I don't know why it couldn't have been him. He's so much better at this than I am. He knows himself so much more, and he'd be a much better rumored savior.

"You're a bit different," Aminah tells me. She helps Gregor and Andrew with some water and a place to sit before grabbing my wrist and pulling me away. "You can't control your powers at all, can you?" It wasn't a question; it was a statement.

I turn red again.

"It's okay. I can tell. You give off a lot more of the pulsating energy than your friend does," she adds quickly, and more gently this time. She pulls my arms out.

"The only times I've done anything with it were by accident. Zander's been teaching me, and I've been trying, but I haven't been great at it," I admit.

That's why I can't be your Nagiisa. I can't be the savior if I'm not even good at this.

"I know, love. We saw the light from all the way out here, and we felt the ground move, too. You don't even know how strong you are. Very few people can move the ground." She looks at me meaningfully. "Most of them have had to train to just to learn how to do it. You did this without training. You've had power seeping out of your veins since you created that light."

She lays my hands out, flattening my palm up towards the sky. "What happened?" she asks.

"What do you mean?" I respond.

"How did you create that light? It must've been something devastating. A Conjurer like you can only release that power if you are seriously hurt or angry," Aminah suggests, eyeing me carefully.

Is it possible for me to turn even redder? Probably. How embarrassing. I can't control my emotions at all. A cold sweat slicks my skin as my fists clench, my body stiffening into a tense coil, fighting against the tide of the haunting memory threatening to overwhelm me.

"It's my father. Well, my adopted father," I begin.

After I've finished filling her in on the details, her eyes shine with tears. "You are a Dominum, Kenna. We haven't seen one in over five hundred years. As far as we know, all the Leaders who were Dominums died in the flooding of the Synkka Meri. Do you know what that means?"

I shrug, remembering what Cersei told me, but knowing it wouldn't hurt to hear it from another party.

"You are a direct descendant of a Leader in the year 500 BN, or the last known year of the Dominums. None of the Dominums back then had children, none that we know of. With you, that means one of them did, just in secret. What a scandal," Aminah continues, grinning.

"So, I'm the secret lovechild of a Leader back in the day?" I want to tell them I already know this, but who's going to believe that a serpent-bird told me that I'm a descendant of Emer? Not that I actually think it's true. It's just laughable.

"I know; it's kind of funny. Who are your parents?"

Once again, I shrug, feeling a tinge of resentment for the people who just dropped me off at Lena and Peter's door. "I was dropped in front of my adoptive parents' house when I was a baby. I have no idea where I'm from or who my family is," I respond. I glance at Zander, who's Conjuring his third tent. "Neither does he. There were three of us dropped in front of our parents' doors when we were babies. We have no idea who our birth parents are, where we came from, or what we are," I recounted.

"Three of you?" Aminah raises her curved eyebrows.

"Kane," I explain, turning back to Aminah, "he was taken by the Soturis when we were younger."

"Dead?" she asks.

"I don't know," I respond, sighing deeply. "Probably. But recently, I keep getting memories of him. Thoughts of him. The memories come back so strong, it almost hurts."

Aminah pats my hands. "Okay. I think I know where you can start."

43

Kenna

"Okay, we're going to practice control first. But first, you have to start feeling and focusing on your surroundings. Close your eyes," Aminah instructs.

I do.

"Now, tell me. What do you feel? What can you hear?"

I don't say anything silent for a bit, but I do it anyway. "I can hear the tents being rebuilt," I start.

"What else?"

"I can hear some people talking. I can hear water somewhere," I continue slowly. "I can hear the tents blowing in the wind. I can hear birds."

"What can you feel?" Aminah urges.

"I can feel a breeze. It's soft, but refreshing. I can feel the heat of the sun," I respond.

"Focus. Quiet your mind," Aminah says.

I focus on my surroundings. It takes a while, but suddenly, I hear an odd sound.

Thud, thud, thud.

Hm. What is that?

"I hear beating," I recognize finally.

"Is it a heart?" Aminah asks lightly.

I fight to focus. The beating is familiar, bringing warmth every time I focus on it. I center on it, making it the primary point in my head. Zander's face appears in my mind.

"It's Zander's," I guess.

"How do you know?" Aminah challenges.

"It's the same feeling I get when I think of him," I respond, trying not to cringe with embarrassment.

"Okay. That's true for people you know. You'll likely be able to tell who it is just by a feeling. For a lot of other people, you might not have any specific feelings towards their heartbeat. Now focus on that beating. What else do you feel?" Aminah says.

I nod and focus again.

Then, as I concentrate on his heart, I feel it, a rhythmic tingle creeping up my spine. I try to stop breathing to see where the pounding's coming from. The feeling persists, a palpable presence.

My facial expression changes because Aminah speaks up.

"Do you feel that? Do you feel that, next to your heart?" Aminah asks excitedly.

"It's like a vibration. Almost like the beating of a drum, except I feel it here," I tell her, patting my chest.

Aminah beams. "That's a call of a Conjurer. Only Conjurers have that. Especially untrained Conjurers who aren't using their powers correctly," Aminah explains.

"But he's using his powers right now," I argue, confused.

CHAPTER 43

"Zander is mostly untrained. He's still not using all of his powers—even if he is trying. He just doesn't know how to. Most of all, this is a signal that he's borrowing power from you and me," Aminah says.

"Borrowing power? How do you borrow power?" My voice rises.

She gives me a reassuring pat on the arm. "He doesn't know he's doing it. As human beings, we're all connected by something. This is a Conjurers' way of connecting. We only have a set amount of power we can expend. Depending on how powerful you are. But we can also borrow power from other Conjurers if we absolutely have to. The more powerful you are, the more you can borrow," Aminah explains.

I frown.

"For example, when you expended that light, you already have an extensive amount of power, so you probably used quite a bit. But most likely, you also used other people's powers, too. My guess is, you unknowingly borrowed power from all the Conjurers that were nearby during that time." Aminah breaks it down for me, and I stare back at her oddly.

"Does that mean that if those Conjurers weren't in Madyor, I might not have been able to create that light?" I ask.

She tilts her head. "It's possible, especially because you aren't trained yet. We don't know how powerful you are just yet. In the future, after more training, you might be able to use all elements to do something similar, without having to borrow," Aminah suggests.

I nod slowly. "Can you prevent yourself from borrowing power?"

"By using your powers to their fullest extent, yes. Only well-trained Conjurers can do this. Even beginner Conjurers have to borrow because they're still learning," Aminah answers.

Then, she takes my hands, her eyes boring into mine.

"The problem with borrowing power is that it can kill the people you borrow from, and it can also kill you as the borrower. If you use too much power that's not yours, you can die. *Tagapamigay* is funny like that," Aminah explains.

My shoulders slump, and I look down at my feet. "Could I have killed other Conjurers in Madyor that day?" I ask, finally looking up.

She looks directly at me. "Yes," Aminah responds. "I imagine you might've hurt some of them, too. Maybe not seriously, since those Conjurers are likely trained. But there's a very high chance you borrowed enough power to slow them down."

So, their rumored savior is also a killer.

"I heard the Conjurers in Madyor were out for days," Aminah adds, chuckling.

I look away. So, I don't really have a choice, do I? I either learn to control this so I can avoid killing someone. Or I don't, and I'll definitely kill someone.

Kenna

"The first lesson is to learn how to find your power so that you can use it and prevent yourself from using other people's powers. Only then will you realize your true potential. Only then can you start masking yourself from other people," Aminah begins. She walks around me, eyeing me carefully. "Close your eyes and try again," she barks.

I do it, focusing on other heartbeats. But in the midst of them all, I find another feeling, another vibration. Not Zander's, but someone else's. I open my eyes excitedly.

"There's another one!" I exclaim.

"That's mine. Good work." Aminah beams. "I'm just going to teach you how to feel it. How to call on it. Once you're a bit more familiar with this, we can move on to using and understanding your actual power. I want you to be able to tell what's an emotion and what's your power. Okay?" Aminah continues.

I nod.

"The only times I've Conjurered were times I was angry or really upset."

"Exactly. You called on your powers using those emotions. Be very careful with your emotions, because they're the easiest way to call on your powers, and the easiest way to lose control," Aminah warns.

She reaches out again and pats my hands. "When you feel your surroundings, use your entire body. Your hands can reach much further than you know. Now, close your eyes." She taps my abdomen. "Your power always starts here. By reaching into your belly, you can awaken it. It will slowly pull in power from the elements you control into your feet, legs, hands, and arms, and you'll feel it move through your entire body as it builds. From there, you can use your hands to release it, which is always the best way because you can control it better. I have heard of some talented Conjurers who can use any part of their body to release it, but I've never tried."

"I felt really warm when I caused the light and the ground movement," I remember out loud.

"Sometimes, this feeling can also change, depending on what you're conjuring. For example, sometimes water or air can feel cold. I suspect that you have a lot of unused power at the moment that's making you feel extra warm."

Ah, that makes sense.

"Now, with your eyes closed, will your power. You don't have to do anything with it, just know you're going to be using it," Aminah says.

"How do I do that?" I ask, hesitant. I'm scared. How do I know that I won't accidentally kill her or everybody in this village?

CHAPTER 44

"Think about it. Feel it. Know that you want to use it," Aminah describes.

I nod, still unsure, but I close my eyes anyway. I don't know exactly what to think about when Aminah tells me to. Think about what? How do you think about power? I think back to when I made the ground move. The warmth in my belly.

"Whoa, whoa," Aminah says suddenly, tapping my arms.

I open my eyes quickly.

"You're pulling too much. Not yet. Don't think about what you've done before. I know it's where your mind is going to go, but do that and you'll start pulling immediately and not from your own reservoir, either," Aminah says quickly.

She pauses to think. "How about this? Think about Zander and how you want to protect him. You *do* want to protect him, right? He's important to you?"

I nod.

"Don't think about him getting hurt just yet; think about how he's important to you and you don't want anything happening to him," Aminah suggests.

I close my eyes again. Zander's face appears in my head. Instantly, I feel warmth, but I don't necessarily know if it's related to my power. I think about how much he's done for me. I want to do the same for him. I want to protect him, keep him safe from everyone that's out to get me.

Suddenly, a surge of energy pulses in my hands and my feet. The energy trickles through my veins, connecting in my abdomen, where it creates a slow bubbling of warmth that I recognize.

"Do you feel the warmth in your stomach?"

I nod.

"Okay, just lean on that. That's your power. Don't pull yet. Just feel it. What does it feel like?"

I sit in that warmth, getting used to the energy, the power. "It's warm. It's like… circling. It feels almost like a stomachache, just because it keeps moving, but more comfortable. I'm not sure if I like it," I admit.

The energy seeps through me, crawling through my body, in my veins, my arms, my wrists. It scares me. What if I explode with it?

"Good. We're going to end there for now. Keep doing that. Just calling it and feeling it. I had an inkling you're the protective kind. Different people use different ways to call on their power. Some use a specific emotion, so for example, you can try getting angry first and see if that works, too, but I always find using an emotion makes it more difficult to control," Aminah says.

My eyes open, the remainder of my power slowly draining out of my limbs, back to where it came from. "What do we do now?" I ask.

"We pack," Aminah says, "and we travel tomorrow. Now that the Soturis have found us, we need to get a move on; otherwise, they will do more than just hurt us next time."

Kenna

"You know, you can also create fake trails, even without conjuring," Gregor suggests, as we make our way towards the encampment's next stop, which is probably not for a few more days.

His eyes are still puffy and swollen, but he doesn't seem to mind at all. This isn't the first time he's been beaten up by a Soturi. The encampment has had several encounters with the Soturis before, so they've created procedures for dealing with unexpected attacks. Even the young kid that the Soturi scared wasn't actually frightened after the incident. She was the most vocal of all kids and always volunteered to be in front so she could act and pretend for the sake of the cause. It wasn't her first time being intimidated by a Soturi. I guess when you're constantly getting scared by your country's supposed protectors, you develop some defense mechanism so you don't feel so vulnerable anymore.

Gregor shows Zander and I how to create fake trails along the way. We deviate from the group's current path, take a horse, and create fake trails throughout. Then, we'd come through our real path and Aminah would teach him to use air to cover up our true tracks.

"How long have you two been traveling?" Gregor asks during one of our training sessions. We ride together at the same pace, while Zander is ahead, deep in conversation with Aminah.

Neither Gregor nor Andrew seems to mind that they got beaten up, and they're not treating us any differently.

"I honestly don't know anymore," I reply. "Maybe a couple of months ago? We had to run right after..." I trail off, wanting to avoid saying it out loud. "Zander didn't want me getting picked up by the Soturis."

Gregor nods. "You love him?" he asks, and I blush.

He's given us some very good advice over the last few days, but I've never been asked about that.

I swallow. He's riding ahead of us. I can't see him well since it's getting dark, but I can hear his voice and laughter. I smile.

"We grew up together. I can't imagine life without him," I respond quietly.

"It's hard, you know. You'll always be in danger," Gregor says. "My kids will never know what it's like to live in one place. They'll never have friends; they'll never have a family outside of us."

I look back at Gregor. "At least you're together."

He nods. "At least we are."

At least the two of us will be. And maybe, just maybe, that's enough for us.

Gregor and the encampment switch responsibilities throughout their travels. There were at least ten other people who took on the responsibility of leading, driving the carriages, and creating false trails. Zander and I offer to take up shifts, too, but Gregor makes us take shifts with him so he can continue to teach us about the land.

Gregor is from Uthaana, too, but in the mountains. He teaches us to recognize good food, plants that are safe to eat, how to find animals to hunt, and how to train and strengthen ourselves by running after the horses. It builds leg muscles, according to Gregor, and to my dismay.

Once we find a place to stay, we help with setting up camp, finding firewood, and cooking food. It's nice. The kids made me think of my siblings, and the older people remind me of Lena. With Aminah teaching us and Gregor slipping in outdoor advice, Zander and I almost feel like we're part of the family.

Almost.

I just can't stop thinking about how this encampment will now be hunted, and all because of me.

The next morning, Zander and I wake up early to hunt and practice with Gregor. He doesn't have any powers, but his extensive experience in the mountains and familiarity with the forests gave him a unique perspective on the natural world. He isn't the most talkative, but whenever he sees something critical to point out, he always does, which Zander and I appreciate.

We walk through the forest, our eyes adjusting to the darkness of the night. I struggle to match Gregor's brisk pace, my breaths coming sharp and labored as the distance between us grows. While Zander attempts to keep an eye on Gregor and match his pace, he always hangs back a bit, just so he can keep an eye on me.

A soft glow emerges on the horizon, gradually dispelling the shadowy veil of the night. The darkness slowly gives way to a beautiful dawn, painting the sky with light shades of pink and orange, revealing the silhouettes of trees. The air is cool and crisp, carrying the invigorating scent of dew-filled grass and earthy soil. The forest is quiet and still, but the rustling of leaves, distant chirping of birds, and soft murmur of the morning breeze add a gentle soundtrack to the tranquility.

Gregor has disappeared from my field of vision already, but I continue, pushing through the tall grass and shrubs that I've had to pass along the way. At least I can still see Zander's outline as he walks in front of me.

Finally, I see a head pop up above the bushes. It hisses at us.

"What?" I call back, and my voice echoes throughout the forest.

A shushing sound responds. We hurry over before stopping to kneel beside him.

"What are we looking at?" I ask.

Gregor silences me with a finger over his lips, and I immediately shut up. I lean closer to hear his voice.

"I remember you telling me about the dryad you encountered awhile back. Do you know how to tell if a tree has one?" he asks, glancing between Zander and I.

We glance at each other before shaking our heads. That would have been a nice skill.

Gregor nods. "Okay, come closer and be quiet," he says, leaning back as he pulls us closer to him.

He points towards a group of trees on the horizon. Right now, even with the initial colors of dawn starting, it still appears as a dark silhouette. The impending dawn is about to illuminate its surroundings, showcasing the vibrant green hues of the foliage.

"Look closely," he whispers. "What do you see?"

Zander and I reach over to look closely at the scenery.

"It's just trees," I say, squinting, trying to look for something to notice, something different.

"Be patient. Keep looking," Gregor encourages me. He pushes my cheek to the right.

In the morning light, the cluster of trees appears like a sparkling oasis, their leaves catching the hint of sunlight as it dances in the gentle morning breeze. As I look on, I notice fog weaving its way across the mountains, casting an ethereal veil over the trees.

All of a sudden, a plume of vapor erupts from one specific spot, mingling with the dense, foggy air.

I gasp, clamping a hand over my mouth.

"Did you see that?" Zander breathes, his eyes glistening with excitement.

I nod. "What was that?" I whisper to Gregor.

He looks pleased. "That, my friends, is a dryad," he says, a smile spreading across his face.

Zander and I both straighten our spines almost immediately, the quick pace of my heart overpowering the quiet beauty of the forest. I fall back, instantly remembering how my mind was so cloudy and how I had wanted to kill Zander just because of her mind control. I crawl backwards to create distance between me and the dryad. I do not want to be anywhere near that thing. I never want to feel something I didn't actually feel; I never want to think something I don't think. I never want that kind of control in my head.

Gregor smiles apologetically. "Don't worry, it won't hurt you. Not right now, anyway," he says. "Dryads won't hurt you unless you piss them off. They're also not very sociable. This is one way to tell if they're there. Sometimes, you'll see them walking around their tree, but it's very rare because they tend to camouflage themselves." Gregor stands from where he was crouched, then walks down into the valley below us, gently pushing through the overgrowth.

The fire. The fire I had started pissed them off. Not only had I hurt creatures because of my inability to control my powers, but I had almost hurt nature and Zander.

With Gregor leading the way, Zander and I proceed cautiously through the forest, our senses heightened as we observe the diverse flora around us. I grip tightly onto Zander's arm.

Gregor points to a red flower in the midst of a tree with white blooms. "There's another sign of a dryad," he says. "Each dryad has a flower that blooms, regardless of the season, and most of the time, it's not the same flower as the tree it's attached to."

Zander and I nod. Gregor's gaze flickers over us before he resumes his steady pace.

"Gregor, what's the most dangerous creature out here?" I ask. I'm already out of breath, even though we're technically going downhill.

He hears me and responds with a grunt, even over the loud rustling of leaves and overgrowth. "There's plenty, really, and it can vary by season," he begins, while he continues walking. I follow right behind him, eager to hear his response. "I think you need to keep an eye out for preyons. Especially since you're a new Conjurer and you have immense power," he finally responds. He doesn't stop, so I struggle to hear his every word.

"What's that?" Zander asks.

He clearly didn't have issues hearing beyond the rustling overgrowth.

"If you didn't have powers, preyons are probably not the scariest thing you're ever going to see in your life. Honestly, they're kind of cute," Gregor adds. "But because you do, they will target you so they can feed off of you and your powers." He stops and looks at us with a warning. "A preyon has the body and wings of a bird; they're enormous. But their heads are similar to a deer's. They have humongous antlers, especially the full-grown ones."

"Have you seen one before?" I ask.

Gregor nod. "I don't have powers, though. It just came for a drink. We were hunting once with my father, and he pointed it out. It was full grown and massive."

Gregor stops walking and turns back to me and Zander. "I think the most important part of a preyon is the fact that they have a shadow of a normal human being, a Conjurer—the Conjurer they just fed on, to be exact. It's hard to keep track of them, because it can change, depending on whom they feed on."

Zander and I exchange a look. We reach a little stream flowing aggressively down from the mountain.

Gregor gestures to the stream. "You always want to drink from moving water. It's safer, and most likely cleaner," he adds, interrupting our earlier topic. "The problem with moving water is that most likely, it attracts other creatures as well."

"Speaking of creatures, where did Tika go?" Zander asks. I shudder, remembering the bobbing creature that had followed us for days.

"Oh! The flumph? I don't know. They come and go as they please. They'll probably be back. Isn't it adorable?" Gregor replies. "I've never been able to get a flumph to attach to me, sadly."

I shudder again, giving Zander a look. Gregor catches that and looks at me suspiciously.

"She's not the biggest fan at the moment," Zander explains. "Tika showed us a memory, and something happened to Kenna."

"Oh!" Gregor looks fascinated. "Was it something interesting?"

I look at Zander, who nods, then back at Gregor. "She was showing me something in her memory. Then, I just found myself present in that location. I don't know if it was still in the memory or if it was current, but suddenly, I was there, like I could touch the caves and water. I even felt and heard the creature call out to me. It was scary." I look away so Gregor doesn't see the fear that threatens to rise in the form of tears.

When I look back, he looks thoughtful. "Tika will likely be back for you. But just so you know, flumphs are great creatures. They can do no harm. They're also pretty useless in a fight. They always mean to do good, to help. I'm sorry you had a scary experience," he adds, shooting me an apologetic smile.

He puts his rucksack, a quiver, and straps that looks like it held a large bow. He pulls out a few arrows from the quiver and unclips the bow from the straps. "Okay, I get that Aminah is teaching you to control your power. But I want to make sure you can also fight physically. Especially if it could save your life," Gregor suggests. He hands the bow to Zander and then pulls out a second smaller bow before handing it to me. "Sorry, it's my daughter's. It's small, but it'll be good enough for you to practice aiming."

I accept, scanning the bow and arrows, my fingers slowly tracing the artwork on the limbs. I've only held one once, a very long time ago. But this bow and the arrows look very different from the ones I held.

"I made it," Gregor says proudly as I run my fingers across the weapon. "This will be great for you to practice, not just aiming with a bow and arrow, but aiming in general. It will help with Conjuring, or if you ever get the chance to grab the gun that those Soturis have," Gregor adds.

He hands Zander a few of the bigger arrows, too. He gestures towards a thicket, its branches rustling slowly in the wind. Gregor circles us, pushing each of us to a specific location before he lets us put together the bow and an arrow.

"Aim there. Hold up your bows and arrows," he instructs, pointing again to the thicket.

Zander walks a bit more to his left before holding up his bow and arrow. Hesitantly, I do the same. I can feel Gregor's eyes as I position myself. Gregor walks behind Zander and pushes up his shoulders before he steps back to glance over his form. He kicks at Zander's shins, and Zander spreads his feet apart. I do the same, looking down at my feet as I try to mimic what he's teaching Zander.

Gregor fixes his arms and hand before he backs away.

"Good," he murmurs. "How does that feel?"

Zander nods. Gregor steps over to me, helping me with my form. I try to remember the feel and angle of my arms and hands over the bow and arrow.

Gregor motions to my hips for permission, and I nod. Then, he plants his hands on my hips, moving me to a better angle.

"See that? That'll give you a better shot," he says, after correcting the rest of my stance. He looks over my form one more time. "Okay, breathe, and then release." Gregor gestures for Zander to go first.

Zander looks straight into the thicket. He breathes deeply. Then, he releases. His arrow pokes into a tree, but it doesn't stick, ricocheting off before landing with a soft plop in the foliage below. Zander nods proudly.

Oof, I'm nervous. I fumble with the bow, then finally release. My arrow barely makes it to the thicket at all. It flails and bounces on the ground. Hm. I didn't think mine was going to make it that far anyway.

Gregor chuckles. "Good, good. Go pick up your arrows. We'll try again."

"Race?" Zander challenges, winking at me.

I laugh. We run to the thicket to collect our arrows, jostling each other playfully along the way.

46

Kenna

I stand with my arms wide open, palms upward. I'm finally on the next phase of my training with Aminah: calling on the elements I can manage. It doesn't start out well. I almost burn down the entire encampment by calling on fire, and then I splash the kids with an out-of-control stream accidentally by calling on water. They enjoy it, luckily, but I never meant to take on that much power. I also somehow made a shrub grow taller, much to the kids' entertainment.

By lunch, I've learned how to take just enough power from the elements not to trigger some sort of reaction.

"The trick is knowing which element to call on and when," Aminah says.

I focus on the little ball of energy in my hands. I call on earth and air and manage not to spin some sort of tornado or make a tree grow. It's warm, comfortable, and very smooth in my hands.

"Good job, Kenna. Yes, get comfortable holding it and molding it. Bounce it around, move it from one hand to another. I've heard some Conjurers can even use other body parts to handle their powers. I've never done it, of course, but other Conjurers have their own ways of managing and handling their powers." Aminah smiles as she watches me play with the energy in my hands.

"It feels so easy like this, like it's moving however I want it to, like I can throw it around and catch it," I say, testing the theory. I throw the little ball of energy in the palm of my hand, not too far, and catch it, balancing it on my fingers. I think it might fall should I lose focus, but I'm not sure exactly how a ball like this dissipates in the air. Will it disappear inside me?

Aminah chuckles.

"Now try gathering more and make it bigger." Aminah circles me, carefully watching my movements and reactions.

I close my eyes, my palms stretch in front of me, focusing on taking a little more from the earth to grow the ball of energy in my hands. I feel the heat enter my feet and travel through my veins and muscles all the way to my hands. When I open my eyes, the ball is slightly bigger than it was before.

"Good job." Aminah beams, delighted.

I grin. Okay, this is kind of fun. Not going to lie, there's a joy, a brimming happiness that I've never felt before when I hold my power. I've never been able to do anything like this. I've never been able to do... well... anything.

"Can you try to take a third element?" Aminah asks.

Ugh, I'm nervous now. I guess I might as well try. I nod at Aminah.

"I'll try." I close my eyes and focus on the small fire lit in the middle of the encampment. The fire doesn't budge. Then, suddenly, the flames grow bigger and wilder, even though there's no wind.

"Focus. Don't be nervous," Aminah warns.

I flick a finger, and the flames travel toward the tents again, engulfing one of them in an orange inferno. I hear shrieks from the people surrounding the tent, each of them grappling off the ground to run far from it. I sigh, frowning, as the ball of energy between my hands start to disappear.

"Put it out," Aminah tells me gently.

I nod and close my eyes, focusing on the air, thinking of it smothering down flames. I continue on to rebuild the fabric of the tent, too. When I open an eye, the flames have died down, leaving black soot all over the tent, but the tent's fabric is still intact. I exhale in frustration, plopping down on a bench, and bury my face in my hands. How am I so bad at this?

"Don't worry so much, Kenna. It will take time. You've only just started practicing," Aminah says, patting my leg as she sits down next to me.

"I can't figure out how to attract a third element. I can't control fire at all," I complain.

Aminah gives me an apologetic smile.

"I wish I could help. I don't work with fire; otherwise, I'd give you tips," she says.

"How many elements do you control?" I ask.

"Two. I was born with air, but I eventually learned how to control earth, too. It took a lot of time and energy and days like this," Aminah replies.

I nod, taking a little comfort in that. "Can someone eventually just learn all of them?"

She shakes her head. "Not without the biology to handle it. A very strong Conjurer can learn up to three elements. But because our bodies aren't technically made to handle that many elements, it can either weaken you or kill you. Some Conjurers spend their entire lives looking for things to help boost their powers. There's two common ways, but they're dangerous and could also kill you," Aminah mentions.

A beat of silence stretches between us when she doesn't elaborate.

"How?" I ask, looking up at her curiously.

Is that what I need? Something to boost my powers? It's like Aminah can see what I was thinking.

"And no. You don't need it. *Tagapamigay* only knows what would happen to you if you get one," she immediately adds, rolling her eyes, then throwing a scowl at me. Her expression changes, and she looks away, deep in thought. "You can spend many, many months waiting for a *rakuuri*. It's a special type of hail that only happens on certain mountains. If a Conjurer is in the same area as a *rakuuri*, it can help them develop another element. But they are extremely rare, and you never know when they happen. I've never known anyone to have experienced it. The second is a special type of water called *lakas*. You can find them only on glaciers in the mountains. According to legend, the glaciers are guarded by cloakers and aboleths and many other creatures, so I've never known anyone to try, either." Aminah shrugs.

"Blights? Cloakers?" I repeat.

"Nasty shits, blights. They are flora, or really, dead flora that will kill you or do everything they can to hurt you. They spread often and easily through other plants. You should ask Gregor about his experience with blights. They're horrible. There are quite a lot of them in this area. I'm really glad Gregor's been in these mountains for years; otherwise, we would've encountered them by now," Aminah explains. "Cloakers, on the other hand, look like creatures that wear cloaks. That's why they're called cloakers. They lurk in caves and dungeons and prey on the injured. I've never actually encountered one."

I cringe. I can barely target anything at the moment, much less try to protect anyone from another creature experience.

"You want to try again?" Aminah asks.

I nod, though I can feel strain in the muscles on my wrists and arms. We've been working all day already—every day since we left the last stop.

I heave a sigh, get up, and then close my eyes again.

First, I call on earth. So far, earth is the easiest out of all the elements to summon. It's like it knows exactly when I need it to come. Then, I call on air. Air is a bit harder, especially when there's an existing breeze. It's hard to tell if I am pulling on air, or if it's just the wind. This time, instead of trying fire as my third element, I decide to focus on water instead. I've only been able to call on water twice successfully, and it hasn't been easy. At least, that's two more than fire.

I focus on the stream beside our encampment. It's fast-moving, but cool to the touch, and refreshing. I think about how it feels, how it looks, and for a second

I think I'm successful because the warm energy turns slightly cooler.

And then I feel a splash of water on my face. I flinch, sputtering, as I fight to open my eyes. I wipe away the dripping water from my face.

I groan, much to Aminah's chuckling.

I hear Zander's laughter behind me, and I spin quickly, using the leftover energy in my arms and hands to push the air and force a pile of leaves onto him. His laughter grows stronger, and I join in.

He approaches, and for a moment, I'm distracted by how handsome he is. He looks refreshed and happy, so different from how tired he's been throughout our travels. Gregor had taken him to practice hunting and fighting closer to the lake, which Zander seems to enjoy more than the Conjuring lessons Aminah provides.

"Hey," he greets me, planting a kiss on top of my head.

"Water being hard today?" he observes.

"Water and fire." I sigh heavily, pursing my lips.

"Well, I can't move either of those," Zander says, smiling encouragingly, "but I'll happily continue practicing with you?"

I beam, unable to control the giddiness I feel.

"I'd like that," I say, grinning.

"Can I take her?" he asks, looking at Aminah.

Aminah nods, shrugging.

Zander takes my hand and starts leading me back towards the lake, my heart skipping a beat as he wraps his arms around my waist.

"We'll go practice by the lake. I'll let you splash me as many times as you want," he teases. I laugh, squeezing his hand. I don't remember the last time I felt like this. Like I am an actual human being with a purpose in this life. Like I'm actually loved.

Kenna

"There are multiple tricks to protecting or masking someone," Aminah says as she flashes her arm.

Zander completely disappears from my view.

My mouth drops. She waves her arm again, revealing Zander, who hasn't actually moved at all.

"What?" Zander's eyebrows knit, looking at my confused expression.

Aminah shifts her gaze to me.

Impressive.

"What's the concept behind it? Do you use air?" Zander asks.

Aminah nods approvingly as she takes steps between Zander and me. "That's right. I just shifted a little air to cover you completely. The problem with this concept is that they can still feel you—your heartbeat, your pulsating, and if a Conjurer or Soturi was close enough to you, they could feel your outline. They'd be able to hit you, no problem. You'd be covered, but you're still susceptible to powers, swords, attacks, anything.

This is also why I asked you to keep still the other day. The stiller you are, the easier it is to mask you. The moment you move, my masking can fail," she adds, her gaze switching between the two of us.

I nod, hanging onto her every word.

"The good thing about it is that it's pretty easy. This is probably level one of masking. You're just moving air. Got it?" She looks at us. We exchange looks before we both nod and turn back to her. "Ready?"

"Yeah." I nod again.

"Think about hiding someone, protecting someone. Then, once you have that emotion locked down, start to pull. Slowly, then move the air over them," she instructs.

I ready myself, then close my eyes, focusing on my intention and emotion, and with the palm of my hand, I move air. Instead, a rush of leaves covers Zander's body from head to toe.

I open my eyes and start laughing at Zander's scowl beneath the leaves.

"Funny," he retorts.

Even Aminah chuckles.

I move my hand again, and the leaves fall from his body.

"The trick is to move just air, which can be more difficult than it seems because most of the time, we use air to move everything," Aminah says.

She grabs two rocks from the ground and plants them on the table in front of us.

"Here," she says, gesturing for us to sit.

Zander and I sit on the bench, pulling a rock out in front of us.

"It should just be air that you're moving, nothing else," Aminah repeats, walking to the other side of the table so she can watch.

I close my eyes and start calling on my elements.

I wave a hand. It hides only parts of the rock. I look up at Aminah, beaming excitedly. She gestures to the rock to try again. It's not there yet, but I at least did *some*thing right!

I look back at the rock and start again. Instead of rushing, I take a deep breath, making sure I think about my intentions before I start. I pull on my power, and the moment I feel it in my fingers, I wave over the rock.

My eyes open. I beam. The rock is gone. I look up at Zander and Aminah. Zander has already moved on to mask a table, and Aminah is coaching him. I look back down at the rock and try it again. I can't contain my excitement when it works a second time around. Could it be true? Can I actually get better at this? I try one more time just in case.

It works again, and I can't contain the euphoria. I get up to try something else, but when I wave an arm, I bring more than just the rock across the field. Two tables tumble and turn, bringing the plates and bottles that were on them crashing into the field. Zander and Aminah jump, and other encampment members scream.

I look up at Aminah sheepishly. Zander and Aminah exchange glances, then they both break into laughter. I scowl, sighing deeply.

I imagine the tables as is, any items sitting on top of them where they were. I call on my power, pausing when I take too much, releasing to give back what I didn't need. When I feel ready, I wave a hand. The tables slowly turn back around, settling themselves back in the original positions. It stops there, but I beam anyway and do it again for the items that were on the table.

I look back at Aminah and Zander, who are already masking humans with Gregor as their victim. I keep that giddiness anyway, tucking it away like a secret.

Okay, now onto bigger things. I move around the table and do the same with the table instead. It doesn't work so easily this time around. I try multiple times before finally managing to cover at least the legs.

My arms hurt. I roll my shoulders and sit back down, my air dissipating, revealing the legs of the table as I slowly let air back to where it came from.

"He's just always so good at what he does and everything he tries," I protest to Aminah, who sits back down next to me.

She pats my knee and looks proudly back at Zander, who's already masking groups of people. I lean over to watch as well, and the smile on his face is infectious. I don't think he's ever done this kind of magic before. He must be proud. I grab my arm, massaging my wrist and arms to dispel some of the tension from the pulling of energy. I feel it in every part of my body, exhausting and tiring my muscles. Zander can practice longer, but I can only do so much in a day without needing sleep and rest.

"Great job, you two," Aminah tells us as Zander comes to join us at the tables again. "Soon, you'll both be able to help me hide each other. Remember, hiding each other is only effective if a Conjurer or Soturi can't feel you." Aminah reaches for two bottles of water on the table and hands one to each of us.

I take one and sip, only to keep drinking. I didn't realize how thirsty I was.

Aminah waits for us to finish before handing us a plate with different types of bread. I take one, nodding gratefully. I can feel the strain in my muscles as I move my arms.

"The more important skill is being able to hide your heartbeat and pulsating from someone else," Aminah begins as Zander and I finish our snacks.

"Ready to start again?" she asks, waiting for us to nod at her and put down our drinks.

"Can you both listen in to each other's heartbeats? Identify your pulsating."

Zander and I focus. He nods first. It takes me awhile, but eventually, I hear the familiar beating.

"Okay. Listen carefully," Aminah instructs. Her hand barely moves.

I snap my head up.

"I can't hear it anymore," I say, staring at Aminah. She nods.

"Good. Now listen carefully."

I lean, trying to listen again.

"It's still there," Zander says after some time. "The breeze is just louder."

"Correct," Aminah says, looking satisfied.

"The trick to hiding someone's heartbeat or pulsating isn't exactly about hiding them in the same way as keeping them from someone's eyesight. Instead, it's more about increasing the sound of the elements you can control so people hear that more than they hear your heartbeat or pulsating," Aminah carries on, "it's not completely foolproof and if a powerful Conjurer focuses just enough, they will be able to hear you still."

Aminah releases, so I hear Zander's heartbeat again, but she continues to talk. "Did you notice it took you a while, though? In battle or when you're confronting someone, you don't have this luxury. You can't just listen and keep talking to someone. It requires concentration, which makes it the better way to protect someone, especially if there aren't a lot of Conjurers in the area."

"How do we do that?" I ask.

"Instead of moving air to cover someone, now you'll be moving elements to increase their sounds," Aminah says.

I frown, scratching the base of my neck.

"Every element has a certain sound. You need to know how it sounds so that you can manipulate it. The hard part for the two of you is that you both can naturally move multiple elements. This means you can hear more than just one. I only have one natural element, so even if I don't focus, I hear air pretty clearly. I don't hear my learned element as quickly or easily," Aminah says.

"Focus on one element first and listen carefully."

I choose air and focus, listening carefully. At first, I don't hear anything. But the more I focus, the more I hear a subtle but swift buzzing.

"It's similar to a breeze, like a soft buzzing in your ear," I tell her.

"Air?" Aminah guesses.

I nod.

"We're going to practice making it louder for a specific person first. This is easier because you can target and focus your energy on the people you're working with. Once you've done that, we'll work on targeting and focusing everyone around you," she instructs.

She looks at Zander. "You ready?" she asks.

He nods.

"Now, target me. Move the air to be louder for me. Be careful not to fill my ears with air, otherwise, I will know. It just needs to be closer."

Zander tries it a few times, filling Aminah's hair multiple times, so she buzzes and flicks at her ears to get it out. By the time he finally makes a successful attempt, I'm already jaded. If he can't do this, how am I supposed to?

"Good job. Keep it there. Focus. Don't use too much. It doesn't need to be a lot; it just needs to be there," Aminah says, listening carefully for Zander's masking.

"If you use too much, you won't be able to do anything else. But if you just keep it there, you can actually do other things while still using your powers to do this." Aminah gestures to Zander. "Try walking around, or talking to Kenna," she suggests.

I watch Zander walk around the table. I can see he's fighting hard to focus.

"Ah, you almost got it. Keep going," Aminah says.

She turns to me. I switch elements and start to listen to earth.

"What did you choose?" she asks me.

"Earth," I reply.

"I can't confirm what they sound like. But would you like to try?" she asks.

I nod.

Aminah motions to Gregor, who is grilling a boar they had hunted earlier today. He looks up at us, waving.

"Can you help Zander practice blocking?" she calls to him. "Gregor doesn't have any powers, but he actually has excellent natural hearing."

Gregor approaches us and nods, jabbing Zander playfully. I chuckle.

"You can hear the pulsing, too?" I ask, impressed.

Gregor nods. "I didn't even have to train for it." He winks at Aminah.

Aminah chuckles.

"Most Soturis have to. It's a matter of focus and knowledge, really," Aminah explains to Zander and me.

She turns back to Gregor. "You would've made an excellent Soturi, honey," she tells him, smiling.

Gregor snorts.

48

Kenna

"You ready?" Aminah asks. It's our third day practicing masking, in our second location with the encampment. Zander is able to mask heartbeats now, mostly with lots of focus. He's practicing how to do it with some distractions now, but it doesn't always work. I'm lagging behind.

See, here's my problem. I can't seem to get past my fear of potential. I can do it all the way here, and I've been able to create little balls of energy with air, water, and earth. But anything past that scares the shit out of me. How do I know what effect it has when I release it? How do I know what it's meant to do? By the time I get to this point, I'm scared or nervous to do anything after it. And then I lose it.

"Okay, I can tell something is up with you. What's going on?" Aminah asks, patting my back.

I sigh.

"I just…" I begin. "There are a lot of expectations on me, and sometimes, I don't know how to manage them.

CHAPTER 48

I…" I heave a sigh, feeling heat sting my eyes. "At home, I was expected to come home with pera and food and be able to feed my siblings. No one else expected me to do anything for them. But now, I feel like I have the expectations of the entire continent." I catch her eye. "I don't think I can do this, Aminah."

She tilts her head, and her eyes soften as I carry on, my voice trembling.

"Everyone expects me to be this badass person who can save the country, the world, and be able to do amazing things. But I can't. I'm… just me. Just me."

She turns to me, her dark eyes gentle. "I'm sorry," she says.

My mouth drops. I don't think anyone's ever said that to me since I've been on this journey.

She chuckles. "I can't imagine the pressure that you must feel right now. You're right, that's a lot of pressure."

I take a deep breath. She has no idea how much that means to me. Maybe I'm not going crazy, after all, though I still wonder if Cersei is even real.

"Real," I hear from the back of my mind, and I scowl, turning to find her outline as I roll my eyes.

"Kenna, it's just you and me here right now. I'm not putting pressure on you at the moment, and the continent doesn't even know you exist yet. Let go of the things you can't control because you won't get there if you keep blocking yourself," Aminah tells me.

I swallow. "How do I do that?"

"Maybe forgive yourself for the things you haven't even tried. Forgive yourself for your past failures. Focus on trying. You're not meant to save the continent in a day."

I look at my feet, kicking at the ground.

I hear her. I do. I just wish there were step-by-step instructions that I could just follow. But I close my eyes anyway, eager to focus on the now.

I can do this. I can do this. I got this.

I take a deep breath, willing myself, knowing that I'm doing this for Zander. For Aminah. For myself. Today. Now.

I do it again. I feel my powers lift, just enough to bring the sound but not the physical ground. I feel it in my fingers, in my hands. I raise it.

Aminah beams.

Kenna

Aminah wakes us in our tent the next day. I'm exhausted after days of practicing. She looks nervous, her hair braided but wild and frizzy, and her eyes wide and rattled.

"They're coming," she explains quickly.

My stomach knots. Zander and I are up almost instantly.

"Are you ready?" she asks, shifting her gaze between us.

The same group of Soturis has made it our way, but it doesn't sound like they're alone. This time, they have a Conjurer in tow. It is faint and probably masked, but we all feel it. A barely audible pulsating amidst the twelve other heartbeats quickly got our attention.

Zander and I nod, exchanging a look. Honestly? I don't feel ready, but I have no choice but to try. Aminah leaves our tent. I can hear her barking orders outside to get the encampment ready.

Zander's face is unreadable. He's always so much more comfortable and confident. I'm so nervous I think my heart is about to bounce out of my chest. I reach up to give Zander a quick peck on the lips before attempting to tail Aminah out of the tent.

Suddenly, Zander grabs me by the waist. He seizes the back of my head, and his lips are on mine. The hair on the back of my neck rises. My eyes widen, but I quickly soften at his touch, my eyes closing, appreciating the short moment together before we might die. We haven't kissed in a while. My hands reach to cup his face, and I fight the urge to just sink into his arms.

I don't know how he knows, but he does. I need this. I need him. Once he releases me, I look into his eyes. His eyes are kind and warm. In my emotional state, this is what I need.

I reach back up and touch his lips with mine again softly, then hungrily, hoping to convey all my emotions in that one kiss. I've enjoyed our time so much lately that I've almost forgotten we're on the run—that we're in danger, and that these people are, too, because of me.

I nestle my forehead against his.

I'm afraid I'll die. I'm afraid he'll die. Everyone might.

So, I say it. Even though I don't absolutely know what it means. Even though I've said it before, in a moment of desperation. I say it because I know we're on the run and I'm afraid I won't get the chance.

"I love you," I whisper.

His eyes soften, and he pushes the hair back from my face as he grins at me.

"Now I'm ready," he says. His smile is confident, instantly replacing the fearful one just before this. He kisses the top of my head and gently pushes me out of the tent, tagging along just behind me.

We stand next to each other, close our eyes, and focus on masking each other. We share a look once we have our masking in place, then we walk over to get in formation with the rest of the encampment, just in time for the heads of our predators to appear on the terrain of the trail, where we expected them to show.

"So," an adenoidal voice speaks, his voice loud and demanding, echoing through the forest. I squint, my eyes catching the Conjurer's face as he appears behind the Soturis. I sneak a quick look at Zander. His face is stony and blank. He'd noticed the Conjurer first, and feel him tense next to me.

This is the same one who'd performed the fire exhibitions on the floats in the last parades at Krag Vinde in Madyor. He's also the same Conjurer who destroyed the village where we last left Callie. I take a deep breath, aiming to control the warmth building in my stomach.

The Conjurer has spiky red hair, dark features, brown eyes, and a muscular build. His left eyebrow has a vertical line in the middle, accentuating the scar on his left cheek. He wears a red *abaya* and walks with a confident stride, sporting the same patronizing glare as the Soturi captain had some weeks ago.

"Is this the traveling encampment you talked about?" he says slowly, modulating almost every word, like he's talking to children.

The captain emerges from the group of Soturis. "Yes." He still has that expression of contempt.

"You think they're hiding them?" the Conjurer asks. He paces around our group, slowly passing through each person in the group, establishing dominance over the encampment.

"Hello again, Captain," Aminah says pleasantly. She turns to the Conjurer with a polite smile. "Hello." She greets the Conjurer directly.

The Conjurer ignores her, continuing to saunter around the group, his beady little eyes inspecting each person with extra care.

"Are you looking for someone, Conjurer?" Gregor asks, his tone respectful.

The Conjurer ignores him, too.

But the captain jeers at him.

"You think you're worthy of speaking to a Conjurer without being asked?" the captain mocks, arrogantly pacing around Gregor.

Gregor looks at him directly. "It was just a question, Captain. Maybe I can help make it easy for him. I wouldn't want him to waste his time." Gregor's words are taunting.

Brave, I note, past the heavy beating of my chest.

The captain smirks. He points his firearm at Gregor. Gregor doesn't flinch. Instead, he moves his gaze to the Conjurer. This slight movement angers the captain, and he seethes.

"If I can be of any help, Conjurer. Please, just let me know," Gregor says.

The captain turns, a nasty smirk on his face. Then he spins back to Gregor, planting a fist on his face.

Gregor takes it with a step back, but he doesn't look at the captain. He shakes off the blood that drips from the corner of his mouth, his eyes focused on the Conjurer.

The captain is livid, baring his teeth like a pissed coyote. He moves to slam another fist into Gregor, and the Conjurer clears his throat. His fist pauses mere distance from Gregor's face. Gregor doesn't flinch.

"Now, now, Captain," the Conjurer says, flicking his eyes onto the captain, dictatorially. This Conjurer took condescending to an entirely different level.

"This isn't the place to prove you have a tiny dick," the Conjurer taunts, his eyes rising slowly to belittle the captain.

The captain's face turns red. I swear I see the veins on his forehead about to explode. I think he'll continue, but instead, he stands up straight, seething and scowling at Gregor and the Conjurer.

The Conjurer wheels back around slowly. His gaze moves from the rest of the encampment to the trio that stands in front. He finally acknowledges Aminah, Gregor, and Andrew, who lead the pack next to the captain.

"You're travelers?" he says to Aminah.

"Correct," Aminah responds. His disdainful tone doesn't seem to upset her.

"How long have you been traveling?" He patrols past Aminah, Gregor and Andrew, his eyes moving from one person to another.

"Just a few months, Conjurer. We're headed toward Madyor," Gregor replies, his gaze still on the Conjurer, even though the captain's standing right next to him, practically breathing Gregor's oxygen.

The Conjurer scoffs, frowning.

"Why would you head to Madyor? There's nothing there," he responds snootily.

"It's cheaper, Conjurer," Andrew responds.

The Conjurer smirks. Even the group of Soturis start to laugh.

"I don't know why anyone would go to Madyor, but you do you," the Conjurer says, shrugging. He starts walking back towards the trail.

I let out a sigh of relief.

Suddenly, the Conjurer stops. "What is that?" he barks.

"What's what?" the captain responds, his voice echoing. He turns slowly, and I catch the fire in his eyes, mimicking the explosive expression that threatens to burst out of his face.

The Conjurer waves a hand, and a sharp crack blasts, followed by a thunderous crash. It starts with the tents. Twenty big tents are pulled from the ground, flying into the air where they float for a moment, before slamming back onto the ground. Then it's the tables.

Suddenly, I feel gravity disappear, and I'm no longer attached to the ground. I'm airborne, my face hitting the branches and leaves of the trees above us. I cower, using my hands to protect myself from the dense brush and branches. Then, my body collides with the ground.

50

Kenna

"Which one of you is it?" the Conjurer roars, his eyes blazing in the same color as his *abaya*.

Aminah quickly motions with her hands, but the Conjurer is too quick.

He counters, lifting her back in the air, and slamming her back down. I watch Aminah's body slump in horror, a motionless grunt slipping from her mouth before silence.

"No!" I yell.

Gregor, Andrew, and the rest of the encampment move quickly, reaching for their weapons before they start to approach the Soturis, who are ready with their firearms and swords raised towards us.

The Conjurer looks triumphant as he makes his way back to the encampment, his eyes passing from one person to another.

His eyes land on me.

"Is it you?" he asks, his voice dripping with outrage.

I stiffen.

Zander motions, using air to rip the Conjurer off his feet and into a tree. He makes another move, using air to trip a few of the Soturis just a few feet away. They stumble and fall, crashing into the rest of their group.

Even in the midst of my fear, a flicker of awe and pride in Zander lights me up on the inside. The encampment takes this as a sign. I hear a yell, and they run to move onto the Soturis. The Conjurer quickly gets back on his feet, looking bewildered.

He seethes, his eyes blazing with fire. His hands motion, calling on that little fire in the middle of our encampment. The flames respond to his call with ease, traveling through the air, finding their place in between his hands. The Conjurer balances his flames between his hands as he looks at us. The veins on his forehead throb with rage.

"So this camp has three Conjurers." He seethes, his eyes focuses on Zander and I. "You think you can fight me?" he yells, spreading his arms out to show his expertise.

Zander immediately grabs me, pulling me back behind him. The Conjurer is vengeful, fuming, as he walks threateningly towards us, the ball of flame still in between his hands. But Zander is ready. He grows another ball of flame in his hands. The Conjurer bursts out laughing, looking at Zander's much tinier ball of flames in his hands.

"You can't fight me," the Conjurer arrogantly declares.

He makes another motion, using his powers to engorge the flame in his hands. He aims the ball at us and releases, but instead of making it all the way across, the ball stops in midair.

My eyes widen. I look around for the other source of power.

Aminah is awake again and alert, her eyes wide as she holds the ball of flames in her hand with air. She uses air to take the fireball and shoves it back onto the Conjurer. The ball of fire hits him square in the chest, his eyes widening as it sends him flying back with the energy. His body slams into the tree behind him, and he slumps slowly onto the ground. He coughs, and red liquid escapes his lips.

The Conjurer wipes his mouth and glares, looking even more agitated. He gets up, spitting out a pool of blood onto the ground. He wrangles his hands, enveloping them with his flames, and sends them Aminah's way. I watch in horror as the flames catch her hair. Aminah flails, working to kill the flames with her powers and her hands. But the Conjurer isn't done. With a single move of his hand, he redirects some of the flames onto us.

Zander immediately moves. I've never seen him do this. Never seen anyone do it. The ball of flames travels fast, and Zander catches it in his hands like an actual ball tossed for a game.

He skids a few steps back, the pressure of the energy strong enough to push him away, but I breathe softly in relief, seeing him control and manage the ball. It surprised him too, because the moment Zander realizes what he's done, his face changes, and he looks up at the Conjurer, the same anger and disdain crossing his face. Zander pulls back and aims, a successful smirk replacing the anger as the Conjurer is hit. He falls back, breaking the concentration that holds the flames that attack Aminah.

Aminah and Zander fall back, forming a protective cover around our people. He forces himself in front of me, and I step back, struggling to see past his tall frame.

The Conjurer pulls himself off the ground, his eyes still glowing from the flames, and with the determination to fight back.

We watch in horror as he slowly lights himself up again, the fiery tongues growing and building from his hands all the way around his body until it looks like he's completely cloaked in flames. He steps closer, his menacing smirk spreading from one side of his face to the other, his eyes eager to witness murder.

"You are going to die today, *Nagiisa*," he declares, his eye catching mine.

I gulp.

His hands smoke from the flames in his hands, but he doesn't notice.

The warmth in my belly grows. With the way he looks at us, I know he's referring to this entire encampment. The kids. Aminah. Gregor. Andrew. Zander.

He looks up, holding his arms outward, inviting his elements into his body to continue building. The fire continues to grow until it is twice his size.

Aminah and I share quick but meaningful glances. I guess I'm about to die. Aminah turns her arms gathering her air, getting ready to release, but it is too late.

The Conjurer releases, and the engorged fiery tongues hit Aminah on the chest. Aminah flies backwards many feet, her entire body combusting into flames.

Anguish shoots through me. "No!" Zander and I yell at the same time, as Gregor, who was fighting with a Soturi, leaps to his feet to run after his wife. He fights to smother the fire with his coat. I look at them across the field, my mind racing, my heart about to burst out of my chest, the warmth in my belly strengthening until I can no longer control it.

The Conjurer makes another move with the rest of his fire. But before the enlarged flames can get anywhere, it stops again, midair. I don't know what I did, or how I did it. But I feel it.

Aminah's face appears in my head. Gregor's. Andrew's. Zander's. I'm angry. No, scratch that. I'm furious. This man can't take any more from us. He already took everything. My life. Callie's. Aminah's. He doesn't get to take any more. Not today.

I hold the flames in front of us, in the middle of the field. Power surges through my entire body, through every vein, and all I can think about is how much I want to kill him. How much I want to rid the entire continent of this being who killed every single person in that village with no consequence.

"You die today," I say under my breath, and my hands release. The fire switches directions, and the fiery tongues swirl back toward the Conjurer.

The Conjurer's eyes widen as he watches the flaming inferno aim for him. He doesn't have time to crouch or avoid it. It's slow, but only at first, crawling over to him, the grass below it burning black. It spirals around him, creating a circle of flames, like a hurricane around its eye. And then, finally, it envelopes him wholly, combusting with the flames, vibrating the ground, the cackles and fervor of the flames enough to echo through the forest. The red and orange fire ignites his *abaya* first, then his hands and feet, before bursting into flames, the explosion reverberating across the forest. The Conjurer's mouth, nose, and then his eyes steadily give in to the tumultuous flames. His screams echo and resonate through every person in the area.

My jaw drops. I can't feel anything. I can't move. I hear his screams, but I don't know if it's still him or my brain reminding me of that awful sound. Zander approaches me gently, but deliberately, grabbing my shoulders first, and then pushing my hands down to release the fire.

The *abaya*, now black, falls to the ground, empty. A black powdery substance is all that's left behind from what used to be a body, and it gradually releases itself into the air above us.

Everyone stops.

I look down at my hands and then onto the blackness of the *abaya* and the ashes that seamlessly merges with the wind. I hear Zander, but I don't know what he's saying. I hear movement, but I don't know what other people are doing. I hear screams, but I can't quite grasp what they're for.

I slowly turn, looking into Zander's eyes. I open my mouth, but I don't know what to say. I am a murderer. I just murdered a human being.

I see darkness looming. For a moment, I resist it. But I'm a killer. Where else do I go? I swallow, then welcome the darkness as it slowly takes me.

Kenna

The skies are dark. I see lightning on the horizon. It's gloomy and gray. I turn. I don't know how I got here.

"Zander!" I yell.

I don't get a response. I walk. I'm in a field. There are no trees anywhere, and I can't see the horizon, just dark and gloomy skies. I sprint into a run, my lungs aching to breathe as I move faster with the wind.

"Zander!" I yell again, as much as I can with my heart racing and my breathing labored.

I bend, clutching at my side, the pain of sprinting rising to my chest. Where am I? I take a deep breath.

"Kenna!" I hear a yell.

I turn and see Inez. She's a distance away, but I see her and wave.

Suddenly, I see a red *abaya* appear behind her, and my heart clenches.

"Inez!" I yell and sprint immediately towards her.

But I can't get to her. She's so… far away. My entire being stops as soon as the Conjurer's arms snake around her neck.

No. No. "No!" I scream as the Conjurer takes her neck and snaps it. Inez's body slumps to the ground. I run faster. "No! Inez!"

I keep running, my tears ricocheting with the wind, but she keeps moving away.

"Kenna!" I hear another yell.

I stop and turn again, squinting, my heart racing as I recognize Soleil's face. She's waving at me too. My eyes widen. I look at Inez on the ground and the Conjurer, then back at Soleil.

No. No. *No.*

"No!" I scream again and run the other way, this time for Soleil. I can't save Inez, but maybe I can save Soleil.

I need to beat him there. I need to save her. I run faster than I've ever run before, ignoring the pain in my chest, the throbbing in my thighs, and the weakness in my ankles.

I need to save her.

I run and I run.

"Soleil, I'm coming. I'm coming, I'll save you," I yell to her, my eyes blurry with tears.

But it's too late. The Conjurer appears behind her, takes her neck and snaps it. I watch the brightness in her eyes disappear.

"No!" I scream. My legs break beneath me, and I feel the ground swallow me. "*No!*"

And then, I'm back in that field again, only this time I see Katleya playing. She waves at me, giggling as she rolls around the grass.

"*No.*" I reach for my powers, wheeling around to look for the Conjurer.

I see him, and I don't let him near them. I pull it. I pull as much power as I can, as I need, roaring as I watch him approach them.

"*No!*" I scream again, but my jaw drops realizing I'm in flames.

My entire body is red, red and orange flames fume out of me, but it doesn't hurt. I use this. I am angry. I am fire. And I will kill you for killing my sisters. I turn back to the Conjurer, the heat in my eyes burning as I let out a ferocious snarl with every step I take. I don't need to close the distance. I will kill you from here if I need to.

The Conjurer laughs, the sound sending shivers up my spine.

I show him my palms, each one bearing balls of flame.

"Are you going to kill me, *Nagiisa*?" he asks, disdain dripping in his voice.

"You killed my sisters," I accuse, my fire burning brighter and brighter.

"Are you sure?" he asks again, sneering. His eyes lock on mine and I've never felt this much anger or power.

I release my palms, sending flames onto him until my fire fully engulfs him.

The Conjurer screams, his entire body starting to combust with the fire. I walk over to him. I don't feel fear; I don't feel remorse as I watch him disintegrate with the flames.

Suddenly, his eyes open and they bore through mine. "Murderer."

52

Kenna

My eyes flutter, and pieces of light slip in. I blink.

For a moment, I forget where I am. But as the pain slowly seeps back through my body, I remember, just as I have every day for the past week. Everything is different.

Aminah is dead.

A Conjurer has died.

This encampment is safe only for another couple of days before the Conjurers and Soturis come back to kill everyone here. But most of all, everything is different now because I'm a murderer.

I hold back tears, blocking out the darkness of my thoughts. I raise my head and find myself on a bed in what looks like the tent we've been staying in for the past few months. Zander sits on a chair in front of me. His eyes are closed, his head is tilted, lying on a fist with his elbow bent on the arm of the chair. I sit up, and my back cracks as I grunt, pain searing from my hip. I stifle back another grunt as I make my way toward the end

345

of the bed. My stomach rumbles. I hear wind blowing outside, and the tent's opening sways. It's dark outside. How long have I been asleep? I feel groggy, but my body remembers the throbbing pain from the massive amount of energy I expended.

I pull my feet out of the bed, gingerly touching the cold ground.

Zander shifts, and I pause, eager to let him sleep longer. His eyes move behind his eyelids, but he doesn't wake. I put on my boots gingerly, savoring the pain with every movement. I deserve pain. I murdered someone. I *should* be in pain.

I slip out of the tent. We're still at the encampment, but I think we're in a different area. I don't see the area where Aminah died, or where I last saw the Conjurer's ashes blowing into the wind. The night is quiet, aside from a small fire burning in the middle of the tents. There's no breeze, but the temperature is cool from the trees that surround us. I walk to the fire and stop, seeing Gregor's familiar face as he sits in front of it, his eyes deep in thought. I can almost see the flames in his eyes, and I shake the memory of the Conjurer away.

"Kenna," Gregor says before I can turn to walk back to the tent.

I'm afraid to respond. I killed his wife. I don't deserve to be here. I suppress tears. I don't deserve to cry either.

But Gregor shoots me a sad smile, patting the space next to him on the bench. I hesitate at first, but he doesn't let me off the hook easily. He watches as I take the space next to him.

"I'm sorry," I say, struggling to keep my voice steady. I shouldn't even be allowed near this man. I killed his wife.

"Me too," Gregor responds, turning away from me and onto the fire. "You know Aminah wouldn't blame you, right?" he says after a while.

But I do. I blame myself.

"Neither do we," he adds.

"Did… did you have a funeral?" I ask.

"We did a few days ago. I'm sorry you missed it." Gregor glances at me for a moment, his eyes drenched in sadness.

"I'm… I'm sorry, Gregor," I say again.

"Kenna, I don't think you realize how much you meant to Aminah. To us," he says after a long pause. I swallow, struggling to hold back tears.

"Gregor… I… I killed Aminah…" I start. "They came for me and killed her. It should have been me."

I feel a hand on my back, and I jolt, looking up. Zander sits beside me, a gentle smile on his face. He wraps an arm around me, and I start trembling. But I shake him away. I don't deserve this. I don't deserve kindness.

Gregor wheels toward me, grabbing my hands.

"Aminah and I—our entire camp—knew the risks of coming for you. We knew the risks of taking you in. It was the highlight of her life to have trained you, to have molded you. To have met you." Gregor squeezes my hands.

My heart sinks. Just like Callie, anyone who helps me seems to be bound to death.

"You have a mighty future ahead of you. All I ask is that you do not waste her death," he says, his eyes bearing into mine.

All I can do is nod.

"You know you don't have to leave, right?" Gregor says to us.

I don't want to. This encampment has been like family to us in the last few months. We trained, we got to eat, and most importantly, Aminah kept us safe.

"They're after me, Gregor. I shouldn't have been here this long, then—then she'd still be…" I trail, my voice cracking. It's dark, so they don't see when I rub my eyes.

Zander pats my knee.

Gregor glances at me kindly.

"You have a difficult path ahead of you, Kenna. Know that Aminah was proud and excited to have been there for you, to have helped you," Gregor says again, his voice soothing and calm. He gestures to his and Aminah's tent, where his kid is asleep.

"One day, Katrine will be proud of the mother she had. The first Conjurer to help you."

I turn back to the fire. I can't control my tears. They stream down until I can't breathe.

Gregor pats my back, so I breathe deeply to stop the tears.

"Will you stick around long enough tomorrow to say goodbye to us?" Gregor asks.

"Yes," I lie.

Gregor slides closer and pulls me aside, wrapping me in his arms. I crumple, sobbing into his chest. When I finally stop, I have the courage to look him in the eyes.

CHAPTER 52

Gregor looks back at me, his face serious. "We're at war, Kenna. Aminah and I knew what we were getting into. When you feel most alone, know that the travelers are here for you."

I've never had anyone say this to me. I've never had anyone outside of Zander or my siblings make me feel welcome.

I nod. He lets go, rising to grab a rucksack and case before he returns to kneel in front of Zander.

"Take this. Don't forget to take all the food that you need. You're going to need it." Gregor pushes the rucksack and case onto Zander's chest. He pats Zander's knee, nods at me, then gets up to head for his tent.

Zander drops the rucksack and opens the case. Inside, is the bow and arrows.

Kenna

Zander and I head out before dawn the next morning.

I don't want to say goodbye. I don't know how. I spent most of my night crying, and I don't want to cause more trouble for the encampment. They've already lost their mother—their Leader. They didn't need me to take more from them.

Zander packs our rucksacks with some food and sets them up on our horses. We whisper our goodbyes to the camp, choose a direction, and trot off.

For some time, neither of us says anything. We travel through the forests, over the mountains, creating fake trails and smells along the way, just like Gregor and Aminah had taught us.

"You okay?" Zander asks when we finally slow to a gentle trot. We've been running for hours, and the horses will probably need some rest soon.

I nod, but don't say anything.

Zander spots a stream nearby and leads us to it. Once we get there, he gets off his horse and reaches out to me to help. I shake my head, waiting for him to turn so he doesn't watch. I swing one leg to the other side of my horse, then slip off his side, my entire body screaming. I deserve it. I need the pain to drive away the guilt. I land on the ground, and even though my legs are killing me, I don't crumple. I stay upright, ignoring the searing ache from my thighs and calves as I tie the horse to a tree, close enough for the horse to have access to the stream.

"Tired?" Zander asks. He grabs fruit from our rucksack and hands it to me.

I nod wordlessly, leaning on a tree. I feel heavy. Like the entire world is on my shoulders.

"I'm sorry I've been a lot lately," I finally say.

He chuckles, looking up at me from where he sat on a rock.

He stands up, approaches slowly, and cups my face in his hands. I don't even try to control it. My eyes heat up, welling with tears. He pushes my hair back from my face.

"I'm sorry about Aminah," he says softly.

I sob, and he kisses my forehead before pulling me into his arms.

A sudden rustling of leaves and movement beyond the trees catches our attention. Zander spins so quickly, I stumble backward. As soon as I find ground, I look up. Zander stands, his hands raised towards someone. His fearful, widening eyes shift to recognition before falling into a horrified frown.

I turn toward the other man and scream. It was another Conjurer: burlier, with short golden hair pulled back into a ponytail, and sapphire eyes, also wearing a red *abaya*.

Zander hits, using air to send the man back a few feet. The Conjurer is ready for it, so he slides backwards, fighting back with air.

His eyes widen, but then he looks up and beams at Zander.

"Wait—" he begins.

I freeze, unable to make sense of what's in front of my eyes.

Zander doesn't listen. He shoots again, and the Conjurer flips onto his back. He groans. The Conjurer pushes himself up, coughing before he gets himself up on two legs again.

"Wait!" he yells, his hands stretched out, his voice more determined.

Zander starts again, but this time the Conjurer is ready. He deflects, pushing back the air Zander sends. He whirls the air around. Zander sees the air come toward me and jumps across, sending me crashing to the ground while he goes airborne, hitting a tree, before slumping down.

"No!" I scream. I stand up quickly, the warmth in my belly ready to be used.

"Wait-wait! Before you hit again, I'm a friend," he rushes out.

He doesn't approach, but he holds up his hands. "I don't want to hurt you," he says again, walking towards us slowly.

Something makes me stop. I keep my arms outstretched, hesitating to fire back with whatever I can at that moment.

"I'm a friend," he repeats.

"I know you," Zander says, coughing, as he struggles to get up from the tree.

"Yes, I know you do," the Conjurer says, his hands still up, palms outstretched towards us in defense.

I look at Zander, confused, then back at the Conjurer. Zander's struggling to get up, so I put my arms down and help him. As soon as he's on his feet, I stand in front of him, putting my body between Zander and the Conjurer. Never again.

"My name is Ronin," the Conjurer introduces himself. He keeps his hands up as he breaches the distance between us.

"What do you want? How did you find us?" I demand, raising my hands again, just in case.

"I've been looking for you two. You've been difficult to find," Ronin says, his breaths short and labored, pushing back his long, golden hair from his face. "I'm a friend, I promise. I won't hurt either of you, and I'm not looking to bring you in," Ronin adds quickly. He bends down, his hands on his knees, struggling to catch his breath.

"I didn't realize you could Conjure yet. I wasn't expecting that," he explains.

Zander and I watch him. Zander was also struggling with his breathing.

"You've been following us even before we went on the run, and yet you're promising that you're not looking to bring us in? What do you want from us?" Zander demands.

I turn to him, my eyes flying wide. What did he mean by following us even before we went on the run?

"If I wanted to hurt you, I would've hurt you the first time I saw you," Ronin responds, looking at Zander meaningfully.

"Wait, what?" I say aloud.

"How did you find us?" Zander asks at the same time.

"It's a long story. But I've been looking for the two of you for a while now. I was hoping to get to you before the Conjurers did, but I don't think I managed it," Ronin admits.

My jaw tightens.

Ronin looks at me. "I followed your power."

"Why should we listen to you? Why should we believe you?" Zander shouts.

I'm hesitant. I can feel Zander's hesitation. After all, this is another fire Conjurer. Our experience with fire Conjurers hasn't been great so far.

Ronin glances between Zander and me. "Because I brought you to Madyor. I protected you by making sure your families were unknown and unlikely to get brought to Ainoa. And I'm the only one who knows about you." He pauses. "I'm the only one that knows who you three are."

Kenna

"What?" I demand.

"Raise your left wrist," Ronin orders. "You both have a scar there, don't you?"

I lift my wrist. I have an old birthmark, similar to Zander's.

"Yes," I respond.

Ronin smiles at us slowly.

"When I was fifteen years old, I went to Eaila with my grandmother," Ronin begins. "My grandmother was looking for something. Finally, my grandmother found what she was looking for in a crate on the boat we boarded together. But then the boat got attacked by rukhs, and she was killed. I only survived because of her."

Ronin's eyes glaze, the memory of it seemingly fresh in his mind.

"Before she died, she whispered to tell me to protect the crate." He keeps talking after he pauses for breath.

"When we landed, I immediately went down to claim the crate, and I found three babies."

My jaw drops. I've always wanted to know where I was from, and now here we are, listening to a stranger. My heart pounds.

"I took the crate, and I brought you all to Madyor. After observing some families, I dropped you at their doors," Ronin says. "I had to burn off the marks to make sure you wouldn't get caught, so you all cried quite a bit for it. I'm sorry." He shrugs.

Zander and I looked at him in disbelief.

"Why Madyor?" I ask.

"It was the farthest from Ainoa. I wanted to make sure you were able to live without getting noticed by the government. The further out of their radar you are, the more successful you might become," Ronin responds.

Zander is shaking now, and I know this information means as much to him as it does to me. "Who were our parents? Why were we smuggled out?" Zander croaks.

"I don't know. You were already on the boat when my grandmother and I found you. Her dying wish was for me to make sure you lived," he continues.

"How did we even survive? I thought any Eailans who left the island were killed because of the curse?" I say, remembering the historical studies we get taught in school.

"They are, normally," Ronin confirms. "But you are the *Nagiisa*. My hunch is that even when you were a child, you were able to protect yourself and the people around you."

I open my mouth to say something, but I change my mind and snap it shut.

CHAPTER 54

"I can't protect anyone. But I was able to do it when I was a baby?" I retort.

I don't believe him at all.

"My grandmother was a high-ranking Leader as a Conjurer. But she'd talked to *Nakijjas,* and they'd all predicted that there would be someone with the power to help overthrow the curse and the government. She did a lot of research and talked to a lot of people. I don't know exactly what brought her to Eaila that trip, but she brought me along. That was my first time in Eaila, and my last time," Ronin finishes.

"Who are you, then?" Kenna asks.

"I'm a high-ranking Conjurer. I've trained and made my way up the ladder, but I've made it my life's mission to keep my word to my grandmother. To protect and train you and to make sure you're ready to do what you're meant to do," Ronin says.

"You didn't protect me from my adoptive father," I mutter angrily under my breath.

"I come to Madyor every year just to keep an eye on you. I tried to be less noticeable, but it's a bit tricky," Ronin adds, gesturing to himself.

I don't say anything.

"Why couldn't you have told us earlier?" Zander asks. His voice is calmer now.

"I can't. This is your timeline. If I'd told you earlier, you wouldn't have been ready," Ronin responds.

Bullshit.

"I'm not ready. I don't know if I'll ever be ready," I tell him, my eyes hot with tears.

He gives me a look that's close to sympathy. "I wanted to keep you away from the Conjurers and the government as long as I could," Ronin adds, "as the moment they take you, it's all over."

I fold my arms. "But you knew I existed. You knew I would become this," I say.

"I-I actually didn't," Ronin says softly, his head hung.

I continue to glare at him, my entire body burning with the anger I'm failing to keep down.

"My grandmother didn't have a lot of time to tell me about any of you, or what any of you could do. All I could do was keep an eye on you until I had a better idea. I had no clue which one of you was *Nagiisa*," Ronin confesses. "I had no way of knowing until…" He stops and looks around.

Then he brightens and points.

Zander and I crane our necks to get a better look. From the forests, we recognize a bouncing creature floating across the grass, its stalks for eyes familiar to both Zander and me. It plops next to Ronin. Ronin grins, smiling at the bobbing creature.

My brow furrows.

"Your true powers didn't fully release until the day that you almost killed your father. After that, there was no hiding you. It's been years, though, and I suspect you must be about twenty-one-years old now, right?"

I nod.

"It wasn't until I met Tika here that I found out which one of you it was and the kind of power you hold," Ronin finishes.

Tika's big eyes focus on Ronin meaningfully.

"No one has ever transported themselves anywhere from a flumph's memory," Ronin adds.

I huff, still suspiciously, eyeing Tika.

"Everyone keeps saying I have so much power. Everyone. All I see when I practice is failure. I can't do it. I can't do anything," I say, raising my arms in exasperation. "Not only that, I killed someone. I *killed someone*. Your rumored savior is a *murderer*." My voice gets louder and louder.

Ronin blows out a long breath. "It takes years to prepare and learn. You can't expect to master this in just a few months," he tells me, just like everyone else has, "and if my knowledge is right, and it usually is, you killed someone who deserved to die." He eyes me with a hint of arrogance.

I glare at him. "You could've taken me somewhere else and prepared me better. I grew up fighting for my life, for my siblings. I-I'm not prepared to do this!"

I'm spinning now, and my entire vision is red and blurry. My body is on fire.

"Not yet," Ronin agrees, "but you will be."

I look at him, disgruntled. It's like he doesn't hear me. I point an angry finger at him, ready to continue my tirade. The wind changes, and Ronin falls backwards, his arms flailing as he hits the ground.

"You could've left my family with more than just five hundred pera! That was not enough to raise a baby!" My voice echoes throughout the forest, but it doesn't register as mine.

Then, I feel a pat on my hand, the coolness of his touch registering finally through all the heat brewing throughout my body.

I turn, blinking, suddenly seeing everything around me, through the red and the tears. Zander's eyes are on me, his brows furrowed. He reaches to hold my shoulders tightly. I watch him take deep breaths and do the same.

"I'm sorry. I was young, I didn't know how much that was or how little it was. I had to get help from some of my assistants to carry the crate, but I made sure you weren't seen. I had people get milk and everything to feed you with. I protected you as much as I could, but I was young and stupid and I didn't know anything then. If I could do everything all over again, I would. But I can't. I'm sorry. I did the best I could with what I had."

Kenna

Zander leads the way on our travels for the next few days. We don't have a specific destination, but Ronin won't let us out of his sight, so he and Tika have followed Zander and me. Eventually, Ronin convinces us to stop at a stream and let the horses drink and rest.

I scan Ronin curiously. It's been days since we've spoken to each other.

"How did you know what we might be?" Zander asks.

"I found my grandmother's diary. It didn't have a lot of information, but it did say we'd have some incredible power coming. Power we didn't know we still had. I don't know if you know this, but we haven't had a Dominum in five hundred years. We didn't even know there could be someone with that kind of power still. We thought the last Dominum died during the flooding," Ronin explains.

I nod, remembering what I'd already been told by others.

"Your grandmother didn't say anything about our ancestry?" I ask.

Ronin shakes his head. "I'm sorry. I know it must be hard not to know where you came from or if you have family. All I know is you're all from Eaila," he replies apologetically.

"You keep saying there's three of us. Are you referring to another boy that was left behind with a family?" Zander asks.

"Yes. There were three of you. Do you know what happened to the third one? He should be about your age," Ronin responds.

"Kane?" I suggest in a shaky voice, exchanging a look with Zander.

"I don't know his name, unfortunately. He looks a bit like you." Ronin gestured at Zander. "But I haven't seen him in a few years."

I respond, saying, "Soturis took him when he was sixteen. We think he might've died. We've never heard from him since." I swallow.

An ear-splitting screech reverberates across the trees.

Ronin snaps to attention, his eyes darting around us. His stance quickly changes, his arms in front of him, his shoulders tense.

"Get behind me quickly," he orders, swinging his arms as he looks around us.

Zander and I duck, diving behind him immediately.

Ronin stretches his arms, pacing back and forth, trying to catch a view of where the screech is coming from.

"Brace yourself. It's a preyon," he quickly explains, without looking at us. "Can you Conjure?"

"Yes," Zander responds quickly.

"A little," I reply at the same time as I crane my neck to get a look. I grip at Zander's arms so tight I'm afraid I might break his skin.

The screech comes again, this time louder.

Ronin braces. He moves his arms, and for a second, he closes his eyes. It doesn't take me long to realize he's calling on his powers. The moment he opens his eyes, they're blazing red, and a flame surges from each of his palms.

I jolt instantly, the growing red flames triggering an unwelcome memory of the other Conjurer. The one I murdered.

My stomach lurches.

Suddenly, another screech echoes across the forest. It sounds closer this time, and my grip on Zander tightens still further.

My eyes catch sight of a shadow of a man walking toward us, and I twist to get a better view, ignoring the pain the sudden movement has rendered throughout my body. My brows furrow. There's no one there but trees.

"Run!" Ronin yells.

A huge shadowy wing crosses us, its feathers hitting me on the head, and I stumble back, my butt hitting the tree behind us. Zander yells, throwing himself out of the way.

Ronin falls, his flames disappearing into him. Another high-pitched squawk sounds, thundering through the ground and forest.

And then, I see it. The head dives between us, piercing its head into Zander's shoulder, thick red liquid spattering all over the verdant grass. Zander howls and flails as his body is lifted into the air.

I gape in horror at the enormous wings as it flies higher and higher. Two majestic antlers protrude from its head, its eyes glittering in the sunlight piercing through the canopy above.

Out of nowhere, a cylindrical flame glides through the air, slicing across the antler that hangs on Zander's shoulder. Zander screams as he falls from several feet above the ground.

"Kenna, protect him!" Ronin roars, sending me into a frenzy, but it works.

I spring to my feet, my hands outstretched, eyes closed. A vision of Zander dropping slower plays in my mind until he lands softly on the bushes.

Once he lands, he coughs, spewing blood from his mouth. I immediately run to him.

The preyon makes another strident call before taking a second dive. I do the only thing I can think of at that moment—I spread my arms as wide as I can, jumping over Zander, covering his body with mine as the preyon takes one more swipe at us.

But Ronin isn't done. He's standing between the trees, looking upwards at his target, his golden hair flowing, his entire being lit red.

His arms move, recreating cylindrical flames. He swirls his arms, and the more he swirls, the bigger the flames. He eyes the target again, releasing as he makes his mark. The flames hit it on its wing, slicing its left one in half. The preyon lets out a shrill cry as it flaps its half-torn wing, stumbling onto a tree. It struggles with one working wing trying to fly out of the area, then changes its mind, jumping from one tree to another instead.

Ronin snarls. He makes another cylindrical motion with his arm before sending a lightning-shaped flame towards the preyon. The flame hits the being square in the chest, piercing into its heart.

The preyon makes one last high-pitched screech, drowning out the loud rustling of leaves, and then a deafening crash rings through the forest air.

Kenna

Ronin drops his arms. A streak of blood lines his forehead. He runs to where I'm nursing the open wound on Zander's shoulder. The preyon had speared its antler into his shoulder, breaking through skin and bone, blood dripping and pooling onto the ground.

If I were better, stronger, more powerful, I might've prevented this.

I cut a piece of my shirt, pressing it desperately onto his shoulder to stop the bleeding. My hands shake.

This is what their savior is. Skin and bones, who can't even protect her friend.

I turn to Zander. I barely feel the tears running down my cheeks.

I'm pathetic.

Zander looks pale, the blood dripping from his mouth starting to clot.

"Tika, go and string together some plantain leaves, now," Ronin orders the flumph, who nods with its eyes and floats away. He approaches Zander, taking the torn shirt from me. The cloth is already soaked in blood.

"Go get some water," he orders.

"I'm not leaving him," I wail.

Ronin spins, his eyes blazing with such ferocity that I'm almost afraid, the intensity of his gaze making the air around him crackle.

"Get. Some. Water," he says, staring me down.

My mouth opened to protest.

"I promise I'll do everything I can to help him," he adds, softening his tone.

I hold on to those words.

Zander's grunting and moaning, his face skewed with pain. I swallow, my heart breaking for him as I slowly back away, then turn and run toward the stream.

I could've helped him. I could've protected him.

I dip the bottle into the stream, catching water, my body turned so I can keep an eye on Zander as I fill it up. As soon as the bottle feels heavy, I get up, twisting the lid on the bottle and run back, positioning myself next to Zander's head. My hands are shaking as I offer Zander some water. He drinks, but he coughs and sputters blood.

There's so much blood.

I stiffen as my stomach sinks.

Ronin bends next to Zander.

"Hey, hey," he snaps at Zander, "open your eyes, Zander, open your eyes."

Zander wrestles to open his eyes, but instead, he takes shallow breaths, his eyes closing again.

"Zander, I'm going to do something, and it's going to hurt quite a bit, okay? I need to close your wound for now, so I'm going to use fire to close it, okay?" Ronin says quickly.

Everything feels like it's going in slow motion.

I can't lose him.

Not Zander.

Not my everything.

He slaps Zander's cheeks, hard. Zander's eyes flutter open. I glare at Ronin.

"You hear me?" Ronin yells.

Zander groans, but nods.

"You have to keep him awake, okay?" Ronin looks at me. I nod.

Oh, I really do belong in *Faahi*. If Zander dies, I'll never forgive myself.

Ronin grabs his shoulder. Zander grimaces.

"Get ready," Ronin warns.

Zander nods slightly, his chest struggling to retract. Ronin opens his hand, revealing a small flame. He grabs Zander's shoulder again and quickly plants his open palm with the flame on it.

Zander screams, the agonizing sound echoing throughout the mountain. I don't think I'll ever forget the sound of it. I wrap my arms around his body, trying to suppress his movements, but also wishing I could take away his pain.

"It's okay, it's okay, only a few more minutes, I promise, it's okay," Ronin whispers to him.

"I'm here," I tell him, over and over again, tears streaming down my face.

And when I can no longer take his howling, I beg Ronin. "Stop, please stop!" I wrangle Ronin's hand away from Zander's shoulder.

Ronin holds up his palm with the flames, pushing me away. "Kenna, I have to close his wound. If I don't, he'll bleed out," he warns, raising his hands again. Ronin turns to me, his eyes blazing the same way as the other Conjurer's had, except softer, kinder.

He grabs my shoulders. "Kenna, you need to be strong for Zander right now. Get. Yourself. Together," he enunciates firmly, his eyes searching mine.

He's right. I blink away the tears and wipe my face with my sleeves.

I stand beside Zander again and close my hands around his. I put my face next to his, kissing his cheeks softly.

Zander's face scrunches, his eyes streaming tears.

Don't worry, Zander. I promise I'll be better for you. Don't worry. I promise. Just live, and I'll do everything I can to make sure this doesn't happen to you again.

"You ready?" Ronin asks.

Zander forces out a weak, but audible "yes."

"I'm right here, Zander," I murmur.

Ronin nods, shooting me a look, before calling his power and planting his palm again on Zander's shoulder. Zander wails.

Zander, I'll protect you next time. I'll keep you safe. I promise. Just please live.

His cheeks are wet with tears, and his mouth bubbles with blood and saliva. It feels like forever. His screams echo throughout the forest. Finally, Ronin lifts his palm, and Zander slumps, his entire body trembling. I've never seen him like this.

This is on me. This is *on me.*

Ronin stands up to help carry Zander to the ground. I make a bed out of leaves and flowers and his coat before helping Ronin get Zander settled.

Tika comes back with some leaves on a string. Ronin takes the leaves and pushes them into the red, inflamed skin on Zander's shoulders.

"He's going to have a bad night," Ronin warns me.

I nod, wiping my eyes again, hiding my trembling hands from him.

Ronin opens his mouth to say something, but changes his mind. Instead, he turns.

"I'll go get something for us to eat," he says and disappears into the trees.

I focus on Zander, his body limp on the ground.

I almost lost him. I really almost lost him.

I bend down to kiss his forehead. He must've drifted into sleep already, but I put my head over his heart to listen to his heartbeat. I close my eyes, relief easing into me as I hear his heartbeat. It's slow, but steady.

Ronin comes back some moments later with firewood and a dead squirrel. He lights a fire easily with a flick of his wrist, then starts to clean the squirrel.

I cover Zander with my coat before sitting down next to Ronin by the fire.

"Won't they catch us?" I ask, gesturing toward the flames.

I'm tired and exhausted. I haven't used my powers since I tried to help Zander fall more slowly to the bushes. That quick moment drained me. How am I supposed to be a savior to anyone?

"It's okay. You're with me," Ronin responds.

I sigh.

Ronin hands me a water bottle, and I drink, staring at Zander.

"What do we do now?" I ask.

Ronin looks at me, a gentle look spreading across his face. I know. I get it now. I didn't want to hear it. But I know.

I sit by the stream, my feet wading in the water. I feel its energy , and I hear it buzzing and cracking as I let my mind focus on it.

Zander's been asleep for days, and I don't know what to do.

"*Do not worry*," a voice interrupts my thoughts, and I nearly jump out of my skin.

I'd almost forgotten about her.

I look up across the stream and I see her outline blending in seamlessly with the green grasses and bushes across from me. Cersei's outline shimmers, then grows brighter and brighter in contrast with the background. Her tail shifts, swaying and glowing orange in the morning light. I can see her face and her body now. I turn, scanning around for Ronin. He's gone to hunt for food. My chest heaves, and I plant my chin on top of my folded knees. I'm exhausted. I haven't been sleeping well. I keep dreaming about the Conjurer and my sisters. Zander. Someone I love dying because of me.

"*Do not worry*," the gentle voice says again.

"How can I not?" I respond despondently. I don't even look at her. I'm too tired, and I know she'll try to make me feel better, but I don't want to.

I don't deserve to feel better.

Why does it feel like everyone around me is meant to die if they help me? There's no point in even getting close to Ronin if I'm going to be the death of him, anyway.

"*That's grim,*" Cersei responds. Clearly, she's listening to the ranting in my head.

Tell me about it.

You try having the same dream over and over again. You try looking at your best friend, knowing fully well you could've saved him if only you were better. You try seeing your siblings' necks get snapped over and over again, until you finally kill the Conjurer again. Only for his eyes to mock you and call you a murderer.

"*I'm sorry about Aminah,*" Cersei says.

I don't look up, fighting the heat brewing in my eyes.

"*Zander will survive. He's strong. And he has a future in store for him,*" she says.

I look up quickly, meeting her eyes.

"What do you mean, he has a future?" I demand.

Cersei glides, her form being entirely too big for the space around us, so she bumps and pushes away the bushes and trees in the area.

"He lives?"

"*This is not his death.*"

I get up on my feet, hurrying back to kneel beside Zander.

He looks so peaceful. He takes shallow breaths, and his eyes flutter behind his eyelids.

My eyes tear, and I look back at Cersei, who's followed me.

"I don't kill him?" I whisper.

Cersei just looks at me with kind eyes.

I cry silently, holding Zander's hand in mine, as tightly as I can.

When I finally look up, Cersei has gone.

Alistair

This morning, I was picked up from my apartment by a Conjurer and two other Iklead Soturis. They usually send someone to pick me up, especially for special meetings at the Iklead, but never by a Conjurer. Perhaps it has something to do with the revealing of my powers the night before. Not that anyone else saw it, but the Conjurers might've felt it. I didn't mean to do it; it just happened. I can't even imagine what my friends might think of me right now, but I've been a bit busy to do something about it today. It's rare to get picked up by a Conjurer. Something big must be happening.

We enter the beautiful Iklead, walk across the pond and into the selection of rooms normally used for higher-level meetings.

None of my escorts said anything to me throughout, but that isn't uncommon. Most Soturis and Conjurers that work for the Iklead are compelled to silence, so they can't communicate with anyone outside of the Iklead about their work. They get tracked and killed if they reveal the secrets of the palace.

No pressure.

We stop in front of a big, beautifully designed golden door. I've never been in this area of the Iklead. "Here you go," the Conjurer finally says. He motions for me to enter, then bends deep. I nod at him slowly and pass him, realizing that he'd only got up once I'd finally passed him. What a feeling. I contain my excitement. I feel powerful, and the warmth in my belly recognizes it too.

I motion to the Conjurer and Soturis, then enter the door. As the door opens, I breathe deeply, taking in the sky-high ceilings, opening to a faux daylight sun all the way at the top. The walls are magnificent, covered with exquisite and intricate markings from the floor, reaching up to the clouds. The floors are gold, shimmering brightly under the faux sunlight. On two sides of the wall, windows rise from the floor, overlooking beautiful verdant gardens. If I hadn't memorized where we'd walked through in the Iklead, I wouldn't have known that it was all fake. I know for a fact we're right in the middle of the castle.

In the middle of the room stands an expansive round stage, with a golden podium facing one side of the room. Ample white seating surrounds it, each chair outlined in matte black, decorated with black roses circling its feet. A red carpet runs through the aisles, also outlined with a black ribbon that hangs loosely from the waist-level posts that begin each row. A majestic emerald and sapphire gem hung in the air, hovering just above the podium.

Near the center stage, I see Leader Chen. The king, rarely seen except on the most important occasions, stands before him. My heart pounds in my chest.

I instantly walk up to them, planting myself in front of the two Leaders before bending at the hip as low as I can go.

The king chuckles, his voice deep and encompassing, rendering an echo throughout the room.

"What did I tell you?" Leader Chen says.

He holds up a hand to signal for me to stand. I do, but I maintain posture, as straight as I can, without looking at the Leaders.

"You're right. He's very well-built. Has good posture, great stance," the king says, nodding as he studies me. I stay still, trying not to melt in front of his majesty.

My eyes train straight down. It's customary not to look the king in the eye. To Ainoa, no one's worthy of having an eye-to-eye conversation with the king—except maybe Leader Chen.

"Hello," the king greets.

"I'm at your service, Your Majesty," I respond.

"You can look up now, my child," the king orders.

I nod.

"Yes, Your Majesty," I respond, but my eyes don't move from the floor.

A heavy silence hangs in the air for a moment until Leader Chen claps.

"You see? Proper training and respect. This child has it all. I think he'd be the perfect candidate," Leader Chen says.

"What do you do, child?" the king asks.

"I am a yellow badge trainer for the Soturi, Your Majesty," I respond, keeping my tone neutral but confident. I don't want the king to think I was nervous.

"How long have you been in service?" the king asks.

"Since I was fourteen, Your Majesty."

He nods. "Where are you from?"

"Madyor, Your Majesty."

Silence stretches around us.

"You don't think that's going to be a problem?" he asks, presumably to Leader Chen.

Leader Chen chuckles.

"What do you think of Madyor, Alistair?" Leader Chen asks, turning to me.

I look up.

"I think the people of Madyor are a complete waste of space. They're poor, untalented, and unworthy of anything. They deserve everything they get. I am completely at Your Majesty's service, because had you not rescued me, I would not be here," I say.

The king stares at me. "You think we rescued you?"

"Of course, Your Majesty. I lived with my father, who beat me up and barely fed me. I probably would be dead had you not sent your Soturis to pick me up," I respond, looking at the floor again.

Another heavy silence. I can almost hear the beating of my heart.

Then, the king starts to laugh. "You're right, Chen," he says finally.

"Do you know what this means, Alistair?" Leader Chen says. He paces around me, as if he is assessing every part of me.

I shake my head. "No, Leader Chen."

"You've been a really great follower, Alistair," he says. "You've followed all of my orders and done everything I've asked for."

"I am your loyal servant, Leader Chen."

Leader Chen beams.

"And that's why I think you'd be perfect," he says.

"Perfect for what?"

"Alistair Strong, we'd like for you to be the next Leader," Leader Chen suggests. He looks at the king, grins, then faces me again. "And your king approves."

58

Kenna

Ronin returns from hunting, dragging the body of a dead deer behind him. He's smiling, talking aloud, presumably to Tika, who's bouncing behind him. I watch as he lights a fire, then starts preparing the deer for cooking. He looks so natural with it, like the fire is part of him and he is part of the fire. My skin prickles as I look at the flames, and I shiver, the memory of the Conjurer's blackened eyes creeping into every part of me.

"It takes time," he says, and I glance at him.

"To learn or to forgive?" I respond after a while.

He chuckles. "Both"

He finishes cleaning the deer meat in the stream before cutting it into pieces for cooking, then placing it on the log he'd set on the fire.

"How does it feel?"

Ronin sits down on a tree stump, near the fire. He looks at me, then waves a hand. The fire in front of us immediately reacts, dancing in tornadoes, streaming as high as the trees above us, but it doesn't catch. It looks absolutely mesmerizing, like an orange spire that's meant to entertain and be admired. Except, it's not just that.

Fire also kills.

He gets up and sits back down in front of me, crossing his legs in front of him. He pulls at my palms, opening them to the air. I give it reluctantly.

He opens his hand, a singular flame sitting on it, swaying in the soft breeze.

"Ready?" he asks. I nod.

He holds his hand next to mine. I watch the flame bounce, then slowly make its way to my palm. I instinctively close my hand, but Ronin pushes it open.

"It's okay," he says, gripping my palm. "I'm right here."

My heart is beating so fast, I can barely hear him.

I feel it. It's hot, but comfortable. Its energy feels like it's scorching my skin, but it doesn't. I flinch, and every instinct wants me to pull away. It's heavy and powerful, the heat as enlightening as it is frightening. I frown, looking up at Ronin, as the flame moves onto my palm. He encourages me with a look and squeezes my palm.

"I'm right here. Nothing's going to hurt you," he repeats, and he slowly pulls his hand away.

I jolt, grabbing his hand. "Don't," I plead.

"Close your eyes," he says.

I do. I don't even feel the tears coming down.

"What does it feel like?"

"I'm scared, Ronin. I don't think I can do this," I tell him. I'm shaking. He squeezes my hand again.

"What does it feel like beneath that fear?"

CHAPTER 58

I force myself to focus. But I can't. All I see behind my closed eyes are the Conjurer's eyes, right before they close and his body dissipates into the air. I'm paralyzed. I'm terrified. I can't breathe. I can't. I can't.

I shake Ronin off, standing up, trembling as the energy disintegrates into my veins, my bones, until it's out of my body. I find the darkest corner I can see, and huddle, enclosing my knees, legs, and eyes in a tight hug, willing those red eyes away.

I don't ever want to feel that way again.

Kenna

I'm not afraid. I'm not afraid. I'm still huddled away from the fire, trying not to look at it.

"It takes time."

Ronin steps over the log to sit on it.

"I'm terrified of it," I say aloud, my brain momentarily rejoicing the moment I say it. Finally, I'm being honest about something.

"When I was five years of age, I killed my caretaker."

I hurt my neck whipping around so quickly to look at him. Ronin doesn't look at me.

"I was young when my powers materialized. Younger than most people. It's rare that a Conjurer releases at four years old, an age way too young to actually be taught how to control it."

Ronin continues playing with his fire, bouncing it from one hand to another. He wiggles his fingers, and the flames do something different. He makes shapes with it, creates a small tree with flames, turns it into an apple, makes it dance. My eyes widen, and I stare in silent amazement, the scene before me a mesmerizing panorama of shape and power. I glance at his face. He didn't seem bothered by it at all. It's like he's doing it with no impact on his energy. Like it's natural.

"But... I come from a pretty powerful family. We're all fire Conjurers by birth, and my grandmother wielded three elements: air, water, and fire. I was just a kid. Unaware of the consequences of what I could do. Soon after I released my power, I accidentally set our entire house on fire. My grandmother found me crying in the middle of it all."

He pauses, the flame he held becoming smaller and smaller until only a candlelight flame protruded above his index finger.

"She got me a fire Conjurer to help take care of me when she had to go to meetings. I really wanted to play outside, but my caretaker wouldn't allow it. My grandmother had made her promise to keep me inside, so I'd stop setting things on fire in the grounds. I got mad. I released power, and I strangled her with fire." He swallows.

My jaw slackens. "But she's also a fire Conjurer, so why couldn't she counter?"

Ronin closes his hands, the flame disappearing into his body. He turns to me finally, his eyes catching mine.

"Because I'm more powerful," Ronin responds.

My eyes bulge. "At that age?"

"I see her face every day. Every day, I remember her eyes the moment I took her life from her."

Was I going to see his face every day for the rest of my life?

"But I don't punish myself anymore for it. It took many, many years for me to forgive myself and to move forward. To not see her every time I wield. To focus on the good instead of the bad."

He opens his hand again, and a small flame starts. He nurses it, and it slowly grows.

"After all, where there is death, there is also light." He extends his hand out to me.

I hesitate at first. But he looks at me with an *"I'm right here"* look, so I hold out my hand, accepting the flame. My body trembles, but I ignore it, focusing on the flame, the energy in my hand.

"The lesson isn't that you've killed someone, Kenna," Ronin says. "It's that your power has consequences, regardless of how or if you use it. The lesson isn't that you've killed someone, because this is war, and you *will* kill someone. The lesson is, what will you do with all that power when there is good and bad? Had Max Meridian lived, how many more would've died? Ask yourself that. I knew Max Meridian fairly well, and I know how much he treasured annihilating villages that don't obey."

I nod and stay silent for a moment. "Then, why do I feel so bad about it, Ronin? Am I broken?"

Ronin looks at me with sadness in his eyes. "Who isn't?"

"I mean, I transported myself to a world that doesn't even exist. I speak to a random dragon that half the time I don't believe actually exists…"

He gasps. "You have a couatl?"

My head spins. I stare at him, my jaw dropping.

He chuckles at my expression.

"I saw you talking to someone the other day," he explains. "When my grandmother passed away, she left diaries of her conversations with Nakijja. The Nakijja said you'd have powerful beings who will hunt you and those who will befriend you. The country hasn't seen a couatl in many, many years, but her diaries said you will most likely have one. I didn't know you'd have one at this point."

I look at the flame on my hand, then back at Ronin. I scan the area for Cersei, wondering if she was listening.

"So I'm not going crazy?"

Ronin chuckles again. "Who isn't?"

60

Kenna

It takes a few more days before Zander wakes up. His wound has stopped bleeding, but it looks more and more infected by the day. I spread some of the green stuff Aelin used to make, but it doesn't help. Eventually, Ronin makes a flat bed to put on top of the horse so we can travel with Zander on the bed. We can't go fast, but at least we're moving, keeping away from Conjurers and Soturis that undoubtedly still follow us, and other creatures that also lurk in the mountains.

Ronin had Tika go ahead so she could warn us about any dangerous creatures, and we follow slowly, keeping a close eye on Zander and his wound. By the time Zander's able to sit up, we've made it some distance from where we were attacked by the preyon.

"Hey," I greet him. I stop my horse so I can take a look at him. "Do you want some water?"

He nods, squinting in the sunlight. His forehead is sunburned again. He reaches over, but pulls back quickly, grimacing and crying out in pain.

"Sorry," he says softly, the pain causing his breaths to slow down.

I stop my horse and pull it onto a nearby tree. I walk over to Zander's horse and do the same thing. Ronin helps Zander off his horse, leading him to a nearby branch to sit. I hand him a bottle so he can drink. Zander pours some water over his face, too.

I sit in front of him and watch Ronin give our horses' food and water.

"Are you okay?" I ask Zander.

Zander blinks, but nods. "I feel weak, but okay," he responds.

He glances over his shoulder. I'd recently stuck fresh plantain leaves to it to help with the healing. His face scrunches as he reaches over to pull them out, but I pat his hand gently.

"Not yet. They're new, so we should leave them there for another day. Your wound may be infected, which is why it's not healing well," I explain.

He nods and straightens, taking another chug of water.

"I have to tell you something," I say.

Zander doesn't respond, but looks at me.

"We're heading to Ainoa," I say quietly.

"What?" he snaps, but then he starts coughing.

I pat his back tenderly. "Please don't be mad," I plead as I rub his back lightly.

"Kenna, we're trying to avoid you getting caught. What will going to Ainoa do for us?" he protests, struggling to get the words out.

"I know, Zander. But we need to," I say. "One, they have better medicine. Whatever this is, we can get it healed quickly. Two, I might be safer there than anywhere else. It's easier to hide me there because there will be so many Conjurers in the area. It will be impossible to find me in the midst of all that power," I add.

Logically, it made sense.

But Zander glares at Ronin. "Was this his idea?" he snaps.

I grab his face and focus it on me. "Hey, he saved your life. If it weren't for him, I would've lost you." I force him to look into my eyes.

Zander sighs.

"I don't trust him fully. But it's you and me. We can do this," I add.

Zander looks at me pleadingly.

"And three, we can get training in Ainoa. You and I can learn to become stronger, and soon, we won't need anyone else. No one else has to get hurt because of us," I finish firmly.

"Kenna, what if he turns you in?" Zander says, still glaring at Ronin.

I sigh. I turn to look at the burly man feeding the horses.

"Then we run," I say.

Zander glances at me. Then, he chuckles until he starts coughing again.

I pat his back gently again. "We need someone to look at you, though. Your wound is infected," I add.

"I'm fine, I'm fine," Zander responds nonchalantly.

I move in front of him and kneel so my face is right in front of his. I look into his eyes before nestling our foreheads together. "I can't lose you," I whisper, lifting my forehead momentarily to look him in the eyes. "I *can't* lose you, you hear me?"

Zander reaches over, wincing as he moves his injured arm, to touch my face. I shift my face to kiss the palm of his hand. He sighs, but nods.

"We'll go to Ainoa, get you healed, get training, and then you and I—we'll figure this out, okay?" I say, my voice firm.

Zander nods again.

I lean over, carefully avoiding any pressure on his shoulder, and slowly and softly touch his lips with mine. He instantly comes alive under my touch. His hands cup my face, trailing my jaw with soft fingers.

"You should've done this earlier; I would've gotten up faster," he teases.

I smile.

"When you're better, we'll have time for that, I promise." I blush red, pulling away, even though every fiber in my body doesn't want to.

61

Kenna

After a few weeks in the forest, we make it to the peak of a mountain, carefully skirting around cloakers and blights, and avoiding areas Ronin had encountered preyons in the past. We stop to camp at a clearing to wait out a windstorm, but as soon as we're packed and ready to move on, Ronin pauses beyond the clearing. I walk over, wondering what he's staring at, but my mouth drops before I can even ask.

The overlook reveals beautiful, lush green forests, dotted with beautiful lakes, rivers, grandiose plants and trees everywhere. On one side of the lake stand tall, dense trees with red leaves, carving a path to other trees bearing pink leaves and white flowers. Other trees sport an array of vibrant colors. From above, it looks like a playground with branches that dip so low they create arms that you can easily slide down on. Water rages from the mountains, becoming slower and calmer in the streams connecting the bigger lakes, building an encompassing river system that must be the reason for all of this beauty. When I squint, I can even spot waterfalls. Stunning. Breathtaking.

"Where are we?" I ask, awestruck.

"Welcome to Ainoa," Ronin murmurs under his breath.

I can't pull my gaze away from the view. "How long have you been away?"

"A while," he responds. He has an odd look on his face, like he's recalling a sad memory.

I don't ask. I have complicated feelings about Ronin, but after he told me the story about accidentally killing his babysitter, I realize he has a lot more demons than I knew. Maybe we all have them, after all.

We get on our horses and start making our way to Ainoa.

When we get even closer to the Highline, we see that the houses are closer together; the streets are narrower, and we finally start to see some people.

Ronin slows to a walk. I spot a group of children running around by a stream, many of them wearing cute little *abayas*. A group of young people are huddled by a house, engaged in an intense discussion. People look absolutely beautiful, their clothes look freshly pressed and brand new, especially in comparison to the faded shirt and pants I have on. We pass a man who's jogging slowly, a tether connecting him to a big dog. As we pass another set of houses, I spot a trash box, and my mouth drops when I notice that it's filled with food and drinks. Sometimes, even Roger's store wouldn't have enough to feed the entire district. And here in Ainoa, trash boxes are filled with food that barely looks a day old, and half-full drinks of alcohol and bottled water.

Bottled water! Who bottles water? Before we started our run from Madyor, I'd always had to collect water from the reservoir and boil it.

I stare at Zander, trying to get his attention long enough to give him a look. He doesn't say anything, but I know he and I are thinking the same thing.

I've never seen this much of anything anywhere. Even the encampment had made sure to use all its resources wisely. They never just threw food away. They always drank their alcohol to the bottom, never threw away resources that they could make into something else.

"Welcome to Ainoa," Ronin says.

I'm not impressed. This is disgusting. The amount of food waste. These could feed my family for many, many months.

Ronin chuckles.

"It's a lot, I know," he adds.

"Why do they waste so much here, Ronin? Madyor is starving," I ask, my voice trembling.

Ronin turns to me. "Do you want the diplomatic answer? Or do you want the honest one?" he asks me.

I think about how many people die of hunger in Madyor.

"What's the honest one?" Zander asks.

"Because they can. They'd rather Ainoa waste it than bring it to Madyor," Ronin responds.

My heart sinks. "They're supposed to be our Leaders, though, aren't they?" I ask.

"Leadership is a funny word," Ronin replies. "Unless you're willing to go against the grind, and by grind, I mean the king and the Leaders, then you're following what has been a problem for thousands of years."

Ronin slows to a trot. He motions for Zander and me to slow down as well. I'm lagging behind Ronin and Zander, so when I finally make it to their side, catching the white-uniformed men walking over to us, my heart begins to race.

Ronin sticks his head out from behind Zander.

"Relax," he hisses, his eyes directly on me. "Just stay with me." He turns back around, pinning his eyes on the Soturis. But his face relaxes as the Soturis approach.

"Hello," he greets, a big smile crossing his face.

"Ronin! You're back!" a toned, dark-skinned man greets him. He wears his white uniform so tightly I can see his muscles trying to push out of it. Despite what I know of Soturis so far, this group of men seemed entirely different. They have friendly expressions and seem genuinely happy to see Ronin.

"You should see who the new Leader is," a shorter Soturi adds, flicking his long hair away from his face.

Ronin grunts under his breath, but his eyes widen.

"I didn't think they'd choose anyone yet," he responds.

"Well. They did." The group laughs, and for a moment, I remember the Soturis that ransacked the encampment. Their laughter seemed a bit more genuine. I can hear my heart beating in my ears.

"Is it bad?" Ronin asks.

"We'll let you decide." The dark-haired Soturi shrugs, waving Ronin on.

Ronin nods and continues walking on. When we're a good earshot away, I shoot Zander a look, letting out a long sigh of relief.

I'm confused, though. How come they didn't say anything about me?

"Did you hide us?" Zander asks, turning to Ronin.

Ronin laughs.

"I don't have to." He clicks to his horse, switching from a walk to a trot. Zander and I follow. He looks eager, and I imagine everything here must be familiar to him. "The Soturis you see here are different from the Soturis you see elsewhere. There's so much power here that they won't bat an eye at anyone who gives off a stronger feeling. There are so many Conjurers in this area, especially new and untrained Conjurers that no one will even try to feel for power because they know it'll be overwhelming. Besides, like I said—I have enough power here that I can protect you," he adds confidently before he turns to me. "That being said, we do have to lie low for a bit. I want you to get the training you need without anyone distracting you."

I barely hear him as he trots further away from me.

Ronin turns a corner, riding faster than he's ever done before. Zander follows closely behind, but I force my horse to slow down. Unlike either of them, I have a much harder time cantering on my horse. But as soon as Zander feels a little too far away, a nervous flutter starts in my chest, so I click at my horse, its hooves drumming against the earth as we canter to keep up. I ignore the pain shooting up my thighs.

When I see Ronin slow from a trot to a walk, I let out a breath. Thank *Tagapamigay*. I didn't like having to run. We had to do it a lot during our travels, but it always caused my thighs to cramp.

"Most people live in the Highline. Important people, higher-level Leaders, Conjurers, Soturis, those who work at the Iklead. I actually have a place in the Highline, too, but I don't spend as much time there," Ronin says loudly, the running barely showing any impact on him.

I'm winded, huffing and puffing behind them, my cheeks cold from the momentary running across this beautiful cobblestone alley, lined by large trees, overgrown vines, and moss. Although the sun shines brightly before we've turned the corner, a dense gray fog blankets this area: damp and cold against my skin.

Ronin stops in front of a brick wall lined with pink and purple flowers, bordered by thick and overgrown green vines. When I look closer, the vines look alive, like they're actually breathing. I squint, my brows furrowing at what clearly must be my imagination.

Ronin closes his eyes, muttering something under his breath, then waves a hand.

For a moment, nothing happens.

A thundering sound booms from the ground. The ivy and vines start to move, slowly at first, then gradually untethering themselves from each other. Once it fully uncrosses, draping itself on the sides like a curtain, an iron gate reveals itself, tall and towering above us, with carvings similar to the ones at the Takkia Rakken marked at the top of the gate. I watch it open and realize my mouth has dropped. The thundering sound begins again, and this time, the iron gates move, screeching as they push open into the estate.

The entrance is gray and foggy, but if I squint and focus properly, I can see the massive building inside, even though it's slightly dimmed by the fog.

Ronin beams at our reactions. "Come on in."

We follow him on our horses, Tika trailing behind us. The iron gate closes automatically, screeching and rumbling along the way. I turn back and watch as a shroud of mist rises above the gate.

"It's masked. No one knows or can get to this place unless I give them explicit access," Ronin explains, without even looking at me.

I shoot Zander a look before gazing around us.

The entire estate is expansive and outrageously beautiful. We could probably fit the entire district of Madyor into it. Towering brick walls surround the entire estate, with thick bushes and vines climbing so high I can't see above them. The pathway to the manor is made of gravel, lined with shrubs that are cut and trimmed to look like pillars. Small white flowers dust each pillar, creating decorative breaks in the mass of dark green, making up the most ethereal garden I've ever seen.

We continue walking, getting closer and closer to the huge manor that stands in the middle of the estate. The closer we get, the bigger it becomes.

We pass a clearing bordered by walls made out of ivy and vines, with shrubs and bushes planted randomly along the area.

"You can practice here; no one will disturb you. You can't hurt anything here either. It will rebuild itself," Ronin says, gesturing to the clearing.

"What?" I mouth to Zander.

Ronin chuckles. He flicks his wrist, and a flame sprouts from his hand. Then, he casts the flame onto a bush. The bush ignites for a few minutes, its leaves burning black. I expect it to disintegrate into the air as the fiery flames take it on quickly and unforgivingly. Instead, the flames die and suddenly, green leaves sprout from the branches, gradually growing back to the same size and shape, pretty much instantly.

My jaw drops.

"My family spent quite a bit of time and energy rebuilding this home and making sure I didn't burn it down," Ronin explains, rolling his eyes.

We reach the manor finally, and I look up at the huge building, towering above us.

The manor is possibly fifty times the size of our house in Madyor, maybe more. I'm appalled by how much Ronin grew up with, and I can't help endlessly comparing it to the past I was lumped with.

Ronin walks us to what looks like stables before he stops, jumps off his horse, and pulls him into the stables.

Zander gets off his horse and then stops to help me off before we follow Ronin into the stables. Even the stables are much bigger than our old homes. Hell, I bet their hay was more comfortable than our beds.

"I'll take you to get healed, then walk you through Highline, and then I do have to check in with the Leaders for a bit. You can get rest after, okay?" Ronin suggests.

Zander and I nod.

I don't know what to expect, but judging from what we've seen so far, I'll bet we'll see more. Tall, expansive houses. Food wasted. Water wasted. Endless alcohol.

Things we don't have. Experiences my family can never have. What Madyor will never see.

Is this what I'm meant to fix? How? How am I supposed to help with such inequality? What can I do to fix a government that's broken from the inside? How am I supposed to fix a mistake a group of Dominumsmade hundreds of years ago?

"We'll go to see the Synkka Meri, too," Ronin adds as he enters the manor.

A shiver runs through my body.

62

Kenna

Our first task in Ainoa is to see a healer. In Madyor, we didn't have healers. We had people who understood dirt and plants and helped concoct pastes to help with wounds. But it didn't come with Conjurer powers. It didn't mean you wouldn't feel the pain anymore or that there wouldn't be a recovery period. But recovery wasn't something you could just skip work for. You had to work, despite the pain, especially if you wanted to eat.

Ronin leads us through a skinny alley. The ground is lined with shiny cobblestones, and the narrow ceiling is filled with colorful flags that glimmer in the sunlight. The walls are red brick, lined with dense moss, with moisture framing the edges of the leaves.

I lean closer to one, patting a finger on the dew. It retracts, but as soon as I lift my finger, it grows back immediately. My finger is dry.

Ronin chuckles.

"It's made to look that way. Calms people down," he explains.

I frown, but continue to follow Ronin and Zander through the alley. Finally, Ronin stops. He turns to the red brick wall on his right, his hand patting around the bricks. As soon as he finds whatever he was looking for, he pushes, a heavy click resounding as he retracts his hand.

The ground responds, creaking and grinding. The wall in front of us disappears, replaced by another alley. Ronin goes in, the disappearance of the wall clearly not a shock to him. Zander and I exchange a wide-eyed look before he follows Ronin. The ground responds as soon as we're in the little alley and I spin, just in time for the alley behind us to disappear behind a red brick wall again. My eyes widen. I raise my hand to touch the wall, to feel if it's actually there.

"Come on," Ronin's voice interrupts, and I drop my hand instantly, turning away to follow Ronin again. I speed up, trying to catch up to the men in front of me with my much shorter legs.

Another door leads us into a house, similar in size to the one I left in Madyor. It's dark, lit only by a few candles floating above us, creating a shadowy dance as we walk deeper into the house.

"Ronin!" a voice shouts.

I flinch, the sound drumming in my ears. After weeks of being on the run, it's weird being inside a house that has four actual walls. A man appears from a door, huge muscles lining his arms, a glorious beard reaching his round belly, and a protective cover over his face. He can barely fit through the door. Ronin bursts between Zander and me, throwing his arms around the man.

I don't think I've seen Ronin smile this wide. The man laughs, his belly reverberating. Ronin steps back and gestures at us.

"Is this them?" the man asks.

Ronin nods.

"Petri, this is Zander and Kenna."

I smile and wave awkwardly, but the man charges past Zander and picks me up off the floor.

"Oh, Ronin, we need to fatten this one up," he says, his belly vibrating with his laughter, "how are you going to save Taiamen when you're so thin?"

Ronin shoots me an apologetic look, and I glare back.

"Petri, we're here for something specific," Ronin cuts in as Zander steps forward to give space between me and Petri.

"Of course you are, ya'll are so busy I never see you unless…" Petri looks at me, then at Zander, who's glaring at him.

"Ay-ay-ay," Petri responds. He heads to a huge black chest, opens it, and starts rummaging inside, muttering to himself.

"Petri is a specialist; he works on specific wounds," Ronin explains to Zander and me. Zander casts a distrusting look at Petri, and I nudge him, shooting him a look. He rolls his eyes at me.

"He works specifically on preyon wounds," Ronin adds.

"Do-do-do preyons cause a specific wound?" I stammer, watching Petri.

Petri ignores me as he continues to rummage in the chest, but his eyebrows are knitted.

Suddenly, Petri stands, looking triumphant, a bottle in his hand.

"Ah!" he says. He turns to Zander and me. "Who is it?" he demands.

Zander steps forward, the expression on his face a display of confusion and distrust.

Petri pulls a chair, planting it in front of Zander.

"Sit," he says. He disappears behind the door he came out of earlier.

Zander gives Ronin a look.

"I promise he's the best," Ronin responds to Zander's dismay.

Zander sits reluctantly. He winces when he lifts his arm to remove his shirt. I grimace, seeing the red splotch on his shoulder. His skin is burned black and warped, with bits and pieces of green from the plantain leaves we'd attached to it. Over the last few days, the color of his skin had shifted dramatically—first vibrant purple, then to a blazing fire red, before finally turning completely black. I look at Ronin again when I realize that Petri's making sounds in the kitchen like he's cutting something up. *Or someone.*

"Trust me," Ronin mouths to me.

I scowl, but I didn't say anything anymore.

When Petri finally reappears, he has two bottles in his hands, a wooden ladle, and a towel.

He hands one bottle to Ronin to hold, flings the towel over his shoulder, and passes the ladle to Zander. Zander eyes it curiously.

"What do I do with it?" he asks, gingerly accepting it.

Petri looks at him with surprise.

"You put it in your mouth, of course! Did you think this would be a picnic? Removing preyon venom is a pain!"

Zander's eyes widen. He turns to Ronin.

"I'll be okay, right?" Panic laces his voice.

Ronin pulls up another chair next to Zander. "Preyon venom is dangerous. It can cause damage to a human body, especially when it's been there for a while. The reason I brought you here isn't that you needed regular healing. Petri is an earth Conjurer. He'll be using his Conjuring powers to pull out the venom that has seeped into your veins and your muscles. He'll bring it back to the earth. You feel weak right now, right?"

Zander nods, his brows furrowing.

"That's from the venom that's made it into your body. But because you've had it in your system for weeks, I'm afraid it'll be painful," Ronin explains.

"What happens if I don't do it?" he asks.

Ronin and Petri share a look.

"You…" Ronin hesitates, "you die. You lose your Conjuring powers. The venom eventually overpowers your entire being."

Zander pales and looks at me as I move to his other side, taking his hand.

Just the thought of it makes my stomach turn, and my vision blurs. "How long will it take?" I choke out.

"It depends on the venom and where it's seeped into. But as soon as it's gone, you'll feel much better, I promise," Ronin says.

"Won't be a cakewalk, that's for sure," Petri grumbles.

Ronin hands a bottle to Zander, but Petri chuckles.

"Oh no, that's for me. Preyon venom, not nice," he says. He grabs the bottle, opens it, and takes a long swig.

"Should I… should I get one, too?" Zander says, chuckling nervously.

"You can't. Alcohol makes it difficult to get the venom," Petri responds. His belly reverberates as he chuckles.

He gestures at the ladle. Zander scowls, but puts the ladle in his mouth and squeezes my hand.

Petri positions himself in front of Zander, his palms in front of his shoulder. "You ready?"

Zander glances at me.

"I'm here," I assure him, squeezing his hand. He nods, then closes his eyes.

Petri gets into position. The moment his hand touches the wound, Zander lets out a bloodcurdling scream.

63

Kenna

It's only been a few hours since Zander was "healed" by Petri, but he was instantly better the moment Petri removed the last bits of venom from the preyon. His color is back, and his energy is back. He's smiling and making jokes. In contrast, Petri's face has turned gray and wrinkled, his tired muscles protesting with every movement as he weakly dismisses us from his home to get immediate rest. Ronin chats with him a little, hands him some pera, and then ushers us out of the alley and into the Highline. According to Ronin, until Petri gives back the venom to the earth, he'll remain weak and gray. But to do that, he needs strength, which probably means days of sleep before he can even attempt it.

Ainoa's main city, the Highline, boasts wide, meticulously maintained roads, a stark contrast to Madyor's cramped, less-kempt streets; everything feels larger, cleaner, and more upscale. The streets are paved with worn red flagstone, its edges softened by years of countless footsteps, the rumble of carriage wheels, and the rhythmic clop of horse hooves—a history etched into the very stone. The streets wind between stone buildings, the sounds of street vendors and cafe chatter mingling with the clatter of restaurant kitchens. A few of the stone buildings tower up into the sky, intricate markings carved all along the sides, just like the Takkia Rakken. Many of them have panoramic windows that reflect the true spectacle of the city.

According to Ronin, some buildings can reach up to the clouds, but Conjurers mask them so the view of the sky isn't impeded.

Then, when we turn the corner to see the Iklead and Voi Makkas, I stop, a tiny gasp escaping my lips. I don't think I've ever seen anything so beautiful.

Ronin chuckles.

"I-I can't tell if it's the beauty that I'm admiring or if it's just shock from seeing something like this here while my entire family is starving in Madyor," I admit.

Zander's arm wraps around my shoulders.

"I feel the same way," he whispers to me. I remember what Aminah had told us about the Iklead. How can something so beautiful be so hauntingly scary?

"The Voi Makkas." Ronin points to the other building, also uniquely beautiful, just not as attention-grabbing as the Iklead. "Is where Conjurers train. It looks small compared to the Iklead, but it's actually about four times the size inside. The reason for this is that it has a tower specifically for each element. You get to focus on harnessing your elements better in each tower."

I guess if I had truly become a Conjurer that would be where I would've spent my entire life.

CHAPTER 63

"Ah, I've got you now." Ronin chuckles, watching our faces.

"I'll mask you if you'd prefer to train there. But truthfully, it's less about the location, and more about the people who train you," Ronin adds.

"I'd still want to take a peek inside, though," I admit shyly.

Ronin nods. "I'll take you in before we start training," he agrees. He leads us towards the Iklead and points to another building.

"That's where we hold events like the Nights of Aava."

"Ainoa has a Nights of Aava?" Zander repeats, in disbelief.

Ronin nods. "We do. Except it's just a ball. It's not like Madyor, where everyone dresses up so they can find suitors. Most Ainoans just use it as a way of socializing," Ronin confirms.

I shake my head. I grew up in a place where it's part of our culture to dress up only so we could be sold to higher-ranking people. Now, here I am, in the land of high-ranking people, who clearly have a disregard for anything and everything I came from.

I resent that this is what the other half of this country is like. That my entire family has to go through this every single year—even though these people just have all of this food and wealth enough to feed three times the size of Madyor for many, many months.

"Come on, I have one more thing I want to show you," Ronin says.

He turns a corner before the terrain starts uphill. Zander and I follow, huffing at the pace he takes. He makes it to the top of the hill faster than Zander and me, barely sweating. His red *abaya* makes him look regal as he waits for us at the top, his golden blonde hair blowing softly with the wind. He faces away from us, his eyebrows furrowing, looking out ahead of the hill.

Finally, Zander and I make it to the top of Ainoa. He and I are absurdly out of breath, but the breeze is nice and refreshing. From here, we can see the Iklead, the Voi Makkas, and all the buildings in the Highline. But over the horizon, just far enough beyond the beautiful lakes and rivers of Ainoa, I catch sight of dark, tumultuous waters, with equally dark clouds and fog hovering over.

"Is that…"

But I already know the answer. My pulse quickens.

"Yes, that's the Synkka Meri. The flooding that was caused by the Dominums five hundred years ago, strengthening the curse on Eaila and preventing any access to the island," Ronin explains.

I look back at it. Shadowy curtains roll and churn above the raging seas. Jagged streaks of lightning split the veils, lighting the chaotic expanse with momentary flashes. Thunder cracks and booms, reverberating across the ground with a deafening roar. It's angry.

I shudder, the hair on my arms and legs rising with the sparks of electricity each time lightning strikes.

"Is it always like that?" I ask.

"Yes. Until the day the *Nagiisa* decides she can lift it." Ronin glances at me.

My brow furrows, and my heart sinks. "I-I don't know if I can do that, Ronin."

"I know," Ronin turns to me, "but I know you can."

64

Kenna

Zander and I make it back to the house just before it gets dark. Ronin tells us to enjoy the night and disappears into the Voi Makkas. By the time we get back to the house, a spread of wonderful food and drinks covers the dinner table. There's no one there, but we assume someone has made it for us, so we help ourselves. Honestly, his table reminds me of the spread at the Nights of Aava. Lots of options, labels on different types of food, different drinks. The privilege of being an Ainoan.

Zander and I enjoy the night with good food before we head into the bedroom. We don't have to share, according to Ronin, but it isn't like we haven't already been sharing a bed.

I clean up first, then Zander goes into the shower.

After I get dressed into my nightclothes, the nicest, softest silk dress and pants that look like they've never been worn, which I'd found folded neatly in one of the many closets in the room; I slip out of the door to our balcony. I look out at Ainoa, over the beautiful gardens on Ronin's estate. Ainoa is breathtakingly beautiful. I can see the lights from many buildings, the towers, the Iklead, even from here. Then, just over the horizon, is darkness, lit up occasionally by streaks of lightning within the veils of shadows of the Synkka Meri. A shudder chases up my spine.

Am I stupid enough to believe it's my destiny to remove that? How could I—me? Little old me, who barely has enough strength to do anything. How can it be my responsibility? The more I stare at it, the more it has me believing I'm headed toward my death.

Suddenly, I hear the glass door open, and I turn. Zander's at the door, gently closing it behind him. We don't have glass doors in Madyor, so he and I have been careful with everything here. A smile spreads across his face as he claims the seat next to me, sinking into the soft cushions underneath.

"Ah." He smiles, closing his eyes as he gets comfortable. Then, he glances at me, his eyes frowning, studying me carefully.

"What are you thinking about?" he asks.

"Just tomorrow," I say, smiling softly. I gaze back at the Synkka Meri, a ripple of its weight crossing my mind.

"Ah, but there's a beauty in that, though," Zander says.

He reaches over and grabs my hand, pulling me gently off my chair and onto his lap. I curl into him, settling comfortably into his chest.

"Yeah? What is that?" I say.

"It's not yet tomorrow," he replies, squeezing me. He pushes the hair from my face.

I smile, then close my eyes as his lips brush against my nose, a light and tender touch.

My stomach churns with a mix of nervous butterflies and thrilling anticipation, wishing for this moment to last forever. A moment where we're together, where we're safe.

Where Zander is safe.

I feel his breath on my nose and open my eyes.

There's something about Zander that makes me feel so at home. But I know if I don't get trained, he'll never be safe. Not with me.

I look into his eyes, trying to read his thoughts.

I notice everything about him at this moment. Scars adorn his forehead, and a small mark mars his cheek. In the moonlight, his eyes are purple, not blue. I caress his cheeks gently, tracing the outline of his jaw with tender touches.

I lean in and touch my lips to his—slowly, delicately, lovingly. His hand wraps around my jaw, and suddenly, he's alive. His tongue caresses mine, and the hairs on the back of my neck rise along with the tiny goosebumps. He moves to trace the contours of my neck with light and subtle kisses.

Oh *Tagapamigay*. It lights a fire in me so aggressive, I barely recognize myself.

I want more. I feel myself arch my back, pushing myself closer to him, aching for his touch, for his lips, for everything. My skin burns with hunger for him.

Zander responds, pulling me closer, his lips traveling from my neck, down to my chest, and then, his hot breath is over the thin silk fabric on my breast. My nipples harden. I feel my center react immediately.

Oh, *Tagapamigay*, I want him. I want this.

I shift my legs over so that he's cradling me, the heat between my thighs amplifying that desire to be even closer. I feel my center meet his, a hardness over his pants. I moan.

Then, he pulls away, and I'm red and blushing, maybe disappointed. His breath is shallow, and his cheeks are red.

His eyes linger on me, and I smile. I love the way he looks at me. I don't feel like I'm nothing in his eyes. I don't feel inferior. I feel… beautiful.

"*Tagapamigay*, you're so beautiful," he mutters in between touches. His eyes trace a slow outline over me, from my face, to my neck, to my breasts.

I want him to touch me. Touch me everywhere. Anywhere.

"I-I…" I start shyly.

"What is it?" he asks, his voice soft and gentle, as he breathes softly above the soft skin behind my neck.

"I never want to lose you," I say sheepishly. It isn't exactly what I want to say, but it's all I can think of right now.

He looks at me, a hunger in his eyes. He cups my face in his hands, kissing me slow at first, and then harder, hungrily, his tongue exploring every inch of my mouth, and when he explores enough, his mouth focuses on that tender curve by my shoulder before traveling down to my breast. I feel his tongue trace the outline of my nipples through my shirt, and I shiver.

A whimper escapes my lips, the sound a testament to my barely contained impatience. I'm wearing too much. I lift my shirt and drag it up over my arms before letting it fall carelessly to the floor.

Zander inhales sharply. His eyes move over my breasts, and before I can breathe out, he leans closer and draws circles of kisses around my nipples.

Oh *Faahi*. If this were my last day, I'll take it.

I adjust my hips, pushing up along his outline, letting him take in my breasts and body. I can't get enough. A quiet moan slips past my lips.

He smiles, lifting his head for a second before moving to my other breast.

I want you; I want to tell him, but I'm too shy.

"I've wanted you for so long," he murmurs in my ear as he kisses my mouth again.

I grip the edges of his shirt and pull it off. He pauses his kisses, and I groan, instantly missing his warmth.

I caress his chest with my fingers, and then my mouth, making a pathway from his neck, trailing gentle kisses over his wounded shoulder.

I can feel the heat of his desire burning beneath me. I lift myself, one breast still in his mouth, and use one hand to help him pull down his pants.

Once his pants fall onto the floor, I gape. His cock stands between his legs, already hard.

My cheeks burn.

I lift myself off the chair and stand in front of him.

My nipples feel taut in the night air, and my skin is soft and cool, and yet, I feel like I'm on fire. His eyes widen, and I feel myself turn red as I grab the corners of my pants, pulling them below my knees and finally my feet. I step out of them, my bare feet cold against the cement floor.

Zander's purple eyes roam over me, and I bite a lip. I've never been naked in front of him, but I love the way he looks at me.

I travel the length of him, admiring, loving his every feature. His strong and broad shoulders. His gangly height, his enormous length. But it isn't just *him* that I love. It's his strength, his determination, his passion, his eagerness to protect me. This isn't just any man. This is *Zander*. This is the beautiful man who protected me, who sacrificed everything for me, who'd throw himself into the fire for me. The man who sacrificed his savings to buy me a dress, the man who sacrificed his earnings so I could bring something home to my siblings.

I reach for him, but Zander beats me to it. He kneels down in front of me, his mouth reaching for the cuts on my thighs. He looks up as he trails a soft tongue over the healing skin on my upper legs.

I moan louder, goosebumps rising throughout my legs. *Tagapamigay*, I want him.

His tongue travels from one thigh to another, and then to the center. I lift my leg, leaning on the chair for support. I tremble at his touch.

"I-I want you," I stutter and beg, feeling his tongue kiss and lick the ripples on my clit.

My entire being shatters. I groan with pleasure, using his head to steady me. I shiver. I want him.

Zander sits back on the chair, pulling me slowly to him.

I've never done anything like this before, but here I am, learning with him, trying with him. Being with him. All I know at this moment is that I want him. *Now.*

He pulls me to him, and I cradle him, careful not to put too much pressure on his wounded shoulder. He moans into my breasts as he holds onto my waist, the tip of his cock sliding around my clit.

It kindles a burning desire I never thought I'd have, traveling through my entire body.

I wrap my arms around him, and he leads me, his length entering as I sink slowly onto him.

I moan again; the friction sends shivers down my spine as my body adjusts to his girth.

From the corner of my eye, I see flames light over the corner shrub.

Zander holds me, one arm on my waist, the other on my lower back. He guides me, in–out–in–out, into a rhythmic dance. Our rhythm starts slow, and then gets faster, mimicking the beating of our hearts.

I adjust my hips and start moving back and forth where it feels good, like I'm riding him. The more I shift back and forth, the deeper he feels. He adjusts me to the left, and I feel him everywhere.

Finally, I let out a loud gasp as we both release, shivering, and I collapse into his arms.

I listen to his fast-paced breathing, nothing in my head, except for Zander and the way he feels inside me, with me.

Then I push on his chest to look him directly into his eyes.

"I don't think I'm going to love anyone the way I love you," I tell him.

"Good," he whispers, touching the tips of my breasts with his fingers, sending goosebumps down my back.

He beams, biting his lips, and I marvel at how freaking beautiful this man is. Then, he looks back at me, his fingers tracing the side of my face. I lean into it, touching his palm with my lips.

"Because I think I'm going to love you for the rest of my life," he adds.

It echoes in my brain like a calling I never want to forget.

I grin.

This is it. This is all I ever want. Be with Zander, to protect him. To love him. To have his love. I'm going to remember this night forever.

"What do we do now?" I ask, cheekily kissing the contours of his neck.

He laughs. He grabs me by the waist, using his arm for support. I feel him slip out, and I groan in response.

"Don't worry, love," Zander says, making sure his still-aroused length grazes my thigh just to tease me. He carries me back into the bedroom, pulling the door closed with his powers before laying me on the bed.

"I plan to have you a few more times tonight," he whispers as he guides his length back into me. I moan excitedly, praying to *Tagapamigay* that this feeling will never end.

Kenna

I wake up early the next day. We were up most of the night, but surprisingly, I feel well-rested, outside of the muscle pain in my thighs and back. I look next to me and smile at Zander. He's buried under the sheets, with a smile spread across his face. I smile back, feeling like a giggly teen. I reach over to kiss him on the forehead, resisting the temptation to jump on him again. He looks so peaceful in his sleep.

I lift the covers and get out of bed, making sure Zander is still fully covered.

After getting dressed, I leave the house with a spring in my step and a newfound confidence that I can take on the world. What could go wrong? Maybe if I go take a look at the Synkka Meri, maybe, just maybe, it won't look as intimidating as it did the first time. Maybe, just maybe, if Zander can love me the way he did, I can do this.

I can be their savior.

I was so overwhelmed yesterday I barely got the chance to take in the fact that I'd made it to Ainoa. I, Kenna Tetanui, made it to Ainoa! I honestly thought I was going to die in Madyor.

I walk past buildings, appreciating the beauty of the more modern designs, the fancier restaurants, and the nicer shops. I wish my family had something like this. Maybe it wouldn't be so hard to actually live. Maybe we'd actually be able to find out who we are or what we want to do if we weren't so busy trying to stay alive.

I continue walking. Even from where I am, I can see the tips of the Iklead already. What a magnificent view! The beautiful gems and jewels on the outside of it are breathtaking, radiating in the morning light.

A familiar voice makes me jump. I spin, scanning for the sound. There aren't a lot of people on the streets yet. It's early; dawn just passed, and the sun just made its way up. Even with minimal people on the streets, it's hard to see where the sound came from. I stop and listen, hoping to catch it again.

I cross the street. It came from this direction. I stop, slipping into an alley.

The voice is from a person standing between three other people. One wears a blue *abaya,* the other two are Soturis. I can't see his face, but he has dark wavy hair and is relatively tall. I can't see what he's wearing either, as the three have stuck to him so close it's like they're protecting him from something.

I cross the street again, keeping a good pace behind them. I crane my neck a few times before hiding behind a wall. He's walking at the same pace as the others, so it's difficult to get a real glance at his face.

But that voice just sounds so familiar. I can't quite place it, but it feels like one I haven't heard in a while.

The Soturis turn in my direction, and I turn around and walk the other way for a moment, praying to *Tagapamigay* no one saw me. I can't even imagine the anger on Ronin's face if I get caught before I've even started training.

I wait a bit before peeking back out onto the street.

They're gone.

66

Kenna

"I wouldn't normally bring you here, but I think it would be a great way for you to see the government, how they operate, and what they do," Ronin explains.

He's invited Zander and me to a powerful Conjurers meeting. Apparently, only certain levels are invited, so Ronin offered to mask us if we wanted to go.

Nerves flutter in my belly. "It will be at the Iklead," Ronin adds, smiling a little.

"Okay," I say, shooting Zander a glance.

Ronin turns to me. "I'll protect you, don't worry," he tells me, eyeing me and Zander.

Zander doesn't even look worried. A few days in Ainoa, and he already looks like he fits in. Maybe this is where Zander truly belongs, after all. He's always so confident and sure of himself.

We follow Ronin into the Iklead. He looks especially formal today, sporting a newer-looking red *abaya*, unlike the one he wore while traveling. On his left chest, he sports a black badge.

Ronin is obviously quite popular, too. Almost every other Conjurer who passes us greets him or tries to get his attention. Ronin barely responds to the greetings.

"Popular, are we?" Zander comments.

Ronin chuckles, shooting him a wary look.

"I'm from a powerful family. People like to kiss ass," he responds when no one's looking.

We stop at the most beautiful room I've ever seen—even more beautiful than the room in the Takkia Rakken. Almost all of it is gold, with tower-high windows looking out into mesmerizing gardens with plants I'd never have seen before. The walls are lined with intricate messaging from a language I don't recognize.

In the middle of the room is a round stage, crowded with some high-ranking Conjurers. They're chatting with each other and laughing.

Zander and I nod.

Ronin motions to a beautiful blonde girl with sapphire eyes quite a good distance away.

"That's Alanna. She's the Leader's daughter. Might want to stay away from her," Ronin warns.

Zander and I follow his gaze back up at the person on stage, who had already started talking.

"We cannot tolerate spending more of our budget on Conjurers who just can't learn. It's a waste of resources," the voice bleats.

Ronin, Zander, and I snap to attention. A resounding mixed reaction from the group echoes through the impressive room.

"Moving forward, we will put everyone to the test. If you can't lead a boat into Eaila and back, you lose your powers," the person continues saying.

"Can you see who it is?" I whisper to Zander.

My heart starts to race. I can feel a weirdly familiar pulling in my gut. A connection of some kind that's making me dizzy.

"I can't yet. I'm hoping he turns," Zander says. He doesn't even bother lowering his voice. Everyone else is so noisy already.

"Why are you doing this?" someone yells.

The person speaking on stage laughs.

"Do you realize how privileged you are? How many resources you have at the moment? If we continue to train those who don't work as hard, you won't have what you have. Do you want that to happen?" he demands. "Do you want to end up in a position where you have fewer resources than you do now, even though you work extra hard?"

The Conjurer looks satiated, nodding.

"You're right, Leader Stong!" he yells, and numerous cheers echo throughout the Iklead.

"You all work hard to be where you are. Do you want to be sent across the Synkka Meri just to die—even though you're the one that grafted?" the man continues.

Suddenly, everyone is nodding their heads. My jaw drops.

"You work hard, you get the benefits. Right?" he demands again, and the entire room blows up in chorus.

"Yes!"

"Right!"

I catch Ronin's gaze, and he shoots me a meaningful but sad smile. "Welcome to Ainoa," he says softly as his face falls. "I'm going outside. Meet me there?" he suggests.

Zander and I nod.

Ronin walks away, his head down. He doesn't even stop to say hello to any of the people who greet him on his way out.

For a moment, I feel bad for him. This was the government he grew up under. This was his government. His people. Yet, it must feel so helpless to not be able to do anything—even though he had this much influence.

"We'll make sure everyone who works just as hard will be rewarded. Like me. I didn't have much when I was younger. I worked hard. Now I'm here. And I will make sure you get what you deserve!" the man goes on.

The crowd erupts.

Zander and I glance at each other. We've only been here for a few days, but our introduction to Ainoa is like a slap in the face.

"Now, you won't ever have to sacrifice yourself for someone else. You fight for Ainoa. You fight for yourself," he continues.

The crowd goes wild.

"Thank you, everyone!" the man says after riling his fans up one more time. Whoever this is, they're definitely enjoying everyone's attention and praise.

Zander and I keep our eyes on the stage, waiting anxiously for him to turn around.

I can see the back of his head now. He's wearing Soturi clothing. He's tall, with wavy brown hair, and his stance is commanding, confident. He waves to his people, a grand smile spreading across his face each time he recognizes someone he knows.

Finally, just before he gets off the stage, he turns fully, facing us.

The color drains from Zander's face. My jaw drops, and a horrified gasp escapes my tight chest.

Kane.

GLOSSARY AND PRONUNCIATION GUIDE

- Taiamen (Tah-yah-men): The name of the country.
- Ainoa (Ay-no-ah): The main district and capital of Taiamen.
- Noppealiik (No-pea-ah-lee-ik): The second-richest district in Taiamen, and the only one with resources to cross the seas.
- Uthaana (Oo-tha-ana): The third-richest district in Taiamen, also home to one of the most volatile volcanoes.
- Madyor (Mah-jor): The poorest district in Taiamen and where Kenna and Zander grew up.
- Eaila (Eh-ya-la): The cursed district in Taiamen, an island set apart by the Synkka Meri with limitless resources.
- Nights of Aava (Ah-a-va): A ball that takes place in every district for three nights. Ainoa provides free food and drinks and people can dance and enjoy the entire night. It's a way to meet people and find families, if they'd like.
- Takkia Rakken (Tah-key-ya Rah-ken): The only building that's important to the government in Madyor.

- Voi Makkas (Voy-mah-kah): This is what the center for Conjurers is called in the old language.
- Iklead (Eek-leed): This is what the palace is called in the old language.
- Synkka Meri (Sink-a Me-ri): The death sea. A powerful curse covered the seas between Eaila and the main islands, casting monsters into the seas to prevent people from entering and leaving Eaila.
- Faahi (Fa-a-hee): This means hell, in the old language.
- Paratiisi (Pa-ra-ti-is-i): This means paradise in the old language.
- Tagapamigay (Ta-ga-pa-mi-ga-i): This is the God who gives, a name from the old language.
- Mt Catapang (Cah-ta-pahng): The volcano in Madyor.
- Rakuuri (Rah-ku-u-ri): Hail that can sometimes fall near volcanoes that double a Conjurer's power naturally.
- Lakas (Lah-kas): Water from powerful glaciers that provide a Conjurer triple their power at a given time.'

9 781969 751004